Simon Scarrow is a *Sunday Times* No. 1 bestselling author. After a childhood spent travelling the world, he pursued his great love of history as a teacher, before becoming a full-time writer. His Roman soldier heroes Cato and Macro made their debut in 2000 in UNDER THE EAGLE, and have subsequently appeared in many bestsellers in the Eagles of the Empire series, including CENTURION and INVICTUS. Simon is the author of many more powerful novels, including HEARTS OF STONE, set in Greece during the Second World War, SWORD & SCIMITAR, about the 1565 Siege of Malta, and PLAYING WITH DEATH, a contemporary thriller written with Lee Francis.

For exciting news, extracts and exclusive content from Simon visit www.simonscarrow.co.uk, follow him on Twitter @SimonScarrow or like his author page on Facebook/OfficialSimonScarrow.

Praise for **SIMON SCARROW**'s novels

'A new book in Simon Scarrow's long-running series about the Roman army is always a joy' Antonia Senior, *The Times*

'Ferocious and compelling' **** *Daily Express*

'I really don't need this kind of competition . . . It's a great read' Bernard Cornwell

'Scarrow's [novels] rank with the best' *Independent*

'Rollicking good fun' *Mail on Sunday*

'A satisfyingly bloodthirsty, bawdy romp . . . perfect for Bernard Cornwell addicts who will relish its historical detail and fast-paced action' *Good Book Guide*

'Scarrow's engaging pair of heroes . . . top stuff' *Daily Telegraph*

'A rip-roaring page-turner' *Historical Novels Review*

'A fast-moving and exceptionally well-paced historical thriller' *BBC History Magazine*

By Simon Scarrow

The *Eagles of the Empire* Series
The Britannia Campaign
Under the Eagle (AD 42–43, Britannia)
The Eagle's Conquest (AD 43, Britannia)
When the Eagle Hunts (AD 44, Britannia)
The Eagle and the Wolves (AD 44, Britannia)
The Eagle's Prey (AD 44, Britannia)

Rome and the Eastern Provinces
The Eagle's Prophecy (AD 45, Rome)
The Eagle in the Sand (AD 46, Judaea)
Centurion (AD 46, Syria)

The Mediterranean
The Gladiator (AD 48–49, Crete)
The Legion (AD 49, Egypt)
Praetorian (AD 51, Rome)

The Return to Britannia
The Blood Crows (AD 51, Britannia)
Brothers in Blood (AD 51, Britannia)
Britannia (AD 52, Britannia)

Hispania
Invictus (AD 54, Hispania)

The Return to Rome
Day of the Caesars (AD 54, Rome)

The *Wellington and Napoleon* Quartet
Young Bloods
The Generals
Fire and Sword
The Fields of Death

Sword and Scimitar (Great Siege of Malta)

Hearts of Stone (Second World War)

The *Gladiator* Series
Gladiator: Fight for Freedom
Gladiator: Street Fighter
Gladiator: Son of Spartacus
Gladiator: Vengeance

Writing with T. J. Andrews
Arena (AD 41, Rome)
Invader (AD 44, Britannia)

Writing with Lee Francis
Playing With Death

SIMON SCARROW

EAGLES · OF · THE · EMPIRE

DAY OF THE CAESARS

Headline

First published in Great Britain in 2017 by
HEADLINE PUBLISHING GROUP

First published in paperback in 2018 by
HEADLINE PUBLISHING GROUP

2

Cataloguing in Publication Data is available from the British Library

ISBN 978 1 4722 5198 5 (A-format)
ISBN 978 1 4722 1338 9 (B-format)

Typeset in Bembo by Avon DataSet Ltd, Bidford-on-Avon, Warwickshire

Printed and bound in Great Britain by Clays Ltd, Elcograf S.p.A

HEADLINE PUBLISHING GROUP
An Hachette UK Company
Carmelite House
50 Victoria Embankment
London EC4Y 0DZ

www.headline.co.uk
www.hachette.co.uk

To John Carr, who started the book club, and for my other reading comrades through the years; Ted, Jason, Phil, Andy, Peter, Trevor, John, Nick, Jeremy and Lawrence.

CONTENTS

Map of Italia, AD 54 — viii

Map of Sinus Cumanus, AD 54 — ix

Map of Rome in the Age of Emperor Nero — x

Praetorian Guard Chain of Command — xi

Cast List — xii

DAY OF THE CAESARS — 1

Author's Note — 457

ITALIA AD54

SINUS CUMANUS AD54
THE MODERN DAY BAY OF NAPLES

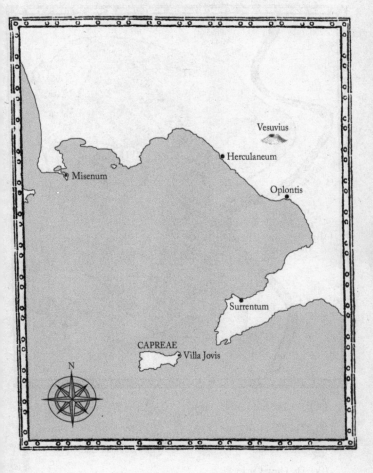

ROME IN THE AGE OF EMPEROR NERO

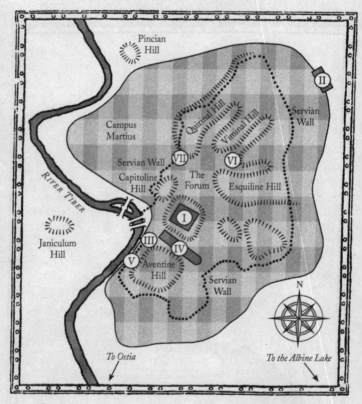

I The Imperial Palace Complex

II The Praetorian Camp

III The Boarium

IV The Great Circus

V The Warehouse District

VI The Subura Slum District

VII Flaminian Gate

PRAETORIAN GUARD
CHAIN OF COMMAND

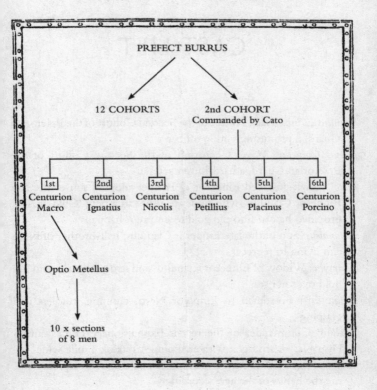

PREFECT BURRUS

12 COHORTS

2nd COHORT
Commanded by Cato

1st	2nd	3rd	4th	5th	6th
Centurion Macro	Centurion Ignatius	Centurion Nicolis	Centurion Petillius	Centurion Placinus	Centurion Porcino

Optio Metellus

10 x sections
of 8 men

CAST LIST

Quintus Licinius Cato: Prefect of the Second Cohort of the Praetorian Guard, a promising young officer

Lucius Cornelius Macro: Centurion of the Second Cohort of the Praetorian Guard, a hard-bitten veteran

Nero: Newly installed Emperor of Rome; adopted son of the late Emperor Claudius, who hopes to usher in a new 'Golden Age' provided he can find the gold to ensure it happens

Britannicus: Son of the late Emperor Claudius; half-brother of Nero and living to regret it

Agrippina: Widow of Emperor Claudius, and struggling to retain her hold over her son

Pallas: First Freedman to Emperor Nero, cunning, ruthless and grasping

Vitellius: Commander of the recent Expeditionary Force sent to Hispania; an aristocrat with an ambitious streak a mile wide

Granicus: Senator, who has lived long enough to see everything and rue the habits of the age accordingly

Vespasian: Former Legate of the Second Legion and senator – an honest and able soldier

Domitia: Wife of Vespasian, a woman with rather more ambition than is healthy for her husband

Amrillus: Senator of Rome

Junia, Cornelia: Wives of Senators

Attalus: Agent of Domitia

Fennus, Tallinus: Spies of Pallas

Lemillus: Admiral of the Fleet at Misenum, an old salt who stays the course

Spiromandes: A Navarch (Squadron Commander) of the Misenum fleet

Pastinus: Legate of the Sixth Legion, with a commendable dislike of lawyers

Praetorian Guard

Burrus: Prefect commanding the Guard, promoted above his abilities

Mantalus: Tribune

Tertillius: Commander of the Third Cohort

Caecilius: Junior Tribune

Second Praetorian cohort

Cristus: Tribune; former lover of Cato's late wife Julia, something of a playboy

Placinus, Porcino, Petillius: Centurions

Metellus, Ignatius, Nicolis, Gannicus, Nerva: Optios

Rutilius: Imperial Standard Bearer

Others

Julia: Cato's deceased wife, of possibly doubtful morality

Lucius: Son of Julia and Cato, something of a handful . . .

Senator Sempronius: Father of Julia, an honest politician, thus something of a rarity

Petronella: Nurse to Lucius, and a woman to be reckoned with

Tribonius: Innkeeper in Subura

Decimus: Doorkeeper at Vespasian's house

Cephodius: A low-life advocate of the lawyers' courtyard in the Boarium

CHAPTER ONE

Rome, late AD 54

It started, as these things always do, over a few drinks. Not that fights were an unusual occurrence in the Subura neighbourhood, let alone in the inn named Romulus and the Wolf, well known for its cheap wine, cheery tarts and those who sold inside information about the chariot-racing teams. It was one of the largest drinking dens in the slum, occupying the entire ground floor of an apartment block on the corner of a small square. A long counter ran along the rear wall where the owner, Tribonius, ran a small team of heavily made-up women who served the customers drink, a limited range of meals, and other services to those with more carnal appetites. Two burly men stood at each of the entrances opening on to the street to check customers for weapons before they were let inside. Some innkeepers declined to take such precautions for fear of driving custom away, but Tribonius had been in business for over twenty years and had an established clientele who put up with the restriction out of fondness for the pleasures to be found within.

On this night, barely a month after the death of Emperor Claudius, it was raining and the streets of Rome glistened in the steady hiss and patter of raindrops. Claudius's demise had been

1

met with a healthy degree of caution and anxiety from the common people of the capital, and that had not been good for business at the Romulus and the Wolf, as many of them kept off the streets as much as possible, fearing trouble between the rival factions supporting the emperor's sons, Nero and Britannicus. The old boy may have been a bit muddle-headed and clumsy but he had kept the people fed and entertained, and more importantly his reign had been stable and not marred by the casual cruelty and ruthlessness of the two emperors before him. But where there are two heirs to the most powerful empire in the known world, there is bound to be tension, to say the least.

Nero at sixteen was the older of the two boys by three years. He was not Claudius's natural son, but the child of the empress, Agrippina, who herself was the daughter of Claudius's brother. Marriage between uncle and niece had required a change to the law, but the senators had found it within themselves to forgive a small matter like incest in order to curry favour with their emperor. And so Nero became the legal son of Claudius. However, Claudius's natural son, Britannicus, resented the imposition of an adopted brother, whose preferential status was soon boosted by his mother's hold over the mind and carnal desires of the emperor. And so, in the final years of his reign, Claudius had unwittingly created a rivalry that threatened the peace of Rome. Even though the empress had rushed to announce that her son had succeeded to the throne, it was well known that Britannicus and his allies did not accept the situation, and the common people were accordingly apprehensive as they watched and waited for the rivalry to be resolved.

A party of Praetorian guardsmen in heavy cloaks entered the square and hurried across to the inn, talking and laughing loudly. As well they might, since the Praetorians were the darlings of the emperors, who rewarded them handsomely for their loyalty. And the new emperor was no exception. Every guardsman in Rome had been given a small fortune when Nero's accession had been announced, and their purses bulged with silver. Tribonius looked up with a broad smile as the soldiers stepped in off the street, lowering their hoods and removing their drenched capes, which they hung on the pegs along a side wall before approaching the counter to order their first drinks. Freshly minted coins were slapped down on the stained and heavily scored wooden surface, and cups and jars of wine were brought out from the back room and handed over to the eager soldiers.

They were not the first guardsmen to provide the inn with custom this night. A smaller group had arrived shortly before and had taken over a corner, seating themselves on benches either side of a table. Their mood was markedly less jovial, even though they too had been recipients of the emperor's largesse, and now their leader turned to look towards the Praetorians at the counter and frowned.

'Bloody fools,' he grumbled. 'What do they think they're celebrating?'

'An extra year's pay, for one thing,' the man sitting next to him replied with a thin smile. He raised his cup. 'A toast to our new emperor.'

The gesture was met with sullen silence from the rest of the soldiers seated round the table, and the man continued in a tone laced with irony. 'What's this, lads? No one going to join me in toasting our beloved Nero? No? They're all as miserable as you, Priscus.'

The leader turned his attention away from the men at the

3

counter. 'Aye, Piso, well there's every reason to be miserable with that chinless wonder on the throne. You've been on duty at the palace as much as me, so you have seen Nero close up. You know what he's like. Stuffing himself with dainties while poncing around with his poets and actors. And he's got a nasty streak too. You remember that time we had to escort him on one of his anonymous trips into the city? When he got into that argument with the old bloke and made us pin the man to the wall while he stabbed him to death?'

Piso shook his head at the memory. 'Not our finest hour, I'll agree.'

'No,' Priscus said through gritted teeth. 'Not by a long way. And he'll be worse now he's emperor. You'll see.'

'At least he paid us off nicely.'

'Some of us,' Priscus replied. 'There's still the lads who've been campaigning in Hispania. They'll not be happy about missing out on their share of the silver when they get back to Rome.'

'You're not wrong . . . Anyway, what makes you think Nero's little brother would be much better if he was emperor instead?'

Priscus thought about this for a moment and shrugged. 'Not much, perhaps. But Britannicus is no fool. And ever since he was an infant he's been raised to prepare to rule the Empire. Besides, he's the flesh and blood of Claudius. It's his birthright to be emperor. Instead, the poor lad's been pushed aside by that scheming bitch Agrippina and that oily bastard Pallas.'

At the mention of the new emperor's closest adviser, Piso looked around anxiously. The inn was the kind of place that imperial spies and informers frequented to listen in on conversations and identify troublemakers to their paymasters at the palace. Pallas was known to show as little tolerance towards those who criticised him as to those who dared to criticise the emperor. However, no one seemed to be eavesdropping and Piso took a quick sip of wine before giving his friend a warning look. 'Better watch your tongue, Priscus, or you'll get yourself, and the rest of us, into trouble. I would have preferred it if Britannicus was our new emperor just as much as you, but he ain't and there's nothing we can do about it.'

Priscus smiled quickly. 'Not you maybe. But there are people who will do something.'

'What do you mean?'

Before Priscus could respond, they were interrupted by a loud laugh just behind them.

'Why, lads, it's our friend Priscus and his dour little shower of mates!'

Priscus recognised the voice at once but did not turn round. He set his cup down instead and spoke loudly. 'Hey, Biblius, why don't you just fuck off and let me drink in peace?'

'Fuck off?' The new arrival stepped round to the head of the table and looked down at Priscus and his companions. 'Now that's no way to greet an old comrade bearing gifts.'

He pulled the stopper from the wine jar under his arm and topped up Priscus's cup before the latter could react, then raised his own cup to the men at the table.

'Now then, lads. Who'll join me in a toast to our mutual benefactor? To Emperor Nero, may the gods bless him!' He drained the cup in one go before throwing it to the floor with a crash and wiping his lips with the back of his hand. 'That's good stuff.'

None of the men had responded to his toast, and he looked at them and cocked an eyebrow. 'What's this? Not going to drink to our emperor? Smacks of disloyalty to me.' He glanced round at his friends clustered nearby. 'What do you think, boys? Seems like this lot don't think much of Nero. Some might say that's more than disloyal. Treasonous maybe. Perhaps they were hoping for that little prick Britannicus to assume the purple? But as it is, our boy won. Yours lost. The choice has been made and your lot just have to stop moaning and put up with it.'

Priscus stood slowly and raised his cup as he confronted Biblius. 'My apologies, brother. Where are my manners?'

He gently twisted his wrist and a thin stream of dark red wine trickled over Biblius's hand. He continued the movement up Biblius's arm, sloshing more wine over the man's shoulder and then up on to his head, where he gave the cup a little shake to get the last drops out. Then he withdrew his hand and stared at Biblius in silence as the latter scowled.

'You're going to regret that, Priscus.'

'Really?'

Priscus smashed the cup into Biblius's face, shattering both it and the other soldier's nose. Then, as his victim staggered back, blood coursing from his face, he shouted at his friends. 'What are you waiting for? Get stuck in!'

With a roar, his companions leapt up, knocking the benches back and upending the table before they charged the other Praetorians, fists raised like hammers. Priscus kept his attention on Biblius. He had always considered the man a stupid loudmouth, and now it was time to teach him a lesson. Rushing forward, he launched an uppercut that crashed into the man's chin, knocking his head up, then followed through with a blow to the guts and then a cross that struck Biblius on the jaw, sending him reeling before he regained his balance.

He glared wild-eyed at Priscus. 'You are dead!' he roared. 'Fucking dead!'

But before he could make good on his threat, Priscus charged forward and threw another punch. Biblius jerked his head back to avoid the blow, but was too slow and took the full weight of it on his throat. Priscus felt bone and cartilage crunch and Biblius let out a grunt and snatched his hands to his neck as he struggled to breathe. Fists raised, and standing in a half-crouch, Priscus waited for the man to respond. But Biblius took another few paces back, clawing at his throat as his jaw worked frantically, his eyes almost popping from their sockets. Then he stumbled against a stool and fell back, landing heavily and cracking his skull on the flagstone floor. He lay staring at the ceiling, then blinked a few times, shuddered, and did not move again.

Priscus approached warily, but the main fight was taking place over by the counter and he was not threatened. He prodded Biblius with the toe of his boot.

'Get up!'

There was no response, so this time he kicked the man. 'On your feet, you bastard, and I'll show you what happens to those who support Nero.'

Biblius took the kick without responding, and the first cold tingle of fear washed up the back of Priscus's neck. He relaxed his fists and cautiously crouched beside the other man.

'Biblius?'

'He's dead!'

Priscus looked up to see one of the bar girls staring down at him. She clutched a hand to her mouth in shock.

'You've gone and killed 'im!'

'No. I—'

7

'He's DEAD!' she cried out.

Some of the Praetorians glanced over, and a few broke away from the fight to see what was happening. Priscus shook his head as he looked down at the man he had felled. He knew the girl was right.

'But it was an accident . . .'

Biblius was dead. Sure as the rising and setting of the sun. And there was only one punishment for those who killed their comrades in arms. He stood up and backed towards the entrance.

'You killed him.' One of Biblius's men stabbed his finger at Priscus.

Priscus turned and ran. Out on to the street without his cloak, into the cold rain. Without thinking, he turned away from the direction of the Praetorian camp and fled, racing down the street as the shouts from the inn followed him.

He had only gone a short way before he heard someone behind him cry, 'There he goes!' He sprinted on, as fast as he could, until he saw the opening to a dark alley ahead and dived into it. He took the first right, then a left, and ran hard. The sounds of pursuit continued for a while before falling away into the distance. Still he ran, putting more distance between himself and his pursuers, until he finally stopped in a street just off the Forum and pressed himself into the shadows of an archway, gasping for breath.

He had killed a man. It had been an accident, a simple accident. But that would not excuse him from the rigours of military discipline. He was as good as dead if he allowed himself to be captured. Particularly if his anti-Nero sentiments were taken into account. The division of loyalties within the Praetorian Guard was making the senior officers nervous enough already. They would be sure to make an example of him, as much to show what happened to those who opposed Nero as to punish him for murdering a brother in arms.

There was only one place he could go now. One place where there were others who thought like him. Who would conceal him until the hue and cry had died down. Others who were waiting for the right moment to overthrow the usurper Nero and kill all those in his faction. They would not be pleased by Priscus's actions, but they needed his particular skills and could not afford to refuse him shelter.

The rain had stopped by the time he had caught his breath and decided on his course of action. Priscus emerged from the archway, straightening his back, and strode away, trying to look like a man who had nothing to trouble his conscience. He knew exactly where he was going and where the future would take him.

CHAPTER TWO

The feast to mark the end of the Sullan games had just got under way when the uninvited guests arrived at the house of Senator Sempronius. It was a modest home by the standards of most aristocrats of his rank, but then Sempronius had never traded on his family name to gain lucrative tax-collecting concessions or preferment. He had even permitted his only daughter to marry beneath her when she wed Quintus Licinius Cato, a young army officer with considerable promise. Though Julia had since died, she had provided the senator with a grandson to continue the family name.

The death of Emperor Claudius, scarcely a month ago, had not come as a surprise to those in Rome, Sempronius reflected. The emperor had been old and increasingly decrepit, and rarely seen in public. His death had been described as peaceful, and the word was that he had slipped away surrounded by members of the imperial family and his closest advisers. His successor had been announced in almost the same breath, causing the more cynical inhabitants of the capital to observe that anointing a new emperor took time to arrange, and that it was likely that Claudius's corpse had been left to corrupt in some side room while his successor's supporters made sure of his position.

And so Nero Claudius Caesar Augustus Germanicus had been presented to the people of Rome as their new ruler. Yet there were rumours that Claudius had been murdered by his young wife. Poisoned. Agrippina may have claimed the purple for her son, but it was no secret that many influential people were resolutely opposed to Nero. The kind of people who might very easily be counted amongst the guests of Senator Sempronius on this chilly December evening.

The rain clouds had gone and the night sky was clear. Tables and couches had been arranged around the sides of the large courtyard at the rear of the house, and the senator's guests were warmed by braziers as they helped themselves to the pastries neatly arranged on the platters placed before them. The host was seated in the place of honour on a raised dais, with the most prestigious guests on either side of him. To his right lay Britannicus – a surly, intelligent youth, picking the crust off a small venison pie as he stared down at it in a desultory manner. Behind his couch stood his illiterate body slave, a hulking former gladiator whose tongue had been cut out to ensure he would never speak of anything he overheard.

Sempronius shifted to his left, and was discussing the recent news from Hispania with a stocky crop-haired senator and his wife when his attention was drawn to his steward, waving frantically from the corridor leading to the front door. Sempronius dabbed his lips with the tips of his fingers. 'Please excuse me, Vespasian. I seem to be needed.'

His guest frowned. 'What?'

Sempronius gestured towards his steward, and Vespasian's wife nodded sympathetically. 'You can never relax at your own social event. How tiresome.'

'Quite. Please pay it no mind, Domitia, and enjoy these

little snacks. I think you'll find that my cook has no equal in the art of baking.'

With a smile Sempronius shifted round and eased himself off the couch and on to his feet. Brushing the crumbs from his tunic, he picked his way along the side of the yard to where the steward was waiting, his expression anxious.

'What's the matter?' Sempronius demanded. 'Is it that bloody lyre player? You did agree the price I said with him, didn't you?'

'It's not that, master.' Croton shook his head. 'There's a man from the palace at the door. Says Pallas sent him.'

'Pallas?' Sempronius frowned. What could the imperial freedman want with him at this hour? No doubt the man was flexing a bit of muscle, now that the boy he had chosen to back was on the throne. Pallas had made a fortune under the previous emperor, and was set to enrich himself even further under Nero. It was one of the more egregious features of the age that humble – not to mention devious – freedmen exercised more power and influence than the Senate. The members of that august body had ruled Rome from the time when the last of the kings had been removed up until the advent of the Caesars. Now the senators lived in the ever-lengthening shadow of the emperors, though many still harboured dreams of a return to the glorious days of the Republic, when men served the ideal of Rome rather than a line of quasi-divine despots afflicted by mercurial fits of cruelty, madness and stupidity.

'Right then. Let's see what he wants.'

The senator followed Croton back through the house to the entrance hall. A thin figure in the blue tunic of the imperial household stood waiting beside the studded door. He bowed briefly before he spoke.

'Senator Sempronius, I bring greetings in the name of Marcus Antonius Pallas, first freedman to the emperor.'

'First freedman?' That was a title Sempronius had not heard before. Clearly Pallas was moving to cement his place at Nero's side.

'Yes, sir. My master bids me inform you that the emperor and his retinue wish to honour you with a visit to your home.'

Sempronius felt his pulse quicken in alarm. 'Did he say why?'

'I was told to tell you it was a social call, sir.' The slave's faint smile betrayed that the senator's anxiety at the news had been anticipated. 'My master says there is no cause for concern.'

'I am not bloody concerned!' Sempronius snapped. 'Who the hell does that jumped-up freedman think he is?'

The slave opened his mouth to respond, but thought better of it and bowed his head in a cursory gesture of deference. Sempronius glared at the man as he forced himself to calm down. 'Very well, when is the emperor coming? I'll need to send my cook to the Forum first thing in the morning. Is there anything in particular he is fond of?'

'Sir, he is coming here tonight.'

'Tonight?'

The senator exchanged a quick glance with Croton. The feast had taken many days to prepare, and now they'd have to call a halt to proceedings and send the guests away as soon as possible.

'At any moment, sir. I was sent ahead to announce his arrival when the imperial retinue began to climb the hill.'

The foot of the Viminal was no more than a quarter of a mile away, and even as Sempronius began to calculate the time it would take the imperial party to reach his front door, he heard the crunch of nailed boots in the street outside and a voice bellowing for the way to be cleared. There was no time to prepare to receive his unexpected visitors. He swallowed nervously and nodded to Croton.

'Open the door.'

His steward slid back the iron bolt and drew the heavy door inwards with a faint rasp from the solid hinges. Cold air wafted into the entrance, carrying with it the stink of ordure and stale sweat and rotting vegetation from the street. Low flames flickering in the small braziers hanging either side of the door cast a faint loom over the paved thoroughfare running past the senator's home. To the left, the street sloped in the direction of the Forum, and less than thirty paces away Sempronius saw a torch being held aloft by a Praetorian guardsman. The plumed helmet of an officer followed behind, and then the dull gleam from the armour of a small column of soldiers. Beyond, two litters swayed gently as their bearers struggled to keep up with the guardsmen. Between the house and the imperial retinue, lit by the wash of light spilling out from a corner tavern, stood several youths, thumbs tucked defiantly into their wide leather belts. Some still held clay cups in their hands.

'You lot! Out of the way, I said!' the Praetorian officer shouted. 'Or you'll feel the flat of my sword on your arses. Move!'

The largest of the youths, his pockmarked face ringed by oiled curls of dark hair, stepped forward and cocked his head to one side.

'What's this, lads? Visitors to our street? I don't recall inviting them.'

His gang, spirits emboldened by cheap wine, laughed and jeered at the oncoming Praetorians.

'On whose say-so do you come into our neighbourhood, friend?'

'In the name of the emperor! Now move aside, unless you want to be thrown to the beasts.'

One of the youths raised his fingers to his mouth and blew a flat, mocking catcall. Their leader drained his cup and suddenly hurled it at the soldiers. It struck the crest of the officer's helmet and exploded into fragments and a spray of dregs.

'Little bastards!' the officer yelled. 'I'll have you!'

He snatched out his sword, thrust aside the man carrying the torch and charged towards the youths. Their leader turned lightly on his heel.

'Time to run, boys!'

With gleeful shouts they rushed up the street, past Sempronius's house, and turned into a narrow alley a little further on, their laughter fading into the distance. The officer sheathed his blade with a muttered curse and continued leading his party up to the entrance, where he shouted an order. The guardsmen halted, and there was a beat before their officer called out their orders and pairs of men trotted on to take up positions guarding the streets and alleys immediately around the senator's home. Once they were in place, the officer waved the litters forward and turned to salute Sempronius.

'Sextus Afranius Burrus, Prefect of the Guard.'

Sempronius had not seen the man before, but knew the name. Burrus was one of the officers promoted in the last months of Claudius's reign, on the advice of Pallas and the empress, and was a supporter of Nero's accession.

There was no time to return the greeting, as the first of the litters had stopped in front of the entrance. The lead bearer quietly called out an instruction and the litter was lowered gently to the ground. There was a brief pause, during which Sempronius could hear a soft exchange of words, before a hand slipped out through the folds of the cloth draped over the litter and drew them aside. Gleaming red leather boots swung out, and then the emperor heaved himself on to his feet, stretching his back. He affected to ignore Sempronius as he offered his hand to his mother, and a moment later Agrippina stood at his side, her carefully arranged hair slightly awry as she pulled up her stola to cover her shoulder. Sempronius glimpsed a small red patch, like a bite mark, on her neck, and instantly shifted his gaze away.

Slipping his arm round his mother's waist, Nero turned to the senator and spoke in a tone that suggested a chance meeting on the street.

'Ah! My dear Senator Sempronius! A pleasure to see you.'

Sempronius bowed. 'The pleasure is mine, imperial highness.'

'I'm sure. But let us not dwell on formalities. We are all friends now.'

'You honour me.'

Nero wafted a hand dismissively before he continued. 'I am told that you are entertaining friends tonight. A feast apparently.'

Sempronius nodded. 'A modest gathering.'

'By palace standards, I am sure. I understand that you have my stepbrother amongst your guests.'

'Yes, imperial highness.'

Nero stepped closer to Sempronius so that their faces were no more than a foot apart. He stared at the senator in silence, and then suddenly tilted his head and tapped him on the chest. 'Like I said, let's keep this informal. You may address me as Nero tonight.'

The passenger in the other litter had climbed out and was approaching. As he moved into the loom of the flames from the braziers, Sempronius identified Pallas. The imperial freedman was wearing a purple silk tunic beneath a soft wool cape. Gold and jewels glittered on his fingers.

Nero turned to him. 'Britannicus is here, just like you said.'

Pallas smiled thinly. 'Of course. The question is, *why* is he here?'

The enquiry was directed at Sempronius, but the freedman continued smiling at the emperor, as if the senator was some flunkey waiting on the imperial party. Sempronius swallowed anxiously. Pallas turned his dark eyes towards him.

'Well, Senator?'

'I worked closely with Emperor Claudius, and got to know Britannicus from an early age. It was my duty to look out for him then, as it is now. I feel I owe that to his father, who was always kind to me and acted as my patron.'

'Very noble of you.' Nero smiled. 'I am sure my late father would be grateful for the kindness you have shown his flesh and blood. Now, if you will be so good as to lead us through to the feast. We're famished. Come!'

Without waiting to be invited, the emperor and his mother swept over the threshold and headed across the modest hall towards the corridor that led through the house to the courtyard. Pallas left orders for Burrus to make sure that no one entered or left the house without first seeking the permission of the freedman, and then strode after them. Sempronius hurried to catch up and fell into stride beside him.

'I'd have appreciated some notice of this,' he said softly but sharply.

'And I would have appreciated some notice of Britannicus's

whereabouts. He left the palace without notifying anyone. He wasn't missed until the imperial family sat down to dinner. When he didn't appear, it didn't take long for one of his slaves to cough up the truth. With things as they are, I am sure you can understand that there might be a degree of suspicion regarding Britannicus's unexplained absence from the palace.'

Sempronius shot him a sidelong glance. If the prince was the subject of suspicion, then the same suspicion would fall upon those he consorted with.

'I am sure there's nothing sinister behind his accepting an invitation to my house. Like I said, we're friends.'

'Friends.' Pallas nodded. 'That's good. Right now a man needs all the friends he can get. He needs to know exactly who he can trust, and who he can't, and act accordingly. That goes for us all, my dear Senator Sempronius, from the meanest slum-dweller in Subura right up to the emperor himself. You understand?'

'Perfectly.'

Pallas patted him on the shoulder. 'That's good. Anyway, we've tracked Britannicus down and can stop worrying now.'

They emerged from the corridor just behind Nero and his mother, and within a heartbeat the steady hubbub of conversation had died away and there was silence, save for the faint trickle of water tumbling into a fountain. Sempronius looked across to the raised dining area and saw Britannicus glance up anxiously.

Then Agrippina clapped her hands together and trilled, 'What a lovely setting! It's like a little bit of rustic charm has landed right here in the heart of our stuffy capital city. And so many familiar faces!'

She glided towards the nearest guests and greeted them by name as they hurried to stand up out of respect.

'Do please remain seated. We did not mean to cause any fuss; we just wanted to slip in and join the party without fanfare. Senator Granicus, what a pleasure. And you, my dear Cornelia.'

Nero stepped forward to join his mother, and then followed her lead as she made her way around the dining area to the dais where Sempronius had been seated with his most honoured guests. The senator turned and beckoned to his steward. 'Quickly, fetch another couch for the top table.'

Nero overheard the remark and shook his head. 'There's no need, my friend. Just slot us in where there's a gap. No need to make a fuss.'

Vespasian and his wife had already risen from their couches and moved aside as Agrippina approached them.

'Are you sure?'

Vespasian bowed his head. 'Please, it's no bother. We'll find somewhere else.'

'Most kind of you.' Agrippina smiled pertly at Domitia. 'What a courteous husband you have. A real gentleman to be sure.'

'Yes,' Domitia replied curtly. 'He is.'

Agrippina turned from them and lay down gracefully on the couch, patting the empty cushions beside her. 'Come, Nero. Sit next to your mother.'

He did as he was told, eyeing up the glazed pastries before him. Pallas, sensitive to his own lesser social status, stood back from the couch and folded his hands together. Agrippina glanced round at the guests, who were still looking on in silence.

'Do continue your meal. Sempronius, please take your place. There. That's better.'

One by one the guests began to talk in muted tones, and soon the mutters rose in volume as people reached out for fresh snacks to refresh their silver platters. Agrippina waited until she and Nero were no longer the focus of attention and then shuffled round to face Britannicus. The prince returned her gaze with a guarded look, but Sempronius saw that his hands were trembling. His stepmother leaned forward and presented her cheek. 'Kiss me, my dear.'

Fighting to contain his nervousness and distaste, Britannicus swallowed hard and craned his neck to touch his lips to her powdered cheek before hurriedly withdrawing.

'Well, here we all are.' Agrippina clapped her hands together. 'One happy family . . .'

CHAPTER THREE

The imperial party made small talk as the first course came to an end and Sempronius signalled to his steward to clear the trays of snacks away. Most of the conversation on the top table was dominated by the young emperor as Nero expounded his views on the merits of Greek culture and the need to bring more art, poetry and music into the lives of the people of Rome. It was one of his favourite topics and one that Sempronius had been exposed to on many occasions when he had been in the company of the imperial family. He had grown used to Nero's grandiloquence on the subject, and was not a little bored.

The emperor brushed some crumbs from the straggly growth of hair on his chin that passed for a beard, chewed quickly and swallowed as he resumed. 'Of course, this is not to say that the more refined of the arts are suitable for the mob. Far from it. While they may well enjoy some ribald mime show, and the more simple tunes, their tastes are more excited by the flesh and blood of the gladiator fights and chariot races. A man may enjoy those diversions, but his true measure is his appreciation of the finer pursuits that are afforded him. Wouldn't you agree, Sempronius?'

'How could I not agree with such a faultless line of argument?'

'Quite. And it follows that most men are not capable of appreciating the arts. It requires a certain sensitivity, a certain aesthetic insight, that one either has or hasn't. It cannot be taught.'

'Is that so?' Britannicus intervened, easing himself forward so that he could see past Sempronius and view his brother clearly. 'Then tell me, is a man born to play a musical instrument, the lyre, for example? If you are right, then why must men be taught to play the lyre?'

Nero sighed. 'You are taking things too literally, brother, as is always your wont. Of course you need to be taught how to play an instrument, but the ability to play it well is innate. Like the ability to sing.'

'Ah, then you might have said so.'

Nero frowned. 'There are times when I grow tired of your pedantry.'

'And there are times when I struggle to endure the imprecise expression of your thoughts, *brother*. I would have hoped for better after Seneca became your mentor and teacher.'

Nero's lips drew together in a thin line. 'I fear you forget yourself. You are addressing your emperor. Be careful what you say.'

'I shall be very careful. I always am. And I note that you have made much play over recent days of your intention to rule in such a way as to tolerate the free expression of ideas, and to ensure that political persecution comes to an end. All part of this golden era that you have proclaimed, presumably?'

Nero was quiet for a moment before he responded. 'If I did not know you better, I'd say that you were mocking me.'

'Clearly you do not know me then.'

'I have warned you to be careful. I have long tolerated your asides and your snide remarks, my dear brother. Take care that you do not overstep the mark. It is true that I was raised in an austere household devoid of books, while you were indulged by the finest teachers your father could find. It is also true that my young years were largely loveless while my mother eked out her life in exile. While you were enjoying the pleasures of growing up in the palace as the son of the emperor. But that has all changed. Your father – *our* father – is dead, and I am emperor. I have the power of life and death over all those who live in my shadow.'

Britannicus shrugged. 'So much for the golden age of free expression.'

'Do not press me, my dear Britannicus. Every man's patience has a limit.'

In an attempt to keep the peace, Sempronius turned to face the emperor. 'You mentioned singing just now. Do you still sing, like you used to as a child? I thought you had a magnificent voice, even then.'

Nero regarded him with a furrowed brow, clearly irked by being drawn away from his confrontation with his brother. 'I still sing, yes. I sing very well as it happens. I have a natural talent for it.'

Britannicus barely stifled a snort and Nero flinched as if he had been slapped across the face.

'It seems my stepbrother disagrees with your judgement about the quality of my singing. Perhaps he thinks he is better than me. Is that it?'

Britannicus shrugged and reached for his wine goblet. He took a sip and licked his lips. But he made no response to answer the question. The air between the two youths was thick

23

with tension and Sempronius found it acutely uncomfortable to be situated between them. He drew a calming breath and tried to bridge the silence.

'I have heard you two sing, and both of you have fine voices. It's a talent to be proud of.'

'What place is there for pride when a talent is gods-given?' asked Nero. 'A true artist needs to strive for that perfection which is the product of his labours and his labours alone. No help from the gods, nor from his fellow man. The life of an artist is one of perpetual struggle. Few men realise that. But it is the waking thought of my every day.'

'Of course.' Sempronius nodded sympathetically. 'You have the burdens of the world on your shoulders, Caesar. An empire looks to you for firm and fair governance. The people of this great city look to you for the supply of grain and the finest entertainments to be found anywhere in the known world. Such demands would test the wisdom of any man.'

Britannicus raised his eyebrows sympathetically. 'But my brother is not just any man. He has the soul of an artist, and feels the death of every creature as a tragedy. Perhaps it would be kinder to lift the tedious duties of a ruler from his shoulders and leave him to pursue his true talents so that he might gift the Roman people his words and music. Let his voice be filled with song rather than the edicts of a stern ruler.'

'Enough!' Nero snapped. 'I've had enough of your snide comments, brother. You have the heart of a snake. And the sinister sibilance of a serpent's voice as well . . .' He paused, and a crafty expression briefly crossed his face. 'There is one way to put my brother's talent to the test, you know, my dear Sempronius. A singing contest.'

'A contest?' Sempronius winced. 'Here? Now?'

'Why not?' Nero scrambled to his feet, standing on the couch as he clapped his hands to draw the attention of the guests. 'My friends! Lend me your ears!'

Once again the diners fell silent and turned towards the head table with curious expressions.

'Sit down,' Agrippina ordered in an undertone. 'You're making a fool of yourself. You are the emperor now, not a prince. You need to show some decorum.'

'I need to show this whelp that he can't defy me any more,' Nero shot back. 'I need to teach him a lesson.'

'But—'

He thrust a finger at her. 'Quiet, Mother.'

Agrippina's brow furrowed and she made to respond, then checked herself and bowed her head gracefully. 'As you wish, my dear.'

'Precisely. As *I* wish. It's my turn to tell people what to do now.' Nero tilted his head back a little to emphasise his authority, and then drew a breath before he addressed the guests. 'My dear friends, as we are between courses, and it is traditional to offer entertainment at such times, I have decided to treat you to a little singing. As you know, I have something of a reputation for being able to carry a note.' He smiled and at his back Pallas clapped his hands loudly. Agrippina joined in, followed by Sempronius. Several others took the cue and hurriedly followed suit, then those slower on the uptake. The young emperor basked in their applause for a moment before waving his hands to quieten his audience.

'What is not so well known is that my brother, Britannicus, also has aspirations to become a singer.'

The prince composed his face and stared into the mid distance, giving no indication of any response to Nero's words.

'As all parents will know, siblings like to compete, and tonight my brother and I will sing for your pleasure. The better singer will be judged by your show of appreciation. And the prize . . .' Nero hesitated and rubbed his thumbs across the pads of his fingers. He glanced at his mother and suddenly grinned. 'The prize will be this ring!'

Before she could react, he leaned over her, took her hand and pulled a large ruby ring from her finger, holding it aloft. 'A prize worthy of a prince or emperor.'

A brief frown flitted across Agrippina's face before she made herself laugh lightly.

Pallas clapped again and the guests, more aware of what was expected now, did the same.

'Without more ado, I present to you Prince Britannicus, who will perform a song of his choice. Not that I imagine there is much of a choice, given his limited repertoire. Sing, brother, sing!'

Britannicus shook his head and said firmly, 'I will not.'

'What did you say?'

'I will not sing. Not for you.'

Nero shook his head. 'Not for me. For them.'

'I won't do it.'

'You will, brother. Because your emperor commands it, and the emperor's word is law.'

Britannicus sneered. 'Your word is worth nothing to me. The imperial crown was never your birthright. My father was emperor. Your father was a dissolute thug who deserved his early death. You are not the stuff that emperors are made of. It is not in your blood.'

Nero glared at him. 'Careful, brother, you go too far. I gave my word to our father that I would protect you if he died. But

26

if you press your luck, I may be moved to break my promise.'

'You would not dare. Not yet. Not while the foundations of your regime are so unsettled. You would not harm me.'

'Not yet. But who can say how long that situation may last? A year, two perhaps. Once my reign has been securely established, I can do with you as I wish. Until then, I will not harm you. But I can harm those close to you easily enough.' He turned to one of the Praetorian guardsmen standing with Pallas. 'You, draw your sword and hold it to the throat of that cur.' He indicated Britannicus's bodyguard. The latter glanced at his master, but before he could react, the Praetorian had wrenched out his blade and stepped over to the bodyguard, raising the point of his sword so that it rested just under the man's chin. The other guardsman quickly stepped in behind the bodyguard, grasped his hands and forced them behind the man's back. The bodyguard looked imploringly at Britannicus.

'Let him go,' the prince commanded.

'I will, if you sing. If you don't sing, he dies.'

Sempronius, who had sat still and silent during the exchange, coughed and looked up at the emperor. 'Imperial highness, this is my home. These are my guests. This is not the place to shed blood. I beg you, release the man. Enjoy the meal. I have already arranged for music and singing. There's no need for this.'

'I command it. That is all the need there is. Now then, sing, my brother. If you want your man to live.'

Britannicus clasped his hands together and bowed his head, as if praying to the gods to intervene and put an end to the confrontation. Then his shoulders slumped in resignation and he nodded. Sliding off the couch, he made his way to the open ground between the tables and composed himself. No one spoke. No one moved. All stared at him, waiting for him to obey the command of his adopted brother.

Britannicus straightened his back, lifted his chin, drew a deep breath and began. His voice was clear, and he sang in a sweet melodic tone.

> *I wake to the rays of the sun in my eyes,*
> *I bathe in the warm embrace of the day,*
> *I lift my head from the bolster and rise,*
> *And with heavy heart I resume my way.*
>
> *From far Britannia I am summoned home,*
> *By a letter salted with my mother's tears,*
> *No more to fight, no more to roam,*
> *No more the soldier of these many years.*
>
> *I am honour bound to grieve my loss,*
> *And my heart is broken by the death,*
> *Of he who gave me life and purpose,*
> *Who spoke my name with his last breath.*
>
> *I am close to where life's round has led,*
> *Where mother waits to embrace her son,*
> *Ere the family gathers to bury our dead,*
> *And honour the glory my father has won . . .*

He hung on to the last word and let his voice fade into nothing as he bowed his head.

After a brief pause, someone began to clap, and Sempronius glanced round to see that Vespasian was applauding enthusiastically and nodding his approval. Others followed suit until almost every guest was paying tribute to the boy's performance. The prince showed no reaction at first, but as the noise reached a crescendo he raised his head and nodded gratefully to his audience. At length he turned slowly towards the head table and looked Nero straight in the eye. The emperor was rigid with anger, his fists clenched tightly against his sides, as his adopted brother returned to his couch. The applause died away and Agrippina took her son's hand and squeezed it to get his attention.

'For the gods' sake, say something. Don't just stand there.'

The spell was broken and Nero relaxed his body and raised a hand. 'A fine song, movingly performed by my dearest brother. So moving, I fear it has quite overwhelmed me. I feel the same grief for the father we both lost so recently.' He raised the back of his hand to shield his eyes and his shoulders gave a theatrical shudder. 'Indeed . . . I am too overcome by sorrow to be able to sing now. And that is a tragedy compounded by tragedy. I would have sung a song to truly make you all weep with emotion. Alas, there is only so much feeling an audience can endure, and I would not add to that stirred by my brother. For it would truly break your hearts. Better that I spare you such tears . . . However, there is no doubt that my singing far surpasses that of Britannicus, and so I win the competition.' He tossed the ring into the air and caught it tightly in his fist. 'The prize is mine.'

'Bravo!' Pallas called out. 'His imperial highness wins!'

'As if there was ever any doubt that I would.' Nero swung his legs round and stood up from the couch. 'But come, little brother, I have a special prize for you. You shall not return to the palace empty-handed.'

Britannicus saw that his bodyguard was still in the grip of the

Praetorians and gave a subtle indication to the man that he was not to resist. Nero placed his arm around the younger boy's shoulders and steered him away from the other guests, along a paved path that ran between two flower beds towards a hedged area at the rear of the courtyard. Sempronius stared after them anxiously until Agrippina cleared her throat and spoke up.

'Well, we've had our little entertainment. Isn't it about time the next course was served? After all, a good host never keeps his guests waiting, nay?'

'My apologies, imperial highness.' Sempronius gestured to attract the attention of his steward. Croton instantly began to snap orders to the household slaves, and a moment later the first of them re-emerged from the house with fresh silver platters to place in front of the guests. More slaves appeared from the kitchen carrying trays of roasted meats, fish and cheese. The first tray to arrive was presented to the top table, and Sempronius tactfully indicated the empress so that the slave set his burden down directly before her.

'Ah! Roast ducklings. And, if I am not mistaken, that's a garum glaze.'

'Very good, your highness. A speciality of my cook.'

'I can hardly—'

They were interrupted by a cry from the rear of the courtyard. As Sempronius glanced back over his shoulder, another cry, louder, cut through the night air.

'Please!' Britannicus shrieked. 'Please, no! Don't!'

His plea was met with a laugh from his adopted brother.

Sempronius made to rise, then hesitated, looking towards Agrippina and then Pallas for a cue. Neither had reacted to the screams, seeming simply to ignore them.

'As I was saying,' Agrippina resumed, 'I can hardly wait to

tuck in.' She picked up her knife and skewered one of the small fowl, shaking it on to her platter and then daintily picking at the meat.

'No!' Britannicus shrieked. 'Noooooo!'

The senator looked round at the other guests for support, but nearly all of them were staring straight ahead. Only Vespasian had sat up, his expression angry as he prepared to get off his couch. Before he could move, Domitia reached out and took his hand, drawing him firmly back beside her. The only other reaction came from a gaunt older man in a senator's tunic, who glared about him before he spoke out.

'Is no one going to do anything? No one?'

Agrippina raised a finger and pointed at him. 'Senator Amrillus, please be quiet. You're ruining the atmosphere. Sempronius's cook has spoiled us. I can vouch for that. This duckling is simply delicious. You should try some, and stop making a scene.' Her tone hardened. 'Sit down.'

The sounds from the far end of the courtyard continued, growing in intensity as Britannicus begged and cried for pity. Now and again Nero swore or laughed mockingly, and all the while the guests, with the exception of Amrillus, forced themselves to pick at their food, not able even to sustain any conversation between themselves. At length the cries subsided. There was a final, wild cry of ecstasy from Nero, and a deep animal grunt, and then all that could be heard was the sobbing of the younger boy.

Sempronius risked a glance over his shoulder and saw the emperor emerge from the hedges into the loom of the light cast from the braziers and torches that illuminated the feast. Nero paused, adjusting his tunic and pulling the hem down, then strolled back to rejoin the guests, his face gleaming with perspiration. The senator looked away hurriedly as the youth's boots crunched on the path. Nero stopped at the end of his couch but made no attempt to return to his place at the feast. He spoke briefly to the Praetorians and ordered them to release his brother's bodyguard. They did as they were told, then the guardsman who had pinned the man's arms behind his back gave him a shove and kicked him behind the knees so that he collapsed.

'I've had enough fun here, Mother. My brother has been taught a lesson I doubt he'll forget in a hurry. Now I'm tired and I want to sleep. We're returning to the palace.'

'So soon?' Agrippina plucked another morsel from the carcass of the duckling and popped it into her mouth. 'Surely we can finish our meal first?'

'Right now, Mother. I'm bored.'

Nero became aware that the others were looking past him, and he glanced back as Britannicus came limping out of the hedges. His knees were scratched and bloody and every step he took made him wince as he cuffed the last tears from his eyes.

'This is an outrage!' Amrillus raged. 'A bloody outrage. Is no one else going to say anything? No one?' He stared round the other guests, challenging them. But not one person dared to respond. One of his friends implored him to be quiet. Amrillus spat in disgust. 'Cowards! Cowards all! Is this what Rome has sunk to? Are we going to sit on our hands while outrages are perpetrated within earshot, and pretend nothing is happening? Well?'

There was no reply, and Nero laughed. 'Oh do be quiet, you old fool. It's just a little fun. Horseplay, that's all it is.'

'Horseplay?' Amrillus sneered. 'If I was a young man again, I'd flog you to within an inch of your life. Come, Junia, we're leaving.' He reached for his wife's hand and struggled to help her to her feet, then without any further word the elderly couple shuffled round the back of the couches and disappeared into the corridor leading to the entrance of the house.

Agrippina quietly called Pallas to her side and the freedman leaned forward to listen as she whispered to him. Pallas nodded and then retreated to pass the order on to the two Praetorians, who strode off in pursuit of Amrillus and his wife. Then the empress stood up and linked arms with her son, and the pair, followed by Pallas, made their exit, not even thanking Sempronius for his hospitality, nor bidding farewell to his guests. Britannicus stopped halfway along the path and eased himself down on to a stone bench before resting his head in his hands, his shoulders heaving with fresh sobs. The prince's bodyguard hurried to his master and knelt in front of him, trying to offer some comfort.

Another guest rose to leave, then others in a steady trickle, hurriedly taking their leave of Sempronius, as he sadly bade them farewell.

'What do you say now?' asked Domitia as she offered him her hand. She glanced round to make sure that they would not be overheard. Her husband was talking in muted tones with three other senators several paces away.

Sempronius shook his head. 'You're playing with fire. I don't want any part in what you're planning. It was bad enough that you involved my daughter. I shall never forgive you for that.'

Domitia was unmoved. 'Julia did what she did out of love for Rome. Never forget that. If only a fraction of her class had the courage and good sense to do the same, then none of us would ever again have to witness the kind of thing we saw

33

tonight. This is how it begins, Sempronius. We saw the same with Caligula, and before him his vile uncle Tiberius. Even Claudius was not immune to the cruel streak of despotism that runs through his family.'

'I don't want to hear this. I don't want to know. You are talking treason, and you'll get us all killed. And not just those who oppose Nero. You'll put others at risk who have no part in this. People like your husband. Those accused of treason are rarely the only victims.'

'Treason?' Domitia sniffed. 'I thought treason meant betraying your state. We've been betraying Rome for the best part of a hundred years, Sempronius. We betrayed our birthright the moment we allowed the Caesars to pass Rome on from generation to generation as if it was a family heirloom. And look where it has got us. We live at the whim of mad and cruel men who treat us as flies to the gods. If only Vespasian wasn't so damned honourable, he would be standing with us. We need to rid ourselves of these emperors.'

'It will be different this time,' Sempronius countered desperately. 'Nero has promised to restore power to the courts and the Senate.'

'And you believe him? All tyrants promise to be benevolent when they come to power. Did you ever hear of one who held to his promise? No? I didn't think so. Nero is no different. Only a fool would think otherwise. He's part of the sickness affecting Rome. Every emperor has abused his power, indulged his base appetites and scandalised Roman society. My worry is that if it continues much longer, we may grow so used to these excesses that we accept them without question.'

Sempronius nodded towards Britannicus. 'Do you think he would be any different?'

'Britannicus believes in the Republic. So did his father towards the end. And that's why Claudius was murdered.'

'So you say.'

Domitia stared into his eyes and clicked her tongue. 'You can't sit on your hands for ever, Sempronius. You're going to have to pick a side one day.'

'I can wait for that day.'

'I don't think so. It'll come sooner than you think. And then all that will matter is which side you are on. It's winner takes all, and we know what happens to losers in that case. Think on that.' She leaned forward as her husband approached and kissed Sempronius politely on the cheek. 'Goodnight, my dear senator.'

As she stood aside, Vespasian clasped hands with his host and nodded. 'It's been an . . . eventful evening, I'll say that at least.'

'Indeed. Your wife and I were just discussing it.'

'We'll be going then. I'll see you in the Senate tomorrow, I take it?'

'I'll be there.'

Vespasian half turned and indicated Britannicus. 'What about him?'

'I'll see to it that he gets back to the palace safely.'

'Good.'

Vespasian placed a hand on his wife's hip and steered her towards the entrance of the house.

'I'm sure we'll see you again soon,' said Domitia. 'I'll look forward to it.'

Sempronius smiled weakly and waited until they were out of sight before he slumped on to his couch and rubbed his forehead.

'By all the gods,' he muttered to himself. 'What am I to do? What?'

CHAPTER FOUR

They could almost taste the fear in the city the moment they reached the city gate on the Ostian Way. The squad of Praetorians on duty hefted their spears and shields as the two officers approached in the thin light of dusk.

'Easy, lads,' Centurion Macro called out and gave a friendly wave. 'We're on the same side. You can lower the spears.'

The optio in command waited until he could see the two men clearly before he gave the order to stand down. 'Sorry, sir. We're under strict orders to check everyone entering or leaving Rome.'

'Oh?' Macro halted just outside the gate. His companion, a taller, younger officer with a vivid scar running from his brow and down his cheek, eased the folds of his cloak aside and stretched his back as he looked along the wall and noted the extra sentries on duty on the walkway and in the towers. As he did so, he revealed the ribbon tied across his scale vest that marked him out as a senior officer. At once the optio stiffened to attention.

'Sorry, sir. Had no idea you were a high-ranker. I'd be honoured if you'd inspect my section.'

Cato shook his head. 'No need for that. We're not on duty. Just heading home for a rest.' He paused and looked at the optio more closely. 'Don't I know you? Yes, I have it now. We talked some months back when the centurion and I were returning from Britannia. Gannicus, wasn't it?'

'Yes, sir.' The optio grinned with delight that he, and more importantly his name, had been remembered. 'It's good to see you again, sir. I'd have thought you'd be back campaigning in Britannia by now.'

'I wish I was. We've just returned from Hispania. Had a hard time of it.'

'You were with the lads that did the operation in Asturica, sir?'

'That was us,' Macro answered, patting the medal harness on his chest. 'Second Cohort of the Praetorian Guard.'

The optio's eyes gleamed. 'The Second? Then it was your lads that gave the rebels a pasting?'

'That we did.'

The optio stood to attention and saluted. 'It's an honour, sir. And you too, sir,' he added as he bowed his head to Cato.

Cato smiled modestly and Macro laughed.

'Oh, make no mistake, Gannicus, the prefect here is not one of those officers who stand by and try to look pretty while the likes of us get stuck in. He's come up the hard way, through the ranks. Cato's one of us.'

'Just on better terms and conditions,' Cato added, and the three soldiers shared another laugh before he continued. 'So, what's the story about the death of Claudius? We heard rumours in Ostia that it wasn't entirely down to natural causes.'

At once the optio's demeanour changed. A mask of cold formality slid into place and he stepped back half a pace. 'That's what the new emperor's enemies are saying, sir. I wouldn't go around repeating them rumours if I were you. The boys in the

Praetorian Guard are happy with Nero and wouldn't take kindly to anyone saying he did his old man in.'

Cato regarded the optio closely and then nodded. 'Thanks for the warning.'

'Just saying, sir. It's best to keep a closed mouth right now. Until the matter is settled.'

'It isn't settled?'

'Not for me to say, sir.' The optio turned away and waved to his men. 'Let 'em pass!'

Macro glanced at his friend, and the latter arched an eyebrow and shook his head. 'Save it all for later, eh? When we're not going to be overheard. Anyway, here we are again, back in Rome, but this time we're the bearers of good news.'

'Not sure that's going to make much difference given the way things seem to be, if Gannicus and his boys are anything to go by.'

They strode beneath the lofty arch of the gate and into the shadowy street beyond. At once Cato was struck by how few people were abroad. Even though it was winter, the streets should be bustling at this hour. Instead they saw only a handful of inhabitants, who regarded the two officers warily as they passed by. Elsewhere they encountered patrols of guardsmen, and men from the urban cohorts tasked with keeping order on the streets. Unlike the Praetorians, the latter had no ceremonial role and were not even regarded as proper soldiers. Armed with staves, they were ready to beat anyone who dared make a show of defiance.

That reality became quite clear as Cato and Macro encountered a squad from one of the cohorts, standing around a bruised youth as he was forced to scrub out a crude illustration of a boy fucking a woman from behind. Her hairstyle was the kind favoured by rich matrons. The air in the neighbourhood reeked of rotting animal fat, and Cato saw a sign above the entrance to a tannery a short distance further on.

'What's all this then?' Macro demanded.

The leader of the patrol looked the two officers over and shrugged. 'Caught this one just as he'd finished his masterpiece. Helped ourselves to a bucket and brush from the tannery there and set him to work.'

The man was carrying a cane, and he slashed at the boy's buttocks. 'Put some elbow grease into it, you little bastard.'

The boy yelped and resumed his scrubbing. Now that they were close to, Cato could make out the names scrawled above the image, making each character's identity perfectly clear: Nero and Agrippina. He gestured to the drawing. 'Has there been much of this sort of thing?'

'More than I'd like. And far more than the new emperor and his mum are happy with. As you can imagine. This little twat's not the first one we've caught today. The last fool is nursing a couple of broken fingers. Won't be up to his tricks again for a while!' The leader of the patrol chuckled. 'And once this one's done, we'll make sure of him too.'

He raised his cane to strike again, but this time Macro moved swiftly and caught his wrist firmly, gave it a wrench and spun the man round away from him. Bracing his leg, he kicked out and the patrol leader went flying face first into the wall, slumping down unconscious with a grunt. At once his men raised their staves and turned to face the two Praetorians. The boy stood in the middle, glancing anxiously from side to side, the scrubbing brush trembling in his hand.

Cato looked at Macro. 'Not sure how wise that was, my friend,' he muttered.

Macro puffed his cheeks. 'Me neither. But what I am sure about is that I don't like grown men who think it's big to bully kids.'

He lifted his vine cane and slapped the gnarled head into the palm of his spare hand as he faced the rest of the patrol. Five men, he noted. Three of whom were overweight and heavy-jowled from spending too much time in the capital's taverns. No doubt using their office to extort free drinks. Of the remainder, one man was grey-haired and wiry and the last was the only one who looked like a threat. His nose was flat, his ears swollen and his shoulders heavy with muscle. A boxer most like, Macro decided.

'I think you and your friend had better go,' warned the grey-haired man.

'And leave the kid to you and that bastard down there? No chance. It's you lot who are going, if you know what's good for you.'

'Macro, I don't think this is a good idea,' Cato said calmly. 'But good idea or not, I'm with you.'

Macro nodded, keeping his eyes firmly on the men two sword lengths in front of him. He tightened his grip on the vine cane as he eased himself down into a balanced crouch. He saw the boxer move first, winding back to strike. Before he could, Macro pounced, charging forward and driving the head of his cane hard into the man's gut, just below his ribcage. The air exploded from his lungs as he stumbled back under the impact. A swift uppercut from Macro snapped his jaw closed and his head back, and he went down heavily. One of the overweight men swung clumsily with his stave towards Macro's head.

'No, you don't,' Cato growled through clenched teeth, and kicked him hard in the side of the knee. There was a dull crack and the man howled in pain as he collapsed. Macro swung his cane at the wiry man and caught him hard on the upper arm, a numbing blow that caused him to drop his stave. The two remaining men drew back quickly, weapons raised but clearly unwilling to get drawn into a fight. Macro grinned at them.

'Come on, lads. What you waiting for? Saturnalia? Or is it that you're only big and brave when you're up against runts?' He took a step towards them, but Cato intervened.

'That's enough, Macro. You've made your point. You two had better get your friends out of here and back to the watch-house. Do it now.'

They didn't need any further encouragement, picking up their injured comrade and their unconscious leader while the boxer climbed to his feet and shook his head to try and clear it. Under the officers' wary gaze, they turned away and headed down the street. The boy laughed with delight and blew a loud raspberry, then hurled the brush after them.

Macro grabbed him by the ear. 'That's enough, you little toerag. I may not like bullies, but I'm a stickler for rules, and I'm pretty sure it's against the rules to go round daubing the walls of this fine city with pictures of the emperor putting one up his mother's arse. Right?'

The boy gave a pained yelp and nodded.

'Then you'd better beat it. Next time we won't be around to help you. So make sure there is no next time. Clear?'

'Yes, sir.'

Macro released his grip and gave the boy a gentle push. 'Now piss off.'

The boy scurried away and dived down the nearest side alley, out of sight, before his rescuers changed their minds about letting him go. Macro could not help laughing as he straightened up. But Cato's expression was serious.

'What's the matter? They deserved that.'

'I don't doubt it,' Cato replied. 'I'm just not sure we want to draw attention to ourselves. You heard what Gannicus said.'

'Ah, it was just a bit of harmless fun, that's all.'

'Try telling that to the commander of the urban cohorts. He's not going to be pleased when he hears that a couple of Praetorians have turned over one of his patrols. And they saw that we were officers. Won't take a genius to track us down, and maybe report us to the palace.'

'But we're heroes of Rome. Who'd want to tangle with us?'

'I can think of a few who might,' Cato mused.

Macro sniffed and turned back to the illustration, taking it in for a moment with his head cocked slightly to one side. 'You know, he's got talent, that boy. Crude, yes, but there's no mistaking the likeness now you look at it. Just hope young Nero there is going at it gently. After all, she is his mother.'

Cato shook his head. 'Macro, sometimes . . .'

His friend punched him lightly on the shoulder. 'Oh, come on. Just having a laugh. Let's get out of here. You must be keen to see your son.'

Cato nodded. It had been some months since he had last seen Lucius, and even then there had been little time between his return from Britannia and being sent to Spain. Now he was determined to remain with his infant son for much longer. Following the death of his wife, Julia, and the settling of the debts she had left behind her, Cato had been forced to sell his home and send Lucius and his nurse to live with his father-in-law. Senator Sempronius had plenty of room in his home, and besides, he was more than pleased to be given the responsibility of raising his grandson.

Sempronius's house was on the Viminal Hill, and Cato and Macro had to cross the almost deserted Forum and climb the hills on the far side, picking their way up the narrow streets between the crumbling piles of cheaply built tenement blocks that eventually gave way to the wealthier neighbourhood on the Viminal. By the time they had turned into the street on which the senator lived, it was late in the evening. Ahead of them they saw a procession of torches being held to light the way of a small column of Praetorian guardsmen escorting two litters.

They stepped off the street into the arched entrance of a tavern to let the soldiers and litters pass by. The last two guardsmen had bundles over their shoulders, and as they drew closer, Cato could see that they were bodies wrapped in cloaks. A grey-haired head lolling between two skinny arms was hanging down the back of one Praetorian. The other body was a woman of similar age. Both were well dressed, and the man wore the red stripe of a senator on his tunic. The curtains of the second litter were open, and by the light of the torch being carried beside it, Cato saw Pallas, leaning back on a cushion, hands behind his head as he stared up with a contented smile.

Cato retreated into the shadows, drawing Macro with him.

'What?'

'Shh. Be still.'

The procession passed by, and then the street outside the tavern was empty again. Cato waited until they were a good thirty paces away before he emerged.

'Did you see who that was?'

Macro nodded. 'Pallas,' he hissed. 'The oily bastard.'

'Yes. I wonder what he was doing here, on the Viminal. In this street. And who was in the first of the litters. And whose bodies those were.'

Macro looked at him. 'You don't suppose . . . ? Not Sempronius?'

'No. Too old. Too thin. Anyway, we'll know soon enough. Come on.'

They hurried down the street to the house of Cato's father-in-law and he rapped loudly on the door. Almost at once it was opened by the senator's steward, who looked them up and down carefully, as was his habit with callers even though he was familiar with the two men on the doorstep.

'Master Cato, and Centurion Macro. We'd heard the expeditionary force had returned to Ostia only this afternoon. You've made good time. The senator will be delighted to see you.'

Croton stepped aside to let them enter. In the hall, there were several other figures, collecting cloaks and being joined by their slave escorts as they prepared to return to their homes through the dangerous streets of the capital.

'Looks like the senator's been entertaining,' said Macro.

'Yes, sir. But the party is over now.'

'Too bad. Um . . .' Macro clicked his tongue. 'Any chance of some tasty leftovers?'

'More than I'd like to think, thanks to the way things have gone.'

Macro gestured towards the departing guests as they made for the open door. 'Their loss. Our gain.'

Croton led the two officers through the house. Just before they emerged into the garden, they encountered a familiar face.

'By the gods!' Vespasian boomed. 'Surely that can't be young Cato and that old sweat Centurion Macro?'

He strode towards Cato and they clasped forearms as the prefect bowed his head. 'Good to see you again, sir.'

'I see they're still keeping you here in Rome, Legate,' said Macro. 'Waste of a damned good legion commander. You should be out in the field. I dare say our troubles in Britannia would have been concluded years ago if you had been put in charge of the province.'

Vespasian allowed himself a smile at the praise. 'Ah well, I could only have managed it if officers like you two were still serving in the Second Augusta. A fine legion, that.'

'One of the best, sir,' Macro responded.

'So what are you two doing here? Last I heard, you were in Hispania.'

Cato nodded. 'Just returned.'

Domitia positioned herself beside her husband and took his arm as his former comrades nodded a greeting at her. She smiled back. 'I take it that the Praetorian cohorts are not far behind you?'

'Yes, my lady,' Cato replied. 'Our ship was amongst the first to arrive. The others will return to barracks the moment they land.'

'Good. Rome needs soldiers it can count on in the days to come.'

Vespasian's brow creased briefly as he glanced at his wife. 'Rome can count on all its soldiers. They're not the problem. Let's not burden these two with matters that need not concern them, eh?'

Domitia forced a smile and squeezed his arm. 'As you wish, my love.'

Vespasian looked tired suddenly. 'Look here, we should meet again when there's more time to talk. Perhaps you'll come to dinner at my house sometime soon?'

'That's very kind of you, sir,' said Cato. 'It'd be a pleasure.'

'Good. Let's make certain it happens. I'll be in touch.' Vespasian patted Cato's shoulder and nodded a curt farewell to Macro before steering his wife towards the entrance. 'Come, my dear.'

Cato gazed after his former commander. 'And what was that all about?' he muttered.

'What d'you mean?'

'That comment of hers about the days to come?'

Macro shrugged and smacked his lips. 'I'm more concerned about the meal to come. Besides, we can find out when we take 'em up on the dinner invitation. No rush.'

'Let's hope not.'

They continued following Croton towards the garden.

Only a handful of guests remained, clustered round the head table and engaged in earnest conversation. As they heard the sound of military boots crunching on gravel, they all turned to look at the approaching officers in the off-white tunics and cloaks of the Praetorian Guard. Then Sempronius stepped forward, his arms outstretched.

'Thank the gods you have returned safely,' he said, embracing Cato. 'And you too, Macro.'

Cato was touched by the warmth of the welcome, but the suspicious looks on the faces of some of Sempronius's guests caused him concern. Then he saw Prince Britannicus, lying on his front on a couch to one side, his cheeks streaked with tears.

Cato glanced at his friend and Macro let out a low whistle.

'By the gods, what has been going on here?'

CHAPTER FIVE

Once the last of the guests had left, Sempronius detailed six of his slaves to escort Britannicus to the house the prince had inherited from his mother, rather than risking a return to the imperial palace. The boy had brushed off his bodyguard's attempt to carry him out to the litter and walked stiffly by himself, face rigid with strain as he fought to hide the pain from the injuries inflicted by his stepbrother. The senator returned to the head table and slumped on a couch next to Cato and Macro. The latter had managed to head off some of the slaves clearing the dishes away and had amassed a sizeable personal feast on several platters arranged in front of him. He was chewing on a chunk of spiced beef from the end of a skewer as Sempronius rejoined them, and nodded at the skewer appreciatively. 'Nice rations, sir.'

'Glad someone is enjoying them. Do you want anything to eat, Cato?'

'Maybe later.' Cato had more pressing matters to deal with. 'How is my son?'

'Lucius is fine. Seems to grow a bit more every day. I reckon he'll be a tall lad, like his father. He has his mother's spirit, too,' Sempronius added wistfully before looking at Cato. 'I'm sorry.

I imagine you are still hurt by what you may think she did. But she was my daughter, and I grieve for her. And her blood runs in Lucius's veins just as much as yours does.'

Cato felt the familiar stab of pain and anger in his heart as he recalled his dead wife's betrayal. But, he noted, the hurt was less than it had been before. Time heals all wounds, he mused. If only because time kills us all in the end. At the moment he felt there was no prospect of him ever forgetting, still less forgiving. But her actions were not the fault of Sempronius, whom he still regarded with respect and affection. So he did not dwell on the subject.

'I'm grateful to you for taking him in.'

'He's my kin. What else would I do? Besides, it's been a pleasure to look after him.'

Cato nodded. 'I thank you anyway. I'll be looking to find myself a new home, once I can afford it. My prospects are good, as long as my appointment to the Praetorian Guard holds. Especially with a new emperor on the scene, anxious to buy his way into the affections of those soldiers charged with protecting him. I should be able to afford something comfortable for Lucius and myself within a few years.'

'Assuming that Nero's reign continues without any trouble flaring up,' said Sempronius. 'Right now, I wouldn't bet on that. Particularly not after tonight's events.'

He briefly recounted Nero's intrusion on the feast, and the outrage he had perpetrated on Britannicus. When he had concluded, Macro wiped his lips on the back of his hand and shook his head.

'Fucking sick in the head, that is. What kind of a man does that?'

'What kind of a man indeed? What kind of emperor will

such a man prove to be? That is the question that is bedevilling Rome. And while there is no clear answer to that, there are plenty who are questioning whether Nero is capable of ruling the Empire. Some are openly calling for Britannicus to replace him. Many more are scheming in secret. Who knows where this will lead?'

'We heard rumours on the way here,' said Cato. 'But matters seem to be worse than I thought. Do you think there's any realistic prospect of Britannicus winning enough support to make a credible challenge for the throne?'

Sempronius considered this for a moment before he responded. 'Hard to say. The Senate is divided on the matter, but few are willing to take an open position. That's the surest way to an early grave these days. Most are waiting for their cue before they support either side. The fact is, far more senators would prefer it if we didn't have to choose either one of them. Neither is a particularly attractive individual. But they are the only choices we have, short of declaring an end to imperial succession and a return to the Republic. And that's the kind of talk that the Praetorian Guard doesn't like to hear. Why would they? As things stand, they're living like pigs in clover. The very last thing they want is to see the back of the emperors and their need for a pampered and privileged bodyguard. To make matters worse, the officers and many of the men have divided loyalties. It's no coincidence that the men chosen to put down the rebellion in Hispania were known to favour Britannicus. That's why they were sent away from Rome until Nero had succeeded Claudius. Who knows what will happen now that they've returned? If Britannicus can win over enough support in Rome, and further afield, he might yet depose his rival. Or he might start a civil war. Something we've managed to avoid for nearly a hundred years.' Sempronius folded his hands together and rested his chin on them in a resigned pose.

Cato reflected on the senator's words. 'You may be right. What if the conflict spills over into the rest of the Empire? I know that the legions in Britannia would prefer Britannicus to be their emperor. And there will be other units who will feel the same way, or whose commanders can be bribed.'

Macro popped a small pastry in his mouth, chewed quickly and swallowed. 'Or it's possible that people will just get used to the new emperor – even if he mistreats his stepbrother – and everything will continue as before. Just saying.'

'We can only hope,' Sempronius replied disconsolately.

The three sat in thought for a while before Cato stretched towards the nearest of Macro's platters and helped himself to a chicken leg. He tore off a strip of meat and worked his jaws slowly before turning to look at the senator closely. 'What about you? If it came to picking sides, who would you choose? Nero, or Britannicus?'

'Not an easy question to answer. In truth, neither. I'd prefer that we return to being a republic. But that choice is unlikely to be available to us. Some say that the Empire is simply too big to be effectively ruled by the Senate, which is riven by factions and rivalries. Maybe Rome can no longer survive without power being controlled by a single individual. If so, we need the emperors. They are all that stand between us and the chaos of the last years of the Republic.' Sempronius watched Cato closely as he continued. 'No one wants a return to that.'

'They might not want it, but then again, they might not be able to avoid it.' Cato poured some wine into a silver goblet and took a sip. 'For the sake of my son, I'll not be taking sides. Not my circus, not my monkeys. I'll leave it all well enough alone.'

Sempronius looked at him with a sad expression. 'Sitting it out may not be an option, my boy. You may choose to try and avoid the situation, but the situation may not avoid you.'

'You could be right. But in the meantime, I'll do my best to keep my nose clean and stay out of it. And if Macro has any sense, he'll do the same.'

Hearing his name, Macro looked up at his companions, trying to recall what had just been said. 'Ah, yes. I'll leave others to their own vices, and they can leave me alone with mine. And with Narcissus gone, we might just be able to get on with being soldiers, instead of being roped into one of his schemes.'

Cato nodded with feeling at the mention of Narcissus, the devious spymaster and imperial secretary of the previous emperor. He had lost favour towards the end of Claudius's reign and had made enemies of the empress and Pallas. Knowing full well the fate the new emperor's imperial secretary had in store for him Narcissus had retreated to his private estate in the country and killed himself. Neither Cato nor Macro grieved for the man. He had coerced them into carrying out his dirty work too many times for that.

The senator smiled. 'I wish I could afford your insouciance.'

'Eh?' Macro frowned.

'If that's your position, then fair enough. Just keep clear of the likes of Pallas, Seneca and Burrus if you want to stay out of trouble.'

They were interrupted by the thin wail of a crying infant coming from the direction of the house, and a moment later a sturdy woman in a plain tunic cinched at the waist wandered out of the corridor. She was gently rocking a small child against her shoulder and stroking its back to try and offer some comfort.

Cato felt a surge of affection well up inside his heart as he saw his son in the arms of his nurse Petronella. As a fresh cry issued from the boy's lungs, he rose from the couch and hurried towards them.

Petronella broke into a smile. 'Why look, my sweet, it's your daddy. Come back from the wars.'

She half turned and lifted Lucius round so that he could see better. The little boy was two years old, with thick, curly dark hair and the lungs of a drill centurion. Cato saw that his eyes were red from crying and his nose and mouth slick with saliva as he blinked at the visitor to his grandfather's house. Then a gleam appeared in his eyes and he raised his head from Petronella's shoulder and beamed. 'Dada!'

Cato could not help a warm flush of love as the child raised his arms and lurched towards him. He reached out and the nurse handed the boy over. He kissed the top of Lucius's head and breathed in the sweet, musky aroma of the child, closing his eyes in bliss. All thoughts of political rivalry, all memories of bloody battlefields and all the bitter anguish of Julia's betrayal vanished in that moment, and he held on to the feeling like the most precious of treasures.

Lucius shifted and looked up at him, his lips wide beneath his snub nose and twinkling eyes. There was a string of tiny white teeth in his smile, and Cato winked at him. 'No biting Dada, eh?'

Lucius laughed and threw his arms round his father's neck as Cato made his way back to the others, followed by the nurse.

'What's the matter with him?' asked Sempronius.

'Colic, master,' Petronella replied. 'It gets most nippers from time to time. He'll go back to sleep soon enough.'

'Good. There's been enough commotion for one night.'

The senator poured himself a goblet of wine and took a large gulp. 'More than enough.'

As Cato sat down, Macro swallowed what he was eating and sat up with a stern expression, arms folded. 'Well now. What have we got here? Young recruit causing trouble? Reminds me of his dad back in the day.'

At the sound of his voice, Lucius whirled round. 'Uncle Mac Mac!' he cried gleefully.

Macro grinned. 'That's right. Your uncle Mac Mac, back from taming those rebellious bastards in Hispania. Let's be having you, lad. You need an inspection.'

Cato set his son down and Lucius approached the centurion. Macro took his shoulders and held him at arm's length, looking him up and down with a stern expression. 'Shoulders back, chest out, chin up. Just so! Ah, you'll be a fine soldier one day, just like your dad.'

Lucius reached down and patted his stomach, looking hopefully at Macro. It took a moment for the latter to realise what the boy was after, and then he pulled Lucius towards him, hoisted him up and raised his bristly jaw to tickle the infant's tummy.

'Now that's not helpful,' Petronella scolded him. 'I'll never get him back to sleep now.'

'Just a harmless bit of fun,' Macro responded, pausing to look at the woman. She gazed back fondly, then became self-conscious and lowered her eyes. Macro tickled the boy again and Lucius screamed with delight, wriggling like a greased piglet, until Macro sat him down, reached over to the platters and selected a small pork pie for him. Lucius's eyes lit up as he sat with splayed legs. He set the pie down between his chubby thighs and began to pick it apart, occasionally popping a fragment into his mouth while the rest of the pastry debris spread across the rich cloth of the dining couch.

'What are your plans?' asked Sempronius. 'Both of you. Now that you are back in Rome.'

'We'll be joining the Second Cohort at the barracks tomorrow,' Cato replied. 'There'll be the usual duties to carry out after an operation. Kit and inventory checks. Sorting out the wills of the men we lost in Hispania, starting the process of finding replacements. Of course, I'll do my best to spend time with Lucius. Until I secure some accommodation of my own.'

'You're both welcome to live here, if you like.'

Macro's eyes lit up at the prospect of enjoying more of the delights of the senator's dinner table, but Cato shook his head.

'You're very kind. But the officers' quarters at the barracks are comfortable enough, and we'll be busy for a while. And if there's any trouble, we'll need to be ready to act the moment we are called upon. But I'll visit as often as I can, if that's agreeable.'

'My home is your home. I have no child of my own to leave it to. If anything happens to me, I have decided to leave it all to my grandson in due course. My will has been altered to reflect that. It has been signed and sealed and left in the care of my banker down in the Forum. Marcus Rubius. He's a good man. You can trust him.'

Cato was taken aback by his father-in-law's generosity towards Lucius. 'I don't know what to say, sir . . .'

'A thank-you would be a nice start.'

Cato regarded him with concern. 'Do you believe you are in danger, sir?'

Sempronius's expression became serious. 'We're all in danger these days. You know what Nero did earlier. If that's the shape of things to come, then we may have landed ourselves with another madman on the throne. In which case, none of us is safe. I pray to all the gods that there's no trouble. And I hope you two have the good sense to keep your opinions to yourselves and resist the temptation to play at politics.'

'Fuck politics,' Macro said with feeling, then shot a guilty glance at Lucius, but the boy was concentrating on making patterns with the crumbs on the couch in front of him. 'Ain't got nothing to do with me any more. Not now that snake Narcissus has gone to join his ancestors. And good riddance to him.'

'I won't miss him either,' said Cato. 'But I fear the elevation of Pallas isn't a change for the better. At least Narcissus had Rome's interests at heart, even if he made a tidy fortune in the process. But Pallas? He's worse than Narcissus. That one is out for himself. And he'll cut down anyone that comes between him and his pursuit of power and riches.'

Macro shrugged. 'So let's stay out of his way then.'

'Easier said than done, my friend . . . Easier said than done.'

CHAPTER SIX

A messenger from the Praetorian camp arrived at the senator's house at first light. He delivered orders for Cato, along with all the other senior officers of the units returning from Hispania, to report to headquarters at noon for a briefing by the acting commander of the Praetorian Guard, Prefect Burrus. The permanent holder of the rank had been an aged and infirm officer even at the time of his appointment some years earlier. Since then he had rarely been fit for duty, and Burrus had assumed most of his responsibilities, being regarded by all as the de facto commander.

By the time Cato and Macro reached the Praetorian fortress mid-morning, the first of the men of the Second Cohort had returned to their barracks. The carts bringing up the baggage and the remaining convalescents were still on the road from Ostia and were expected at dusk. For the soldiers it was a relief to put the hard conditions of campaigning behind them, and they were keen to resume the comfort of decent beds, regular hot food and shelter from the elements. In addition, there was the chance to catch up with their comrades in the cohorts that had remained in Rome and boast of their exploits in Hispania. After that, they were keen to indulge in the pleasures afforded by the greatest city in the known world.

But first, they were required to go through the usual routine of units returning to base after a period of service in the field. Their arms, armour and kit needed cleaning and repairing, and lost and damaged items had to be reported to the quarter-master's clerks so that replacements could be drawn from stores. Rations and kindling and fuel had to be fetched to the barrack blocks, which themselves had to be swept out and scrubbed down to restore them to a state that would be acceptable to the sharp-eyed optios and centurions when the daily inspections began again.

If the process was burdensome for the rank and file, it was even more so for their officers, who were obliged to resume their administrative duties. For Cato and Macro, who had only been appointed to the Praetorian Guard mere days before the Second Cohort marched off to campaign in Hispania, there had been very little time to make their quarters comfortable, and not much opportunity to familiarise themselves with the routines of their new posting.

Unlike the cramped barrack blocks of legionary fortresses, which were generally built to house a century of eighty men, the Praetorians' barracks were constructed on a far larger scale, big enough to accommodate an entire cohort of nearly five hundred men on two storeys. Cato opened the doors to the large mess room and entered, followed by Macro, who was holding his wax slate and stylus at the ready to take notes. As the cohort's commander moved round the room, opening the shuttered windows, light slanted across the long tables and stools, unused since the guardsmen had marched off to war several months earlier. A light skein of dust covered the furnishings and the flagstone floor, and thick cobwebs hung in the corners and along the sturdy timber beams that crossed the room. Rats had got in and gnawed through some sacks of wheat that had been left beside the row of cooking stoves lining one of the walls. Spilled grain and small, dark rice-like turds lay scattered about the torn cloth. Cato stirred the detritus with the toe of his boot.

'I want a section in here to clear all this up. Dust, cobwebs, the lot.'

Macro nodded and made an entry on his slate. 'There won't be anyone on fatigues yet, so it'll have to be the first of the lads to get here.'

'No reward for being diligent then, eh?'

Macro clicked his tongue. 'That's the army way, sir.'

Cato pointed at the wooden shutters. Some of the paint was peeling and a few of the slats had fallen out. 'Get them to sort those out. Same goes for the rest of the block.' He paused and sniffed. 'And have the drains cleared out. Smells like something has crawled in and died.'

Macro made another note and they moved on. The first arrivals had already returned to their section rooms, and they leapt up and stood to attention as the two officers continued the inspection tour. They were immediately set to work, despite having just completed the march from Ostia. Cato had only visited the clerks' office briefly before the cohort had departed, and now he had time to take in the shelves piled with scrolls and slates and felt a dull dread at the prospect of catching up with the cohort's records over the coming days.

The prefect's quarters were on the second storey at the end of the barrack block, overlooking the open ground between the barracks and the wall of the camp. There was a narrow balcony sheltered by the building's eaves, and Cato gazed out over the wall to the vast sprawl of tiled roofs of the capital beyond. It was an impressive view and he looked forward to those moments when he could sit and take it in over a cup of heated wine. The rest of his quarters consisted of a comfortably appointed sleeping chamber, an office, a modest dining room, and storerooms for his personal effects. There were also two cells with palliasses for slaves or servants.

The only slave Cato now owned was Petronella. The others had been sold by Julia, or disposed of by Cato along with his house to cover the debts his dead wife had left behind her. Petronella was needed to look after Lucius, and Cato made a mental note to find himself a personal slave or two the moment he had time to visit the slave market. He had a small amount of money left over from the sale of the house, and was owed six months' back pay. More than enough to find the man he needed, some fine food and drink for his pantry for when he entertained other officers, as well as some new clothes. Having discovered Julia's infidelity, he had disposed of the small wardrobe she had bought for him while he had been fighting in Britannia. He had not been able to bear the thought that the garments might have been worn by her lover in his absence.

'Has Optio Metellus returned yet?'

'I'll check on that as soon as I can, sir.'

'Once you have found him, tell him he has been promoted to chief clerk. Unfortunately for Metellus that makes him responsible for the clerks' offices and living quarters, as well as mine. I want this place spotless before nightfall, or I'll want to know the reason why. Tell him I'll need blankets and a mess kit from the stores until I can sort out something better.'

'Yes, sir.'

Cato took a last look round his accommodation and then undid the clasp of his cloak and tossed the thick material over one of the stools standing beside the long table in the small dining room. 'There's plenty for you to get on with, Macro. I'll be in my office. Have the strength returns sent to me as soon as they're ready.'

Macro nodded and was about to leave when a final thought struck Cato. 'Last thing. I don't want Tribune Cristus in the barracks. He can find a room at headquarters. If he has any personal effects, have them taken there.'

'As you wish, sir.' Macro did his best to keep his expression neutral. Cristus was the tribune assigned to the Second Cohort as the unit's nominal commander before Cato's appointment. Just as in the legions, the tribunes were young men from aristocratic families, putting in a few years of military service before they began their political careers in earnest. Many regular soldiers regarded them as little more than a nuisance, although Macro had known some who had proven their worth. One such was Cristus, who had done well in the recent campaign. However, he had also been Julia's lover, and Macro could understand his friend's reluctance to have the man accommodated any closer to him than absolutely necessary. 'Will that be all?'

Cato thought briefly. 'Yes. I'll see you later, once the evening watch goes on duty. We can catch up over dinner.'

As Macro saluted and strode away, his footsteps sounding along the corridor, Cato made his way through to his office, where he leaned on the window frame and looked down. More men and carts were arriving all the time, and shouted orders and the braying of mules echoed off the surrounding buildings. A small number of guardsmen from the cohorts that had remained in Rome looked on, and there was the occasional exchange of good-humoured ribbing. Cato watched them for a little longer, wondering if these same men could be divided by political factions to the point that they would be willing to shed each other's blood. It seemed unthinkable at that moment, but he was well aware of the bloody history of Rome's civil wars in the previous century.

The armies of Sulla and Marius, Pompey and Caesar, Octavian and Antony had all torn at each other's throats, blindly following men who feigned patriotism and promised everlasting glory, and the spoils of war, to any who would take up a sword in their name. Had such a time come again? he wondered. The last emperor had come to power at the behest of the Praetorian Guard. His predecessor, Caligula, had been murdered by guardsmen. And now Nero had been sure to present himself at the camp, along with a chest of treasure, to seek their support the very moment that Agrippina had announced the death of her husband. There was no question that the Praetorian Guard held the keys to power, and yet Cato wondered just how aware the common soldiery was of this state of affairs. He had little doubt that the officers had grasped the essential truth, and that therefore he and Macro would have to tread very carefully if they were to survive the simmering conflict between the factions of the two rivals for the purple.

After the previous night's events, Britannicus would be harbouring a burning desire for bloody revenge against his stepbrother. And Nero and his advisers must surely be aware of that. In which case, why had they not acted yet? Why not finish the job; have Britannicus seized and murdered and lay any fear of a power struggle to rest? The only thing that made sense to Cato was that they were afraid of the consequences of such an overt act. If Nero were to murder his rival, the boy's supporters amongst the senators and army officers in Rome, and further afield, might be moved to act. Either that, Cato mused, or perhaps someone was calculating that Britannicus's presence could be used to exert some measure of control over Nero. If the latter was the case, then it would have to be someone close to the emperor. Someone like Pallas, or Agrippina. Or maybe Nero's mentor, Seneca, and his sidekick Burrus, the acting commander of the Praetorian Guard. It was possible that the emperor's inner circle was divided; that there was a faction within the faction.

Cato took a deep breath and drew back from his speculations. As long as the tension between Nero and Britannicus did not break out into armed conflict, it made little difference to him who came out on top. And little difference to the men of the Praetorian Guard, or the teeming masses of Rome. They would rather be bystanders in the deadly game of politics that was played out behind the scenes as each emperor came and went.

A knock on the door frame of his office interrupted his thoughts, and he gratefully turned away from the view of the city and stepped back inside. Optio Metellus was waiting on the threshold. He carried a blanket roll under one arm and a skillet and cup in his other hand.

'Your pardon, sir, but Centurion Macro told me to bring you these.'

'In my sleeping chamber, please.'

Once Metellus returned, Cato sat down behind his desk and idly ran a finger through the dust, leaving a bright streak of polished wood visible in the thin grey film. 'I take it that Macro also told you that you have been promoted to chief clerk?'

'Yes, sir.'

'That comes with double pay. And you'll have to earn it. First job is to find the other clerks and get my quarters cleaned up.'

'Yes, sir.'

'Then I want the strength returns brought here, together with the wills of those we lost in Hispania. They'll be in the strongbox at headquarters I imagine.'

'That's right, sir. I put them there myself before we left.'

Cato could not recall having given the order, and was impressed that Metellus had taken the initiative. But initiative was one thing. Acting over and above the requirements appropriate to his rank was quite another. 'In future you will inform me of any such actions you undertake. Is that clear?'

'Yes, sir.'

Cato looked at him sternly to make sure, and then stood up. It was nearly midday, as far as he could estimate. 'I have to attend an officers' briefing. Make sure you've carried out my orders by the time I return. Oh, and bring me something to eat. Bread and meat will do.'

'And to drink, sir?'

It was a cool day, and being thin and sinewy, Cato was inclined to feel the cold. 'Heat some wine. And get a fire going in the brazier.'

'Yes, sir.'

Cato strode through to the dining room and picked up his cloak. He felt a touch of guilt over the peremptory tone he had adopted with Metellus. His mood had been soured by his reflections on the political situation, and now he realised he had allowed himself to take that out on the optio. He hesitated at the door to his quarters and turned back to the man.

'Just so you know, I consider that you've earned the

promotion. You served with credit in Hispania. I'm sure you'll continue to do so back here in Rome.'

'Yes, sir. Thank you, sir.'

The man's expression masked any more pronounced reaction, and Cato stared at him a moment before he nodded. 'Carry on then, Metellus.'

CHAPTER SEVEN

As the trumpets announced the change of watch at noon, the doors to the commander's office were opened by two guardsmen, and a moment later Burrus appeared in full dress uniform. He wore a spotless white tunic, rather than the off-white issued to the other men and officers, and a gleaming silvered breastplate covered his torso, with red leather strips hanging at the waist and from his shoulders. A broad red ribbon was tied around his midriff, with the ends neatly tucked so that two loops hung down just below the rest of the ribbon. Like many officers who had been directly appointed to senior ranks in the army, he had won no decorations and so had no medal harness, unlike many of the men standing before him, who had earned their promotions in the field and proved themselves in battle. Burrus wore a thin gold torc around his thick neck, and a thin band of dark hair curved round the sides of his head. The few strands that were long enough were combed artlessly across his crown in an effort to deny the baldness that was obvious to any onlooker. He was well enough built, Cato decided, but the effect of manly prowess was undermined by his withered right arm, which he did his best to keep tucked behind his back.

'Commanding officer present!' bellowed the First Spear of the Guard, its most senior centurion.

The officers rose as one and stood to attention. Their commander raised his chin a fraction and regarded them loftily for a moment before nodding. 'At ease, gentlemen. Please be seated.'

Cato, Macro and the other prefects, tribunes and centurions lowered themselves on to the cushioned benches of the briefing room. Like everything else in the Praetorian Guard, there was a degree of scale and comfort here that was markedly superior compared to the situation in Rome's legions spread across the Empire and defending the frontier. The headquarters was more like a modest palace than a military administration building. The entrance to the outer courtyard passed beneath a lofty arch, and marble columns lined the large open area before the main building. Sejanus, the commander of the Guard who had persuaded Emperor Tiberius to authorise the construction of the camp, had expended a fortune on the project. His ambitions may have won him infamy in the annals of history, but his successors and the men of the Guard were quietly grateful to him for his unstinting profligacy with imperial funds. Not only did they have barracks that were the envy of every soldier in the Empire, but there was also an exclusive bath-house and a gladiator arena attached to the camp.

Even the briefing room was impressive. The ceiling rose high above, and the walls were decorated with murals depicting glorious military actions from Rome's past, all of them featuring luminous, larger-than-life images of the emperors from Augustus to Claudius. Cato noticed that a section of a panel to one side of the door through which Burrus had entered had been scraped back to the plaster and the figure of a youthful warrior had been outlined in charcoal. Nero, it seemed, was already in the process of joining his predecessors in this hall of fame.

Burrus positioned himself directly in front of the assembled officers and addressed them. 'Gentlemen, it is a pleasure to welcome you back from your service in Hispania. Having spoken to the commander of the expeditionary force, Senator Vitellius, I am told that you and your units acquitted themselves in the finest tradition of the Praetorian Guard. In particular, Vitellius singled out Prefect Cato and Centurion Macro and the men of the Second Cohort, for their courage and determination in defending a vital silver mine against the army of the renegade Iskerbeles. I understand that the senator will be proposing to the Senate that the unit be accorded a decoration for its sterling service. Prefect Cato! Centurion Macro! Please stand.'

The two officers exchanged a brief look of surprise and then rose from their benches and stood erect before their peers and the commander. Vitellius had been their long-time enemy, and had even tried to engineer their elimination, so why was he now doing his best to elevate them to the status of public heroes?

'Rome is in your debt, and you have won the respect of us all.'

The other officers stamped their feet to show their appreciation, and the sound rose to a crescendo and filled the chamber. A few men cheered their names, until Burrus raised his good arm and called for quiet.

'Although the prefect and the centurion have only recently been transferred to the Guard, they have already honoured us. We Praetorians are indeed fortunate to have such men join our ranks. I expect to see them both add even greater lustre to our reputation as the finest body of soldiers anywhere in the Empire, or even beyond.'

The officers stamped their feet again, and Burrus gestured to Cato and Macro to resume their seats. When the noise had faded, he continued.

'As you men recently returned from Hispania will know, we have a new emperor. And it is our duty to serve Nero as loyally as we served Claudius before him. The men who remained here in Rome have already sworn an oath of loyalty to Nero, and I am sure that all of you will be eager to follow their example as soon as possible. To which end, there will be a full parade of the Praetorian Guard tomorrow morning, where those officers and men who have not taken the oath will be given the opportunity to do so.' Burrus took a step back. 'Are there any questions?'

Cato glanced round as a tribune from one of the other cohorts stood up. 'Sir, we heard the news about Claudius the moment we landed in Ostia two days ago. We also heard rumours about the manner of his death.'

Burrus regarded the tribune coolly. 'And what rumours would those be, Mantalus?'

The man shifted uneasily. 'Some people were saying that he had been poisoned.'

'Poisoned?'

'By someone close to him at the palace, sir.'

'Really? Was a name mentioned?'

Cato saw the anxious look on the tribune's face as he made to reply. 'Begging your pardon, sir, but I am only repeating what I heard.'

'And what did you hear, Mantalus?'

'Sir, just some loose talk in a local tavern. Some drunken loudmouth. That's all.'

'What, precisely, did this loudmouth say?' Burrus demanded.

'He said . . . he said that Agrippina had poisoned the emperor.'

There was a stillness in the room for a moment, then Burrus smiled thinly. 'And do you believe this extraordinary claim? Do you believe that a devoted Roman wife would commit so heinous a crime? Do you believe that?'

'No. No, of course not, sir.'

'Then I suggest that you never repeat such an outrageous remark in front of me, or any other Praetorian, ever again. Is that clear, Tribune Mantalus?'

'Yes, sir.'

'Be so good as to sit down. I will speak to you later, and you can tell me exactly which tavern you were in when you heard that scurrilous remark. With luck we will be able to identify the individual who uttered the words, and then he will have to answer for his treasonous views.'

Cato had listened with a growing sense of concern. So this was how the new emperor's reign was to begin. The ruthless suppression of any dissent, and the hunting-down of those who dared to question the means by which Nero had come to power. Tribune Mantalus was a marked man now, and Cato wondered how long it would take for Pallas to learn of his comment and find some suitable way of making an example of him.

'Jupiter's balls,' Macro whispered. 'Ain't that a bit heavy-handed? If we're expected to hunt down every drunken bastard who opens his mouth, then we're going to have our hands full.'

'I fear you may be right,' Cato replied softly.

'I didn't sign up to bump off drunks. I joined the army to fight barbarians and defend Rome. That's what. Not this bullshit.'

Cato noticed that some of the officers nearby were glancing in their direction. 'Later, Macro. Now isn't the time.'

'Any more questions?' asked Burrus.

Another officer rose, this time a centurion. His craggy face was lined with a thin growth of silvered beard and a stubbly head. He showed no sign of nervousness at the treatment of the previous questioner as he spoke up. 'Sir, most of us have heard about the bonus the new emperor paid out to the lads who were here in Rome when his accession was announced. A year's pay for the rankers and five years for officers. Is that right?'

Burrus nodded.

'Paid out in silver, on the day, I heard.'

'Yes, so?'

'Well, sir, what I'd like to know is when we can look forward to receiving our bonus.'

There were murmurs of agreement from many of the other officers, and they looked steadfastly at their commander as he made his reply.

'I have been directly informed by the emperor's freedman, Pallas, that the bonus will be paid to the rest of the Praetorian Guard as soon as possible. There is insufficient silver in the treasury to cover the cost at present. A consignment of silver is expected from Hispania any day, now that the rebellion in the mines of Asturica has been put down. Largely thanks to the efforts of Prefect Cato.'

The centurion shot a glance at Cato and gave a brief nod of gratitude before focusing his attention on his commander again. 'So how long will we have to wait until we get our share, sir?'

'I can't say.'

The reply was met with muted grumbling from the centurions, and now, before Cato could restrain him, Macro was also on his feet. 'Lads! Lads! If I might say something . . . Thank you.' He turned towards Burrus and began. 'Sir, I am new to the Guard, like you said. Perhaps there are some here, you included, who might think I am talking out of turn, but I got my transfer to the Guard the hard way. I've fought in Germania, Britannia, Parthia, Aegyptus, Judaea, Syria, Creta and now Hispania.' He patted the polished medals on his harness. 'I've earned these. I've shed blood for Rome and my mates, and that's the same for most of us in this room. Right?' He looked round and the veterans nodded, and not a few called out their support.

'You see, sir, I feel that me and the others here have earned that bonus. While we were out there in Hispania, fighting the rebels, the rest of the Praetorian cohorts were comfortably tucked up here in the barracks. The biggest danger to life and limb that they were facing was choking to death on cheap wine. So you'll understand that we might take it hard that they were given their bonus on the day, while those of us who were actually out there fighting for Rome are going to have to bloody well wait for our share. Assuming we actually get it at all.'

'You'll get what's coming to you, Centurion Macro. I give you my word on it.'

'Sir, if you'll pardon me for saying so, I've lived long enough to have had plenty of men give me their word, only for them not to follow through with it.'

Burrus's eyes narrowed. 'Are you questioning my integrity, Centurion?'

'No, sir. Just those who have let me down before. I haven't

known you long enough to pass judgement.'

'Very well then, do you question the word of the imperial palace?'

Cato hissed. 'Careful, Macro. For gods' sake.'

His friend collected his thoughts before he continued. 'If you are asking me if I question the word of the emperor, then of course not. Nero is the emperor and if he personally guarantees our bonus, then I will believe him. If, however, I have to rely on the word of one of his advisers, like Pallas, then you'll have to forgive me if I seem at all doubtful of his integrity. I know the type. Those greasy little Greek freedmen are out for themselves and they'd steal the coins off the eyes of their dead mothers. So if you don't mind, sir, can you tell us whether the promise that we will get our share of the bonus comes directly from the emperor himself?'

Burrus clasped his hands behind his back and straightened up to his full height. 'The emperor is a busy man. The weight of the Empire lies on his shoulders and he needs time to get used to the burdens of the office. However, I am confident that he will turn his attention to this matter as soon as he can, and that you will all receive what you are due, just as the other cohorts have done.'

'So the answer's no then, sir?'

Some of the officers could not help a quick laugh, while others muttered, and there was no mistaking the frustration and anger in their tone now. The blood drained from their commander's face, and he took a sharp breath and bellowed across the room.

'Silence! Sit down, you two! Sit down at once!'

Macro and the other centurion resumed their seats, and the rest fell silent as Burrus glared at them.

'You dare to question the word of your commanding officer? You dare to question the word of the imperial palace? Who in Hades do you think you are? This is the Praetorian Guard. The most loyal unit in the entire army. It is our sacred duty to obey and protect the emperor and his family. That is the oath we swear and the oath we renew at the start of each year, and at the commencement of a new reign. It is not your right to question me, and it is not our right to question those who the gods have placed over us. If I am told that you will receive the bonus, then I have every expectation that you will receive it. And so should you. That is the end of the matter.'

He thrust his jaw out and glared round the room, daring any of his officers to challenge him. 'Tomorrow Nero will be here to accept your oath of allegiance. I want every man turned out in spotless kit. Every inch of your armour is to gleam like glass. Woe betide any slovenly soldier who lets down the Guard. He and his entire century will be assigned to fatigues for a month on half-pay. That goes for his officers as well. And if I hear one more complaint about the bonus, or any further doubts about my integrity or that of any official at the imperial palace, then I will personally have that man's balls for breakfast. Anyone who is bloody foolish enough to question the integrity of the emperor will be crucified in front of the entire corps of Guards. On all of that you have my word, gentlemen, as the gods are my witnesses. Dismissed!'

With that, Burrus turned on his heel and strode swiftly through the doors and out of the room. The guardsmen pushed the doors to behind him as the First Spear Centurion bellowed, 'You heard him. Dismissed!'

At once there was the scraping of benches and the buzz of conversation as the officers rose and made their way to the entrance of the chamber and into the main hall of the headquarters building.

'Nice going,' said Cato. 'You got on the right side of your commanding officer very adeptly there.'

'Just saying what everyone else was thinking.'

'Sometimes there's a reason why everyone thinks something yet no one says it. Not out in the open at least.'

Macro shook his head. 'Look here, Cato, you and me have finally got ourselves a plum posting. It don't come any better than the Praetorian Guard. We've earned it, many times over. Especially after what happened in Hispania. Why should we lose out on what those bloody idlers who remained in Rome got?'

'You heard the man: we'll get what we're owed.'

'Really? You really believe that?' Macro sighed. 'Because I bloody don't. Not until I can feel that silver in my hands. And I dare say almost everyone in this room feels the same, as do the rest of the lads who served in Hispania. It's all right for the bastards who remained in Rome. They've got heavy purses and they're living high off the hog in the best taverns and whorehouses in Rome.'

'Centurion Macro?'

They turned to see one of the centurions from another cohort. An older officer, with wiry streaked hair. His face was scarred and he wore a patch over his right eye. He nodded a greeting and clasped Macro's forearm. 'I'm Centurion Appius. Just wanted to thank you for what you said. It's what that upstart Burrus needed to hear.'

'Upstart?' Cato cocked an eyebrow.

'He ain't a proper soldier and he ain't even a proper gentleman. New money and all that.'

Cato had met this kind of prejudice before and still wondered at the degree to which soldiers preferred to serve under men with noble ancestry rather than men who had merely performed noble deeds. Burrus, it seemed, had neither quality and was therefore doubly damned in the eyes of the veterans he commanded. Still, he was the senior Praetorian prefect, in charge of the entire corps, and it was the duty of every officer and common soldier to respect the rank if not the man. Cato had heard enough.

'We're new here, Centurion Appius, and we'll make our own minds up about Burrus.'

'Yes, sir.' The centurion had realised that he had overstepped the mark in sharing such confidences, and now a more professional mask slipped over his face. 'All the same, it's an honour to have you serving with us, sir. You and Centurion Macro.'

They exchanged a salute and Appius turned and strode out of the chamber. Cato and Macro followed the last of the officers outside and into the hall. Light was streaming through the windows high above. As he walked into a beam of light, Cato blinked for an instant and then looked down at the frayed hem of his tunic, the rust spots on his scale vest and the worn and cracked leather of his sword strap, casualties of the hard campaigning in Hispania.

'The Second Cohort's not going to get much rest today and tonight if we're going to have a good turnout at tomorrow's parade.'

Macro nodded, a happy gleam in his eye at the prospect of getting the men and their kit into shape. 'Don't you worry, sir. I'll have 'em looking so good, no one will believe they haven't been preparing for this for months, and may the gods show mercy to any soldier that lets the cohort down, because I fucking well won't!'

CHAPTER EIGHT

Metellus indicated the stack of waxed slates on Cato's desk. 'The strength returns, sir. I've indicated the names of the dead, and the wills are in the box beside the desk. There were only a handful of men who hadn't prepared one. Their names are on the slate on top of the pile.'

Cato's gaze shifted to the piles of folded documents in the box, each sealed with the ring of the cohort's standard bearer, the man whose duties included maintaining the guardsmen's pay and savings records as well as helping them to complete their wills, witnessing them and ensuring that they were kept safely.

'Very good, Optio. Now you'd better see to your kit for the parade. When you're done, take care of mine. Pick the best of my spare tunics. Make sure any tears are stitched and any stains removed. Dismissed.'

'Sir!' Metellus saluted and marched from the room, closing the door behind him. Cato hesitated a moment before he sat at his desk. So many wills. So many men lost in Hispania. It had been a desperate struggle against great odds and at times it had seemed that defeat and death were certain. If it was true that fortune favoured the brave, then he and Macro must be amongst the bravest men ever to have served in the army. But he did not feel particularly brave. It was just blind luck that he had survived long enough to achieve his present rank. A pace to either side and he could easily have been cut down by a javelin, arrow or slingshot. Or run through by a sword thrust. Of course they had not emerged from battles unscathed. Macro's body bore many scars, and Cato touched the hardened line of white tissue that stretched down from his own forehead, past his nose and across his cheek. Some day their luck would run out. Either he or Macro, or both of them, would be killed in battle. And if not that, then killed by the hand of any of the other great slayers of soldiers: sickness, starvation or accident.

He crossed to the brazier and added two more logs to the blaze. There were still a few hours of daylight left and he could work by the light coming through the open window, even if that admitted the cold air. When night came, he would shut the windows and continue in the glow of the lamps hanging from the stand on his desk.

With a sigh he sat on his stool and started going through the strength returns. He had lost two centurions in Hispania and their centuries were now commanded by optios until such time as replacements were appointed. Of the five hundred soldiers, clerks and mule drivers he had taken on campaign, over two hundred had been killed in battle, and then there had been the steady trickle of those who had died from their wounds on the return march. It would take a while before the cohort was brought back up to full strength. There would be plenty of applicants, since the service conditions and pay of the Praetorian Guard were second to none. But their numbers would be winnowed down through the selection process of determining height and fitness, followed by character references and interviews. There would also be a small number of men transferred into the Guard from the legions as a reward for good service.

The latter – veterans with fine records – would be a valuable addition to the Second Cohort, it was true. But they would also be depriving the legions of their continued service, and to Cato's mind it made little sense to take good men from units defending the frontiers of the Empire and send them to the Praetorian Guard, where there was very little chance of them putting their experience and skill to good use. But that was always the way in the army, he reflected. There was often an ineluctable and unquestioned way of doing things that defied reason.

Once he had read through the strength returns, he marked down a few names that he deemed suitable for promotion to fill the places of the lost centurions. Two optios had distinguished themselves in the Spanish campaign, Ignatius and Nicolis. The former had only just been appointed to the rank before embarking on the campaign, but he had proven himself a popular and natural officer and Cato was happy to promote him again. Some old sweats might complain, but Ignatius was sure to win them over soon enough. The other optio, Nicolis, had a more studied approach to his duties, but both men would be valuable additions to the ranks of the cohort's team of centurions. That would mean two more vacancies for the rank of optio, and a standard bearer to appoint.

Cato set such considerations aside for the present and turned his attention to the wills. He lifted the wax tablet on top of the pile and counted the names of those who had died and not left a will. Twenty-six of them. Their savings, kit and other possessions would be divided amongst the surviving members of their section, as was the custom. In return, funds from the cohort's funeral club would be used to pay for tombstones to set over their graves. The tombstones would join the others along the Via Patricus that ran past the camp. Cato picked up the cohort commander's seal and pressed it into the wax to authorise the distribution of the dead men's property.

Then he turned his attention to the most time-consuming task. He picked up the first will, reading the name with a faint look of distaste. Centurion Gnaeus Lucullus Pulcher. Pulcher had been a brutal, heavy-set man, prone to bullying others. He had also been given a secret assignment to ensure that Cato did not survive the campaign in Hispania. If it had not been for Macro, he would have carried out his mission. As it was, he was past troubling Cato any more, buried back in Hispania in a mass grave with the rest of the Praetorian dead.

Cato broke the seal, opened out the document and began to read. He had no idea what to expect, and was therefore surprised and not a little moved by the tender message Pulcher addressed to his mother and older sister, who worked a smallholding in Campania. To them he left everything in his possession at the camp, together with a considerable sum in savings held by a banker in the Forum. No doubt the rewards accrued from his undercover work. Still, Cato reflected, the two women were blameless and would welcome the security Pulcher's bequest would grant them. He drafted a brief note to Pulcher's mother to inform her of her son's death in action, making no mention of the darker side of his career. He gave details of the banker for the mother to contact, then wrote a note to Metellus authorising the auctioning of the dead man's belongings, and directing the optio to ensure that the sums realised were added to Pulcher's savings. Then he moved on to the next will.

Dusk was settling over the city when Metellus returned with a tray of food and a small jug of watered wine. He set them down on the corner of the desk before lighting the oil lamps and closing the shuttered window to keep out the cold night air.

'There's a woman to see you, sir. I told her to wait outside your quarters.'

Cato lowered his stylus and looked up. 'Who is she?'

'Says her name is Petronella, and that Senator Sempronius sent her to you.'

'All right, show her in.'

Metellus nodded and left the room. He reappeared a moment later and waved the nurse through the door before closing it behind her. Petronella approached the desk and bowed her head. She was carrying a heavily laden sidebag slung across her shoulder and she shoved it behind her back before she spoke. 'The master sends his compliments and asks to know if you will be joining him and your son for dinner tonight.'

'Not tonight.' Cato indicated the remaining wills. 'Too much work still to do. Send him my apologies and say that it is my hope to return to his home tomorrow evening.'

'Yes, sir.'

'Is that all?'

She nodded.

'Very well. You may go. Oh, wait. It's getting dark. I'll have a couple of the men escort you back home.'

'No need, sir. I can manage. Be a brave footpad who chanced his arm with me.'

Cato smiled. It was true that Petronella was well built, and no doubt having lived in Rome most of her life had made her streetwise, but right now the city felt like a simmering cauldron.

It was better to take precautions, especially after nightfall.

'Very well, then please escort my men to your house and keep them safe. They'll have to take the risk of coming back to camp alone.'

'It's all right, sir. I insist. I don't want to be no bother.'

Cato was too tired to continue such a discussion and simply waved her away. 'As you wish, but get moving, while there's still some light in the sky.'

As the door closed behind her, he shook his head at her foolhardiness, and then turned his attention back to dealing with the remaining wills.

Once she had left the prefect's quarters, Petronella did not return to the senator's house directly, but made instead for the section of the barrack block allocated to the First Century, at the far end of the building on the ground level. The centurion's accommodation was far less lavish than the cohort commander's: a sleeping cell, one room for pantry provisions with a thin sleeping roll for a slave under the shelving, and an office that was shared with the century's sole clerk. The latter looked up as the nurse crossed the threshold uncertainly. He quickly took in her full figure, round face, jet-black hair, dark eyes and full lips. Her simple clothes indicated her status and how he might be able to address her.

'And what can I do for you, my lovely?'

'I'm here to see Centurion Macro.'

'Oh?' The clerk did not hide his disappointment. 'He's in his room. This way.'

Rising from his stool, he gestured to her to follow him down the short, narrow passage between the pantry and the centurion's latrine and paused at the door at the far end.

'Don't suppose you might want to share a little wine after-wards?'

'I don't think so. I'll need to get back home.'

'Pity. Another time, perhaps?'

She pursed her lips non-committally, and he sighed and tapped on the door.

'What now?' Macro barked irritably from within.

The clerk opened the door and stepped aside to wave the nurse in. Macro looked up from the end of his bed, where he was sitting as he rubbed wax into the leather of his medal harness. His brow creased in surprise at his unexpected visitor. Petronella blushed and stepped hesitantly across the threshold, swinging the sidebag round in front of her.

'Sorry to interrupt, sir. I just brought you some things from the senator's house.'

Over her shoulder Macro could see the clerk looking his visitor up and down from behind, a faint approving smile on his lips.

'That'll do,' the centurion snapped. 'Get back to your duties.'

The clerk scurried off, leaving Macro and the nurse looking at each other awkwardly, until she crossed to the small table where he kept his mess kit and began to unload the contents of her sidebag. Sausages, a cold glazed chicken, three small but ornately plaited loaves of bread and a selection of sweet tarts. Macro's eyes lit up appreciatively as she explained, 'You seemed very hungry last night, sir. And there's plenty of leftovers, so I thought of you up here with your soldier's rations and thought you could do with something better to eat.'

Macro looked at her curiously. 'You came up from the senator's house just to give me these?'

'Oh no, sir! I was sent here with a message for Master Cato, but I thought I'd bring these just in case you were hungry, like.' She looked concerned. 'Didn't mean to impose, sir.'

'Impose away!' Macro grinned as he stepped up beside her and looked over her offerings with delight. 'And if there's any more where this came from, then I'm your man.'

Petronella smiled quickly and bit her bottom lip rather than risk a reply. There was a moment's silence before she darted across the room to fetch the small stool beside Macro's bed and set it down beside the table. 'There. Sit and eat, sir. Have you any wine I can fetch for you?'

Macro was struggling not to show his amusement and pleasure. 'In the pantry. Bring a jar, and two cups.'

Petronella looked scandalised. 'Oh, I couldn't.'

'Yes, you could. I insist. After all, I think I am going to need a little help with all this food.'

'But I have to get back to the house to look after Master Lucius . . .'

'Once we've eaten. I insist.'

She was doubtful for a moment, then nodded impulsively and hurried to do Macro's bidding. A moment later she returned and set the jug and cups down, then realised she had no place to sit. Macro stood up.

'Take my stool.'

'I can't let you stand, sir. Not while I sit; it wouldn't be proper.'

'Nor is it proper for a centurion to entertain women in the barracks. So we're quits. Now sit down. In any case, I have no intention of standing up to bloody well eat.'

Macro strode through to his office, ordered his clerk to sit on the floor and returned with the man's stool. 'There. Now let's not waste any more time. Tuck in.'

Conscious of the nurse's need to get home, they ate with the emphasis on haste rather than taste, jaws working furiously and crumbs regularly falling on to the table and the floor. They paused only to sip wine. And from time to time they glanced at each other self-consciously and exchanged a happy smile. At length all that was left was the detritus of the small feast, and Macro sat back and slapped his stomach, letting rip a belch before he could help himself.

'Ooh, fuck. Sorry about that.'

Petronella exploded with laughter, choking on her last mouthful of wine as she fanned her face furiously with her hand. Macro was alarmed and reached round to slap her on the back.

'Careful . . .'

Once she had recovered, the nurse blinked the tears from her eyes and smiled. 'Haven't laughed like that for years.'

'Really? You don't seem the type not to.'

Her smile faded. 'Being a slave, you get used to guarding your feelings . . .' Her eyes widened in alarm. 'Not that I'm saying that Lady Julia was hard on me, master. Nor the senator.'

'It's all right. You can speak your mind freely. I ain't going to tell anyone. I don't suppose being a slave is everybody's idea of good times. The gods know I've seen what slavery can be like . . .' Macro recalled the mine in Hispania. A ghastly place where men, women and children had been worked to death, or were buried alive whenever ramshackle mineshafts collapsed. Even the most minor infraction of the harsh discipline resulted in an agonising and lingering execution to serve as an example to the other slaves. With difficulty he shook off the memory and forced himself to smile at Petronella.

'Now then, let's get you home.'

'I can manage on my own, master.'

'I don't doubt it. But I think you'll find that I am used to getting my own way. So let's be having you.' Macro swept up his military cloak and fastened the clasp before gesturing towards the door. 'After you, my lovely.'

CHAPTER NINE

'I swear to Jupiter, Best and Greatest, this sacred oath that to the leader of the Roman Empire and people, Nero Claudius Caesar Augustus Germanicus, supreme commander of the army, I shall render unconditional obedience, and that as a brave soldier I shall at all times be prepared to give my life for this oath . . .'

The voices of the men from the six cohorts that had returned from Spain echoed off the surrounding barrack blocks and then died away. Cato, standing alongside Macro and the standard bearer of the Second Cohort, lowered his hand, and his men neatly followed suit, as did their comrades in the remaining units. It was a new oath, drafted by Pallas, and had been issued to the Praetorian Guard and all other units in the army. Cato did not like its wording, which conspicuously made no mention of the Senate and people of Rome. This was a naked appeal to the loyalty of the soldiers in the name of Nero alone. No previous emperor had dared to go so far in expressing the reality that all had known but few had been willing to openly admit: tyranny had returned to Rome. The spirit of Tarquin the Proud, the last king of the city, who had been overthrown hundreds of years before, was as good as reborn.

On the podium facing the assembled guardsmen, Burrus lowered his withered arm and stepped aside to make way for the new emperor. Nero was finely dressed for the occasion. He wore knee boots of purple leather, and a silk tunic and cloak of the same colour, laced with golden patterns of Greek design. His silver breastplate was richly decorated with golden lions facing each other across his chest, and the ivory handle of a sword projected from a silvered scabbard. A wreath of oak leaves circled his brow, and he carried an ebony sceptre studded with jewels, with a small gold eagle at the top.

'Cuts quite a figure, eh?' Macro muttered. 'Almost looks as if he was angling to get deified right now.'

'Shh!' Cato hissed.

Nero puffed out his chest and raised his chin as he slowly swept his gaze over the units assembled before him. Cato was acutely conscious that the Second Cohort's ranks were far more thinned out than those of the other cohorts. But then they had borne the brunt of the action in Hispania. The emperor took a half-step forward, close to the edge of the podium, and Pallas instinctively raised a hand towards the emperor, as if to stop him from toppling off the platform, but just managed to restrain the gesture in time. The freedman thrust his hands together behind his back to ensure that he did not repeat his mistake. Nero raised his sceptre and held the small golden eagle aloft as he addressed his guardsmen in the traditional style preferred by teachers of rhetoric.

'My dear comrades in arms . . .' His voice, though melodious enough, strained to be heard across the ranks of the soldiers standing to attention. 'Although you have sworn an oath to me, you should know that I have sworn my own oath, before Jupiter, Best and Greatest, that I will be a servant of Rome, and a brother to all who bear arms in the service of Rome, whom I am honoured to call my comrades.' He raised his arms as if to embrace the soldiers massed before him, and there was a ragged cheer from some quarters, but most looked on silently.

'Rome is on the cusp of a new golden age,' Nero continued. 'Gone are the days of the tyranny of Tiberius, the chaos of Caligula and the corruption practised by so many under my dear adopted father, Claudius. From this day Rome will be a shining beacon of all that is civilised, all that is best in the world, and our friends, and our enemies, will look on in awe.'

'When's he going to get to our money?' muttered the standard bearer.

Macro glanced round and glared at the man. 'Shh!'

The standard bearer opened his mouth to protest at his superior's hypocrisy, then saw the dangerous look in Macro's eyes and snapped his jaw shut instead.

'But they will not look to Rome with awe alone,' Nero continued. 'They will regard us with terror, and will tremble at the prospect of defying us. Fear will be their watchword. Fear at the might of Roman power and the bravery and ruthlessness of our all-conquering soldiers who bring down fire and fury on all who defy us! There is no part of this world that we dare not enter, no part that does not lie beneath the shadows of our standards. No enemy we cannot defeat. No enemy we are afraid of. No enemy that will ever surpass our superiority at arms. The Roman Empire will last a thousand years and more, as long as the gods will it.'

Cato sucked in a long breath between his teeth. While he was used to the windy rhetoric of generals on the eve of battle, the words of the new emperor were even more hyperbolic by some measure. And quite untrue. Cato had not seen much evidence of fear and trembling amongst the British tribes he and Macro had faced in recent years. Nor had the people of Hispania been cowed by the shadow of Rome's standards. They had risked all, against superior odds, to defy their Roman masters. And what of the massacre of the three legions in the depths of the German forest when Augustus was emperor? Or the humiliation of the crushing of seven legions under Crassus before that? Humiliation gilded by the Parthians killing Crassus by pouring molten gold down his throat. No, the truth was that even if Rome was held in awe, there was as much defiance as there was fear to accompany that awe. Cato had read his history and knew the cardinal lesson that it taught: all empires come to an end.

Still, he mused, Nero's speech was flowery and uplifting enough and showed that the vast sums spent on his education had not been entirely wasted.

'The men of the Praetorian Guard have proven their valour time and again. No more so than the men on parade today. Your exploits in Hispania have won fresh renown for the Guard and crushed the spirit of rebellion that still lingers in the ungrateful hearts of the less civilised peoples there. And no unit is more deserving of our praise than the Second Cohort. Step forward, Prefect Cato, and the standard of the Second!'

Cato stiffened his spine and turned on his heel to march along the front of the parade ground, the crunch of the footsteps of the standard bearer close on his heels. To his right he sensed the respect of the men he was passing. When he reached the podium, he turned sharply and stamped his boot down to come to attention before the emperor. The standard bearer fell in alongside, the shaft of the standard held a foot clear of the ground and perfectly vertical.

Above them, Nero regarded them with lofty approval for a moment before gesturing with his spare hand. From the rear of the podium Pallas advanced, carrying a velvet-covered tray upon which rested two golden rings, one an arm brace, the other a broad circle decorated to resemble a laurel wreath. He went down on one knee beside his emperor and bowed his head respectfully.

Nero drew a deep breath. 'The Second Cohort was instrumental in the defeat of the rebellion led by the renegade Iskerbeles. The men of the Second showed great courage and skill at arms in the face of an enemy that outnumbered them ten to one. The Senate have voted to honour the cohort with this wreath as a sign of the gratitude of the Senate and people of Rome, and as their powers are vested in me, I am pleased to bestow the award. Standard bearer! Advance your standard!'

The soldier slid his left foot back smartly to balance himself and lowered the shaft towards the podium so that the tip was a foot from the emperor's midriff. Nero reached to his side for the wreath and slipped it over the point, then eased it down to the cross brace from which the heavy folds of the standard hung. Later the wreath would be fastened round the shaft, below the two awards the unit had already won. He withdrew his hand and the standard bearer waited an instant before returning to attention, standard rising high so that all the other guardsmen could see the new decoration glittering in the sunlight.

'Prefect Cato,' Nero intoned. 'To you we owe our thanks for the inspired leadership you showed to the men under your command. I do not recall ever having seen an officer decorated twice within the space of a year!' He smiled, and Cato felt a twinge of self-consciousness as he recollected the silver spears that Claudius had bestowed on him and Macro some months earlier after their return from Britannia. They had been sent back to account for the disastrous campaign that had resulted in the loss of almost an entire legion, along with its commander. But politics being what it was, and Rome being in need of something to celebrate, they had been lauded as heroes instead. At least there was no question that the current award had been earned. By them and all the others in the Second Cohort.

Nero reached for the golden bracelet and held it out, raising his voice to ensure that he was heard by every man on the parade ground. 'For courage and inspired leadership we award this symbol of our gratitude to our comrade Quintus Licinius Cato, commanding the Second Cohort of the Praetorian Guard!'

Cato stepped forward to accept the award, noting the solid weight of the golden decoration. He slipped his hand through and squeezed the sides to hold it in place on his right forearm, which he then raised in salute. Behind him, the guardsmen roared his name, quickly finding the rhythm so that the word echoed off the surrounding barracks and built to a deafening crescendo. He felt his breast swell with pride as he gazed directly into the eyes of the emperor. It was strange, Cato thought, how the high and mighty were apt to forget a face. Cato had saved Nero's life a few years earlier and the boy had been fulsome in his gratitude. Yet there was no trace of recognition in his expression now. Back then Cato had been playing the part of a ranker, and such people are eminently forgettable by those at the pinnacle of society, he reasoned. Conversely, he was surprised that none of the rankers seemed to recognise him or Macro from their earlier, undercover, service in the Praetorian Guard. Perhaps they dare not, given that Cato and Macro ranked so high above them in turn. Nero stared back a moment and then giggled nervously, before raising a hand to hide his inappropriate mirth. He recovered his poise as the cries died away, and lifted his sceptre to gain the attention and silence of the soldiers. As quiet fell, he spoke to Cato.

'You may return to your men, Prefect.'

Cato and the standard bearer turned about and marched back to the depleted ranks of the Second Cohort, falling in beside Macro.

'Well done, sir. No more than you deserved.'

'Thank you, my friend. We've all earned this.'

Nero had retreated to a cushioned stool towards the rear of the podium and sat down. Behind him stood two German bodyguards and a slender young woman in a shimmering silk stola beneath a blue cape. He reached for her hand and held it to his shoulder, gently caressing her fingers.

'Who's the woman?' asked Macro.

'No idea.' Cato shook his head. It was not Claudia Octavia – the daughter of Claudius – whom he had been coerced into marrying to strengthen his ties to the previous emperor. 'Not his wife, that's for sure.'

Before they could continue the conversation, Pallas approached at the front of the podium and drew his shoulders back to address the men. 'Glorious soldiers! You have seen how much the emperor holds you in his affection. What man could not? You are the heroes of Rome. No! The heroes of the entire Empire! No soldier can match the exploits of the famed and feared men of the Praetorian Guard! Let's hear you tell the world what they can expect from the Guards! Victory! Victory! Victory!'

He pumped his fist into the air and the chant was taken up by some of the men, but when they realised they were in the minority, they fell silent again. Pallas made one last attempt on his own before giving up and lowering his arm, his expression betraying his anxiety.

'Such self-control! Such modesty! As befits the most noble of men. I should have known the quality of you before I spoke.'

'Where's our money?' a voice demanded.

'Aye!' cried another. 'The money!'

'Silence in the ranks!' bellowed one of the centurions. 'I'll beat the living shit out of the first man I see speaking out of turn.'

'Where's the money?' someone else piped up from the rear of the formation.

Others joined in and the chant swelled into a frustrated roar. Pallas raised his hands and shouted something, but Cato could not make out the words above the din. The imperial freedman began to wave his hands to try and emphasise his point, but it was as if he was a feather trying to hold firm in the face of a howling tempest.

'WHERE IS OUR MONEY? WHERE IS OUR MONEY?'

A deeper voice sounded close by, and Cato turned, shocked to see Macro cupping his hand to his mouth. If the officers were starting to join in, it meant control had slipped out of Pallas's fingers, and the mood would soon turn ugly if nothing was done about it. Fortunately, one of those on the podium had grasped the danger. Nero jumped to his feet and rushed forward, sweeping Pallas aside and waving his gilded sceptre to win the attention of the guardsmen.

'Friends! My dear comrades!'

Gradually the chanting ceased, and the emperor forced a smile as he called out to them. 'You shall have your money! Just the same as the men in the other cohorts. Not one sestertius less. I swear this on my life. But you must appreciate that such a vast sum is not readily available at present.'

There was a groan from the ranks, and a handful of angry shouts. The emperor continued heedlessly. 'The imperial treasury is nearly empty. But a convoy of silver bullion is on its way to Rome even as I speak. It will be here in a matter of days, and then you will have your reward. I would sooner pluck out my own eyes than deny you what is rightfully yours. Trust me. Trust your emperor!'

He paused, trying to gauge the mood of the soldiers. The muttering and isolated shouts continued unabated. Nero's smile began to fade and he took a step back. At once, Burrus came forward, stepping in front of the emperor and cupping his hands to his mouth as he bellowed. 'The parade is dismissed! Officers! Dismiss your men! Back to barracks! Now!'

Cato turned to face the Second Cohort. He could see the anger in their faces and the furious gestures some were making towards those on the podium. The situation was getting out of control. Discipline was crumbling. He must act.

'Second Cohort! Stand to attention!'

He caught Macro's eye and nodded desperately. Macro filled his lungs and repeated the order with a roar, raising his vine cane and advancing on the front rank of the first century. The men there knew better than to defy their ferocious officer and snapped into position. Those on either side and behind followed suit. The other centurions and optios had also turned on their men with furious shouts and swipes of their canes. Very quickly the Second Cohort was standing as still and silent as they had been at the start of the parade. Their example spread to other cohorts, and gradually discipline was restored.

Cato looked up to see that the imperial party had descended the rear of the podium and was hurrying away towards the main gate of the camp. Only Burrus remained. Arms clasped behind his back, chin up, he glared at his men.

Cato filled his lungs again. 'Second Cohort . . . dismissed to barracks! Officers! Get the men moving!'

Century by century they were quick-marched away from the parade ground. Cato fell into step beside Macro and the standard bearer, his heart beating fast.

'Well,' Macro muttered. 'That could have gone better.'

'Indeed.' Cato shook his head. 'We'll have to keep our eyes and ears open, my friend. I fear Rome is going to be as dangerous a place to be as any battlefield we have ever known.'

Once the Second Cohort had returned to barracks, Cato, Macro and the standard bearer made for the farrier's works, where all three looked on with pleasure and pride as the wreath was securely fitted to an iron collar fastened around the standard's shaft. It was a menial task that the standard bearer could have carried out by himself, but the two officers had felt compelled to witness the fixing of the first decoration the Second Cohort had won since they had been transferred to the unit.

The farrier finished the job and examined his work closely for a moment before he handed the standard over. 'There you are, sir.'

Cato looked up at the wreath and smiled. 'It looks fine.'

'Fine indeed.' Macro nodded. 'And there'll be more to follow.'

Cato clicked his tongue. 'I'm not so sure. I may be wrong, but I don't get the impression that Nero will be the kind of emperor who enjoys going on campaign. Like as not, we'll be spending our days escorting him to and from Baiae, or controlling the mob on public holidays. Not much chance for the Second to distinguish itself doing those kind of duties.'

'I suppose not . . .'

Cato passed the standard to the bearer. 'Guard it well, Honorius.'

'Yes, sir.'

The two officers emerged from the workshop just as a light rain began to fall. A breeze had picked up, and Cato drew his cloak closely around his body and hunched his chin down into the folds as they made for the barracks.

'What do you reckon about the silver convoy?' asked Macro. 'Do you think he was telling the truth?'

Cato shot him a sidelong glance. 'You ever met an imperial freedman who did?'

'Point taken. But now is the time for Pallas to go against type. You saw how it was. If the lads don't get their silver, and quickly, there's going to be trouble.'

Cato left Macro to assign the sentry roster for the night and made his way back to his quarters. He was looking forward to taking off his armour and heading back into the city to see his son. There would be a chance for a few hours of play with the boy before Petronella fed Lucius and put him to bed.

The door to his quarters was open, yet there was no sign of Metellus within. Cato felt a faint sense of unease as he made for his bedroom. There was the creak of a chair in his office, and Cato froze. His hand slipped to the pommel of his sword as he stepped lightly to the entrance and looked cautiously round the door frame. Seated behind his desk, smiling, was Pallas. Cato did not smile back. Pallas was cut from the same cloth as his predecessor, Narcissus, and could not be trusted. His presence here could only mean trouble of some kind.

'Prefect Cato, I think it's time we talked . . .'

CHAPTER TEN

'I have nothing to say to you,' Cato responded as he strode into his office. 'And I'll thank you to get off my chair.'

Pallas's expression was cold for an instant before the ready smile returned and he rose and fetched a stool from the side of the room to set down beside the desk. Cato slung his cloak over the back of the chair and swept his hand across the cushion, as if to clear away something unpleasant. Then he sat down and stared at the freedman. 'I fail to see that there's anything for us to talk about.'

'Really?' Pallas arched his eyebrows. 'I had thought you intelligent enough to realise there might be plenty for us to talk about.'

'Then I'm glad to have disappointed you. So if there's nothing else . . . ?'

'Don't play the fool, young man. You used to be Narcissus's creature, and I knew him well enough to know that he only picked the best to serve him.'

'Narcissus is dead. In any case, I never served him. I was coerced into working for him.'

'It comes to the same thing. Volition is a delusion.'

Cato was tired, and had no appetite for verbal sparring,

particularly with a man he had come to regard with wary loathing. 'I assume you crept into my quarters for a reason.'

'Other than to congratulate you?'

Cato made no reply, but stared back, stony-faced, until his visitor shrugged. 'Very well, then. I came to make you an offer. I need good men I can rely on. Men who know how to be ruthless, and more importantly, discreet. You and your friend Macro have proven that you are just the kind of men I am looking for. With Narcissus dead, you need a patron, and I need you to serve me, in the interests of Rome. I will not ask you to do anything you weren't willing to do for Narcissus, but I guarantee that I will reward you both more generously than he ever did.'

'We're not for sale.' Cato sat back and stretched his shoulders. 'We're done here, Pallas. You can leave now.'

The freedman gave a dry laugh. 'I think you mistake me for someone who is offering you a choice.'

Cato shook his head. 'I know exactly what you are. Cut from the same cloth as Narcissus, but still nothing more than a jumped-up freedman with an inflated sense of his own influence and worth. I should have you flogged out of camp for daring to address me as you do.'

'Try that, and I will have your skin for a doormat,' Pallas said tonelessly, and the hairs on the back of Cato's neck rose. 'I suggest you hear me out. You have no choice, in any case. That is the same for all men that I approach to serve me. Especially men who have family to consider . . .'

Cato felt the blood turn cold in his veins as he lowered his hands below the desk and clenched them into tight fists, fighting to control his anger and fear. 'Are you threatening my son?'

'Not if I don't have to. So don't make me, and I am sure we

can come to a mutually beneficial arrangement. Lucius is a lovely little fellow, and it would grieve me if you gave cause for him to come to any harm.'

So there it was, thought Cato, his Achilles heel. A man needed only one weak spot to be undone, and foul creatures like Pallas were adept at finding such weaknesses and exploiting them without mercy, or any semblance of morality.

Pallas was watching him closely, a thin, calculating smile on his lips. Cato felt as if the imperial freedman was reading his mind, and mentally shivered at the prospect. Besides the fear he felt for his son, other feelings swelled to the fore. Anger, and hatred, and a rapidly growing desire to draw his sword and plunge it into the black heart of the man sitting across from him. The urge was so strong, it scared him, and he swallowed nervously before he could trust himself to speak again.

'I need time to think.'

'Of course you do. You have only just returned from a tough campaign. You need to recuperate. I understand that. I can wait a while before you make any decision about my offer. Besides, I have every confidence that you will do the right thing once you have thought through the situation. But please don't make the mistake of thinking you can test my patience. As you may have noticed, there's a certain tension in Rome these days. Some people are unhappy at the idea of having Nero for their emperor. They may make trouble. If that happens, then I need to know I can count on you. And your friend, Centurion Macro.'

'Leave him out of it.'

'I wish I could. But he's as devoted to you as any family hound. I might as well take advantage of the chance to have such a formidable fighter on my side into the bargain.' Pallas eased himself up and adjusted the folds of his cloak as he gazed down at Cato. 'You know where to find me. And I certainly know where to find you and yours. Remember what I said, Prefect. Think it over, but don't take too long. Five days should suffice. After that, if I hear nothing from you, I shall take it that you have turned me down. Which would make you my enemy.'

'Why? Why should I be your enemy? Any more than your friend? Why can't you just leave me alone? I have no interest in politics. I couldn't care less who is emperor. Just let me serve your master by doing what I do best – soldiering.'

Pallas could not help a brief chuckle of amusement. 'My, but you soldiers can be breathtakingly naïve at times. Or at least you pretend that you are. Kindly respect my intelligence, Prefect. I know you have plenty of brains as well as brawn. You would not have risen to your current rank so swiftly otherwise. Nor would you have survived the cross-currents of the political world had you not been so quick-witted and sure-footed around such individuals as my former adversary Narcissus.'

'I despised him, as I despise you now.'

'Ouch . . .' Pallas nodded his head in farewell. 'I'll be seeing you again soon, Cato. One way or another. But remember, you are only of use to me as a friend. Anything else I will consider a threat, and act accordingly. Goodbye for now.'

He turned and paced out of the room, leaving the door open behind him. Cato listened to his light footsteps fade into silence before he hunched forward over his desk and cradled his head in his arms. He was tempted to offer a prayer to the gods. A plea to bring down fire and destruction on Pallas, and all men like him. In exchange, Cato would devote himself to honouring the gods in every way he could for the duration of his life. But what was the point? he reflected. When had a prayer ever been answered? He recalled his childhood, and the many times he had earnestly beseeched Jupiter to rid him of a bully, or grant him some treat. Try praying harder, his father had advised. As if there was some quantum of effort required to pass a certain threshold before the gods deigned to pay any attention.

Cato let out a groan of despair, then rose wearily and took off his armour. Once it had been neatly laid out on his clothing chest, he retrieved his coat and left the barracks. Outside, the rain was falling steadily in a gusty wind, and he pulled his hood over his head before he turned and strode swiftly in the direction of Sempronius's house.

Cato returned home in time to spend an hour with Lucius in his room. Sempronius had bought the boy a set of wooden soldiers, and for a while Cato was able to forget his predicament as he set the soldiers up again and again, only for his son to bowl them over with his pudgy fist and then laugh madly. After a while, Cato picked two of the soldiers up and began to tell Lucius tales of his and Macro's adventures, while the boy half listened and played with the folds of his father's tunic.

At length, Lucius looked up, eyes wide and expression serious.

'Daddy is a soldier?'

'Yes,' said Cato.

'Do you fight bad men?'

'That's how I got this.' Cato indicated the scar on his face.

Lucius regarded him silently, and then suddenly reached up and touched the scar, running his small fingers over the hard white tissue. He made a face and snatched his hand back.

'Is Uncle Mac Mac a soldier?'

'Yes. The best soldier there is.'

The boy picked up one of the wooden figurines. 'Me too. When I am big.'

Cato grinned and lightly tousled his son's soft hair. 'Not for a while yet, I hope.'

The door creaked open as Petronella entered. She beamed at the sight of father and son playing on the floor together. 'I'm afraid it's time to feed the young master, sir.'

'No!' Lucius frowned. 'I want to play!'

'Now, now.' Cato wagged his finger. 'If you want to be a soldier, then you must learn to obey orders. Particularly if they are issued from someone as formidable as Petronella.'

Lucius folded his arms together and scowled.

Cato struggled stiffly to his feet. He stretched his back, then bent down to pick his son up and kissed him on the top of the head before passing him to the nurse.

'Will you be taking dinner with the master and Centurion Macro, sir?'

'Macro's here?'

'Oh yes, sir. He arrived an hour before you did.'

'What's he been doing?'

'Talking to me in the kitchen, sir. While I prepared some gruel for Master Lucius.'

'Really?' Cato could not help smiling at the thought of his friend taking a shine to the nurse. He could see it now, easily enough. She was firmly built and attractive enough, just the kind of woman Macro admired.

'If you have finished with my senior centurion, would you mind asking him to join me in the senator's dining room? Send us wine and something light to eat. Is the senator at home?'

Petronella shook her head. 'He went down to the Senate

102

first thing. Hasn't returned yet. He'll want dinner when he comes in. I'll see that something's prepared for the three of you, sir.'

Cato looked up as Macro entered the dining room. 'I had no idea you were joining us for the evening.'

Macro shrugged. 'Thought I'd drop in and see how the little lad's doing.'

'Just to see him, eh? Not anyone else?'

Macro met his amused gaze and then rolled his eyes. 'Fuck it. All right, I came to see Petronella. What's the harm in a soldier enjoying a little female company, without having to pay for it first?'

'Nothing wrong with it at all. She's a fine-looking woman.'

'Yes, she is. She's got a big heart as well. And that ain't the only thing that's big on her.'

'I noticed.' Cato poured him a cup of wine and passed it over. 'There.'

They sipped quietly for a moment before Macro spoke up. 'So what's on your mind? Something's happened.'

Cato had already decided to tell his friend about Pallas's visit to his quarters. Macro listened in silence, and when Cato had finished, he let out a long sigh. 'Shit.'

'Quite.'

'What are you going to do?'

'I am not sure there is much I can do. Not with Lucius's safety being put at risk. Seems that when Narcissus died, we just traded one back-stabbing bastard for another.'

'What the fuck have we ever done to deserve it?' Macro growled as he clenched his fist around his cup. He thought briefly. 'You're going to have to get Lucius out of Rome. Find

103

somewhere he'll be safe. Somewhere Pallas can't find him. Then he's got no hold over you and you can tell him where to stick his offer.'

Cato nodded. 'I was thinking along the same lines. I just wish I knew who I could trust to look after him. The senator's already being watched by Pallas's spies, I'll bet.'

Before they could discuss the matter any further, they heard the sound of the front door being closed and voices in the atrium. A moment later, Senator Sempronius entered the dining room. His thinning hair was plastered down and his toga had been soaked in the downpour sweeping over the city.

'Good to see you both. I'll just dry myself and change, then we can eat. And talk. It's been an interesting day down in the Senate. Very interesting indeed.'

He returned shortly afterwards in a fresh tunic, just as one of the kitchen slaves brought in a large pot of venison stew and ladled it into three large samian-ware bowls. Sempronius picked up his spoon and fished out a chunk of meat. He tested it carefully but it was too hot to put in his mouth, so he blew gently over it.

Cato could not restrain himself any longer. 'Sir, you mentioned your day in the Senate . . .'

'Oh yes. Well, the cat's definitely amongst the pigeons now. There was a vote on the deification of Claudius. The sort of speeches you'd expect, about his peerless contributions to the security and welfare of Rome. The motion was passed unanimously, as anticipated. But one wonders what Jupiter and the others will make of us mortals voting on whether we should be divinities.'

Cato smiled. 'A bit hubristic, one might think.'

'Exactly so.' Sempronius took the plunge and put the

meat in his mouth; he winced, and then chewed quickly before swallowing. 'That's good. Very good. Anyway, that was the easy business of the day. It's what followed that raised the temperature. There were a few procedural matters, then the floor was opened for other business. Some were already leaving their seats when Granicus stood up to put forward a motion.'

'Granicus? Haven't heard of him.'

'Not surprised. He's a bit of a fossil. Amazing he is still alive. Comes from one of the oldest families, but they've been down on their luck financially and might not even qualify for the Senate when the next census is taken. So Granicus hasn't much to lose. Which is why he put the motion forward, I suppose. He wants the Senate to act as guardians for Nero and Britannicus until Nero reaches the age of twenty-one; during that period, the Senate is to be empowered to rule on Nero's behalf.'

Cato shook his head in disbelief. 'He's signed his own death warrant.'

'You may be right. But it's not just him. Several other senators came to his defence when the imperial lackeys tried to shout him down. The debate, such as it was, got quite heated. At one point the master-at-arms had to intervene to break up a fist fight.'

Macro wiped his mouth and looked at the senator shrewdly. 'And which side of the fence did you come down on, sir?'

'Neither. And I wasn't alone. Most of us ended up squatting on the fence.'

'Sounds uncomfortable, and crowded.'

'Exactly. That's what surprised me. Not many were willing to openly commit themselves to Nero's cause. For sure, the Nero faction outnumbered Granicus and his supporters two or three to one, but the rest? Who knows?'

'Typical politicians, too scared to even fart before they know which way the wind is blowing,' Macro snorted, then recalled at whose table he was sitting. 'Present company excepted, sir.'

Sempronius shook his head. 'No need to apologise. It's been a long time since senators have had the guts to speak their minds. Usually they do whatever the palace tells them to and make a great show of supporting the will of the emperor. Now, however, there's a feeling that the imperial succession is unfinished business, and the Senate is waiting to see who is going to come out on top.'

'Surely there's not much doubt about that?' said Macro. 'The Praetorians have sworn to serve Nero. And he's the one on the throne. Job done as far as I can see.'

Cato clicked his tongue. 'Not if the mood on the parade ground earlier today is anything to go by.'

'I heard about that,' said Sempronius. 'Awkward moment by all accounts.'

He took a few spoonfuls of stew before he continued. 'Made more awkward still by the situation in Ravenna. There's a legion in camp there. The Sixth. They're waiting for transports to reach Ostia so they can ship out to Lepcis Magna. They were supposed to have sworn the oath by now, but there's been no confirmation from them. Nor any word from the fleet at Misenum, as yet.'

'Sounds like a mutiny brewing,' Macro mused.

'Not yet. But I have no idea which side they will come down on, and I dare say it's causing a few sleepless nights up at the palace.' Sempronius shook his head wearily. 'We live in exciting times . . . Oh, I nearly forgot!' He turned to Cato. 'I ran into Vespasian's steward as I was leaving the Senate. He had a message for you. Vespasian has invited you to his house for a meal tomorrow night.'

'Oh?' Cato thought a moment. 'Why not send the message to me directly?'

'He must have heard that you're my house guest.'

'I suppose . . . What time?'

'Second hour of the night.'

'Hmm. Not sure if I'll have the time . . .'

'You can go, sir,' Macro intervened. 'I can be trusted to look after the lads for a few hours. Besides, it'll give you a chance for a good chinwag with the legate. It's been a while. I expect he'll be glad to hear how things have been going in Britannia.'

Cato nodded. 'Yes, I think we'll have a lot to discuss.'

Sempronius smiled. 'I imagine you will. A lot to discuss indeed . . .'

CHAPTER ELEVEN

It had been dark for some time when Cato stepped up from the street and rapped sharply on the door of Vespasian's home, which lay off a quiet side street on the Janiculum Hill. It was an affluent neighbourhood, with just a handful of ramshackle tenement blocks clustered around the nearest crossroads. A candle inside a lantern illuminated the space in front of the door so that visitors could easily be identified from within. Without warning, the shutter behind a small iron grille snapped aside and a pair of eyes regarded him.

Cato had borrowed a neat but plain toga from Sempronius to lend him a respectable appearance for the visit to his former commander. Even so, he felt self-conscious under the gaze of the man behind the door.

'Prefect Quintus Licinius Cato.' He introduced himself calmly. 'I am expected.'

There was no reply, then the slot closed and the faint scrape of bolts sounded before the door swung inwards. A youthful, thickset man with dark features emerged, glanced both ways along the street then hurriedly ushered Cato inside. He closed the door and slid the locking bolts back into place. The house was quiet, Cato noticed. No sounds of voices from within, and little illumination, as if the place was deserted. At once he was on the alert, senses straining for the first sign of danger. His hand slid down to the handle of the dagger hanging inside his cloak.

'Where is your master?'

The doorkeeper returned his stare without expression, and Cato took a pace back, watching the man for any telltale sign of hostility, but there was no bunching of muscles, no easing himself down in preparation to spring. Instead he nodded towards the atrium, and Cato noticed the dark opening of a passage beyond.

'I said, where is your master? Answer me.'

The man touched his lips and shook his head.

'You're a mute?'

He nodded, and waved Cato towards the passage.

'You first.'

The man shrugged and then strode across the atrium with a rolling step that made his broad shoulders sway slightly. He had the physique of a boxer, or a wrestler, Cato decided, and he kept a modest distance from the man as he followed him. There was a steady drip from the tiles overhanging the shallow pool in the atrium, and the surface was riddled by intersecting ripples; it briefly put Cato in mind of the complexity and duplicity of the political world of Rome. Then he pushed the thought aside and focused on his surroundings, still wary of the suspiciously quiet and darkened interior of Vespasian's home.

As they entered the passage, Cato could barely make out the broad back of the man, and he closed his fingers around the handle of his dagger, ready to draw it in an instant. Then he saw a faint strip of light glowing along the bottom of a door, and the soft scrape of the doorkeeper's feet came to a halt as he knocked gently. Cato did not catch any reply before the door was opened and a warm orange hue spilled out into the passage, casting a large shadow on the wall.

The doorkeeper stepped aside. Keeping an eye on the man as he stepped past him into the room, Cato saw that he was in a large study. One wall was lined with shelves heaped with scrolls. A large desk stood at the far end; beyond it another door. In front of the desk were two couches either side of a low table, upon which stood a large bronze candle holder. Four candles provided enough illumination to see that there was only one other person in the room. Domitia, the wife of Vespasian. She rose from the couch and looked past Cato.

'You may leave us, Decimus.'

The doorkeeper bowed and gently closed the door behind him. Cato heard his footsteps padding away, back towards his post at the entrance to the house. Domitia approached him, a warm smile on her face.

'It's a pleasure to see you again, Cato. Always a pleasure, in fact. Ever since I knew you as a boy in the imperial household. You have come a long way since then.' She looked him up and down. 'Quite the man these days. Man and soldier. More than a soldier, a hero.'

Cato felt uneasy when praise was lavished on him, and he shifted awkwardly. 'It is a pleasure to see you too, my lady. But forgive me, I was under the impression that I had been invited to dinner with the legate. Is he not here?'

Domitia looked at him for a moment before she replied. 'No. Vespasian left Rome today on a hunting trip with some of his old army companions. So we won't be disturbed.'

This was acutely uncomfortable, thought Cato. He was alone in a room with the wife of a senator, and it smacked of scandal. She read his expression and chuckled.

'I can assure you that I haven't asked you here to seduce you, Cato. As it happens, I am that increasingly rare thing in Rome these days – a loyal and loving wife.'

'Then why was I told that your husband had invited me to dinner?'

'A necessary subterfuge. It would have been inappropriate to ask you to come and see me alone at this hour. Besides, I doubt you would have accepted the invitation. Nay? But here you are. Now come and sit down.'

She returned to her couch, but Cato did not move. 'So why am I here?'

'We'll come to that in a moment. But first, are you hungry? I can send for food and drink if you like.'

Cato did not feel like giving her an excuse to keep him here should he feel the need to depart quickly. For now, though, his curiosity outweighed his anxiety. 'Thank you, but no.'

'As you wish . . . Please, my boy, sit down. It is not conducive to having a comfortable conversation when one of us is seated and the other is standing there like a pallbearer.'

'My lady, there is nothing at all comfortable about this situation at the moment.'

'All the more reason for you to sit down.'

There was a moment's stillness before Cato relented and took his place on the couch opposite Domitia.

'That's better.' She smiled again. 'You wear your unease on your sleeve, Cato.'

'Can you blame me?'

'Very well. I'll get to the point.' Domitia collected her thoughts. 'From what I recall of your early days in my husband's legion, you were something of an idealist. Most soldiers choose to enlist for loot, adventure or to escape drudgery or scandal. But you were given no choice, as I recall. You were sent as a condition of your father's will. And yet you served willingly, and with an exemplary devotion to duty. You demonstrated your courage and ability from the outset, and have been promoted to your present rank with what some might regard as unseemly haste. But that is not your fault, my dear Cato. There will always be envy of those who excel. Such people tend to make the rest of us feel a little inadequate. My question to you is, would you be prepared to give your life for the good of Rome?'

'I have risked my life for Rome often enough, and have the scars to prove it.'

'So I see. But my question was slightly more nuanced than that. I asked if you would give your life for the *good* of Rome.'

'Ah, I see. That depends how you define good.'

'Precisely. It's easy to be patriotic. Any fool can love Rome and be prepared to die for it. But that is not enough. What matters is to determine what is good for Rome, and what is to its detriment, and then act to advance the former and prevent the latter. That is the true work of the patriot. That is the cause that is worth fighting for and, if need be, dying for.'

'I see . . . And you are the one who should determine what is good for Rome?'

'It has to be someone, Cato. Would you prefer that it was Agrippina, or that loathsome son of hers, Nero? Or that creature Pallas?'

Cato almost flinched at the mention of the freedman's name, and he recalled the sickening dread he had felt at the threat to harm his son. He despised Pallas, and saw him clearly for what he was: a grubby little opportunist with the cold cunning of a snake. But that made him all the more dangerous, and therefore Cato would be a fool to make an enemy of him.

'My lady, I am a soldier. I have taken an oath to obey the orders of my superiors. It is for them to decide what is good for Rome, not me.'

'Rubbish. You are not a fool, Cato, and nor am I. So don't insult my intelligence by claiming that you have no political views.'

'If I have such views, they are mine and I do not have to share them with you.'

'Then you *do* have views.' She leaned forward and jabbed a finger at him. 'If that is the case, it is your duty to act on them. To do what you think is best for Rome.'

'As I said, I am a soldier. My duty is very simple. It is to obey orders. Nothing more.'

Domitia did not hide her frustration. 'What is it, Cato? Why are you being so obstinate? You can speak freely to me.'

'That is a bit rich, my lady. You question my views and yet you have told me nothing of the purpose of inviting me here, in secret. I take it that there is more to this than simply a cosy chat about my political views. What do you want from me? Speak plainly or I will take my leave of you.'

'All right . . . as you wish.' She folded her hands together. 'Many years ago, I came to realise that Rome's interests and those of the emperors were not one and the same. When all power is vested in one man, there is a temptation for that man to rule for himself only. I'm afraid I do not have any faith in the notion of a benign dictator. Experience has taught me that the concept is no more than an oxymoron. No one man can be trusted with the fate of Rome. That is a truth that was known to our forefathers, and that is why Rome became a republic. It is also why the Liberators cut Caesar down. It is why their example lives on even to this day. There are people like me who still believe that Rome only has a future if we return to republican government. Otherwise it is condemned to a process of tyranny, corruption and decadence that will eventually bring about the fall of the Empire. That is why it is my duty to oppose the emperors. That is why it is your duty too. If you truly serve Rome.'

Cato responded coldly. 'I defy anyone to question the service I have rendered Rome.'

'I don't question it, Cato. Rome needs you now more than ever. Which is why I must ask you to help me and others like me.'

'No. I can't.'

'Can't? Of course you can. You can choose to act as you will.'

'My answer is still no.'

She sighed, and there was a pause before she tried another tack. 'It is not just simply a question of serving Rome well. There would be something in it for you too, Cato. I know you are short of money. That you had to sell your home to cover the debts run up by Julia. I am sorry about her death, by the way. She is sorely missed by all who knew her.'

'Not by me,' he said through gritted teeth.

Domitia gave him a searching look. 'I don't believe you . . . Be that as it may, if you were to join our cause, and Nero falls, along with those who follow him, then the Praetorian Guard will need a new commander. I cannot think of a better man to replace Burrus than you.'

'Me?'

'Why not? You have a fine record. You are a soldier's

soldier, as they say. You have proven your courage, and the men of your cohort respect you and would follow you anywhere you chose to lead them. And where they go, others will go too. You would be the most powerful soldier in the Empire. And richly rewarded, I'm sure.'

'And what would I have to do to earn such a reward? What precisely do you and your co-conspirators have in mind?'

'Conspirators?' Domitia frowned. 'No, we are patriots, as I said. Our ambition is to remove Nero from power and replace him with Britannicus.'

'Swap one emperor for another? I thought you wanted a republic?'

'I do. But revolutions succeed best when they take the people along with them. We have had emperors long enough for the mob to get used to them. Britannicus will prepare the ground for a return of power to the Senate and people of Rome.'

'And why would he want to do that? If I have come to know one thing about emperors, it is that they do like to hang on to power.'

'Britannicus is different. He believes in the Republic.'

Cato laughed. 'Britannicus is a mere boy; how does he know what he believes in?'

'He is no ordinary boy. He is wise far beyond his years, and he knows that Rome must become a republic again if the Empire is to survive. Once he is on the throne, he will slowly return power to the Senate. When the time is right, the Senate will vote itself supreme power in all respects and Britannicus will agree to relinquish his title.'

'You really think he will do that?'

'I do,' Domitia replied earnestly. 'I am staking my life on it.

So are all the others who support the cause. There are hundreds of us, Cato. Senators, equestrians, some legionary commanders, and many of your fellow officers in the Praetorian Guard.'

Cato rubbed his brow wearily. There were so many things that could go wrong. So little detail, and so much trust in Britannicus and his intentions. The whole thing was rife with danger and uncertainty.

'I cannot help you. In truth, I share your desire for the return of the Republic. But I fear it is too late to reverse the tide of history. The emperors are here to stay.'

'You cannot truly believe that, Cato.'

'I do . . . Besides, I cannot risk helping you. I have already been approached by Pallas. He wants my loyalty. And he has threatened my son if I refuse him. For that reason alone, I cannot help you. I cannot even be suspected of being associated with you and your cause. So you see, I have no choice. Rest assured, I have no sympathy for Pallas, nor any wish to help him. But I will not make him my enemy. For Lucius's sake.'

'I see.' Domitia stared at him for long enough to make him uncomfortable. Then she nodded. 'I understand the delicacy of your position, Cato. So I will say no more for now. All I ask is that you consider what I have told you. If you wish, we can talk again. But first, swear to me, on the life of your son, that you will not breathe a word about what we have said tonight.'

'I swear it,' Cato replied solemnly. Then he stood up. 'I must go now.'

'Very well.' She remained seated and bowed her head in farewell.

As Cato left the room, Domitia listened to his footsteps receding in the direction of the atrium.

'Well? What do you think?' she asked softly.

The door behind the desk opened and a figure emerged from the darkness. A man dressed in a plain tunic. 'He'll come round to us. I am sure of it. He just needs to be given the motivation to see what he must do. And that I can arrange, very soon . . .'

CHAPTER TWENTY

CHAPTER TWELVE

Over the next two days, Cato's attention was taken up with finalising the details of the last of the wills, confirming promotions and working through the applications from those seeking the places of the men of the Second Cohort who had fallen in Hispania. Though many of the vacancies would be filled by men promoted from the legions, there would still be some recruited directly. They would have to meet certain physical criteria, but more importantly they would need a reference from a figure of standing. Most of the documents were genuine, but more than a few were forgeries of a varying standard. Often there was an additional promise of a bribe, which the more venal kind of officer was willing to take. But Cato's priority was to ensure that the Second Cohort was as fine a body of soldiers as he could make it. If they were called on to fight again, then the quality of the men mattered rather more than the amount they could afford to pay Cato for a place in the Praetorian Guard.

Meanwhile Macro was working the men hard at cleaning and repairing the barracks, and carrying out regular drills and inspections to ensure that they were as well turned out as they had been before they had left for Hispania. Following the poor reception of the news about their delayed bonus payment, it was the intention of both officers to keep the men occupied as much as possible. Bored soldiers will talk and drink, and it would only take one hothead, or agent provocateur, to stir up fresh trouble. Cato was all too aware of the fervid atmosphere in the city as the tensions between the supporters of Nero and Britannicus grew day by day. There were clashes in the streets between rival gangs, broken up by the urban cohorts. Britannicus had moved out of the palace into the large house on the Aventine that he had inherited from his mother. There he was surrounded by the company of German bodyguards that had once protected his father and now felt honour bound to serve his son. Their numbers were supplemented by scores of veterans from the legions who had served in Britannia and now swore allegiance to the boy who had been named to honour their campaign.

It was late in the afternoon of the second day that Cato was summoned to headquarters by the commander of the Praetorian Guard. Burrus was seated at his desk as a clerk showed Cato in, and barely looked up as he waved him forward.

'Just a moment . . .' He finished reading some figures on a waxed tablet and then pressed his ring seal at the bottom before snapping the tablet closed and placing it to one side. 'There.' He glanced up at Cato as he slid a sheet of papyrus towards him. 'Orders from the palace. You are to take a half-century to the house of Senator Granicus and arrest him. He is to be taken to Pallas for questioning. You are commanded not to harm him, nor any of his household, unless there is any resistance. Is that understood?'

'You want me to arrest the senator?'

'That is what I said. You seem to be doubtful. I am sure

your orders are easy enough to comprehend.'

Cato picked up the sheet and read the instructions through. The order was authorised with the emperor's name and seal. It even specified Cato by name to lead the arrest party.

'Straight from the top, as you can see,' Burrus said tersely.

'From Pallas at any rate . . . But why send a cohort commander to do the job, sir?'

'Do you think you're too good for this kind of work?'

'No, sir, I—'

'No doubt it is because a senator is being arrested. He merits someone of senior rank. That is how these things are done.'

'I apologise, sir. I am not familiar with the protocol of this sort of situation.'

'You will be soon enough. It is a common requirement for Praetorians.' Burrus's lips lifted fractionally into a slight sneer. 'Even war heroes have to take their turn. So if you don't mind, pick your men and arrest the senator at once. Dismissed.'

Macro cast his eye over the soldiers forming up in the lengthening shadows outside the barracks. Cato had given orders for them to leave their spears and shields behind. After all, they were only going to arrest an old man, not fight a battle. In helmets and armour, and carrying swords, they were intimidating enough.

'Are you sure you don't want me to deal with this?'

Cato shook his head. 'The orders were clear. Pallas wants me to do it. With things the way they are, it would be best not to draw attention to ourselves. We'll do our duty, obey orders and keep our noses clean while Nero and Britannicus and their followers battle it out. It's not our fight, Macro.'

The centurion smiled. 'Not our circus . . .'

'. . . not our monkeys.'

They shared a laugh, and Macro patted the purse hanging from his belt. 'I'll stand you a jug of wine when you get back to Sempronius's house.'

Cato arched an eyebrow. 'You seem to be a pretty frequent visitor to the senator's home these days.'

'The place has its attractions.'

'The place, or my son's nurse? Oh, come on, my friend. It's not as if the pair of you are making any secret of it.'

Macro rubbed his chin. 'She's a fine woman. I like her well enough, and she seems to like me.'

'But she's a slave.'

Macro's expression became serious. 'That's right. Your slave.'

'And you wish she wasn't. Is that it?'

Macro nodded.

'Do you want to buy her from me?'

'You could use the money.'

'True. I'll give it some thought . . . But I'm glad you like her. You could do with a good woman. And while we've got ourselves a nice billet in the Praetorian Guard, you can take the chance to enjoy something of a family life.'

Macro looked doubtful. 'I'm not sure I'm the kind to settle down.'

'Most men do eventually. I had hoped for that myself, but . . .' Cato left the thought unfinished and slapped his friend lightly on the arm. 'We'll have that drink later, if you can tear yourself away from Petronella, eh?'

They exchanged a salute and then Cato strode forward to take his place at the head of the small column of soldiers. 'Detachment . . . advance!'

Macro watched them tramp towards the gate leading into the city, until they rounded the corner of the adjacent barracks and disappeared from view. It pained him to see his friend treated in such a cavalier fashion by the imperial freedman and the commander of the Praetorian Guard. But Cato had good reasons to play along with them. He could not afford to make enemies amongst the powerful political players in the capital. Better to stay out of it, suffer the humiliation and survive.

'Ah well,' Macro sighed as his thoughts turned to the prospect of sharing a jug of wine. A little drop of the good stuff had a way of making light of difficulties. But first he'd spend a few hours with Petronella. Now she really did have a way of making the problems of the wider world melt away when he was in her arms . . .

As the late-afternoon sun sank towards the horizon, Cato led his men down the Vicus Patricus, the air already tinted with the blue hue of a winter evening. It was cold too, and the inhabitants of Rome were huddling indoors to keep warm as they prepared their evening meals in the communal cooking spaces – the only places the commoners were allowed to light fires, due to the risk of a conflagration in the densely built-up heart of the city. Cato had been given directions to Senator Granicus's house on the Janiculum Hill, not far from Vespasian's home across the Tiber. It had been one of the wealthier parts of the city for generations, with a handful of fine public gardens, bequeathed to the people by rich patrons no doubt seeking a kind posterity.

He wondered what the senator would be doing this evening when the soldiers arrived. Would he be eating dinner alone? Or would he be with his family and friends? It struck Cato that he had no idea who the man was, beyond the meagre details that

Sempronius had supplied a few days earlier. Granicus appeared to have caused offence by raising the prospect of limiting the powers of the two princes. That was enough to see him taken from his house at night and dragged away for questioning. If that was the kind of place Rome had become, then maybe Domitia was right to desire change. To wish for a return to a time when no one man had absolute power and was beyond being called to account.

The Praetorians descended the Viminal Hill and entered the Forum, opposite the looming mass of the imperial palace. Torches and braziers were already being lit along the terraces overlooking the city, and Cato noted that the number of men guarding the entrances and patrolling the perimeter of the palace complex had been doubled. A party of drunken revellers gave way to them, cheering the Praetorians as they passed through and continued along the street that ran at the foot of the Capitoline Hill. Ahead lay the Tiber, and as they crossed the river, the breeze carried the stench of the outlet of the great sewer a short distance along the bank. Cato quickened the pace across the bridge and soon they were climbing the slope of the hill towards the house of Senator Granicus.

A high wall surrounded his home. The whitewash had long since faded, and some of the plaster had cracked and fallen away. Patches of the wall had been daubed with adverts, curses and crude cartoons. Above it towered the boughs of poplar trees, dark against the velvet twilight sky. Cato ordered a section to cover the small gate at the rear of the house while he and the rest of the men approached the front. The entrance had a small portico, two pillars on either side of the wide steps leading up to the weathered door. Detailing a section to cover each end of the street in front of the house, Cato led the remainder up the steps and drew his sword. He rapped the pommel sharply against the door several times before he sheathed the weapon and waited for a response.

Moments later the grille slid open and a voice called out tremulously, 'Who is there?'

'The Praetorian Guard. Open up. I have an imperial warrant for the arrest of Senator Granicus.'

'I w-will let him know you are here, sir.'

'No! You will open the door at once, or we will break it down,' Cato bluffed. He had little doubt about the sturdiness of the door. It would take a battering ram to smash it open. 'At once, d'you hear!'

There was a muted exchange from within, then the sound of bolts scraping back. The door opened, and a nervous-looking boy stood on the threshold. He was wearing a plain tunic and was bare-footed.

'Where is your master?' Cato demanded. 'There's no point in him trying to escape. I have men surrounding the house. Where is he?'

The boy opened his mouth but the words did not come, and he shook his head instead, trembling. Cato stepped forward and brushed him aside, then turned to his men.

'Search the house!'

'Wait!' A voice called out from inside the darkened hall and a figure shuffled forward. By what little light remained in the sky, Cato made out a tall man with wispy white hair about a mottled pate. He was so thin that his skin seemed to hang on his bones. He too wore a simple tunic, but his feet were shod with light slippers. Confronting Cato, he drew himself up and looked down his nose at his visitors.

'I am Senator Marcus Granicus Sapex. You say you have

come to arrest me?' He spoke loudly, as if declaiming to the Senate. 'On what charge?'

Cato took the warrant out from his sidebag and held it up. 'Treason, sir.'

'Treason? I have committed no such crime. I have merely exercised my right to speak in the Senate. Young man, I am a patriot. I have served Rome loyally for over sixty years. It is a rank offence to accuse me of treason.'

Cato replaced the warrant. 'I am sorry, but it is not for me to question the validity of any charges. I just have orders to arrest you and deliver you to the imperial palace. If you'll please come with me, sir?' He gestured towards the street.

Granicus made no reply; he merely stood still and regarded Cato with a severe expression.

Cato sighed. 'Sir, you can come with me, or I can order my men to force you to accompany us. I would rather not subject you to such an indignity if I can avoid it.'

'This is an outrage,' Granicus responded coldly. 'But I have come to expect no less from the string of tyrants that have humiliated our traditions and made Rome no better than any of the corrupt, despotic kingdoms of the east. I have been prepared for this moment for a long time. Let's go.'

Without waiting for a reply, he stiffly descended the steps into the street. The boy looked on anxiously. 'Master, what should I do? Should I ask them to—'

'You will do nothing,' Granicus snapped. 'Just stay here and wait for me to return.'

The boy nodded and then disappeared inside, heaving the door closed with a squeal from the old hinges. The senator looked round scathingly at his captors. 'Praetorian Guard, eh? This lot wouldn't have lasted a moment against my boys of the

Twelfth Legion when we served in Pannonia. Those were real men, not pampered louts like this shower. And you . . . yes, you!' He stabbed a gnarled finger at Cato. 'You're their officer, I take it. What is your name?'

'It doesn't matter what my name is.'

'Kindly do me the courtesy of telling me who is responsible for this outrage. I will have your name, young man. I am a senator of Rome, from one of the oldest families in the bloody Senate, and you will show me the respect I am due.'

The old man's shouting had roused some of his neighbours. A door on the opposite side of the street opened fractionally and an anxious face appeared in the gap. Cato squared up to Granicus. 'Very well. My name is Prefect Quintus Licinius Cato, Second Cohort.'

A glimmer of recognition glinted in the old man's eyes, and he nodded. 'The war hero, eh? And these men too?'

'We have all just returned from the campaign in Hispania, sir.'

Granicus looked at the soldiers again and took a deep breath before continuing in a much calmer voice. 'That was fine work, my boys. Fine work indeed. I, uh, apologise if I seemed a bit hasty just now.'

'Hasty?' a voice grumbled. 'Not 'alf . . .'

'Quiet there!' Cato scowled in the direction of the comment, though he had not identified the speaker. He turned to the senator. 'We'd better go, sir.'

Granicus nodded imperiously, and the party marched to the corner and along the side of the house to pick up the squad at the rear before retracing its steps towards the Tiber. Cato fell in beside the men who had been watching the rear gate. 'Any sign of trouble?'

'No, sir. Just someone taking a peep at us through the grille, that's all. Quiet the rest of the time.'

It was as he suspected then, Cato reflected. Granicus had had guests when the Praetorians had come calling. People he had not wanted to reveal. But that was not Cato's problem. His orders were to make this arrest and no more, and he was damned if he was going to be the cause of anyone else's misfortune this night.

He increased his pace and rejoined the senator. The old man held himself aloof, as if the soldiers were his personal escort and he their commander. It was a fine act. Cato was amused, and soon found himself feeling a little admiration for his prisoner. As they reached the bridge, he addressed the senator quietly. 'Why did you do it, sir? Why put such an inflammatory motion in front of the Senate? You must have known it would end like this.'

'Of course I did. As to the why, I have lived a long and full life. Three wives, four sons, all dead now, alas. I commanded a fine legion and was governor of Sicily for a while. I have nothing to be ashamed of. Or so I thought, until I looked back on my years in the Senate. There was a time when, if only enough of us had stood up to be counted, we could have restored the Republic. But we sat on our hands and did nothing. And now look where we are. Ruled by a grinning monster who is still more boy than man.'

He paused and looked sidelong at Cato as they paced over the ancient bridge spanning the Tiber. 'I have little time left to me in this world, one way or another. If Pallas doesn't do for me in the next few days, then Charon surely will. What have I to lose? And yet I might still regain some measure of pride before I go into the shadows. Be the man I once was, one last time. So I said my piece, and to my surprise, a handful of my peers backed me. I tell you, Cato, I have not felt such purpose and peace of mind for decades. If I am to pay the price now, I think it was worth it.'

'I'm glad you feel that way, sir.'

'Are you? Why should you feel glad? Do you agree with my point of view?'

Cato cursed himself for his open comment, and glanced at the nearest Praetorians for any sign of reaction, but none seemed to be paying their commander and his prisoner any heed. He lowered his voice before he responded. 'Sir, you have my sympathy for your plight, but that is all. I have no further view on the matter.'

Granicus sniffed. 'You'd be a very unusual man if that were true.'

Cato shrugged and said nothing more as they made for the street that ran along the rear of the imperial palace. He felt relieved that he would soon have completed his unsavoury task and could return to barracks. Ahead he could see the modest gate that led into the administration quarters. A squad of Praetorians stood guard by the light of a brazier standing to one side. At sight of them, Granicus began to slow his pace and spoke in a low, urgent tone.

'Listen, I may well never see the light of another day. If this is my end, then hear me, Prefect Cato. You may be a soldier, but you are also a Roman. It's good Roman blood that runs through your veins, not some watered-down piss-poor wine. You have no excuse to stand idle while our empire is treated as the plaything of a hereditary incompetent. People must act to put an end to this. That includes you. I'm sure you are no fool. You must surely see that the new regime will be a disaster for

Rome. And if you can see that, then in all conscience you must do something about it.'

'I told you, I am a soldier, and that is all. And I'll hear no more from you.' Cato rapidly increased his pace and left the old senator in his wake.

As the column approached the sentries, Cato called a halt, then drew the warrant from his bag and held it out for inspection.

'I have a prisoner to be delivered to Imperial Secretary Pallas.'

The optio in command briefly examined the warrant and returned it. 'I was told to expect you. Your men can wait here, sir. I'll have someone accompany you and the prisoner.'

'Thank you.'

The optio turned to assign a man to the task while Cato had the senator brought forward, then the three men entered the palace and climbed a plain stone staircase to the offices used by the emperor's clerks and advisers. Their way was lit by the glow of oil lamps in brackets mounted on the walls, and Cato could see that the rooms on either side were dark and still. At the end of a long corridor they stopped outside a door, and the sentry pushed it open and gestured to the senator. 'You're to wait in here, sir.'

Cato made to follow, but the sentry took a half-step to block him. 'Just the senator, sir. That's what the optio told me. You're to wait out here for Pallas.'

Cato seethed with frustration at this cavalier behaviour, but swallowed his irritation and nodded. 'Very well . . . Just a moment.'

He stepped past the man to inspect the room. It was plain enough, with a window high on the opposite wall. Too high for Granicus to attempt an escape. Apart from two long benches on opposite sides of the room, there were no other furnishings. The senator would be secure enough here, Cato decided. There was no other way out. He stepped back and ordered the sentry to shut the door.

'Where's the imperial secretary?'

'I'll find him and let him know the prisoner is here, sir. If you'll excuse me?'

Cato gave a curt nod, and the sentry marched away down the corridor. Cato relaxed against the wall and rubbed his eyes. He felt tired and was sorely looking forward to his first good night's sleep since returning from Hispania. The interior of the palace felt cold, and the silence was oppressive. He stretched his shoulders and comforted himself with the thought of the soft bed waiting for him in his quarters. At the same time he tried to dismiss any thought of the senator's earlier comments: he did not want to regard him as anything more than a duty performed.

A faint cry of surprise came from inside the room, then a dull thud and the scraping of the feet of one of the benches.

Cato froze, ears straining. Then he eased himself away from the wall and turned towards the door, putting his hand on the latch and lifting it. The door began to swing towards him as he called into the dark room. 'Sir? Are you all right?'

There was an explosion of movement from the shadows and a burly man smashed into the door, slamming it back against Cato, the impact driving the wind from his lungs. He tumbled back on to the floor and the man tried to leap over him, but Cato just had time to snatch at his ankle and the man came down heavily on top of him, shoulder first. The blow was numbing and Cato lay inert, blinking as he gasped for breath. The sleeve of his assailant's tunic had ridden up, and there on his upper arm was a tattoo. A scorpion. Then he rolled away from Cato, on to his feet, sprinted down the corridor and turned the corner into another passageway.

Cato slumped on to his back, desperately trying to breathe as movement began to return to his limbs. He let out a strained groan, then sat up and hugged his knees for a moment before climbing back to his feet. He rested a hand on the door frame and stood on the threshold of the room. 'Senator . . . sir . . . ?'

In the pool of light cast by the oil lamps in the corridor, he saw the bench lying on its side, and close by, the spread-eagled body of Granicus, face down. The shaft of a dagger protruded from between his shoulder blades, and blood stained the cloth of his tunic, dark and glistening as it spread. Beyond, a rope hung down from the high window in the opposite wall. Cato rushed across the room and knelt beside the body. Granicus was still moving feebly, so Cato eased him gently on to his side, feeling the warmth of the blood on his hands as he did so. The senator's throat convulsed and a red froth spewed from his mouth.

'Oh Rome . . . Oh gods . . .' He choked. 'Not yet . . .'

Cato had seen many men wounded on battlefields, and knew that if there was any hope of saving Granicus then the bleeding had to be stopped. He tore off his own neck cloth and held it ready as he grasped the handle of the dagger and pulled it out in one steady motion. Granicus let out a deep groan and arched his back. Blood pulsed from the wound and Cato thrust a fold of the cloth into the torn flesh, cramming more in and pressing it down tightly as he tried to keep the old man from struggling. He was so intent on his work that he was not aware of the sound of footsteps until the men were almost upon the room.

'Hold on, sir.' Cato spoke urgently into Granicus's ear. 'Help's coming.'

The senator's frail body was trembling uncontrollably now, and his breathing was a savage series of gurgled gasps as blood filled his lungs and throat. Suddenly his body went quite stiff, then spasmed violently and went limp in Cato's arms.

'What is the meaning of this nonsense?' a voice demanded as the door swung wide. 'Why have you brought the senator to this room—'

Cato looked up and saw Pallas standing outside. The imperial secretary's expression was etched with horror at the gory spectacle on the floor. Behind him stood two Praetorians, heavy-set men in worn tunics spattered with dried blood. Torturers.

There was an instant of tense stillness in which Cato was only aware of the blood pounding through his ears. Then Pallas thrust his hand out. 'Murderer!'

CHAPTER THIRTEEN

It took no more than a heartbeat to realise how the situation would appear to Pallas and the others. Blood was smeared over Cato's hands, and even if he spoke the truth, the fact that he had been discovered with the body and the murder weapon would point to a very different conclusion.

His instincts took over and he jumped to his feet, sprinted towards the wall under the window, caught hold of the rope and began to haul himself up. The suddenness of his action startled Pallas, but only for a moment, and the imperial freedman stepped aside and shouted at his torturers: 'Take him!'

They sprang forward, charging across the room. One hurdled the body, while his comrade slipped on a slick of blood and pitched forward on to his hands and knees. Cato already had one hand on the window frame. As he began to pull himself up, he felt the rope jerk violently beneath him. He let go of it with the other hand and reached up, scrabbling for purchase. Teeth gritted, he pulled himself up. The shutters were half closed, and he head-butted them open. Fingers snatched at his right calf, then slid down and tightened around his ankle, pulling hard. Cato felt his grip loosen, and he tensed his fingers painfully as he lashed out with his foot. On the second attempt he caught his assailant's knuckles between his boot and the wall, and there was a gasp of agony as the man let go of him and swung back down on the rope.

'Don't let him get away!' Pallas cried out from the doorway. 'Or I'll have your hides!'

Cato braced the toe of his left boot against the roughly plastered wall as he swung the other leg on to the sill and then carefully heaved himself up and over so that he lay on his stomach, breathing hard. Now he could see that the rope had been tied around the centre post of the shutters, with one end trailing into the room while the other dropped down a sheer wall for some thirty feet before ending coiled up behind one of the bushes that ran along a narrow terraced garden overlooking the Forum far below.

Meanwhile Pallas's men had discovered a better way to get at their prey, and while one leaned against the wall and cupped his hands to hoist the other up, his comrade was rapidly rising towards Cato.

'No. You. Don't!' Cato raised his left leg and kicked down hard. The nailed sole of his boot struck the torturer squarely in the face, crushing his nose and jerking his head back. He blinked, dazed by the blow, and Cato struck again. This time the man let go of the rope and fell, taking his comrade with him. Cato snatched at the rope and yanked it up, the end flickering just beyond the final attempt to grasp it before it was too late.

He could not help a quick triumphant grin as he tossed the coils of the rope down the outside wall and swung himself off the sill and began to descend hand over hand.

'Fools!' Pallas snarled. 'He'll get away! Don't just stand there! Raise the alarm!'

Boots clattered across the flagstone floor and pounded down the corridor. Cato paused, and twisted round to examine the garden. There were two sentries at each end, guarding the entrances to the palace. He hesitated. It would be risky to continue climbing down and chance being spotted. How Granicus's murderer had managed to slip into the garden was a mystery for now, but Cato would not be able to leave it undetected. He could see that clearly.

There was only one thing for it, he realised, and he bunched his muscles as he pulled himself back up to the window and clambered in. The room was deserted except for Granicus's body, under which blood was slowly pooling. Cato lowered the shorter part of the rope back into the room and then climbed down, dropping the last few feet. The murder weapon still lay close to the senator's body and he snatched it up, wiping the gore from the blade and handle. It was a standard-issue army dagger, he noted as he tucked it into his belt the opposite side to his own sheathed blade. Then he hurried to the door and looked cautiously out into the corridor. There was no movement apart from the gentle wavering glow of the oil lamps. He ran for the corner where the murderer had disappeared and plunged into the gloom of a narrow passage.

There was scant lighting here, the wan glow of small lamps interspersed with stretches of darkness. But there was no time to proceed cautiously. He had to get away from the palace as swiftly as possible, and it made sense to head in the opposite direction to where Pallas would direct his search parties. This was also the route taken by Granicus's assassin, who might only be a short distance ahead of Cato. He ran on, the sound of his boots echoing off the walls close on either side. Suddenly he saw a splash of light framing the end of the passage. A woman in a blue palace tunic carrying a tray passed the opening. Then another, heading in the other direction. Cato slowed to a walk as he neared the junction, breathing deeply and brushing down his cloak.

As he stepped into the light, he saw that he was in an access corridor used by the slaves and servants of the palace. He recognised it from his childhood and knew that the banqueting chamber was to his left and the kitchens to his right. Slaves hurried to and fro with fresh food and drink, and empty platters and jugs. Few of them spared him a glance. He turned towards the kitchens, and saw a young woman on her hands and knees beside a bucket, cleaning up a large spillage of soup. He stopped beside her.

'Did you see a man come out of that passage a few moments ago? Running, perhaps.'

She looked up, and her exhausted expression turned to anxiety when she saw the Praetorian officer looming over her. Cato pointed at the passage and asked the question again.

'Yes, master. I saw him. Red cloak, dark hair?'

Cato could barely recall the colour of the cloak, and nothing of the man's face, but it was not likely to be anyone else. 'That's him.'

The slave pointed back over her shoulder. 'He went that way, master.'

Cato hurried on. It occurred to him that if the alarm had been raised, he could pretend to be running with the hounds, looking for the fugitive; who would question a prefect of the Praetorian Guard?

He felt the heat of the kitchens before he descended the short flight of steps leading to the entrance. A great waft of warm air brought with it the heavy scent of woodsmoke and roasting meat. Two slaves carrying a suckling pig on a silver platter passed him as he stopped on the threshold. Even though he had visited the kitchens as a child, the memories had faded and he had forgotten the scale of the operation required to feed the emperor and his guests. A vast space was broken up by thick supporting pillars and low arched ceilings. Pans and cauldrons spat and steamed over stretches of iron grills, watched over by sweating cooks, as children hurried to and fro with bundles of split logs to feed the fires. Elsewhere pigs, goats and haunches of beef and venison were turned on spits by slaves stripped to the waist, bodies running with perspiration. Orders were bellowed across the room, barely distinguishable above the cacophony of clattering pots, the bubbling of cauldrons and the faint crackle of burning wood. Steam and smoke mingled to create patches of almost impenetrable haze, lit from within by the glow of flames. Any hope of spotting his prey here was dashed.

Close to the entrance was a table behind which sat a fat, sweating man overseeing the dispatch of food to ensure that the banquet ran as seamlessly as possible. Cato crossed over to him as the man was totalling up a series of columns on a large waxed slate.

'Can you—'

The man did not look up from his work but raised a finger to indicate that Cato must wait. Anger surged in his blood and he slammed his fists down on the table. The slave dropped his stylus and recoiled on his stool, nearly falling off.

'A man came in here a moment ago. Not one of the kitchen staff. Red cloak and dark hair. Did you see him?'

'Y-yes, sir.' The heavy jowls quivered as the man nodded vigorously.

'Where is he? Where did he go?'

The clerk looked up and scanned the kitchens, then pointed towards some long tables beyond the spits where slaves were slicing the roast meat and arranging it on platters. Thirty paces away Cato caught a glimpse of red and saw a man with his hood raised helping himself to a joint, chewing as he leaned against a pillar, trying not to draw attention to himself.

'Do you know him?' Cato demanded as he pointed the man out.

'No, m-master. I thought he was one of the guardsmen, sent here on some errand. Never seen him before.'

Cato turned away from the clerk and continued into the kitchen, moving steadily so as not to attract attention. Keeping the man in sight as much as possible, he began to work his way round to approach him at a perpendicular angle, so that he would close him down whichever way he might attempt to flee. A short distance ahead he saw a cloud of steam swirling from the top of a large cauldron and moved to position it between himself and his prey so he could get closer without being seen. Reaching down to his belt, he drew his dagger and paced steadily closer.

He was only three paces from the cauldron and the steam, and ten more from the murderer, when a burly slave with a thick strip of cloth wound about his sweating head stepped forward and clattered a heavy lid down on the cauldron. The sound made the man look up just as the steam parted and his eyes met Cato's.

His reactions were as quick as any Cato had ever seen. At almost the same instant that he apprehended the danger, he threw down the hunk of meat and sprinted to his left, along the edge of the kitchen, where the space was less constricted by those preparing the food. Cato thrust his way through and ran after him. The man had twenty paces' lead as he raced towards a narrow staircase at the far end of the cavernous kitchen. A young boy trotted into his path and was instantly bowled over, landing hard against a pile of firewood. Split logs tumbled around the child and Cato stumbled over them, nearly losing his balance, and then he was clear. The murderer had reached the stairs and raced up them, taking three steps with each bound. Cato followed, his leg muscles straining to keep up. At the top of the stairs was an open yard filled with carts, some still harnessed to mule trains. Scores of slaves were unloading provisions, overseen by clerks with waxed tablets. Rush torches blazed in iron brackets and cast a lurid orange glow over the scene.

Cato stopped at the top of the stairs, searching for his man, desperately trying to pick him out from the seething crowd in the yard. There was an arched gate at the far end guarded by a pair of Praetorians, giving out on to a street; he decided that was where the murderer would make for. He worked his way along the side of the yard, constantly scanning the faces passing by. He was halfway to the gate when he saw a cloaked figure on the far side of the yard, just ahead of him. He wore his hood up and was moving purposefully, weaving through the muleteers, merchants and slaves. Cato increased his pace, pushing his way forward as he angled across towards the gate in an attempt to reach it before the murderer.

The man turned to glance back as he neared the gate, and Cato cupped a hand and shouted across to the Praetorians. 'That man in the cloak! Stop him!'

The nearest soldier spotted Cato as he moved clear of the crowd. Recognising his rank, he lowered his spear tip towards the murderer. The latter slowed his pace, raising his hands as if in surrender, then dodged aside, snatched the shaft and thrust it back, catching the Praetorian off balance so that he half spun and fell to his knees. His comrade rushed to his aid, spear raised to strike.

'No!' Cato bellowed. 'I want him alive!'

The command checked the soldier, and the murderer once again demonstrated his blindingly swift ability to react, wrenching the spear from the fallen Praetorian and thrusting the shaft between the legs of the remaining sentry before sweeping it round and carrying the man off his feet so that he crashed on to his back. Then he released his grip and dashed out into the street.

Cato ignored the plight of the Praetorians and sprinted through the gate after him. Carts lined the side of the street stretching along the wall of the palace, and the figure running in the direction of the Great Circus was clearly visible in the almost deserted thoroughfare. Cato was breathing hard as he continued his pursuit, the footsteps of both men echoing off the buildings on either side. His heart pounded in his chest and his limbs burned with the effort of keeping up.

Ahead loomed the vast length of the Circus, where chariot races thrilled the Roman mob; now, though, the structure lay in the dim light of the stars and the arches were each like some dark maw leading down into the underworld. At the sound of their approach a handful of hopeful prostitutes emerged from the pitch black of the archways to call out, offering their services even as the men raced by.

Cato was the taller of the two, and he was sure he was gaining fractionally. He knew he must run the man down before his strength began to fade. He forced himself on, lengthening his stride. The murderer's lead began to narrow as they neared the end of the Circus, where the charioteers and their teams prepared for their races. A short distance beyond lay the Forum Boarium, a warren of warehouses and stalls close to the Tiber. If his prey managed to reach the Boarium, then Cato feared he might elude him.

They ran on, the street now sloping slightly so that their pace increased. The entrance to the Boarium was an aged arch; it had once been richly decorated, but now the paint had peeled and crude graffiti covered the columns on either side. They were no more than fifty paces from the arch when a patrol from one of the urban cohorts emerged. At the sight of the two men, the optio in charge raised his club.

'Oi! You two! Stop right there!'

The murderer did not even slow down, but swung left into a narrow alley between two tenement buildings. Cato thought fleetingly about calling on the patrol to help him, but in the time it would take him to explain the situation, his prey would have made good his escape. Instead he turned into the alley and ran on blindly. This was a slum area, fog-ridden for much of the winter and swarming with mosquitoes during the height of summer. At night the cold air accentuated the stench of sewage, sweat and rotting refuse. A trickle ran down the alley, and Cato's boots splashed through the puddles where the foul water pooled. He could hear the footsteps of his prey now, and his laboured breathing. The man was close. Very close. Cato readied his dagger and ran on.

Then, suddenly, he was aware that his were the only footsteps in the alley, and he slowed to a stop, chest heaving, and looked around, straining his eyes to pick out any details. A short distance ahead, just beyond a shuttered tavern, was a crossroads.

Raising his dagger and lowering himself into a well-balanced crouch, he crept towards the junction, muscles tensed as he braced himself to receive an attack from the alleys on either side. Still there was no sound of movement above the blood pounding in his ears and his own heavy breathing. As he stepped past the arched entrance to the inn, something warm and soft pressed up against his leg, and he let out a gasp of surprise and lashed out with his boot. The shrill screech of a cat filled the alley, and he saw the tiny shape scamper across the junction and into the narrow street on the far side.

'Shit . . .' Cato muttered as he lowered his dagger slightly and drew a deep breath.

A great weight struck him square in the back, carrying him across the alley to strike the far wall. Rough plaster scraped the skin from his forehead and the air was driven from his lungs with a loud grunt. The force of the impact stunned him, so that he dropped his dagger and collapsed on his front, feeling the cold cobbles and the dirt and slime of the alley against his exposed skin. His attacker knelt across his shoulders and grabbed his hair, then wrenched his head back and lowered his mouth close to Cato's ear.

'That's twice I've taken you by surprise, Prefect.' The man spoke in a soft, menacing tone. 'I thought you were supposed to be a good soldier. You're as green as a recruit.'

He reached out to pick up the fallen dagger and brought the edge of the blade to Cato's throat. 'I could kill you now. Just a flick of my wrist is all it would take.'

'So why . . . don't you?' Cato gasped.

'Believe me, I'd like nothing more. I'm paid to silence people, not set them up. But orders are orders. It's important that you are found alive. That's what Pallas says. He wants you paraded in front of your men to confess your guilt. You'll be known as the soldier who butchered an old man. Only then will you be put to death.'

'But I'll speak the . . . truth. I'll tell them I had . . . nothing to do with it.'

The man laughed harshly. 'Good luck with that! In the meantime, I'll be keeping your blade. Nice thing like this ought to pick up a good price in the Forum.' He shifted as he bunched his fist around the handle of the weapon and raised it. 'Goodbye, Prefect . . .'

'Wait!'

The word was hardly out of Cato's mouth when his assailant slammed his fist into the back of his head, knocking him out cold.

The man rose slowly and stood over the prefect's body. He gave it a contemptuous prod with the toe of his boot, then glanced round and set off up the alley. The sound of his footsteps faded and the only noise left was Cato's ragged breathing.

A short while later, the cat returned, padding on silent paws. It lifted its head cautiously and sniffed, then began to lick the blood oozing from the tear on Cato's forehead.

CHAPTER FOURTEEN

Macro's body slowly relaxed and then, with a contented sigh, he rolled off Petronella and flopped on to his back beside her. That was the second time they had had sex that evening and he was feeling quite pleased with himself. He was breathing heavily and licked his dry lips before he spoke. 'Well, that was a treat, that was.'

Petronella snorted and propped herself up on an elbow so she could look down at him. Her heavy breasts rested on the side of Macro's chest. 'Treat? What, you think I'm some sort of snack? Something you can take as and when you feel peckish?'

'Peckish?' Macro gave a sly grin. 'I think a better word for it might be peckerish.'

Her eyes narrowed in disapproval, and he laughed and slapped her lightly on the flank. 'Easy, my girl. I was just joking.'

'Well, don't you go having a laugh at me, Centurion Macro.' She poked him in the side to emphasise the point and then shuffled down, lowering her head on to his chest as she stroked his stomach.

Macro wrapped one arm around her shoulders and tucked the other behind his head to prop it up. By the light of the oil lamp on the table beside the bed he could just make out the details of the guest room Sempronius had assigned for his use. It was a little larger than his simple cell at the barracks, with a dressing table and chair, a clothes chest and a heavily patterned Parthian rug on the floor. A fresco depicting soldiers, horses and sundry enemies of Rome ran around the top of the wall. But without doubt, the best item in the room was the large bed, with its thick mattress and comfortable bolster. For Macro, used to the rigours of sleeping on campaign and the rough-and-ready accommodation of forts and fortresses, the sheer comfort of the bed was a revelation. And all the better for having a comely woman to share it with.

His thoughts drifted back to the previous evening, when he had sauntered down from the Praetorian camp, whistling contentedly as he looked forward to seeing Petronella again. He had stopped to buy a jar of wine from a nearby tavern, to share with Cato once the prefect had returned from arresting Senator Granicus. Petronella had greeted him at the door; she had been playing with Lucius in the atrium. Sempronius had a dinner invitation, and so they had prepared a meal for themselves and the boy and eaten it in the kitchen before putting Lucius to bed. Petronella had sat on a stool nearby while Macro told the boy a story about the wild tribes in the mountains of Britannia, and the sinister druids who led them.

'You'll give the boy nightmares,' she had warned.

'It's nothing compared to the nightmares the barbarian kids back in Britannia will be getting when their parents tell them all about me.'

'That isn't going to help Master Lucius to get to sleep either, is it?'

Macro ruffled the boy's hair. 'You can take it, can't you, my lad? You've got your dad's blood in you.'

Lucius nodded happily and then grabbed Macro's ear lobe and tugged. 'Tell me another druid story, Uncle Mac Mac!'

'Not tonight, Lucius. Little soldiers need their sleep.'

With the lamp extinguished, Macro had followed Petronella out of the boy's room on the colonnaded side of the house that overlooked the garden. Above, the night sky was clear and stars glittered across the velvet expanse, cold and hard-looking, but somehow both majestic and comforting in their permanence. Macro's life had been one of continuous hazard and change, and the view of the heavens gave him some small comfort. He had been a soldier for over twenty years and soon his enlistment would expire. Like other veterans, he could accept a discharge and choose between land and a cash gratuity and settle into retirement. Or he could re-enlist for a further period. It was tempting to do the latter. Soldiering was all he knew, and he was good at it. But he was beginning to feel the effects of age and knew that he would only ever become weaker and less able to fight from now on. Not that it meant he couldn't kick the shit out of any barbarian who crossed his path for the next few years at least, he reflected contentedly. But it was something to think about.

As was the possibility of taking advantage of his current posting to the Praetorian Guard, with the promise of generous bounties paid by the emperor. With those, and his not inconsiderable savings and campaign loot, Macro could retire in style and comfort. All that he was left wanting was a good woman.

He had glanced briefly at Petronella then, and felt his heart stir a little as she raised her face to the stars, her skin looking like the finest porcelain.

'It's a fine night,' she said.

'Fine indeed.' Macro nodded. 'Bloody fine.'

They stood in silence for a moment before she muttered, 'I'm cold.'

Macro looked at her. 'You need to fetch a cloak then. Or a stiff drink of heated wine.'

Petronella had sighed patiently. 'Or you might offer to put your arms around me, you pillock.'

Macro was shocked at her effrontery. Then he laughed out loud and faced her, hesitating a moment before he enfolded her loosely in his arms. She pressed against his chest, and he was aware of the faint odour of straw coming from her hair. A good smell, he thought. She raised her face and stared up into his eyes, then her lips lifted in a smile.

'So then . . . ?'

Macro leaned forward to kiss her, and she pressed her lips gently against his. Soft and warm, he thought. Nice . . . Very nice indeed.

At length she drew back and shook her head mischievously. 'I was starting to wonder if you were ever going to do that.'

'What? Why wouldn't I? You, er, you're a fine woman. Lovely. That's what I think anyway.'

'Not much of a lover, I take it?'

Macro frowned slightly. He had never really thought about it. He imagined he was as lustful as any man. He had been with more women than he could easily remember, and some of them he hadn't even had to pay for the privilege. There had been attractive women and plain women, and some he had felt a passable measure of affection for. And now there was Petronella, and for some reason he felt compelled to be with her. She spoke her mind. She made him laugh, and then there was that undeniable sensation she sparked off in his loins.

Petronella shifted her stomach against his groin. 'Ah, I thought I could feel something stirring.'

'Yes, well. Perhaps I should . . .' Macro made to pull himself away, but now she held him firmly in her arms. He was surprised by her strength.

'I'll tell you what we should do.' She kissed him again. This time Macro felt his reserve start to melt away, and he ran a hand up her neck and softly stroked her hair. She purred, and he let his left hand slide down to her buttocks.

'That's the idea,' she whispered. 'Now let's go and find somewhere quiet.'

'This is quiet.' Macro nodded towards the garden.

'It's also bloody cold. You've got a nice large, warm bed in your room.' She winked at him. 'Be a shame not to put it to good use . . .'

Macro smiled fondly and took Petronella's hand, raising it to his lips and kissing her fingers. She stirred.

'What's the matter?'

'Nothing,' Macro replied. 'Just feeling happy. Peaceful.'

'I imagine that's unusual for a soldier.' She eased herself up and stroked his cheek thoughtfully. 'I'm glad if this brings you some peace.'

Macro stared up at the ceiling, his eyes moving to the fresco. The faint movements of the flame of the lamp seemed to make the figures shimmer slightly and come alive. He felt a waft of cool breeze through the shutters and then his mind was filled with a vivid memory from the previous winter when he and Cato had been part of the retreat from the druid island of Mona. Snow had fallen deeply across the mountains as the Roman army had struggled to reach the nearest legionary fortress. They had been harried every step of the way, frozen and starving, constantly having to turn about and fight their pursuers off. An image formed of a Celtic war axe shattering the helmet of the man next to Macro, the blade cleaving right down to the collarbone so that his head split open like a water melon.

Macro's face convulsed at the memory. He had not recalled the incident at any time since the campaign. Why now? Why here, in the arms of this woman he already felt a considerable affection for?

'What is it?' Petronella cupped his cheek.

Macro shook his head, hurriedly trying to banish the memory from his mind before anything more terrible still should flow on from that horrifying image. He felt cold and sick, but more than anything, tired. The weariness had set in during the voyage home from Hispania, and had stayed with him, even though he tried his best to ignore it. He had heard men talk of the battle sickness that afflicted some veterans. It was spoken of with some embarrassment and pity, and he had wondered if the true number of those afflicted was greater than his comrades were prepared to admit to. Or were too ashamed to admit to.

'It's nothing,' he lied. 'Just a little worried about Cato. He should have returned to the house hours ago.'

'There must be a good reason for the delay. He doesn't seem like the type to come to any grief.'

'You're not wrong there.'

Petronella rested her head on his chest again. 'You're fond of him, aren't you?'

'Fond? I suppose so. Not sure that's the right word, though. He's my commanding officer.'

'I think he's something more than that to you.'

Macro thought a moment. 'At times he's more like a brother,

or a son, or both. I don't know,' he concluded uneasily. 'He's just a brother in arms, like any other soldier a man has grown used to serving alongside. That's all.'

'If you say so.'

'Anyway, that's enough questions from you. My turn. There's something I'd like to know.'

'Oh? What's that?'

'I get the feeling you've been waiting for this moment. Do I take it that you've been keen on me ever since we returned from Hispania?'

'Before then. When the two of you returned from Britannia. I thought there was something about you that I liked even then. A directness. I felt I knew you at once. That's not something I've felt with many men.'

'You've known a lot of men, then?' Macro said lightly.

'Yes . . .' She moved her head off his chest and rolled on to her side, away from him, before she continued. 'That was when I was younger. Before I was sold into slavery.'

'Sold? Why?'

'My father. My dear drunk decurion father could not cope with my fondness for men. He said it shamed him. He warned me to put an end to it or he'd put an end to me. He said having a slut for a daughter was humiliation enough, without taking into account the damage it was doing to his reputation. He wanted to be a leading figure in the town senate. When it came down to it, my mother persuaded him to spare me. So I was sold off instead. His last words to me were that he hoped I would die a raddled whore in a cheap brothel in Subura.'

'He said that?' Macro growled.

'That, and more. I try to forget. Luckily I was bought by a kindly old soul who wanted a nurse for his daughter. I raised his children before I was sold on to Lady Julia nearly two years ago.'

'Is he still alive?'

'My first master?'

'Your father.'

'No. He was burned alive, along with my mother, in their house. An accident apparently. Luckily my little sister wasn't there. She'd married a local farmer a few years before. I only found out about the fire when she came to my lady's house to tell me the news.'

'A pity your father died,' said Macro. 'I'd have liked to meet him. Just the once.'

She took his hand and squeezed it. 'It doesn't matter now. He's dead and I'm a slave. The world goes on.'

Macro shifted uncomfortably. 'That's something that can be changed. You don't have to die a slave. I'll speak to Cato about it.'

She was silent for a moment. 'I don't expect anything from you, Macro. I am not in your bed because I want a reward. I just wanted you to myself for however long you'd have me. That's all.'

'All right. But I'll still have a word with Cato . . .'

A sharp rapping at the entrance of the house interrupted their conversation. After the briefest delay it came again, longer, louder and more urgent. Macro swung his legs over the side of the bed and reached for his tunic. 'Who the fuck is it at this hour?' he muttered.

'Let the doorkeeper find out.'

'He might appreciate someone to back him up.' Macro slipped his tunic on and then crossed to the chest by the door where his cloak, boots and sword belt lay. He slipped the belt over his head and adjusted the scabbard so that it hung comfortably at his hip. A shuffling noise from the bed drew his attention, and he saw Petronella slipping on her own tunic.

'No. You stay here,' he ordered.

She stood up and stared at him firmly. 'We can argue about it later. Let's go.'

Macro flashed her a grin. 'That's my girl.'

Barefoot, they padded through the house towards the front door. The pounding was louder than ever as a voice shouted, 'Open the door. In the name of the emperor!'

The doorkeeper had emerged from his cell, blinking and uncertain on his feet, and Macro realised the man was drunk. The centurion reached the door first and turned to him. 'Has the senator returned?'

'Yes, master.'

'Then go and rouse him. Tell him we have guests.'

As the doorkeeper staggered off, Macro slid back the grille with a sharp snap and looked out on to the street. An optio from the Praetorian Guard stood with his dagger raised, ready to strike the door again with the haft. Behind him was a squad of guardsmen.

'Open up!' the optio barked.

Macro shut the grille and motioned to Petronella to stand away. Then he slid the locking bolts back and lifted the latch to swing the heavy door open. The optio stepped boldly into the entrance hall. 'Come on, lads.'

Macro let the squad enter before he squared up to the junior officer. 'What's the meaning of this, then?'

The optio looked him up and down with a dismissive expression. 'You'd better watch your tongue if you know what's good for you. Where's your master?'

Macro reached down and tapped the scabbard of his army-issue sword. 'You'd better watch *your* tongue, my lad. Unless you want to be up on a charge for insubordination. I'm Centurion Macro of the Second Cohort, Praetorian Guard.'

The optio looked sceptical, then his eyes widened as he recognised the name and recalled the face. He stiffened his spine and snapped his shoulders back. 'Sorry, sir. Thought you was part of the household.'

'So I gather. What are you doing here, Optio?'

The man held up a small scroll. 'I've an arrest warrant, sir.'

'For Senator Sempronius?'

The optio shook his head. 'No, sir. It's for Prefect Cato.'

'Cato?' Macro started in surprise. 'What in Hades do you want Cato for? He's one of us. There must be a mistake.'

'I don't know about that, sir. All I know is he's to be arrested for the murder of Senator Granicus. We've orders to take him alive if he's here.' The optio turned to his men. 'Search the house.'

The Praetorians filed by and began to spread out through the house. Macro turned to Petronella. 'Go to the boy and make sure he is looked after. Anyone touches a hair on his head and they'll answer to me.'

The nurse nodded and scurried off, leaving Macro and the optio together.

'Murder, you say?'

'Yes, sir.'

'But he was only sent to arrest Granicus.'

'I don't know much about that, sir. Just that he killed the senator up at the palace. The imperial secretary's got hundreds of us out searching the city for him. I was sent here because

Sempronius is his father-in-law and the prefect might turn up. If he's here, we'll find him soon enough.'

There was an edge to the last comment that Macro did not like. An intimation that if Cato was hiding here, then Macro was in on it. He was about to take the man to task when Senator Sempronius came striding towards them, pulling a cloak on over his loincloth.

'What the hell is the meaning of this outrage?' Sempronius thundered. 'How dare you invade my home at this time of night?'

The optio turned to face this fresh attack and swallowed nervously as he held out the warrant. 'We're looking for Prefect Cato, sir. He's wanted for murder.'

'Murder?' Sempronius's eyebrows rose as he exchanged a look with Macro. Then he took the warrant and broke the seal, moving over to the lampstand to one side of the door. He held the warrant up and read quickly.

'Cato's murdered Granicus? But that's absurd. Why, in the name of all that is holy, would he do a thing like that?'

More to the point, Macro thought, where was Cato? Where?

CHAPTER FIFTEEN

The first thing that Cato was aware of as he regained consciousness was a terrible pounding agony on the back of his head. He gritted his teeth and clenched his eyes shut for a moment as he breathed deeply. At once his lungs filled with the rank odour of the filth he was lying in, and he retched. He blinked his eyes open. It was dark and he was in a narrow alley, and yet he had no recollection of how he came to be in this place. He eased himself on to his knees and cradled his head, retched again, and then was sick, vomiting into the foul trickle of water and sewage that ran down the alley, feeling his stomach wrenched up through his chest as his abdomen clenched tightly and the acid contents of his gut splattered across the alley. The urge to throw up came again and again, and between each bout the pain in his head throbbed unbearably. At length there was nothing more to expel, and he sat back against the wall and breathed as easily as he could.

'What in Hades is going on?' he mumbled.

A fleeting movement caught his eye and he saw a scrawny feral cat trot over to the vomit, take a sniff, then recoil, before pacing to the opposite side of the alley and sitting down to watch him.

'You're not much help, are you?'

He reached behind his head and felt a thick crust of dried blood matted into his hair. Further delicate examination revealed a large bump and a cut in his scalp. He winced. It was cold. Bitterly cold. He drew his knees up and hugged them, and tried to concentrate. Though he had no recollection of where he was, he could recall the arrest of Senator Granicus. The comments the senator had made to him as Cato took him to the palace. Then a door flying open and someone crashing into him. Afterwards, a body with a knife in its back. Granicus.

With that, the rest of the details flooded back into his mind like a torrent. Cato was suddenly very alert, eyes and ears straining as he looked from side to side. There was no sign of his assailant. The man who had murdered Granicus and set Cato up to take the blame for the killing. There was no sign of anyone. How long had he been unconscious? He could not tell. But what was certain was that he was in danger. No doubt Pallas had squads of Praetorians and men from the urban cohorts scouring the city for him. And if they found him, there was no question but that he would be held responsible for the murder. Nor was there any question who had framed him. This was the work of Pallas. The imperial freedman had insisted that Cato make the arrest in person, and then escort the prisoner to the palace. There he had chosen the room in which Granicus was to wait, and as soon as the senator was in place the killer was given the signal to enter the room and carry out the deed. If Cato had not heard the sounds of the brief struggle, then doubtless the killer would have used the rope to escape the same way he had entered the room.

Cato recalled the details of the pursuit through the kitchen and into the streets, and then . . . nothing. He traced his memories back and saw the tattoo again. A scorpion, tail ready to strike. The scorpion had been the emblem of the Praetorian Guard ever since Sejanus had adopted it in honour of the birth sign of his master, Emperor Tiberius. So the murderer was a Praetorian, Cato mused. And no common soldier at that. He was superbly conditioned, with the fastest reactions Cato had ever seen. He could have killed Cato, but he chose to let him live.

What was it the man had said? Pallas wanted Cato found and taken alive so that he could be paraded before Rome as the killer of Senator Granicus. Of course, Cato would protest his innocence and point the finger at the killer, but Pallas would be sure to ridicule his explanation, and who would believe Cato? He had been found, daubed in the victim's gore, in the presence of two witnesses who would back up whatever testimony Pallas gave. It was a neat trap, Cato conceded. His only hope of salvation lay in finding the real killer and forcing him to tell the truth. And what hope of that was there? It was all very well knowing that the man was a Praetorian, but there were several thousand men in the corps. It was possible that he had been discharged, in which case Cato's prospects of tracking him down were even more daunting.

To make his situation far worse still, Cato was a hunted man. He must not let himself be caught before he had uncovered the identity of the true murderer and proved that he was working for Pallas. Until then he must disappear into the general population of Rome, become simply a face amid the mob. The first thing to do was to change his appearance. Starting with his clothes. His cloak and tunic were now smeared with excrement and blood from the cut on his head. Even so, they were of good quality and would instantly set him apart from others in this neighbourhood. He needed to get rid of them.

He stood up, wincing at the throbbing pain in his head, and cautiously made his way up the alley into the heart of the slum, quietly trying the latches on the doors as he passed. All were bolted from the inside. Just before he reached the next junction, he heard voices, and hurried back until he reached an arched shopfront, where he pressed himself into the corner. A lurid red glow spilled into the junction, and a moment later a man with a flickering torch appeared at the head of a party armed with cudgels.

'So where is he, then?' one of the men grumbled. 'I thought this is where that bloke said we could find him.'

'Maybe he was having us on,' another added.

'Quit your jabbering!' the torch-bearer snapped.

They paused and debated which way to continue their patrol, before the leader decided to continue straight on and they trudged out of sight, the glow of the torch fading swiftly behind them. Cato waited until he could no longer hear their voices before he emerged from the arch and padded cautiously to the corner of the junction. The patrol was already some distance off, and he let out a relieved sigh before crossing the junction.

A short distance further on he came to a narrow arch leading through into a communal yard shared by the surrounding tenement blocks. There was a small fountain in the centre of the yard dating back many years, to when this part of the city had not been so built up. Water splashed into a large basin, overflowing into a series of troughs before the run-off flowed into a gully that ran out of the arch. Cato waited a moment to listen, but no one was about. He went to the fountain and stripped off his cloak before leaning his head under the spout. The water was bitterly cold, and he stifled a gasp as he let it run through his hair, loosening and washing away the matted blood. He ran his fingers over the welt in his scalp and winced at the sharp pain. He was tempted to wash himself, but then thought better of it. The grime and filth would add to his disguise.

Looking round, he spied a covered area in the far corner of the yard beneath which stretched some drying lines. A meagre collection of garments hung from them. As he headed over towards them, he heard the rattle of a chain and a dark shape detached itself from the gloom and trotted forward before being brought up short with a loud clink. A watchdog. Cato instantly feared that the animal might give him away if it started barking. But instead he saw its tail wag as it sniffed curiously. He stretched his hand out and approached cautiously. The dog strained at its collar, licking Cato's fingers as soon as they came within reach. He eased himself forward and stroked under the dog's chin as the tongue worked eagerly across his palm.

'There's a good boy,' Cato whispered. 'Nice and quiet now.'

After making a fuss of the animal, he moved on towards the clothes line. There was an assortment of tunics and cloaks, most patched and frayed, together with a felt cap. There was also a large linen laundry bag with a strap to one side. Cato stripped and took down the most worn-looking tunic and cloak he could find, along with a cap. He hung his own clothes in their place, ruefully imagining the delight on the face of the man who discovered the exchange. The tunic had a sour smell and the cloth felt coarse against his skin as he slipped it on. The clasp of his own cloak was of fine silver and Cato was loath to lose it. Instead he tucked it into his purse and fastened the replacement cloak with a plain iron clasp that was attached to it. His sword belt and dagger felt reassuring under the cloak. There was only one further personal feature to hide – the gold wrist band. He wondered why his assailant hadn't robbed him of such a valuable item, but then reasoned that the man would have a hard time explaining away something that precious. Picking up the laundry bag, Cato placed the wrist band inside and slipped the strap over his head.

Satisfied with his new appearance, he returned to the dog and stroked it gently on the head, then patted its flank reassuringly. 'I doubt Cerberus is going to be losing any sleep for fear that you might replace him, my furry friend.'

The animal butted its head against Cato's thigh, and he gave it a last pat before easing himself away. The dog looked up and gave a whimper as it stared after the shadowy figure crossing the yard, then retreated to its corner, where it laid its head between its paws with a deep sigh.

As he emerged into the alley Cato looked up and saw the first light hues of the coming dawn in the sliver of sky visible between the tenement blocks rising up on either side. His stolen clothes smelled foul, but between them and the streaks of dirt on his exposed skin, he would not be taken for a prefect of the Praetorian Guard. Pulling the cap down tightly, he set off in the direction of the Viminal Hill. He had no doubt that one of the first places that Pallas would send a search party was the house of Sempronius. Cato would have to approach the place very carefully. He had to make sure that Lucius was safe, and also speak to Macro. He needed his friend's help to track down the murderer of Granicus. If the man was still a serving Praetorian, Macro would be able to continue the search in the barracks.

Of course, it was possible that Pallas would be keeping Macro under observation in case Cato tried to make contact. That was what he would do if he were in the imperial secretary's position, Cato mused. In which case, perhaps it would be better to stay away from the centurion and not involve him. The odds against Cato were bad enough. It would not be right to put his best friend at risk into the bargain. But who else could he turn to for help? Who else could he trust?

By the time Cato reached the street on which Sempronius's house lay, the sun had risen. Dark rain clouds were rolling in from the east and quickly obscured the pale disc, so that a chilly gloom hung over the city. A breeze whipped up fallen leaves and blew them down the street into Cato's face. He hunched down in his cloak as he headed to a tavern a short distance away. Although there was plenty of seating inside, he chose a bench with a view of the street and sat down with a handful of other early risers; the usual cluster of clients killing time before they made their way to the houses of their patrons to seek employment for the day, or a handout so that they could return to the tavern for another drink.

A skinny girl with a spotty complexion and thin greasy hair came to take his order.

'Honeyed wine.'

'Jar or by the cup?'

'Just a cup.'

She gave him a quick appraising look before she spoke again. 'That'll be two asses. In advance.'

Cato scowled at her. 'I can pay.'

'Sorry, sir. The landlord's rules. If you're not a regular, then you pay up front.'

161

'Very well.' He huffed as he reached down to the purse hanging from his belt. He took out a sestertius and handed it to the girl. 'I'll want the change. I'd like to tip, but my rule is that if I'm not a regular at a tavern, I'll keep the change first and see if I get good service up front.'

She glared at him briefly before turning on her heel and scurrying over to the counter, returning with a cup that she set down sharply on the bench beside him. When she had gone again, he took a sip and then sat with the cup in his hands as he watched the street. A handful of slaves emerged from various houses, heading down to the Forum to buy the day's groceries. A few pedlars went from door to door with their wares, making the odd sale. A short distance beyond the entrance to Sempronius's house a beggar squatted in the shelter of a buttress, his one leg stretched out in front of him. He occasionally raised a mess tin and rattled it at passers-by. All the while the clouds thickened overhead.

The first drops of rain pattered down, and people pulled their hoods up if they had them, or increased their pace to get to shelter before it poured in earnest. Soon there were very few people left on the street. Cato noted that the beggar did not move, but shifted a little to work himself as far into the angle of the buttress as possible.

'That has to be a very keen beggar, or else someone who is obeying his orders,' he mused in an undertone.

Just then the door of the house opened and Macro stepped out. The nurse stood sheltered on the threshold, and at her side was Lucius, sucking two of his fingers. Cato felt a surge of despair at the sight of his son. It was painfully tormenting to see him and not be able to be with him. Macro kissed Petronella, patted Lucius on the head and then stepped down into the street, striding in the direction of the Praetorian camp. As he passed the beggar, he paused, and there was a brief exchange, then he tossed a coin into the tin and moved on.

Cato waited for the door of the house to close before he set his cup down and stood up, ready to set off after his friend. The beggar, however, was already using his crutch to get up. He glanced both ways along the street, then stuffed the mess tin beneath his battered cloak, tucked his stick under his arm and followed Macro at a distance, at an impressive pace for a man with one leg.

Cato glanced up at the sky. The rain was falling hard now, hissing off the flagstones and running off the roof tiles. With his cap pulled down and his shoulders hunched, he stepped into the street and began to tail the two men ahead of him.

CHAPTER SIXTEEN

It had been a sleepless night as Macro went over what little he had gleaned from the optio in command of the Praetorian search party. At dawn, Petronella had stirred, and dressed to begin her daily duties, leaving him brooding. None of it made much sense. He could not believe that his friend would cold-bloodedly murder a defenceless elderly senator. What reason could he possibly have to carry out such an outrage? There was no doubt in Macro's mind that a mistake had been made, at best; at worst, some double-dealing scoundrel had set his friend up. Either way, someone was going to pay for the trouble they had heaped on Cato's shoulders. On that, Macro was firmly resolved. And if it turned out to be the work of that oily reptile Pallas, then Macro was going to rip his heart out and feed it to the crows.

The search party had made thorough work of their task, searching every room in the house, as well as under the eaves and in the dusty and dank cellars beneath the house. Some furniture had been moved and overturned, and not a few expensive bowls and ornaments had been knocked over and shattered. The alarming noises and the shouting of soldiers had woken Lucius up and caused him to burst into tears before

Petronella was allowed to go to him and comfort the boy. She had finally managed to calm him down after the soldiers left, and remained at his side, stroking his fine hair as he dropped back into a troubled sleep, twitching and moaning from time to time.

The optio had left them with a stark warning. The imperial palace had decreed that anyone who offered shelter or succour to the fugitive would be condemned to death alongside him. Which was getting things a little out of order, thought Macro, since normally a trial usually preceded execution. Perhaps it was a sign of the times and this was the way that Nero's regime intended to conduct itself. If so, then Rome was set to become every bit as dangerous a place as the most far-flung outpost of the Empire.

Macro tried to push such gloomy prospects aside by shifting his thoughts to Petronella. She had come as something of a surprise to him. While she might be Lucius's nurse, and the property of Cato, she had quick wits and a fiery personality when roused. She had also proved to be a tigress in bed, and Macro, never usually one for playing down the roles assigned to men and women by nature, had surprised himself by allowing her to straddle him and ride him until he was spent, at which point she folded forward and held his head between her hands and kissed him until he had recovered enough for a second helping of her delights. The mere memory of it caused a tingling sensation in his groin, but there was not time to indulge his reverie. Even though the cohort had resumed its daily routine, there was still the drudgery of administration to be taken care of. Besides, he would be in a better position to find out more about the search for Cato up at the Praetorian camp than loitering here at the house of Sempronius.

Throwing back the bed covers, he got up and dressed before joining Petronella in the kitchen, where she was feeding Lucius. The boy had not slept well thanks to the intrusion of the night before, and was moody and refusing to co-operate as he sat cross-armed and tight-lipped while his nurse offered him a spoon of gruel.

'Ah, come now, little man. What's your father going to say if he hears you've become mutinous?'

'Don't care.'

'Well, he might. And let me tell you, no one, no matter how brave, ever refuses to do as your dad says.'

Lucius's eyes widened.

'That goes for me too. He scares the willies out of me. I've seen him snap men in two for not eating their food.' Macro shuddered theatrically, and a moment later Lucius leaned forward and opened his mouth wide so that Petronella could feed him.

'That's the way!' Macro grinned, then helped himself to a bowl.

Petronella shook her head. 'That's the way to terrify the poor mite, you brute.'

'Whatever gets the job done.'

Macro ate quickly, and the others accompanied him to the entrance of the house, where he slipped his sword belt on and wrapped himself in his cloak before opening the door. It was raining outside and Petronella winced. 'You're going to get soaked.'

'A little rain never hurt a soldier.' Macro kissed her, and then smiled at Lucius and patted him on the head. 'Be a good soldier today and obey your nurse here, understand?'

'Yes, sir.' Lucius smiled.

Stepping down into the street, Macro strode off towards the Praetorian camp. Despite the rain, his thoughts turned to the plight of his friend, on the run and no doubt falsely accused. He was determined to do what he could to help Cato. But he would need help. Sempronius could be counted on, and there was Vespasian too. The former commander of the Second Legion held the two of them in high regard, and Macro felt confident that he would speak up for Cato when he returned to Rome. All the same, there was no denying the peril his friend was in.

'Spare an ass for an old soldier down on his luck.'

Macro looked at the pitiful beggar huddled in the shelter of a buttress supporting the high garden wall of one of Sempronius's neighbours. He stopped and regarded the man, touched by this living proof of the harsh life and poor rewards endured by many of those who had given their best fighting for Rome.

'Which unit were you with, brother?'

The beggar raised a hand in salute. 'The Tenth, sir. Was with 'em for fifteen years before I lost my leg.'

'How did it happen?'

'Some barbarian bastard's axe nearly took it off at the knee, the gods bless you, sir.'

'Too bad.' Macro fished inside his purse and gave the man a sestertius. 'Get yourself out of the rain and have a hot meal.'

'Thank you, sir. Most generous.'

Macro nodded a farewell and continued on his way, head down into the rain angling towards him. A sestertius *was* a generous amount to hand to a beggar, but little enough for a former comrade in arms. Especially when he had nowhere to go to in the middle of winter. Macro hoped that Cato had food and shelter at least. Wherever he might be at that precise moment.

★ ★ ★

Cato did not dare to follow the beggar too closely, in case the man turned and saw him and became suspicious. Maintaining a safe distance, he tailed him, with Macro a similar distance ahead, up the street towards the city wall. At the Viminal Gate, the sentries passed Macro through with an exchange of salutes. The beggar gave a brief account of himself before he was let through, and then hurriedly hopped forward to catch up with Macro. Cato hesitated a moment, thinking quickly, and then strode up to the gate. Fortune was with him, as he recognised none of the men on duty. The nearest of the soldiers moved to block him.

'All right, sunshine, what's the big hurry?'

'My father's funeral is this morning. I'm already supposed to be there. He's being cremated today.'

The Praetorian glanced up at the rain. 'That's wishful thinking.'

'Please, my family are expecting me.'

'Not so fast. Wait there.' The soldier turned to call over his optio. 'This one says he's going to a funeral.'

The optio came forward and looked Cato up and down. 'You might at least have dressed for the occasion.'

Cato raised his sleeve. 'It's all I can afford. I work in a fullery. You know what they pay me?'

'No. And I don't much care.' The optio jerked his thumb at the gate. 'Be on your way.'

Cato nodded his thanks and hurried on, under the arch and out along the street on the far side. For a short distance the pillars of the Marcian aqueduct provided a little shelter from the wind and rain, until the structure took a dog-leg to the right across the road and stretched away towards the hills to the south. Cato strode as fast as he could to catch up with the beggar and Macro, and then kept pace with them. The suburb was less densely built up than the city within the walls, and the strict fire regulations did not apply here, so that smoke rose from many chimneys as people did their best to keep warm through the winter months. The Praetorian camp was half a mile from the gate, and Cato could see its walls and towers rising above the roofs of the buildings in between.

Ahead there was open ground, and Macro made his way along the side of the camp until he reached the gate opening on to the road. He was challenged by the sentry, gave the password, entered and disappeared from view. The beggar found himself a spot opposite the camp, sheltering under a tiled lean-to on the back of a tavern, the Guardsman's Return, where he settled down to keep watch. Cato turned into a side street before he was spotted and then worked his way round until he came back to the road a hundred paces further on from the beggar. The only shelter available to him was a cypress tree, and he used the trunk for cover as he stood and waited.

The morning wore on and the rain continued unabated. Cato's clothing, cheap and worn, had been soaked through on the walk up the Viminal Hill and he felt each gust of cold wind keenly, so that before long he could not stop himself shivering. It was of little comfort to know that the beggar must be enduring similar hardship. In any case, it was more than likely he was one of Pallas's spies, and that put paid to any shred of pity that Cato might have felt for him. Quite rightly, the imperial secretary had calculated that his prey would be keen to contact Macro, and Cato now had misgivings about his plan to seek out his best friend. If Macro was being watched, then it would be hard to get to him. In addition, he would be putting Macro's life in danger. He knew his friend well enough to know that if their positions were reversed, Macro would look to him for help and Cato would respond without an instant's hesitation. Even so, he could not help feeling a degree of guilt over his actions as he waited for his friend to emerge. That might take hours, it might take all day. Cato's only hope was that Macro would be sure to seek the warm embrace of Petronella come the night.

The hours passed interminably and Cato felt the cold seep into his flesh and bones, so that by the afternoon there was not a part of him that retained any warmth at all. At noon the rain eased off and settled into a steady drizzle beneath a leaden sky. From time to time an individual, or a squad of Praetorians would emerge from the gate to go about their duties, and Cato scrutinised them closely in case Macro was amongst them. But there was no sign of his friend's distinctive stocky physique, and Cato resigned himself to further discomfort and boredom.

Late in the afternoon a trumpet sounded the change of watch. Shortly afterwards a crowd of off-duty soldiers emerged and crossed the street to the tavern, and soon the air was pierced by laughter, singing and shouts. A careful searching glance round the trunk of the tree revealed that the beggar was still in position and keeping watch, though he was making the best of it as he accepted coins from the soldiers, on top of whatever reward Pallas was paying him, Cato mused miserably.

He began to feel hungry, and recalled that he had eaten nothing since the previous midday; now his stomach was starting to complain, to add to the throbbing in his head. He tried to take his mind off his miserable situation by fathoming the possible reasons behind his being framed for the murder of Senator Granicus. It was hard to believe that Pallas would do anything so elaborate as a result of being affronted by Cato's reluctance to work for him. After all, the imperial freedman had seemed certain that his veiled threat to harm Lucius would be enough to compel Cato to do as he wished. So why attempt to destroy him? It did not seem to make sense . . .

Unless it had something to do with the high regard that Cato enjoyed within the ranks of the Praetorian Guard. Throughout the Empire soldiers tended to be loyal to commanders who had proven their valour. It was no different in the Guard corps, although generosity also helped to win loyalty, as Sejanus had discovered when he had engineered imperial bribes to be paid to the Praetorians. In the present situation the reverse was motivating the soldiers. The failure to reward the loyalty of the units recently returned from Hispania had proven to be a very egregious matter indeed. The men were discontented. Meanwhile, one of their commanders was riding high in public favour. Cato could see how those two factors might be perceived by Pallas as posing a threat to Nero.

In which case it would occur to Pallas that one solution might be to get rid of him in such a way as to destroy his reputation. And the slaying of an elderly senator in cold blood would be more than enough to damn him in the eyes of the mob, and more importantly in the eyes of the Praetorian units. There was another benefit in such a scheme: the elimination of an opinionated senator whose bold line was causing embarrassment to the new emperor and his regime, and encouraging others to speak out in favour of limiting Nero's power. Some might even speak in favour of returning to the Republic.

On that, at least, Cato had mixed views. The Republic had been dead for a hundred years – that was when Julius Caesar had assumed dictatorial powers for life. And civil wars had raged for decades before and after his fateful decision to seize absolute power. It was Augustus who had realised that there was no going back; that the only way to bring peace within Roman society was through ruling with a firm hand and an iron heart. Keep the mob happy and the question of how they were ruled would remain a matter of supreme indifference to them. Keep the upper echelons of society living in fear and they would be cowed into a show of indifference. Some of them, like Granicus, might speak out, and pay the price for doing so; others, like Domitia and her companions, would continue the struggle against the emperors in secret. They might claim their plotting was determined by lofty ideals, but Cato was cynical enough to think that their real ambition was to reclaim the power that the aristocracy had wielded before the age of the emperors.

Cato sighed. He was a believer in the ideal of the Republic, but in practice he could no longer see how it was in the best interests of Rome and her people. Too much had changed. Rome had come to rely on the emperors and their imperial freedmen.

At that moment he caught sight of another figure leaving the camp.

CHAPTER SEVENTEEN

It was Macro, no question about it. Cato watched his friend march out and turn towards the Viminal Gate. He strolled past the Guardsman's Return, checked himself, hesitated a moment and then about-turned and entered the tavern.

'True to form,' Cato muttered through chattering teeth. He wished, fervently, that Macro had gone straight home. At least that would have given him the chance to get his limbs moving again and some warmth back into his body. He stamped his feet and rubbed his arms vigorously as he waited. Fortunately, Petronella's charms outweighed the pleasures of a night's drinking, and Macro soon emerged, wiping his mouth on the back of his hand before continuing on his way. The beggar waited a moment before scrambling up and hobbling after the centurion. Cato followed on.

Once they were back inside the walls and the buildings crowded the street, he closed the distance on the two men ahead of him, fearful of losing them amongst the other people hurrying along with the hoods of their cloaks drawn up. He knew that there would be little chance of speaking to Macro if he returned to Sempronius's house, which was sure to be watched front and rear. He must find a way to get to him before then. A hundred paces ahead, he saw the junction where Macro would turn left on to a less-frequented thorough-fare. That presented the opportunity he sought, Cato realised swiftly.

He took the first side alley and ran down the filthy cobbles, turning parallel to Macro and the beggar and running hard to get ahead of them and lie in wait. There was the opening on to the street where they would pass by; Cato kept back in the shadows as he caught his breath and felt the familiar tension in his limbs at the prospect of action. A handful of people passed by, then he heard the crunch of military boots and pressed himself back against the wall of the building on the corner of the street. Macro marched past, a contented smile on his lips. He burped and patted his chest. Then he was out of sight. Cato edged forward, hearing the dull rap of the crutch on the flagstones. The beggar lurched into view, staring fixedly ahead as he passed by.

As Cato stepped out behind him, he glanced back and saw there was no one in sight for at least fifty paces, and even then it was an elderly couple, arm in arm, who were unlikely to intervene. He increased his pace, coming up behind the beggar. At the last moment the man turned anxiously, and Cato lunged forward, grasping his crutch and wrenching it from his hand. With a sharp cry the beggar pitched forward, hands extended, catching the folds of Cato's tunic. His fingers slipped and slid down and then locked powerfully around Cato's ankle.

'Help!' he called out. 'Help me!'

The elderly couple stopped and stared ahead, uncertain what to do.

Cato tried shaking himself free of the beggar's grip, but the man was stronger than he had seemed and held on. Taking the risk that he might lose his balance, Cato kicked the man in the side with his spare foot, to no effect. Then, in desperation, he raised the crutch and struck out at his head. The man ducked and took the blows across his shoulder, still trying to cry for help as the wind was driven from his lungs.

'That's enough, you bastard!' Macro's voice roared, and before Cato could look up, his friend had punched him in the kidneys, then grabbed his shoulders and hurled him bodily across the street. Cato struck the wall at an angle and went down with a winded groan, the crutch dropping at his side. Macro snatched it up and brandished it like a club.

'What the fuck has the world come to when toerags like you decide to rob defenceless cripples?' He paused and looked at the beggar. 'Hang on, haven't I seen you before? Ah, yes, the lad from the Tenth.'

He rounded on Cato again. 'You just compounded your mistake, my friend. No one turns over an army veteran and gets away with it. Not when Centurion Macro can help it.'

Cato threw up an arm to guard his face. 'Wait!'

'Bollocks to that!'

The crutch came sweeping down and Cato just had time to throw himself to one side so that the blow glanced off his ribs. Even so, he cried out at the sharp pain. 'Stop!'

Macro drew back, making ready to strike again.

'For fuck's sake, Macro!'

His friend froze. 'Cato? Can that be you, lad?'

Cato propped himself up with one arm and swept the cap from his head with his spare hand. 'Yes, and thanks. You could have killed me.'

'Ah, don't exaggerate . . . Maimed, maybe.' Macro's expression became serious. 'What the hell is going on? You're wanted for murder one moment, and you're mugging cripples the next. We'd better talk.'

'Surely, but first we need a few words with our friend there.' Cato pointed to the beggar, who had slowly been shuffling away from the encounter.

Macro turned towards the man. 'Him? Why?'

'Because he's been spying on you all day.' Cato climbed back to his feet, then tentatively touched his side and winced.

'Spying? Spying for who?' Macro demanded.

'Pallas. I've got that right, haven't I?'

The beggar glanced anxiously at them as he reached the wall of the nearest building and backed up against it as firmly as he could. 'Leave me alone. I'm just a veteran, boys, begging for a living, that's all. I don't work for nobody.'

'Liar!' Cato spat. 'Let's get him somewhere quiet and I can tell you what's happened, before we speak to this one.'

Macro nodded, and was reaching down to lift the beggar to his feet when there was a sudden movement, a flicker of steel, and he recoiled in surprise at the gash on his forearm. Blood surged from cut flesh and Cato looked down to see that the man had pulled a concealed knife and now held it out threateningly.

'Stay away from me, if you value your lives!'

Macro hefted the crutch and grinned savagely. 'I ain't going nowhere, my friend. And neither are you!'

He smashed the crutch down heavily against the side of the beggar's head, snapping it to one side and knocking the man out. He slid on to his side with a long, low sigh, the knife slipping from his fingers, then lay still.

'Jupiter! I hope you haven't killed him.'

'No chance,' Macro said confidently. 'Just a tap on the head.

If he's a veteran like he says, then he's used to it. No more than a nasty bruise and a thumping headache if I'm any judge of it.'

Cato looked up and down the street. The elderly couple had backed off towards the main thoroughfare and he feared they might find help for the stricken beggar. 'We'd better get moving . . .'

With dusk deepening the city's shadows, Macro and Cato found a small but neatly kept brothel, and talked the owner into letting them rent a private room for a few hours. The man looked them over and clicked his tongue at the one-legged cripple hanging limply between them. 'Whatever turns you on, friends.'

Macro scowled at him, and ordered a couple of jars of wine before handing the money over from the beggar's purse. With Macro supporting the man's shoulders and Cato his feet, they climbed the narrow stairs to the first storey and along a corridor to the door of the room they had paid for. Muffled, and not so muffled, groans and possibly genuine cries of pleasure and pain sounded from the other occupied rooms, and Macro made a mental note to give the place a try some day. Then he remembered Petronella and guiltily put aside such a prospect. He suspected she might be the kind of woman who did not like to share her man with others. Just as he balked at the idea of sharing her.

The room was small, scarcely eight feet deep and six across, and airless, the only furnishing a soiled straw mattress that stank of sweat. There was a shallow alcove above the mattress with jars of cheap scent and lubricating oil, and three wooden dildos of different shapes and sizes. A candle burned from a bracket on the far wall, giving just enough light to see by. They dumped the unconscious beggar on the mattress and leaned his crutch up against the wall before they sat on the floor. The owner appeared at the door with two jars and three battered leather cups and set them down. He hovered a moment until Macro spoke.

'If you're looking for a tip, forget it.'

'It's not that. I just, er, don't want anything dodgy going on, with your friend there. Don't want my establishment getting an unsavoury reputation.'

'Unsavoury reputation?' Macro snorted. 'Go on, gerradavit! Before I knock your block off.'

The owner beat a hurried retreat and quickly closed the door behind him. Macro picked up a jug, pulled out the stopper and sniffed. 'Hmm, not as bad as you might think for a place like this.' He poured each of them a cup and handed one to Cato. 'Here. That'll warm your cockles.'

'Thanks.' Cato took a sip. It was rough stuff, but it felt good to have inside. He eased off his drenched cloak. 'While we're waiting for him to come round, I'd better explain what's happened.'

'I imagine it'll be quite a tale, judging from the condition you're in, brother.'

Cato collected his thoughts and gave an account of everything from the arrest until the point Macro ran into him, literally. His friend listened attentively, hands clasped round his leather cup. When Cato had finished, he drained his wine and sat back against the wall, resting his hands on his knees.

'I thought Narcissus was bad enough, but that Pallas puts the old snake right in the shade. Question is, what can we do to clear your name?'

'We start with the murderer. I'm certain he's a Praetorian. And he has that tattoo I told you about.'

'A scorpion.' Macro nodded. 'I hate to break it to you, lad, but there's going to be more than a few of the men who have a scorpion tattoo.'

'Maybe, but the pose was quite specific: a striking scorpion, and here on the arm.' Cato indicated on his own limb. 'I agree, it's not much of a starting point. But it's all I have for now. Unless we get something out of hopalong here when he comes round.'

Macro ground his right fist in the palm of his left hand. 'Oh, we'll get something out of him all right. I'll make sure of it.'

'There's something else we need to do,' Cato continued. 'I want Lucius taken somewhere he's going to be safe from Pallas. I think Pallas is anticipating that I'm going to be tracked down quickly. If that doesn't happen, I fear he'll take Lucius and threaten to harm him to make me turn myself in. He may already be thinking along those lines.'

Macro grimaced. 'That's pretty low, even for scum like him.'

Cato shrugged. 'It's exactly what I'd do in his place.'

'Sometimes I'm not sure I wholly like your train of thought, lad. It's one thing to be bright, quite another to be an utter scheming bastard.'

'If you're going to best people like Pallas, you have to think like them. They live by a different standard, Macro. The trick of it is to learn the rules of the game and then play it better than anyone else. Only a fool thinks there's any virtue in being a good loser.' Cato sighed. 'I want Lucius kept out of the way until this matter is resolved, by one means or another.'

Macro considered this for a moment and nodded. 'I think I

know someone who can help us on that front. Petronella has family who own a small farm not far from the city. Lucius would be safe there.'

'Petronella? I had no idea her family owned anything. Come to that, I didn't even know she had a family.'

'Why would you? She's just your slave.' Even as he uttered the remark, Macro felt a surge of empathy for his woman, and at the same time a faint disappointment in his friend for expressing ignorance of Petronella's life beyond her servile legal status.

Cato had not missed the shift in Macro's tone. He looked at his friend closely, seeing the hurt there. 'I did not mean to sound dismissive. I barely know her and just hadn't given it any thought. I know she means something to you. I'm sorry.'

The apology was well meant, Macro realised. 'I know. It's just it makes the situation a bit difficult . . .'

Cato thought a moment before he continued. 'This isn't merely a passing fancy of yours, right?'

Macro shook his head. 'I don't think so. She's a good woman. There's something about her I can't help wanting more of.'

Cato gave a wry smile. 'Centurion Macro, I do believe there's a romantic soul hidden beneath that crusty exterior.'

Macro frowned. 'You can fuck right off if you take the piss out of me.'

'I'm not, believe me. It's just a side of you I don't think I've ever seen. Look here. If Petronella can take care of Lucius and keep him safe, then she's yours. I'll give her to you.'

'Really?' Macro's heart warmed to the suggestion at once. Then came the guilt. It would demean both him and Petronella to have her passed from one master to another so that he could take advantage of her being a slave. That was not what he wanted. If there was a future in their relationship then it had to be on the basis that she chose to be with him. 'Listen, Cato. If she does what you want, then you set her free. I'll take my chances with her after that.'

'That could be your choice, if I gave her to you.'

'No. If she agrees to help us, then you free her.'

Cato nodded.

A groan from the mattress drew their attention to the beggar, who was stirring. He rolled his head slowly from side to side and blinked his eyes open. 'What happened to . . .' He stopped speaking as soon as he became aware of the two men close by, and shuffled back on the mattress. 'You . . .'

Macro smiled cruelly. 'Yes, us. Now then, my friend, I think it's time we had a little chat. But where are my manners? First, let's share a drink.'

He poured wine into the third cup, filling it almost to the brim before he passed it to the beggar. 'There. Get that inside you.'

The man hesitated, and Macro pressed the cup into his hand, spilling some wine on the sleeve of the beggar's tunic.

'I paid good money for that. It's bad manners to refuse a drink from an old army comrade. Drink up.'

The beggar shook his head. 'I don't want it.'

'It's not an offer, mate. It's an order.' Macro drew his dagger with his spare hand and tapped it against the beggar's stump. 'Do it.'

The man raised the cup to his mouth and took a gulp.

'There you go,' Macro said encouragingly. 'Not so bad, eh? Keep at it.'

Watching Macro anxiously, the beggar quickly drained the

cup, spilling dribbles either side of his chin. As soon as he was done, Macro took the cup back and Cato refilled it.

'Again.'

They repeated the process until both jars were empty, and before long a dazed look filled the beggar's eyes and he slumped back against the wall.

'Nothing like a good drink, eh?' Macro patted him on the hand. 'So, it's time we talked. Let's begin with your name. Your real name.'

'Gaius Fennus.'

'We're pleased to make your acquaintance, Fennus. I seem to recall you saying you're a veteran of the Tenth Legion. That true?'

The man shut his eyes and shook his head.

'Thought not. I'm not sure I like men who claim to be former army comrades. Let's be clear then. You work for Pallas?'

Fennus smacked his lips lightly, and his reply when it came was slurred. 'Yes.'

Cato leaned forward. 'You spy for him. Which means you almost certainly know other spies who work for him. Tell me, have you seen one about my height, with dark hair? He's a Praetorian, and he has a tattoo on his arm. A scorpion. Do you know him?'

'N-no. Never seen him.' Fennus shut his eyes and his chin slumped on to his chest.

Cato reached for the collar of his tunic and gave him a firm shake so that his head cracked back against the wall.

'Ouch! What you do that f-for?' The man's eyes were open and he regarded Cato with an offended look. 'N-no need for that, friend.'

'Then tell me the truth. Do you know the man?'

'No. It's the truth. Swear it is.'

Cato glanced at Macro and the latter raised his eyebrows. Cato shook the beggar again. 'Bullshit. You tell me the truth or I'll smash your brains all over the wall.'

'Wh-what?' Fennus raised a hand and waved it feebly in drunken protest. 'No n-need for that. Told you, it's the truth.'

Cato was quiet for a moment. 'All right. Then what about Sempronius's house? Are there any other of Pallas's men watching it?'

Fennus nodded. 'Another one at the b-back.'

'Any others?'

'No.'

'Be sure. If you lie to me, you'll pay for it.'

'Not lying. Just one.'

Cato released his grip and eased Fennus back before he turned to Macro. 'Not much help to us.'

'No. So what now?'

Cato thought a moment. 'You go about your duties and see if anyone knows about a guardsman with that tattoo. Also, speak to Petronella. If she can get Lucius hidden away, then you can tell her from me that I'll set her free.'

'Thank you. What about you?'

'I'll lie low. Find myself a place to hide. We'll meet back here as soon as you've made sure Lucius is safely out of the way.'

Macro nodded towards Fennus. 'And him? What do we do with him? Not such a good idea to let him report back to Pallas and tell him about our little drinking session. Might be better if he disappeared.'

'Yes. Time we all went for a short walk.'

* * *

Cato gave a denarius to the brothel keeper to buy his silence. Then, Fennus supported between them, they left the tavern and ventured out into the dark streets. Heading down towards the Forum, they came to a small square with a public fountain. There was no one else in sight. A short distance from the fountain they found what Cato was looking for: a sturdy wooden hatch covering an opening to one of the sewer tunnels that ran beneath the city and emptied into the Tiber.

'Hold him up,' he ordered, and transferred the man's weight to Macro. Reaching down, he slipped his fingers into the recessed handle and heaved the hatch open, laying it on the ground. A nauseating stench rose from the black opening and Fennus stirred.

'What is th–that stink?'

Cato braced himself, then drew back his fist and swung it in a vicious uppercut that snapped Fennus's slack jaw closed and cracked his head back. The beggar let out a soft groan and slumped unconscious in Macro's arms. Cato shook his fist and winced at the pain from the jarring impact. Then he took a last look round the empty square before turning to Macro and nodding. The centurion eased his burden towards the dark maw of the sewer, dangled the beggar's foot and stump over the edge and released his grip. Fennus dropped, striking his head on the rim of the opening before he was snatched from sight. A deep echoing splash sounded from below, the swirl of water, then silence. Cato eased the hatch back into place and faced Macro.

'We can't afford to take the risk of meeting unless it's absolutely necessary.'

'I agree. We'll need a signal of some kind. We can use the

bath-house in the next street along from Sempronius's place. There's a lean-to in the yard at the back. If you need to talk, chalk a C on the wall, right up beneath the tiles. If it's me that needs to speak, I'll mark an M.'

Cato nodded. 'Good. Then if either of us makes our mark, we'll meet in the steam room at noon the next day. Agreed?'

Macro thought briefly. 'That's sound enough. Just need to make sure I'm not followed.'

'Quite.'

'Meanwhile, you take care, Cato. Don't get caught.' They clasped forearms.

Cato smiled thinly. 'Don't worry about me. Save your concern for the bastards who set me up. When I find them, they'll go the same way as Fennus. By Jupiter, Best and Greatest, I swear it.'

CHAPTER EIGHTEEN

'Leave Rome?' Petronella's eyebrows rose in surprise. 'But why?'

Macro glanced round the garden, but the only person in sight was a slave raking up dead leaves beneath the apple trees in the far corner. It was a cold morning; the sky was overcast and the air felt clammy. He turned back to Petronella and gently took her hand. 'We have to get the boy out of the city. He's not safe here. And we need to go today.'

'Why so soon?'

Macro had been rehearsing this conversation since first light and had decided to tell the nurse only what she needed to know, for her sake as much as anyone else. 'Look, my dear, Cato has been framed for a murder he did not commit. He's on the run and they're looking high and low for him. They're confident that they'll catch him soon. But I'm not so sure. The lad's got more brains than all the librarians in Alexandria. And he's wilier than a fox. If anyone can keep out of their clutches, it's Cato. Which means that his enemies will have to try other tactics to lure him out. They'll use Lucius as bait, or they'll simply threaten to harm him unless his father surrenders himself. That's why we have to get him out of here and keep him somewhere he can't be found.' Macro paused to let this sink in before he continued. 'And it's not just the boy. I'm worried about you.'

'Me?'

He nodded. 'Whatever's going on, you can be sure that there'll be trouble brewing. You've seen what it's like out on the streets. Nero and Britannicus have rival gangs of supporters, who are clashing whenever they get the chance to have a punch up. The Senate is divided and there are rumours that some army units are ready to rise up against the emperor. If that kicks off, then Rome is going to be a dangerous place to be. Better that you aren't around if it happens.'

Petronella looked at him anxiously. 'But what about you? You won't be safe here either.'

'I'm a soldier. I'm used to it, and I can handle myself well enough to get by.'

She did not look convinced, and Macro felt his heart warmed by her obvious concern. He took her other hand as well and leaned forward to kiss her on the forehead. 'I'll be fine, I promise. I've faced hordes of barbarians in the past and given them a kicking, so that oily little scrote Pallas ain't going to be the one who takes me down.'

'It's one thing to face your enemy, but to have your back turned to people like him . . .'

Macro chuckled. 'Point taken. I'll keep an eye out all round.'

'So where shall we go? Lucius and me?'

Macro pressed his lips together briefly before he replied. 'That younger sister you told me about. The one who married a farmer. Can you trust her, and her man?'

'I'd trust her with my life. I don't know her husband. All I know is that Lucilla told me that he was a good man.'

'Which is just what we need right now. And I'll make it worth his while to keep you both safe.'

'What if he is not prepared to hide us?'

Macro smiled. 'Trust me. Silver can be very persuasive, and so can I, if it comes to that. Now then, how far is this farm from Rome?'

Petronella thought a moment. 'It's about ten miles south of the city, just off the Appian Way. I visited it once, shortly before I was sold by my father.'

'Not far then.' Macro squeezed her hands. 'There's no time to waste. I want you to pack some clothes for you and the boy, and anything else you need. Keep it light as you can. Make sure that no one sees what you are up to, and don't speak to anyone if you can avoid it.'

'What about the master?'

'Senator Sempronius is still asleep. I looked in on him before we talked. I had a few jars of wine with him after dinner last night; he'll be sleeping that off long after we've gone. It's best he knows nothing about this. It would serve no purpose to tell him. Understood? Just get your things ready and wait for me by the rear gate to the house. I'll knock five times. Don't open it for anyone else.'

She nodded, then noticed the distracted look in his eyes. 'What are you going to do?'

'Just need to make sure we aren't followed.'

It had started to rain again as Macro left the house. He glanced both ways along the street, but aside from a few figures hurrying along, there was no sign of anyone watching the front door. They were there, though, he knew. Fennus would have been missed by now, and that meant that whoever replaced him would be taking every care to ensure they were not detected.

He pulled the hood of his cloak up and stepped into the street, striding away in the direction of the Praetorian camp. He glanced from side to side at open shops and taverns, trying to spot anyone watching him closely. But despite his alertness, nothing seemed untoward amongst those he passed along the street. Two hundred paces from the door, he took a turning into a side street that led in the direction of the camp by a more sheltered route. The rain was light enough for him to hear the sound of footsteps behind him a moment later, but he continued steadily, without looking round. Ahead, two men were wheeling a heavily laden handcart towards him. He moved aside to let it pass, and then stepped back into the road.

At once he turned about to follow the cart, crouching slightly as he did so. As it passed the opening to a tiny dark alley, he stopped and ducked down to look between the wheels. His tail was moving to the side of the street to avoid the cart, and Macro realised that for a moment the vehicle would block the man's view. He ducked into the alley and pressed himself against the wall, drawing his dagger. The sound of the wheels rumbling over the cobbles filled the street, and then he heard the hurried crunch of boots breaking into a trot as his tail realised he had lost sight of his quarry and raced to catch up. A dark cloak flurried past the alley, and Macro sprang out behind the man and thrust him hard in the back so that he lost his balance and crashed face down on to the ground. Before he could react, the centurion had clenched his left fist in the man's hair and brought his dagger round, resting the blade against his throat.

'Get up. Quick as you can, if you want to live.'

His pursuer was winded by the fall, and struggled to his feet, breathing hard. Close up, Macro could see that he was a short, scrawny man in his thirties, clean-shaven and wearing the blue tunic of a member of the imperial household beneath his plain brown cloak. Dragging him into the alley, Macro pressed his head hard against the wall and moved the point of the dagger round to the small of his back, pushing the tip in just far enough that he could feel the point.

'Listen carefully,' he hissed in the man's ear. 'I know Pallas sent you to watch me. I also know there's another man watching the rear of the house. Right?'

'I don't know what you're talking about. If you want to rob me, then just take my purse and leave me.'

'Nice try, friend.' Macro pressed the dagger home a little further, and the man flinched. 'Let's have another go. You and your pal are watching the house of Sempronius. I want to know where your friend is, what he looks like, and his name. And I want you to tell me now, before I have to hurt you.' He ground the man's cheek against the brick wall to emphasise his demand.

'I told you, I have no idea what you are talking about! Please, take my money and let me go.'

Macro sighed, then yanked the man's head back and slammed it into the brickwork. 'You're not listening, and I'm not some fool fresh off the boat from Macedonia. Last chance. Tell me what I want, or the real pain begins.' He pressed his dagger in a bit further and felt a slight resistance before the material of the cloak and tunic gave and the point pierced flesh. The man let out a muffled cry.

'All right! I'll talk!'

Macro eased his hand back. 'That's better. Get on with it.'

'The other man is Tallinus, wearing a green cloak.'

'Where is he positioned?'

'Selling trinkets outside a bakery, almost opposite the gate.'

Macro leaned closer to his ear. 'You wouldn't be lying to me, right? I'm not the type who takes kindly to liars.'

'I swear it's the truth, on the life of my mother!'

'Somehow I think she'd be more than a little disappointed about how you've turned out, working for that cold-blooded rat Pallas and all.' Macro wrenched the man's head back and slammed it into the wall. He did it again, and this time the bricks crushed the man's nose with a soft crunch and blood gushed from his nostrils. He released his grip and the body collapsed. 'Night, night.'

Sheathing his dagger, Macro leaned out into the street and saw that his actions hadn't attracted any attention from the handful of people clustered around the shops a short distance away. He was about to step out of the alley when he paused, reached down, fished for the man's purse and helped himself to the coins there. 'Don't mind if I do, thanks.'

An array of cheap-looking rings, necklaces and wristbands lay on a red cloth spread over a small barrel in the shelter of the bakery's awning. Pallas's spy was leaning against the wall, arms folded as he kept watch on the gate further down the street. Two women with coarse urban accents were haggling with the baker as Macro casually strolled up on the spy's blind side. He waited a moment to ensure the women and the hapless proprietor were fully preoccupied before he approached the spy.

'That looks nice.' He pointed down at the display. 'That necklace there. With the red stone. Can I have a look?'

The man stooped to pick the item up, and Macro's dagger was at his side in an instant. 'Keep hold of the necklace,' the centurion said quietly. 'Both hands, as if you're holding it up to show me. Do it, Tallinus.'

The spy held the necklace up.

'Now turn and walk slowly over to Sempronius's gate. No sudden moves, mind, or I'll gut you where you stand.'

The man looked over the necklace at Macro. He was young, with dark, intelligent eyes and a sparse beard. 'Anything you say, Centurion.'

They made their way down the street, Macro keeping his blade in the man's side as he walked half a pace behind. When they reached the gate, he rapped five times with his knuckles, keeping a close eye on Tallinus as he did so. A moment later the bolts slid back and the gate opened a fraction. The look of relief on Petronella's face as she saw Macro faded the instant she glanced towards the spy.

'Who's this?'

'One of Pallas's dogs. Let's get off the street before anyone pays us too much attention.'

Petronella opened the gate wide enough to admit the two men, then closed it and slid the bolt into place. Lucius, his back towards the gate, was squatting on his haunches a short distance away, playing with his wooden soldiers. There was a stable to one side of the gate and a long, low shed opposite. The door to the shed was open and Macro gestured towards it.

'In there. Keep your hands up where I can see them.'

Tallinus did as he was told and ducked under the low lintel just as Lucius looked round and smiled and ran towards Macro.

Macro glanced aside. 'Stay back, boy!'

There was a blur of movement as Tallinus hurled the necklace at his face and Macro instinctively raised his hands to protect himself. At once the spy grasped the wrist of Macro's knife hand and dragged him into the shed, swinging him round in a neat pivot. Despite his slight stature, Tallinus was strong and deft, and his sudden attack had caught Macro by surprise. Now the surprise was over, and Macro gritted his teeth and bunched his spare fist to strike back. Before he could move, however, Tallinus swung a foot behind his left leg and pushed hard, forcing the centurion back so that he overbalanced and fell.

'Macro!' Petronella shouted in alarm from outside. Tallinus just had time to kick the door back in her face before he fell on top of Macro, still fighting for control of his knife hand. The impact was numbing and the back of Macro's head cracked hard against the floor, and then the full weight of the spy landed on him, driving out what little breath remained in his lungs in a pained gasp. At once Tallinus wriggled up and knelt astride the centurion, straining to turn the dagger so that it pointed at Macro's throat. Macro's spare hand came up, clamping round the other man's forearm in an effort to push the blade away. At the same time he was desperately struggling to breathe in ragged gasps. The gleaming point closed on the pulsing skin of his throat and a brief thought flashed through Macro's mind. How ignominious it would be to die in a garden shed in Rome, rather than sword in hand facing an enemy army.

'Not . . . now . . . friend,' he grunted, summoning his last reserves of strength as he locked his wrist and fought back. Above him the spy's teeth were bared, and spittle sprayed on to Macro's face. Tallinus leaned forward, pressing with his full weight. The point of the blade edged down remorselessly, and Macro felt his powerful muscles burning with the effort of holding the dagger back. Despite the cold, he felt sweat break out on his brow. He could not stop the man, and if he tried to take his left hand away and lash out, it would only hasten his end.

The blade trembled slightly as it came down, and Macro succeeded in angling it away from his throat. The point touched the folds of his cloak and pressed on. He could feel the slight pressure on his shoulder, growing quickly, and he tried to yield before it. Then came the first sharp, burning sensation as the point tore through the cloth and pierced the skin. The strained expression on Tallinus's face twisted into a manic look of triumph as he sensed Macro's strength fading.

'And they warned me you were dangerous,' he snarled through gritted teeth.

Both men's attention was so fixed on the struggle that neither noticed the door swing open behind them. Petronella saw at once that her man was losing the fight, and with a shriek she rushed up behind Tallinus and wrapped her left hand around his throat, while her right clawed at his eyes. Her teeth closed tight on his ear and tore at the cartilage as a keening howl swelled in his throat.

He released his left hand and tried to punch her in the side of the head, but the angle was difficult and the blows were only glancing. Petronella held on. Beneath them, Macro was fighting back, thrusting the dagger up and slowly turning it away so that it was at right angles between them. The nurse had succeeded in getting two fingers into the socket of Tallinus's right eye, and he clenched it tightly shut as her nails probed, gouging into the flesh of his eyelid, pressing on the ball and causing him terrible agony. He stopped trying to punch her and grabbed her hair instead, trying to rip her free.

'Fucking bitch!' he snarled through his constricted throat. 'I'll kill you!'

As he heard the spy's threat, Macro felt rage surge through every muscle in his body. He twisted the dagger so that it faced Tallinus again, and in one continuous movement pressed the tip of the blade into his stomach and on through the soft flesh and organs, right up to the hilt. The spy's body tensed and he choked on a low howl. Macro began to tear the blade down diagonally with a slight sawing motion across Tallinus's stomach. The acrid smell of blood and stomach acid caught in his nostrils, and he felt a warm, sticky flow drench his hands and drip down on to his tunic.

The spy released his grip on the centurion's wrist and began to slump forward. Macro tried to shift him away, but Petronella was still choking him and gouging his eye.

'Let him go,' Macro gasped. 'And help get him off me.'

There was a pause as the red mist cleared from her mind, then Petronella released her grip and stood up. At once Macro heaved his pelvis and thrust the mortally wounded spy away. Tallinus fell on to his back and lay writhing, as blood and fluids oozed from his ruined eye. The nurse helped Macro to his feet and clasped his face between her hands.

'Are you all right? Are you wounded?'

Macro shook his head and gasped. 'Just winded.'

'Thank the gods.' She drew his head down and kissed him hard. 'I thought he'd kill you, my love.'

'My love?' Macro raised his eyebrows and smiled.

Then the groans from the stricken spy drew his attention and he turned towards the man. Tallinus's tunic was torn across his midriff, and blood-streaked viscera bulged beneath the hand he had clamped across the wound. His other hand rose and covered his eye socket as he let out a series of gasps.

'He's done for. Won't die for a bit, though.' Macro tightened his grip on the dagger. 'Not unless I help him.'

He knelt down beside Tallinus and shook his head. 'Sorry, friend. But you chose to work for Pallas. This is your reward.'

Tallinus's good eye opened and rolled up. 'Just . . . do . . . it.'

Macro nodded, and placed the point of the dagger in the soft tissue under the man's chin, then glanced up at Petronella. 'You might want to look away.'

She retreated to the door, wiping the blood and eye fluid from her fingers, just as Lucius appeared, toy soldier in hand. Before he could see anything, she shuffled him away from the shed.

'What's Uncle Mac Mac doing to the man?' Lucius piped up.

'Helping him go to sleep. That's all.'

'Sleep? But it's morning.'

'Uncle Macro's friend is not feeling well . . . Come on, let's play.'

Macro turned back to the spy. Tallinus had arched his neck to expose his throat, and Macro could see the pulse flickering beneath the skin. 'On three . . . One!'

He punched the blade up through skin and bone, into the brain, and worked it around as blood spurted from the spy's nostrils. He ripped the blade out and Tallinus's body spasmed wildly, then collapsed inert, a last long sigh of breath escaping his lips. Pausing to wipe the blood from his blade, Macro sheathed the weapon and did what he could to get the gore off his hands and arms. A large patch of blood had stained his tunic, but there was nothing he could do about that for now.

Looking round, he saw a large pile of old rags and bundles of kindling wood next to some brooms in the far corner of the shed. He dragged the body across, positioning it as close to the wall as possible, then piled the rags over it and covered them with the kindling until it was completely hidden. Then, taking the broom, he did his best to erase the streaks of blood on the dirty flagstones. He paused to adjust his cloak so that its folds covered his tunic, and hurriedly brushed his hands over his hair to smooth it down before he left the shed.

Lucius was crouched down holding a soldier and making it fight with another held by the nurse squatting opposite. He looked up at Macro.

'The man. Where is he?'

'Ah, yes. Well now, he's er, fast asleep, little 'un. So we'd better get going, eh?'

Looking down, Macro was aware that there was still blood on his hands. He crossed to the long, low trough running in front of the shed and quickly washed the last traces away.

'There! All done. Now let's go.'

Petronella rose and picked up a bag of her spare clothing. Macro took the boy's pack and Lucius hurriedly put his soldiers in his sidebag and then held the nurse's hand. Opening the gate, Macro let them pass through before he closed it, and then the three of them set off in the direction of the Appian Way, the old road that led south to the rich farmland and vineyards of Campania. Lucius walked between the two adults, eagerly taking in the details of everything they passed, as children do.

Macro puffed his cheeks. 'One other thing. Thanks. You saved my life back there.'

Petronella smiled back. 'Any man who tries to get his hands on you has me to answer to. Same goes for any woman, by the way.'

'I'll bear that in mind,' Macro laughed. Then his expression became serious. 'But first, we have to get out of Rome . . .'

CHAPTER NINETEEN

A section from one of the urban cohorts was on duty at the Appian Gate when Macro, Petronella and Lucius reached it later that morning. They had managed to cross the centre of Rome without attracting any unwanted attention. Every so often Macro would glance round to see if anyone was following them, but there were no familiar faces behind them. Once, as they turned a corner, he hung back to make sure, and a handful of people turned after them, none of whom even glanced at him. He studied each one before he caught up with Petronella and Lucius again, and then kept a lookout to see if any of them reappeared. By the time they reached the gate, he was confident that they had managed to escape the attention of Pallas's spies.

One of the sentries raised a hand to halt them as they made for the left-hand arch of the gatehouse. 'Good morning, citizen. What is your purpose in leaving the city?'

Macro gestured to Petronella and Lucius. 'Taking my cousin and her boy to see relatives in Lanuvium.'

'I see.' The sentry gave them a cursory glance, then turned his attention back to Macro. 'Are you a soldier?'

'That's right. I serve with the Praetorian Guard.'

'Just a moment then, sir.' The sentry turned and called his

optio over. A rotund, heavily jowled man approached, thumbs tucked into his belt.

'What's up, Nerva?'

'This one's a soldier, sir. From the Guard.'

'Oh?' The optio stepped in front of Macro and looked him up and down. 'Which unit?'

Macro had already decided there was little point in lying. Far better to pull rank and bluff his way through the checkpoint. He raised himself to his full height. 'I'm a centurion in the Second Cohort. And you'll stand to attention when you address a superior officer.'

The optio whipped his thumbs out and clasped his hands to his sides. 'Sorry, sir. Second Cohort, you say?'

'What of it?'

'We have orders to be on the lookout for a man from that unit. An officer.'

'And you think it's me? What description do you have?'

The optio thought briefly. 'Tall, thin, in his twenties. Name of Quintus Licinius Cato, sir.'

'Well, my name's Macro, and do I look anything like your description?'

'No, sir. I suppose not.'

'Suppose not?' Macro snorted. 'Do they promote any old fool in the urban cohorts these days? Eh?'

The optio flushed, and at his shoulder the sentry struggled to stifle a grin.

'It's obvious I'm not your man. Neither is my cousin or her boy.' Macro patted Lucius on the head.

The boy looked up at the optio and smiled bashfully. 'My daddy's a soldier. Uncle Mac Mac says he's the bravest soldier in the army.'

'Is that right, sonny? That's nice for you.'

'Er, quite so,' Macro responded with forced calm. 'But there's no time to stop and chat about that. So let's not be bothering these busy men.'

Lucius stared at the optio earnestly before he announced, 'This one is a fat soldier, Uncle Mac Mac. Very fat.'

The optio's brow furrowed, and Macro could see he'd have given the boy a thick ear but for the presence of a superior officer.

'Yes, he is fat. A spot of drilling in the legions would sort him out, but that's work for another day. Come. Let's go.'

But Lucius was having none of it. 'My daddy's thin. And brave. Everyone says so.'

Macro could see the optio's frown deepening as he began to think. He stepped in front of Lucius and bent down. 'You know, lad, there are times when a good soldier knows when to stop talking and start walking.'

Lucius stared up at him. 'This time?'

'Yes, this is an excellent time for it. So button your lip and stand to attention, like I showed you.'

Lucius shuffled his little boots together and stood like a beanpole.

'That's better.' Macro straightened up and shook his head at the optio. 'Kids, eh?'

'Yes, sir. I have five nippers of my own,' the optio replied proudly.

'Then you have my profoundest sympathy, brother.' Taking Lucius by one hand, while Petronella took the other, he barked, 'Guards detachment! Quick march!' And with Lucius giggling with glee, they strode through the arch and out of the city, watched by the bemused men of the urban cohort.

When they were a safe distance along the road, and the

soldiers had turned their attention to other traffic, Macro let out a deep sigh of relief. He gave Lucius's small hand a gentle shake.

'You nearly landed us right in it there, little man.'

'In it? In what?'

Petronella shot him a warning look and Macro changed what he was about to say. 'In deep trouble. That's what. Look here, Lucius, do you know what a secret is?'

The boy shook his head.

'It means that there are some things you must not talk about.'

'What things?' he chirped.

'Things like your daddy. Until you see him again, it would be best if you did not talk about him to anyone. Is that clear?'

Lucius looked disappointed and pouted slightly. 'Not to you?'

'Not unless I say so.'

He looked up at his nurse and tugged her hand. 'Not to Petty?'

'No one,' Macro said firmly, wagging a finger.

Lucius bit his lip and drew his brow down, refusing to meet Macro's eyes. A moment later his bottom lip was quivering as he began to quietly cry.

'Oh well done, you brute,' said Petronella.

They continued in silence, apart from the mewling of the little boy. On either side of the Appian Way spread the tombs: imposing structures built in a bid to immortalise the greatest families, and the more modest ones of those less affluent, or less concerned with posterity. Scattered amongst them were the simple tombstones of ordinary people, often abandoned and then forgotten by the generations that came after them.

After a while, Petronella paused to speak comfortingly to

Lucius, while Macro climbed a small knoll and looked back towards the city. There were several other people on the road behind him but none seemed to be in any hurry to follow him. He rejoined the others, hoisted Lucius on to his shoulders, and they continued along the road. From time to time the boy sniffled and cried. At length he muttered, 'I'll bet he can't keep this up for long.'

'How much are you willing to wager?' Petronella tapped her nose. 'I'll take any bet you're prepared to make. I could use the money for my buying-myself-out-of-slavery savings.'

Macro looked at the boy and nodded. 'A sestertius says he dries up by noon.'

'A whole sestertius!' Petronella scoffed. 'How brave of you. Make it ten.'

'Four.'

'Seven.'

'Five.'

'Done!' The nurse spat on her hand and Macro slapped it, faintly suspecting that he might just have made a mistake.

'. . . three . . . four . . . five.' Macro handed the coins over as they stopped by the fifth milestone they had passed since leaving Rome. Then he eased the boy from his shoulders and set him down gently. The sky had cleared a little and the sun shone through breaks in the cloud; it was as near to midday as either of them could guess.

Lucius was still crying, until Petronella took one of the coins and pressed it into his hand. 'Here. That's your cut.' The little boy's tears stopped at once. His eyes gleamed as he took the silver coin and held it up to examine it, before tucking it in the tiny purse in his sidebag.

'Nicely worked,' Macro growled. 'I'm not sure who scares me more. You and the kid, or Pallas and his gang.'

Lucius sat down and let out a theatrical sigh. 'I'm tired.'

'We all are, poppet.' Petronella took a canteen out of her bag and handed it to him. 'Drink something. It'll make you feel better. Then we'll have a little rest and carry on.'

'Don't want to carry on . . .'

'Your daddy wouldn't say that, would he? Try to be like him.'

'Why?'

Petronella shook her head. 'We're not playing that game.'

Rome was no longer in sight, and the countryside on either side of the road was now largely rolling farmland and orchards, whose produce fed the teeming masses of the capital, though the occasional tomb was still to be found, where a relative had decided there was a particularly fine view, or it was simply a peaceful spot.

'How far to the place your sister lives?'

Petronella took a swig of water, then stoppered the canteen and placed it back in her bag. 'We take a track to the left just beyond that hill up ahead. Then it's a mile or so from there.'

Macro thought for a moment before he spoke. 'I hope she and her man are the welcoming kind. If they do decide to turn us down, and my charming nature fails to impress, we'll have to find somewhere else for you and the boy. I can pay for accommodation, but I'd rather not leave you in lodgings where you're amongst strangers.'

He allowed them time only for a brief rest, conscious that he needed to return to Rome the same day. He would be missed if he was not in barracks for the night, and that might cause questions to be asked. With Lucius protesting loudly that his feet already hurt, he swung the boy up and back on to his shoulders, and they set off again, passing through more farmland, interspersed with copses and small woods. The sky began to cloud over, and Macro feared that it would rain before they reached the farm. Then, just over a mile along the track, they came to two small brick pillars either side of a rutted lane that ran through an orchard of apple trees. Just visible above the tops of the trees was a tiled roofline.

'This is the place,' Petronella confirmed. She led the way and Macro followed on, as Lucius pretended to shoot arrows at imaginary barbarians hiding amongst the trees, with a lisping *phut* as each 'arrow' was loosed.

Soon they reached open ground in front of the farm. A shoulder-high wall surrounded the buildings, and there was an arched gateway leading into the compound. Inside they found a small courtyard with a lemon tree growing in the middle, a bench beneath it. The house was the familiar design, with an open centre around which the rooms ran. The front door was open so that they could see into the interior as they approached. A thin trail of smoke curled up from a chimney towards the rear of the building, and the sound of an axe splitting wood came from the inner courtyard.

Macro paused a short distance from the house. From experience he knew that it was best to announce an approach to a friendly camp when it wasn't expected. He gestured to Petronella to stop, and then drew a deep breath and called out: 'Hello, the house!'

There was a pause before a figure in a long tunic appeared in the entrance. When she stepped out into the daylight, Macro saw a rake-thin woman with a pinched face, her dark hair braided and tied back. She stopped dead when she saw

Petronella and raised a hand to her mouth in surprise.

'Well, aren't you going to greet your sister?' asked Petronella, holding out her hands. She moved forward and Lucilla rushed up and hugged her tightly.

'Who's that?' a voice demanded.

Macro saw a man striding through the short hall, axe in hand. He must have been more than ten years older than his wife. His hair was dark and curly and his eyes were keen and set in a plain, broad face. A farming life seemed to agree with him; he was well built and moved easily, Macro noted. In another life, he would have made a fine soldier. He hesitated as he came out of the farmhouse and looked his visitors over.

'Lucilla, who are these people?'

His wife released Petronella and turned round with a warm smile. 'This is my sister.'

Petronella raised a hand in greeting. 'We have never met, but you must be Marius. This is Centurion Macro, of the Praetorian Guard. His commander is my master. And the boy is my master's son.'

Marius nodded. 'And what brings you here, to our home?'

'That is best explained indoors,' said Macro. 'Beside a warm fire, over a bowl of soup or stew, and once I have relieved myself of this little bundle of mischief.'

The farmer pursed his lips for a moment. 'Make yourself at home then, Centurion. This way. Lucilla, some food and drink for our guests.'

'Yes, my love.'

Freshly laid logs hissed and crackled in the hearth as Macro pushed his bowl away and wiped his lips. 'Ah, that was good stew. Quite a cook you have there, Marius.'

On the opposite side of the table the farmer nodded as he mopped his bowl with a chunk of bread. Petronella, at Macro's side, was happily chatting with her sister, while at the end of the table Lucius had fallen asleep, head resting on his arms as he breathed easily. Macro was conscious of the forced march he must make to return to Rome by nightfall, and cleared his throat.

'Down to business. As you might have guessed, this ain't a social call. The boy's father is in trouble, and he can't afford to have Lucius taken as a hostage. So he needs to be kept somewhere safe, where he won't be found. Same goes for Petronella, as she is responsible for him. It was her idea to bring him here.' Macro looked directly at his host. 'Can you help us?'

Marius considered the request and clicked his tongue. 'As you can see, we've only got a small farm, and I barely grow enough to pay my creditors and sustain us. Two extra mouths to feed is going to make life difficult.'

'I can work for you,' Petronella interrupted. 'And the boy can help in his way. We won't be a burden.'

'Besides,' Macro added, 'I'll pay for their keep.'

He took out and opened his purse and counted out fifty silver coins. 'That's more than enough to cover them for at least a couple of months. When the trouble's over, I'll pay the same again. It's easy money, friend. All you have to do is look after them and keep 'em out of sight.'

The farmer's eyes gleamed as he looked at the dull sheen of the coins. As his cupped hand moved to draw them towards him, Macro took him by the arm. 'Just so we are clear, do we have a deal? It's just that I'm the type who likes to be sure that we are agreed. I tend not to look kindly on anyone who breaks faith with me. If you're happy with the terms, then take the money. If not, we'll find somewhere else.' He smiled. 'No offence intended, it's just that there's not a great deal of trust around at the moment.'

Marius nodded solemnly. 'We have a deal, Centurion. Besides, Petronella is family, and I'm the type who likes to look after his own.'

It was a plain enough rebuff, which pleased Macro. He would have been less comfortable if Marius had simply taken the money without comment. The man clearly had strength of character. Macro removed his hand, and after a beat, Marius drew the coins across the table towards him and heaped them into a small pile.

'I'd better be going,' the centurion announced, rising from his stool.

'It'll be dark before you reach the city,' said Petronella. 'Couldn't you stay the night and head off first thing in the morning?'

Macro shook his head. 'I've got to get back to Rome. I'm expected at the camp. Besides, Cato needs me on hand.'

'But the road might be dangerous at night.'

'Not for me it won't. Any bandit who fancies his chances is in for a rude shock.' Macro glanced at Lucius. 'Take care of him.'

'Of course. I'll guard him with my life.'

Macro touched her cheek. 'I know you will.'

He made brief farewells to Lucilla and her husband, then Petronella walked him to the wall of the farm and clung to him briefly before drawing herself away. 'Take good care of yourself, Macro. Try and stay out of trouble.'

He laughed. 'I only wish I had the choice. But I'll come back for you, I swear it, and the gods help anyone who tries to stand in the way of that.'

He adjusted his cloak, gave Petronella a wink and then turned and marched away, through the trees and out of sight. The nurse caught the distant sound of his cheerful whistling, and smiled faintly. Then a faint rumble of thunder drowned the sound out, and she looked up to see dark clouds filling the horizon in the direction of Rome.

CHAPTER TWENTY

'Nice . . . very nice workmanship indeed.' The merchant held the gold wristband up to the light streaming through the window high on the wall of the small room at the rear of his shop, just off the Forum. The fine detailing of the pattern etched into the gold and finished with silver inlay was clear to see. 'If I'm not mistaken, this is the work of Epidarus of Alexandria. It bears his mark here, just along the rolled edge, do you see? Of course, that is no guarantee of authenticity. Most forgers are adept at re-creating such marks. However, I have seen examples of his work before, and I can distinguish between a fake and the real thing. This is definitely the creation of Epidarus.' The merchant lowered the wristband and regarded Cato. 'Which rather begs the question of how you came by it. You sound like an educated man, yet you look like a common street beggar. I take it this piece is stolen?'

'I came by it honestly,' Cato responded. 'The question is, what will you give me for it?'

The merchant set the wristband down on the small sheet of red silk on his desk and leaned back in his chair. 'That is an interesting question. A fine piece like this would normally fetch a very high price. I could make a small fortune selling it to some senator, or even the emperor himself. I have heard that Nero has very refined tastes, and pays handsomely to prove it. But I can't sell this.'

'Why not?'

'Because it is more than my life is worth. I don't know how this came into your possession. I really don't want to know. But as surely as the sun rises, it is stolen, whatever you may say. If I try to sell it and it is recognised, as it doubtless would be, then I would be accused of profiting from stolen goods at the very least. I would be ruined, if I was lucky. More likely exiled, or even put to death. So I cannot sell it.'

Cato was losing his patience. 'If you won't buy it, then I will take it to someone else who will.'

'I don't think so. Every goldsmith or jewellery merchant will tell you the same thing.'

'We'll see about that.' Cato reached for the wristband, but the merchant moved quickly and flicked the cloth over it.

'Don't be too hasty, young man. I said I couldn't sell this. Not as it is. But I could melt it down for the gold and silver. Of course that would destroy any value that is attached to the craftsmanship, but that very craftsmanship is what makes it unsaleable. The only practical value this trinket has to you is its weight in precious metals. I would be prepared to pay you a decent price on that basis.'

Cato smiled cynically. 'I wondered when you would come to that.'

'Then you have no reason not to consider my offer.'

'How much?'

The merchant felt for the wristband and pulled it out from under the fold of silk. He tested its weight in his hand and pursed his lips. 'Two hundred denarii.'

Cato scoffed. 'Even I know it's worth ten times that.'

'If I was to sell it to a collector, I dare say I would get even more than that for it. But I am only prepared to pay what it is worth to me. Two hundred denarii. You won't get a better price.'

'Three hundred.'

'Two hundred, and that is all. My final price. Take it, or take this somewhere else.'

Cato sucked in a deep breath. He wished he had the inclination to drive a harder bargain. But he needed the money to pay for lodgings and food.

'Very well, I'll take two hundred.'

They shook on it briefly, then the merchant wrapped the wristband in the silk and placed it carefully in a strongbox re-inforced with iron bands. He opened a smaller box and counted out the coins before handing them over to Cato. 'There.'

Cato swept them into his large leather purse and drew the cords tightly before attaching it securely to his belt.

'You might want to count that,' the merchant suggested. 'Just to be sure that I haven't cheated you.'

Staring hard at the man, Cato raised a finger in warning. 'If you have cheated me, then I'll be back to make you pay for it. Same goes if you let anyone know about our little transaction. You have no idea how to find me, whereas I know exactly where you are. You had better remember that.'

The merchant affected a hurt expression. 'I am an honest trader, and a discreet one. You have no cause to insult my integrity.'

Cato left the back room, sweeping the bead curtain aside, before striding through the shop and out into the street. There were many other jewellers, gold- and silversmiths, as well as hawkers with small stalls, crowding the area. Even though the weather was gloomy, the Forum and surrounding thorough-fares were filled with people. In addition to his poor clothing and the streaks of filth on his face, Cato now had a pronounced stubble, and he felt confident that he would not be easily recognised. All the same, even in a city the size of Rome, there was a danger of running into men from his cohort, or other officers in the Guard. So he pulled up his hood and turned away from the Forum, making his way towards the Esquiline district, well away from the route taken by off-duty Praetorians heading into the heart of the city to savour its entertainments.

As he climbed the steep road leading into Subura, the most notorious slum in Rome, the tenement blocks grew taller and closely packed so that little natural light seemed to pene-trate to the grubby streets. There also seemed to be little movement of the air, and he wrinkled his nose as he breathed in the foul air. The streets and alleys were narrow and twisted between the ramshackle blocks where the city's poorest inhabitants lived in crowded, crime-ridden proximity to each other. Even the men of the urban cohorts were reluctant to patrol the slum, which made it the best place for Cato to hide out while he tried to find Granicus's murderer and clear his own name.

Not far from the Esquiline Gate, in the heart of the district, Cato came to a small square. A rowdy crowd stood outside a tavern as two men, stripped to the waist, fought with hands bound with leather straps. Their technique was clumsy, far below the standard of boxers who fought in the arena. But what they lacked in style they made up for in brutality, and blood oozed from cuts on their faces. Opposite the tavern stood three teetering tenement blocks, propped up by thick weathered timbers. A sign outside the entrance to the middle building advertised rooms to let, and that details were available from the concierge within.

There was a small recess inside the wide doorway with a stool, and to one side a low door. Cato leaned forward and knocked; a moment later he heard someone coughing before the latch on the other side lifted and the door swung inwards. A stooped man in a plain but worn military tunic emerged and limped into the light. Now Cato could see his wrinkled skin and wizened expression as grey eyes swiftly looked him up and down.

'There's no work for you here.'

'I'm not here about work,' Cato responded. 'There's a sign outside saying you have rooms available. I'm looking for a place to stay.'

'The terms are a month up front and half a month damage deposit. Are you good for that?' the old man asked doubtfully.

'I can cover it.'

Cato saw an old brand on the man's forehead that at first glance he had mistaken for a wrinkle. 'You're a veteran, I think?'

The man's eyes narrowed. 'What of it?'

'Nothing. It's just that my father served,' Cato lied. 'I recognised the cut of your tunic and the brand of Mithras. Which unit were you in?'

'Twenty-First Rapax legion. Just made centurion when some barbarian bastard cut my hamstring. Honourable discharge.'

Cato was surprised to see a man of the rank of centurion

reduced to living in such a hovel, scraping a living as a concierge. The veteran read his expression.

'I know what you're thinking. I got the full gratuity, but I was cheated out of it by a banker a few years back. Like a lot of people. You fight for Rome and some swindler in a slick toga sweet-talks you into taking on a loan you can never repay. Don't know how those bastards can live with themselves.'

'Very comfortably, I should imagine.'

The veteran frowned and waved his hand. 'Come on, then, I'll show you the rooms.'

He led the way up a narrow staircase whose boards creaked loudly beneath their boots. Four storeys up, he stopped on a gloomy landing. One of the doors was open, and a thin young boy, no more than five years old, sat listlessly on the threshold staring at the two men.

'Don't mind him.' The veteran nodded. 'He's a halfwit. Good for nothing. Don't know why his family don't sell him off, or take him across to the other side of the city and abandon him. It's not like they don't have enough mouths to feed.' The cry of an infant from within the apartment emphasised the point.

The veteran turned to the door at the far corner of the landing. It opened on to a room barely ten feet across. A single window, with a grubby woollen curtain to one side, provided enough light to see by. A large crack ran from the ceiling to the floor on the wall to the right, while another door opened on to an even smaller room opposite. A coarse sackcloth bedroll lay on the floor, chewed in places by mice, or rats, so that grey strands of straw stuck out. The only other items of furniture in the rooms were a pair of stools, and a slop bucket with a lid. Cato lifted it off and grimaced at once.

'I'll have the boy take that out and empty it. Should have been done when the last tenant left.'

'What happened to him?'

'He died. Found him dead just inside the door when I came to collect the rent. Been gone several days, judging from the smell. Well, there it is. Two rooms. Good size, with views towards the Forum.'

Cato looked out of the window at the square below. The boxers were still going at it, though they were tiring now, and badly bloodied. All he could see were the rooflines of the buildings surrounding the square. 'I can't see the Forum.'

'Like I said. Views towards the Forum, not views *of* the Forum. Ten sestertii a month. And another three if you want the boy to take away your slop and bring a bucket of water up to your room each morning. Food can be arranged. The wife does a pot of gruel at night. I can have a bowl brought up by the boy for another three.'

'Call it fifteen all in, and we have a deal.'

The veteran made a show of thinking this over, and then gave a sour smile. 'You're ruining me, but I like your face. Fifteen it is. You have it on you?'

Cato went to the other room so that he would not be seen, took out his purse and counted out the coins, then returned to hand them over to the veteran. 'That's a month's deposit and first month's rent. One other thing. I don't want anyone asking questions about me, and I don't want you or anyone giving any answers.'

The other man frowned. 'You in trouble?'

'Let's just say there's a girl involved, with an angry father who is not ready to be a grandfather.'

'Aha, I thought it was something like that.' The veteran chuckled and tapped his thin nose. 'You're safe with me, young man. Been in trouble once or twice myself, when I was back in the ranks.' He placed the coins into his own purse with a light jingle, tightened the strings and then tapped a finger to his forehead in farewell. 'I'll leave you to it then.'

The door closed behind him and Cato let out a long sigh as he took in his surroundings again. Now that the man had mentioned it, there was a faint odour of rotting flesh lingering in the air. Or perhaps he was imagining it. It was hard to tell over the more overpowering stench of damp, sweat and the foul odour from the slop bucket. The walls were plain, except where a previous occupant had scratched a small picture of a mountain, the base of which was covered with vines and farmhouses. Cato smiled. He thought he recognised it: Vesuvius, down in Campania. He had visited Herculaneum once with his father when he was eight years old. A happy summer, he recalled. He had played on the beach, beneath a bright sun. The smile faded. His father was long since dead. And now Cato himself was being hunted down, hiding out in this crumbling tenement block in the heart of the most wretched slum in Rome.

He hoped that Macro had found a way to get Lucius safely out of sight. With his son beyond the reach of Pallas, Cato would be free to concentrate his efforts on finding the murderer of Granicus. Not that he had any idea how he could achieve that yet, since there was so little information to go on. Just the probability that the man was a Praetorian, and the tattoo. It fell to Macro to see what he could discover from within the Praetorian Guard. Meanwhile, Cato would investigate the tattoo. The murderer was likely to have had the work done by someone in Rome. Someone might remember his face, and better still, his name. And then there would be a reckoning, Cato promised himself that.

CHAPTER TWENTY-ONE

CHAPTER TWENTY-ONE

The next day, the sun finally shone from a clear sky. Cato went into the Forum and bought a waxed tablet and stylus, then sat in the corner of one of the taverns close to the Great Circus, carefully sketching the image he had seen on the man's arm. The pose of the deadly creature had been quite specific. Tail raised to strike, claws spread wide and the body presented at an angle. It took him nearly an hour before he was satisfied with his work. Then he finished his wine and crossed the city to the Viminal quarter, close to the streets most frequented by off-duty guardsmen.

A short distance along the Vicus Patricus, he came across the first tattoo parlour. A range of images, together with prices, were chalked on boards either side of the door. He entered and found himself in a long, narrow room. Near the door was a table, and on a shelf along one wall were the pots of dye, needles and bloodied cloths that were the tools of the trade. A dark-skinned man in a felt cap was examining the image of an eagle he had just completed on a teenager's shoulder. He dabbed a smear of blood with a cloth and cocked his head one way, then the other, before straightening up and patting the youth on the back.

'There you go, young Skaro. You'll be the envy of the other recruits in the Anglianus mob.'

The boy craned his neck to look down at the tattoo and smiled. He paid his fee, then pulled on his cloak and left the parlour, nodding to Cato as he passed.

The tattoo artist sized Cato up. 'What can I do for you, sir? Something patriotic? The name of a loved one?'

Cato shook his head. 'I'm after something special. I have a mate who had a nice piece done. But he was drunk at the time and can only remember that he had the tattoo in this district. Thing is, I'd like to get the same as him. Here, let me show you.'

He took out his waxed tablet and opened it for the other man to see. The artist looked a moment and then scratched his chin. 'Not one of mine, that's for sure. This kind of thing's popular with the Praetorians, but I haven't seen one quite like that. If you like, I can have a stab at it, so to speak.'

'I'd rather get it done at the same place as my mate.'

The artist shrugged. 'As you will. I'd suggest you try Perseus at the top of the street. He gets a lot of Praetorian trade.'

'Thanks.' Cato closed the tablet, nodded a farewell and left.

The sunshine seemed to have improved the mood in the capital. Far more people were abroad, and had left the hoods of their cloaks down. Much as he was tempted to hide his features, Cato realised he was far more likely to stand out with his head covered. So he went on his way trying to seem as unconcerned as the other people in the street, though still fearful that he might be recognised. That morning he had seen the first of the wanted notices daubed on a wall in the Forum. It had given a detailed description, together with the promise of a reward of a thousand denarii for information leading to his capture. So

Cato had smeared dirt on his face to help conceal his scar. The reward was a large enough sum that it would tempt many who knew him, and excite many more with the prospect of winning enough to buy their way out of Rome's slums for life. They would not stop to question if he was innocent or not. Nor would they even care.

Perseus's tattoo parlour was set on the corner of a busy junction. The name of the proprietor was painted in swirling black letters against a white arm with the hand pointing down at the entrance. Inside was a large room with three tables and some benches. Two of the benches were occupied, and tattoo artists leaned over them concentrating on their work. A heavily made-up woman, her smock lowered to her stomach, gritted her teeth as a man created a flower pattern over her breasts.

Cato coughed to attract attention. 'I'm looking for Perseus . . .'

The man working on the woman glanced up. 'Who's asking?'

'Gaius Antonius.'

'What's your business?'

'Looking for a friend.'

'Aren't we all? But I doubt Perseus is your type.' He laughed and the others joined in knowingly. Then he called out towards the back of the shop: 'Hey, boss, there's a man to see you.'

Cato turned to look and heard a creak as someone climbed off a chair or bed. A moment later a stooped man, almost a dwarf, walked stiffly into the room. His neck was twisted to one side and he had thick dark hair tied back in a ponytail. His sharp eyes immediately fixed on Cato. 'You want something?'

Cato crossed to the empty table, set the tablet down and flipped it open. Perseus came over and stood beside him. He was barely tall enough to get a decent view of the illustration as

Cato tapped the tablet. 'A friend of mine had this design done, and I'm trying to find who did the work.'

'Oh? Why's that?'

'I'm thinking about having the same.'

'Then you've come to the right place. That's one of my better pieces. Designed it exclusively for my Praetorian customers.' He looked up at Cato. 'You don't look like a guardsman, so I can't help you, friend.'

'A pity. Is there much call for this design?'

'Not much. It costs more than basic tattoos, thanks to the shading effects.' He raised a finger to scratch his chin. 'Most go for the simpler images, the kind of thing these amateurs can cope with.' He gestured dismissively at his employees, who chuckled with derision.

Cato described as best he could the man who had fled from the scene of Granicus's murder, and Perseus thought a moment before he responded.

'Could be a couple of my customers. You got a name?'

'I was hoping you could help me with that,' Cato said quietly.

At once the man looked at him suspiciously. 'What kind of friend are you?'

'The kind who pays well for information he is seeking.' Cato drew aside his cloak and tapped his heavy purse lightly. 'Perhaps it's best we discuss this in your back room.'

Perseus weighed his visitor up, then nodded. 'Follow me.'

He led the way to the door. Cato saw that the room beyond was a combination of office and storeroom. A low stool sat before a table with short legs across which were spread a series of tablets bearing the business's accounts. Perseus sat on the stool and crossed his hairy arms.

'Right, what's this really about? You an informer?'

'Something like that.'

'Then you'll be willing to pay a good price for what you're after. I know your type. You only get out of bed for a decent share of the spoils.'

'I'll pay a fair price for information that helps me find the man I'm looking for. You have the names of those customers who had this tattoo?'

'Yes. Two men. One's a regular, got some lovely art on him. Practically a walking gallery these days.'

'Then it's the other one I'm interested in. He only had the one image I could see.'

'All right, what are you offering for the name?'

Cato reached into his purse and took out ten sestertii. Perseus sneered in contempt. 'Ten? You're insulting me. I don't sell my customers out for any less than twenty.'

'I'll give you ten now. Ten more if I find him.'

'Fifteen now. Five later.' Perseus tapped his chest. 'I got a reputation to uphold. I can't have people knowing I'll rat on them for loose change.'

'But you'll do it for a fair price,' Cato responded cynically. 'That's some reputation you have there, friend. Fifteen, then. But if I find out you've been leading me up a blind alley, I'll be back for my money, and more. I've got a reputation to uphold as well.' His voice hardened. 'As most of those who have tried to cross me have lived to discover.'

'Most?' Perseus sniffed.

'That's right. The others didn't live long enough to regret their mistake.'

There was a brief uncomfortable silence before Perseus gave a quick nod. He waited for Cato to add five more coins, then swept them from his visitor's hand and put them straight into a strongbox beneath his desk. Then he locked the box and put the key, on its chain, around his neck, tucking it out of sight beneath his tunic.

'The name?' Cato prompted.

'Marcus Priscus. That's what he said it was, at least. Came in a couple of months back. He'd been celebrating a promotion and had had a skinful. Wanted something special. That's why I remember the name.'

'Marcus Priscus? You're sure?'

'For twenty sestertii, and your attitude towards those who let you down? I'd better be sure.'

'That's right.' Cato put his tablet back in his sidebag and pulled his cloak over his purse. 'If I find him, I'll be back to pay the rest. Meanwhile, you don't breathe a word of my reason for visiting you. Understood?'

Cato spent most of the time off the streets in his cold and malodorous rented rooms. He ventured out only for food, as the fading light helped conceal his identity, or to go to one of the lesser used bath-houses where the steam room provided anonymity. Several days later, Cato was sitting in the steam room of the bath-house of Alpicius, not far from the home of Sempronius. This was his second visit to the establishment, after he had left a sign for Macro to meet him there. He did not like being seen two days running, but his jaw and cheeks were now covered with bristles, and he had also bought a leather band to wear around his head to add to his disguise. As the Praetorians had their own bath-house just outside the camp, there was minimal risk of anyone recognising him, and the thick steam swirling around the room helped to conceal him further.

That morning he had hidden the majority of his remaining coins under a floorboard in the corner of the smaller room at the tenement block, keeping enough in his purse only to cover daily expenses. It was a necessary precaution, as none of the apartments had locks on the doors, only bolts within to secure them at night. As he recalled his dismal lodgings, Cato grimaced. At night, the room he slept in was cold, and the thin blanket he had bought in the market was barely adequate. Worse still, the place was alive with cockroaches, some emerging from within the ruined mattress he was attempting to sleep on. He had felt them scuttling across his bare skin and had soon given up trying to brush them off. In contrast to the barracks and camps that he was used to, filled with the snores of men, and muted conversations, the tenement resounded with the wailing of infants, voices raised in argument, and the cries of the beaten and those enjoying carnal pleasures. The constant noise, along with his concern for Lucius's safety and the endless turmoil over his own predicament, had prevented Cato from getting much sleep, and now he closed his eyes, leaned back on the marble bench and began to drift off . . .

A hand shook him roughly, and his eyes blinked open to see Macro standing in front of him.

'Wakey, wakey, lad,' the centurion chuckled. 'You were dead to the world. Why, I feared you might just be dead!'

Cato rubbed his eyes and shifted himself into an upright position. 'Jupiter's balls . . . I need a bloody good night's sleep.'

'You haven't secured the best of billets, then?'

'You can't imagine . . . How is Lucius?'

'He's safe. Petronella's got him out at her sister's farm south of Rome. No one knows where.'

224

'What about Sempronius?'

'I told him that before you'd gone on the run you'd given Petronella orders to take Lucius away from Rome for a while, until things settle down. He wasn't happy, but there's nothing he can do about it. I claimed I had no idea where she might have gone.'

'Good. The fewer who know, the better.' Cato mopped the sweat from his brow as Macro sat down a short distance away and leaned forward, resting his elbows on his thick thighs. 'Any news from the barracks? How are the men taking the news about me killing Granicus?'

'Most of 'em don't believe it. They know you, lad. They know you're not a murderer. A heartless taskmaster, yes. But not a murderer. The rumour mill has it that you were set up by someone, and some of the stories are as wild as you might expect. I overheard two of the men saying you were caught in the act with the emperor's mother, and this was Nero's way of paying you back.'

Cato shook his head. 'I only wish I knew the full truth. But I've got something now. The name of the killer. Or at least the name he gave when he had his tattoo done. Guardsman Marcus Priscus.'

Macro made a mental note of it. 'I'll check the rolls of the cohorts as soon as I can. If he's our man, then we'll need to have a word with him.'

'We can't send him off the same way we sent Fennus. I need him alive so he can confess to the murder and say whose orders he was acting on.'

'And after that?'

'After that, he can join Fennus.'

★ ★ ★

After Macro left the bath-house, Cato stayed on for a few more hours, preferring to remain there rather than spend time with the cockroaches back at the tenement. He used the weights in the gymnasium before finishing with the hot room and a dip in the cold pool. As dusk settled over Rome, he left the bath-house feeling relaxed and in better spirits than at any time since the murder of Granicus.

It was only a few days to go before the annual holiday of Saturnalia, and already statues, temples and shrines were being dressed with garlands. Cato passed a chain gang of slaves laden down with sides of beef and pork destined for the table of a wealthy patron preparing to feast his clients. There would be six days of celebration, followed by more two days later when the feast of the Birthday of the Unconquered Son would mark the closing of the year. A year that he would not miss, Cato reflected ruefully. It had begun with the bitter retreat from the druids' island of Mona in Britannia, following which Cato and Macro had been sent home to report on the disaster. It was shortly after his return to Rome that Cato had discovered his dead wife's infidelity, before being sent to Spain to quell a rebellion in the mining region of Asturica. And now he had been framed for a murder and forced to abandon his men and his son and go into hiding. Not for the first time he wondered what he had done to deserve the unswerving attention of malevolent fate. Surely there were other men more deserving of the kinds of misfortunes heaped on his shoulders?

Shouting from further down the street broke into his thoughts, and he craned his neck in alarm as he instinctively feared that he had been recognised. But all he saw was a gang of drunken youths strolling towards him arm in arm, laughing and talking far more loudly than necessary, as young men in their cups were wont to do. As they passed a fishmonger, one of them stumbled against a trestle counter and a shower of sardines fell into the street. At once an elderly woman in a bloodied apron emerged, brandishing her gutting knife.

'Oi! You little bastard, watch your step!'

The youth backed off, hands raised, grinning. 'Keep your hair on, Grandma. You'll do someone a mischief with that blade.'

'Pick those fish up and put 'em back.'

'Try and make me.'

'I'll have none of your cheek, you cocky sod.'

'Haven't you heard? It's a new golden age. A new emperor. Now Nero's in charge, says he's going to make Rome great again. Rome belongs to the young. So you can piss off and pick up your own fish.'

The young men continued on their way and Cato stepped to the side of the street to let them pass. But one of them caught his eye and held up a canteen. 'Have a drink, friend!'

Cato shook his head. 'I'm all right, thanks.'

'Bollocks! Have a drink with us.'

Cato saw that some of those in the street were looking in his direction. Fearing any trouble that would draw even more unwanted attention, he forced a smile, took the canteen and raised it to take a quick sip. The wine was as rough as any he had ever tasted and seemed to burn as it passed down his throat. He handed the canteen back and grimaced.

'By the gods! What is that stuff? Tastes like horse piss.'

The youths roared with laughter, and there was a ghastly moment before Cato rejected the notion that he had been tricked into drinking urine.

'Might as well be piss.' The youth nodded. 'But it's the

cheapest wine in Rome. And it'll be flowing like water once the Saturnalia begins.'

He slapped Cato on the shoulder and the gang moved off. Cato hawked up some phlegm to clear his throat of the foul brew and spat into the gutter. At least the holiday would mean the streets would be packed and he would be lost in the crowd. And the Praetorians and men of the urban cohorts would be too busy keeping order to spend time searching for him. He felt his spirits lift at the thought as he continued on his way to his lodgings.

Even the sour stink of the Esquiline slum did not diminish his optimism, and he whistled contentedly as he climbed the stairs to his rooms. Closing the door behind him, he hung his cloak on the single peg, and then, with night falling over the city, curled up on the mattress, huddled beneath his blanket. He was exhausted, and even the prospect of another night in the cockroach-infested tenement did not prevent him from falling into a deep, dreamless sleep.

So deep a sleep that he was not woken by the shouts of alarm, the pounding of feet on the stairs; nor did he stir as the smoke entered the apartment. Instead, his body relaxed in the warm air as the flames began to eat their way up the building towards him.

CHAPTER TWENTY-TWO

The crash and roar of falling masonry woke Cato, and he sat up with a start, head thick with sleep and a dull ache. He yawned and took a deep breath, and instantly began coughing as an acrid sensation burned his gullet. The room was dark, but a rosy hue glimmered around the thick woollen hanging covering the small window that overlooked the square. At once the drowsiness fell away, and Cato covered his mouth as he rose from his bedroll and crossed the room, tripping over his boots and bundled cloak and barely managing to remain on his feet. Now his eyes were smarting, and he narrowed them as he reached for the makeshift curtain with his spare hand and drew it aside. A bright red glare flowed into the room along with a blast of hot air, and he recoiled. Now he could see the thin trails of smoke curling in under the door.

'Oh shit,' he muttered. He snatched up his cloak, sword belt and boots, and then hesitated. In the corner of the room was the bucket of water he paid for daily. He picked it up, with the cloak resting over his arm.

Moving to the door, he lifted the latch and cautiously opened it. The landing was thick with smoke, and as he hurried to the top of the stairs, he could see a lurid glow below. The doors of two of the other apartments were open. The heat rising up towards him was stifling. He started heading down, but got no further than the floor below before he was forced to stop. Here there were more open doors, and he ducked into the nearest to escape the fierce heat.

There was only one room, and three bedrolls took up most of the floor space, together with a small chest, lying open with what remained of the occupants' valuables still inside. Cato glimpsed a crudely carved figure of a gladiator. On the other side of the room was a large shuttered window, and he rushed over and opened it. Smoke billowed past, lit from beneath. A small, rickety-looking balcony looked out over the square, and he carefully stepped out on to the narrow strip of boarding. The main blaze was to his right, and as he craned his neck, he saw that most of the heart of the building had already collapsed, spilling burning timbers into the square, along with bricks and chunks of plaster. The fire had spread to the adjacent tenement blocks. A crowd of onlookers stood at a distance, their faces lit up by the flames as they watched in horrified awe.

'Look!' a voice cried out. 'There's still people inside!'

The gasp of the crowd was audible even above the roar of the flames, but no one moved to help. Cato did not blame them. What could they do to save him? He must look to himself. The balcony was almost fifty feet above the street and he dared not let himself drop that far. The fall would kill him, or cripple him at best. There had to be another way. If only there was some rope . . . He thought about cutting up his cloak and the clothing scattered about inside the room, but by the time he had fashioned enough to reach down the front of the building, it would almost certainly have been consumed by the fire, and him along with it.

A burst of sparks and a bright yellow tongue of flame flared up in front of the balcony, driving him back inside. There was only one thing for it. He must try to get through the flames and escape from the building, or at least descend far enough that he could find a window from which he could drop to the street without injuring himself.

He set everything down and hurriedly put on his boots, belt and cloak. Then, picking up the bucket, he doused himself in water. There was not nearly enough to drench the cloak, and he glanced round and saw two more pails in opposite corners of the room. The first also contained water, and he poured that over himself, but the other was filled with urine, collected to sell to a fuller's business. Gritting his teeth, he raised the bucket and sluiced the contents over his cloak, trying not to notice the sharp tang that filled his nostrils. Then he drew the garment tightly about himself and made his way back to the landing. The heat was even worse than before, and he hesitated at the top of the stairs before pulling his hood up over his head.

At that moment, he heard a cry from above. A high-pitched call for help. A child's voice. He cursed under his breath, but there was never a doubt in his mind about what he would do. He turned on his heel and ran back up the steps to the next storey, towards the sound of crying. As he took the last stairs two at a time, he saw a small boy, barely more than an infant, standing on the threshold of one of the apartments. He was barefoot and wore a threadbare tunic, and both hands covered his mouth as the smoke caused tears to streak down his cheeks.

'What in Hades are you doing here?' Cato demanded, furious that someone had abandoned the child. He rushed over and snatched him up, then turned back to the stairs. At once the boy started struggling violently, thrusting a bony hand back towards the doorway.

'Mama! Mama!' he cried shrilly.

Cato paused, then turned back quickly. In for a sestertius, in for a denarius . . .

The apartment was comprised of two rooms, like his own, but there was no sign of anyone in the first, just a few small heaps of rags, some wooden platters containing abandoned meals, and a basket of cheap trinkets. Striding quickly into the second room, Cato saw a woman lying on her side, snoring. A man was sprawled beside her beneath a soiled blanket. There was much less smoke in here, and Cato took a deep breath. An empty wine jar lay beside the bedroll. He put the boy down and shook the woman.

'Wake up! Wake up, you fool! The building's on fire.'

She stirred without opening her eyes and coughed before turning away from Cato towards the man, who lay unconscious, jaw hanging open as he breathed deeply. Cato yanked her roughly back and shook her again, more forcefully this time. 'For fuck's sake, wake up!'

Her head lolled from side to side and she frowned as she muttered an insult. Cato slapped her hard across the face. Her eyes blinked open and she flinched from him, raising her hands to protect her head.

'What? What are you doing? Don't hit me! Please!'

There was terror in her eyes and Cato could only guess at the kind of abuse she endured. He took her hands and spoke directly. 'You have to come now.'

'No . . .'

'Now! If you want to live.'

She shuffled back against the wall and reached to shake the man beside her, but he was too drunk to respond, other than to growl in his sleep and smack his lips. Cato stood up and kicked him hard, desperate to wake him; still there was no reaction. Only the woman could be saved with her boy then, he decided. He grasped her arm and tried to pull her up, but she attempted to wrestle free, and the boy, who had been standing watching, leapt towards her and locked his arms around her neck, crying in terror.

As Cato stood back helplessly, he heard the sound of boots clattering up the stairs. A moment later a man ran across the other room and burst through the door. In the red glare of the flames outside the window, Cato could see the scorch marks on his cloak and the dark smears on his face. His cheeks were lined and his neatly trimmed beard was streaked with grey. Cato guessed he must be a decade or so older than himself.

'Cato, we must get out of here! Come!'

'Who in Hades are you? How do you know me?'

'There's no time to talk. Come on.' He gestured towards the landing. 'We have to move, sir! Right now.'

Cato shook his head. 'We have to get these people out of here.'

The man looked at the occupants of the apartment. 'They're beyond help. If we try to save them, we'll die too. Please, sir. Let's get out while we can.'

Cato sensed that the man had a military background and firmed up the tone of his voice as he made a decision. 'We'll take the woman and the boy, then.' He leaned down and pulled the boy from his mother's arms, and the child let out a shrill cry of panic. 'Hush, lad. We're taking her with us.'

With a sharp hiss of frustration, the other man grabbed the

woman, hauled her to her feet and wrapped the blanket around her.

Outside there was another crash of masonry, and the floor shifted under Cato's feet as grit rained down from the floorboards above.

'Let's go!'

He led the way back to the landing, the boy tucked inside the cloak, while his new-found comrade heaved the woman over his shoulder as she made a feeble attempt to resist his efforts.

'Let go of me, you bastard.'

'Shut your bloody mouth. Unless you want to choke on the smoke.'

The heat rising up the stairwell felt like the door of a bread oven had been opened in Cato's face, and he flinched as it stung his flesh. He hesitated only a moment before he plunged down into the swirling smoke. He tried to breathe through his nose, but the air was hot and acrid in his throat and he choked and coughed as he hurried to the next flight of stairs. Two more storeys to descend before they reached the ground, he thought as he continued down. The next landing was ablaze, and sparks burst from burning door frames and floorboards as the air filled with the roaring crackle of the flames that were consuming the base of the block. He tried to work his way across the landing, but ahead of him the fire was even more intense and he was forced to retreat.

'We can't go on. Go back. Back!'

He kicked open a door and strode through the smoke to the front of the building. The floorboards beneath his feet were lined with the glow of the flames raging beneath, and he knew it was only a matter of moments before they caved in. The shutters of the window overlooking the square were open, and he leaned out to call down to the crowd.

'Get a blanket! Get something to catch us!'

There was a brief stillness before one of the onlookers rushed over to the inn on the corner and tore at the awning outside the entrance. Others went to his aid, bringing the awning as close to the burning tenement as they could before spreading it out and holding it tightly.

Cato drew back from the window and opened his cloak, pulling the youngster free. There was a ten-foot gap between the building and the awning, and he judged it as best he could, tensing his muscles. The boy sensed what was about to happen and opened his mouth to scream.

'Quiet!' Cato roared. 'Be still!'

He looked at the upturned faces of the men below. 'Get ready! One! . . . Two! . . . Three!'

He launched the boy out of the window and he fell backwards, arms and legs flailing in the short flight before he landed on the awning, which shimmered under the impact. The air being driven from his lungs silenced his cries, as did the shock, and at first Cato thought he had come to harm. Then, with relief, he heard the wailing resume and turned away.

'Now the woman.'

His mysterious companion nodded and heaved her off his back and on to her feet. Her eyes were smarting with tears from the smoke, and she coughed as she tried to breathe. Cato pushed her towards the window. 'You're going to have to jump. It's the only way out of here.'

She looked down and recoiled in alarm. 'No!'

Cato pressed her gently. 'You have to. Your son's already down there.'

'It's too high. Too high. It'll kill me.'

'It won't. But the flames surely will.'

As if to underline his point, a floorboard near the door suddenly gave way and a yellow tongue licked up into the room.

'I can't do it!' She retreated to the side of the room and pressed herself against the wall.

'There's no time for this,' the other man said. 'Leave her, or we'll all die.'

Cato felt a sudden surge of anger. 'I thought you were here to save lives?'

'I was ordered to save yours.'

'Ordered? Who are you? Who sent you?'

Before the man could reply, another section of the floor collapsed, and smoke and flame billowed into the room. The woman screamed and Cato instantly turned back to her. 'You must jump. Your son is waiting for you. Do you want to make him an orphan?' He reached out and took her hands firmly. 'Here, let me help you.'

As he attempted to ease her away from the wall, her eyes flitted to the window and she flinched back and struggled to free herself. 'Let go of me! Let go!' She managed to snatch one hand away and slapped him hard on the side of his head so that his ear rang.

'Leave her!' the other man shouted.

'You go first. I'll deal with her. Then I'll jump.'

'Leave her, I said. I'll not warn you again.'

Cato had had enough. 'Just fuck off—'

He lurched forward as a massive blow struck the back of his skull. There was a brilliant flash of white, then utter darkness as he lost consciousness.

CHAPTER TWENTY-THREE

For a moment there was nothing. Then a stirring of light and thought and awareness. A sensation of heat as he felt his body being moved, then lifted. Despite a vague awareness of his surroundings, Cato could not think clearly. As if he was wallowing in a stew of perceptions randomly jostling against each other.

'Get closer!' a voice bellowed nearby. 'Closer, I said!'

Then Cato was hoisted up, and the air was alive with flares of light, and his lungs burned with smoke and he coughed and retched. A sudden jerk, and he was floating for an instant, weightless, then he landed hard against something coarse that yielded only a little as the air was driven from his lungs and he blacked out again . . .

The nightmare was long, and unrelieved. Cato was trapped in a burning forest, flames leaping from bough to bough as he and Macro struggled to find a way through the fire while they tried to protect Lucius from burning branches tumbling from above. Then ahead he saw the trees part to reveal a river and a boat. A man he recognised – Tribune Cristus – sat at the oars, while a woman stood on the bank, her back towards Cato as he cried out to her to wait for them. She turned and he saw that it was Julia. She smiled, and as they ran towards the safety of the boat, she casually climbed over the stern and pushed it away from the bank. A moment later Cristus stroked it away into the middle of the current, and as Cato, his son and Macro reached the edge of the river, it was far beyond reach. They could only watch helplessly as the boat left them to their fate, and the flames loomed closer and closer, the glare increasing in intensity . . . slowly resolving into a rectangle, a window frame high on the wall opposite his bed. The brightness of the light took a moment to adjust to as Cato slowly opened his eyes and stirred.

'Ah, he's awake at last.'

He turned his head to one side and his blurry vision made out a woman sitting a short distance from the bed. She had a scroll in her hands, which she rolled up and placed on a side table as she stood. Cato's lips were dry and his throat was sore, and he could only manage a rough croak as he recognised her.

'Domitia . . .'

She approached and smiled down at him. 'Wait. You need to drink first. My surgeon has prepared something for you. Can you sit up?'

Cato nodded and eased himself up slowly until his shoulders were supported by the wall behind the bed. As he became more wakeful, so he became aware of the stinging pain in several areas of his body. He was wearing a fresh tunic and lying on a soft mattress, with some sort of glistening salve spread over the burns on his arms and legs.

'How . . .' he started to say, and then winced at the raw pain in his throat and chest.

'I told you. Wait.' Domitia leaned down to pick up a small

flask from the floor beside the bed and removed the stopper. 'Drink this.'

Cato took the flask and raised it to his nose and sniffed. There was a faint odour of mint; the smell was not unpleasant, so he took a small swig. The liquid was thick, almost the consistency of cream, and it felt cool as it passed down his throat, soothing the pain there. He took another swig before Domitia stayed his hand.

'That's enough for now. You're to take it in small doses through the day. Until the pain passes.' She took the flask and replaced the stopper. 'I expect you are wondering how you came to be here?'

'It had crossed my mind.' Cato shifted to make himself a bit more comfortable before he continued. 'How long have I been here?'

'Two days. You took quite a knock to the head. You stirred a few times and muttered something, but I didn't catch the sense of it. My physician says that it is not unusual for a blow to scramble the senses for a few days. Do you remember the fire?'

'Yes . . .' Cato frowned. 'There was a woman and a child.'

'The boy was saved. His mother, alas, did not survive.'

An image of Lucius flashed through Cato's mind. 'What happened to him?'

'Who knows? If he's lucky, someone will take him in. If not . . .'

Cato felt a sharp pang of pity for the nameless child. The streets of Rome were a merciless place to grow up. Even if the boy was fortunate enough to find a new home, the chances were that he would be condemned to work in a back-street sweatshop the moment he was old enough to survive such employment. Cato was grateful that Lucius would never know such an experience. Such was the result of an accident of birth. One child, now an orphan, almost certainly doomed to a life of misery, while the other, blessed by fate, more than likely to benefit from a comfortable upbringing and the prospects of a prosperous career. If Lucius lived long enough. And that very much depended on Cato proving his innocence.

As he reflected on the fate of the boy and his mother, he recalled the stranger who had risked his life to save him. 'There was a man there. He was the one who saved me?'

'That's right. He brought you here after you jumped from the tenement.'

Cato frowned as the details flowed back into his memory. 'I didn't jump. He threw me.'

'He had to. It was the only way to save you.'

'But he knocked me out as I was trying to save the woman.'

Domitia nodded. 'He told me. He said there was nothing else he could do.'

'Who is he?' Cato asked suspiciously.

Domitia hesitated and took a breath before she replied. 'He works for me and my friends. His name is Attalus. He's been following you for the last few days. Making sure that you were safe. Luckily for you, he was on hand when the fire took hold. When you didn't emerge with the others in the block, he went in to find you. Otherwise, you'd have shared the fate of the woman you tried to save.'

Cato took this in. 'How did he know where to find me in the first place?'

Domitia smiled. 'I sent him to keep watch on Sempronius's house. I was sure you would try to see your son, or contact Centurion Macro. You were quick enough to spot Pallas's men and deal with them, but Attalus is altogether a better agent and stayed out of sight as he followed you.'

'And why did you set him on my tail? Why would you want to keep me safe? Especially after I told you that I wanted no part in your schemes.'

'Why do you think? We knew that Pallas was aiming to get you on his side. We also guessed that if he failed to win you over, he would do his best to destroy you.' Domitia folded her hands together. 'It seems we were right.'

'Then why not bring me in when I needed a place to hide?'

'Because we could not be sure that you would accept our help. You turned us down last time. I took the view that it would be best to wait until you approached us. Sooner a volunteer than a pressed man, as they say. Then the fire forced our hand, and here you are. The main thing is that you are safe. You can stay as long as you need to.'

'As long as I throw my lot in with you and your friends, I assume.'

Domitia shrugged. 'That's up to you, Cato. I'd rather you joined us, of course. But since you are on the run and wanted for murder, I'd say it would make sense to join us.'

'I'm innocent. Pallas framed me for that murder.'

'I believe you. Truly. Your problem is going to be convincing everyone else.'

Cato closed his eyes for a moment, feeling the weight of despair settling on him once again. 'I have to find the man who killed Granicus, and force him to confess.'

'I'd say that's not going to be easy. Of course, if Britannicus was to become emperor, I am sure he could be persuaded to ensure that you were exonerated. And then you could resume your life and career in peace.' She paused to chuckle lightly.

'Well, hardly peace, given your profession. But at least you wouldn't be forced to live in hiding like a common criminal, always looking over your shoulder for fear that you were being tracked down. I have sons myself, Cato. They're being raised on our country estate. I can imagine how much you miss being with yours.'

Cato tried to keep his expression neutral. 'Lucius is safe, at least.'

'I know. I'm sure your nurse's sister is looking after him well.'

Cato felt a chill trickle through his heart. 'How did you know?'

'Simple enough. Attalus is not the only agent working for us. Another man followed your friend Macro.'

'Did anyone else follow him?'

'If you mean Pallas's men, not as far as I know. Lucius is quite safe. Be thankful for that at least.'

It was a relief to know that his son was out of Pallas's clutches. But there would be no chance of Cato raising the boy himself as long as he was being hunted. And until he could locate the real murderer, and force the man to tell the truth, he would be a fugitive. That was already starting to take on the feeling of a futile quest. Reluctantly he began to reconsider whether he should ally himself with Domitia's cause. She and her friends were playing for high stakes, but if they won, and he was on their side, he would be sure to have his name cleared and to reap rich rewards besides. But first he needed to know more. His gaze returned to Domitia and fixed on her shrewdly.

'Lucius is safe?'

She was silent for a moment before replying. 'From us, you mean?'

'Yes.'

'Of course he is, Cato. What do you take me for? I and my friends want an end to the arbitrary rule of hereditary despots, monsters like Caligula and fools like Claudius alike. And I fear that there is every chance that Nero will turn out as insane and cruel as the former. Rome cannot afford another emperor like that. Britannicus is a lesser danger at the very least. He understands that imperial powers must be curtailed, and that Rome should return to being a republic at the earliest possible opportunity. The purpose of our cause is to end the aberration of a dynasty of despots and return power to the hands of the Senate and people of Rome. Surely you would support such a cause? From what I know of you, I believe you desire that as much as I do. Am I wrong?' She arched an eyebrow.

Cato kept his expression blank as he thought through what she had said. It was true that he had no great love for the institution that Augustus had first foisted on Rome, but then he had little faith in the aristocrats who had ruled Rome before. It was their mistakes and naked ambition that had led to the bloody conflicts between a succession of warlords before Octavianus emerged as dictator of Rome, assuming the title of Augustus. Who was to say the whole calamitous process would not be repeated if Britannicus won the day and abolished the principate, handing power back to the Senate? And yet at present, Cato's future, and that of his son, seemed to hang on the success of Britannicus, Domitia and her fellow plotters.

'How can I be sure that there's a decent chance you will succeed?'

'There's no such thing as certainty in politics. All I can say is that we have prepared the ground as well as we can, and that we have been planning for this moment for some years now.

Preparations have been made. The playing pieces have been patiently positioned and we await only the right moment to seize power.'

'And when will that be?'

'On the day of Britannicus's fourteenth birthday.'

Cato nodded. That was the traditional occasion that marked the passage from childhood to manhood. Britannicus's birthday was in February, less than two months away. 'And what exactly will happen on that day?'

Domitia collected her thoughts before she replied. 'It will begin with a vote in the Senate. Sempronius will put forward a motion questioning the legality of Nero's accession. You can imagine the feigned outrage that will provoke. There is no chance of the motion being passed as things stand, but it will allow us to identify our most vociferous opponents, who will be dealt with later. At the same time the Sixth Legion will be camped outside the city, on the road to Ostia. Their legate and most of the senior officers have already thrown in their lot with us. They will enter Rome in support of those Praetorian cohorts that support Britannicus.

'And that's where you come in, if you decide to join the cause. Your men are loyal to you. If you appear at the morning parade and call on them to swear loyalty to Britannicus, then I imagine their example will win over most of the remaining Praetorian units. At the very least it will sow seeds of confusion, long enough for the legionaries to take the city. After that, we take the palace, depose Nero, and arrest him, his mother, Pallas, Seneca and Burrus. We proclaim Britannicus the true heir of Claudius, and present him to the Senate. At which point I imagine there will be plenty of new-found support for Sempronius's motion. Holding a sword to a senator's throat has a rather more direct effect than any amount of carefully constructed rhetoric.'

'I imagine so.' Cato smiled briefly. 'However, I don't see that my role is critical to the success of your venture. You already have the Sixth Legion in your pocket.'

'But they're not much use to us unless we control the gates of the city and ensure that they are open when the legion marches. For that we need to control the Praetorians, or at least enough of them to grant us access to the capital. Besides, if you can win them over, there's every chance we can take control without bloodshed. You could save the lives of many, Cato.'

'But not Nero and his circle, I take it?'

Domitia sighed. 'They cannot be permitted to live. Or else we may find ourselves on the receiving end of what we are about to dish out. They will be arrested and we shall say they are being sent to Caprae. However, they will not reach the island alive. By the time their fate is known, Britannicus will have cemented his grip on power and no one in Rome will have the stomach for any attempt to resist the new regime. As for the rest of the Empire, the legions and their commanders will accept the outcome, or be bought off easily enough.'

Cato considered all he had been told. 'You seem to have thought of everything.'

'We have tried to. As I said, we have been preparing as thoroughly as we can for some years. As proof of that, it's time you met one of the leading figures behind our plans. I'll be back in a moment.'

Domitia left the room, and Cato's gaze returned to the window. Outside the sky was clear and larks occasionally swept past. He could hear the sound of distant footsteps and voices as he waited, and realised he must have been brought to a seldom-used part of Domitia and Vespasian's home. That would make sense. Slaves gossiped as much as anyone in Rome, and his presence would soon be betrayed if he was recovering in the main part of the house. He became aware of his burns again and winced as the stinging intensified. He flexed his limbs and sat up straight. Aside from the burns and the pain in his throat and irritation to his lungs, he was in fair shape. More than fit enough to carry out the duties Domitia and her friends had assigned to him, if he joined their plot.

At length he heard the sound of footsteps. The lighter patter of Domitia's sandals, and the heavier stride of a man. Shadows appeared in the corridor outside the room, and then Domitia stepped across the threshold.

'Here you are, Cato. Meet an old friend.'

She stood aside, and a slender figure stepped out of the dimly illuminated corridor and into the pool of light cast by the sunshine pouring through the window.

'Greetings, Cato.'

Cato felt a sudden mixture of shock and the cold dawning of realisation that he should not regard this as much of a surprise at all, given what he knew of his visitor.

'I was told you were dead, Narcissus . . .'

CHAPTER TWENTY-FOUR

Macro glanced round one final time to check that he was not being followed. It was late in the day, and the last rays of the setting sun bathed the highest buildings in a warm glow. But everything else was in shadow, and a cold blue hue seemed to infuse the air in the streets. The entrance to the yard behind the bath-house was off a quiet back street, and besides Macro there were only a handful of other people hurrying by. None seemed to pay him any attention and no one paused to loiter further along the street. He nodded to himself before he entered the yard. There was an elderly slave responsible for maintaining the fire beneath the bath-house that kept the hypocaust system warm for the customers. As usual, Macro tipped him a sestertius to mind his own business.

'Thanks, master.' The old man touched the coin to his brow.

'Any sign of my companion?' Macro asked.

'Not since the last time you asked after him.'

'No?' Macro frowned. He had heard nothing from Cato for several days now, despite having left his mark and waiting in the steam room as arranged. Even though Macro had every confidence in his friend's ability to look after himself, it was deeply worrying. If Cato were to be tracked down, killed and disposed of, Macro would never know. He clung to the hope that if Cato was found, he would be more use to Pallas alive than dead, and tried to console himself with the thought that lack of news about his friend was not necessarily a bad thing. He sighed and turned his attention back to the slave. 'If you do see him, tell him he needs to get back in contact with me at once. Got that?'

'Yes, master. And what about the other man?'

'Other man?' Macro felt his stomach tighten. 'What other man?'

The slave smiled and tapped his nose. 'That will cost you, master.'

Macro sighed and gritted his teeth. Stepping forward, he grabbed a knot of the man's wiry hair and thrust his head sharply against the wall beside the open doors of the hypocaust oven. With his spare hand he drew his dagger and lightly prodded the point into the soft folds of flesh under the slave's chin. A bead of blood oozed out and trickled down the edge of the honed blade. The heat from the oven bathed the legs of both men.

'You don't get to fuck about with me, you worthless piece of shit. I said, what other man? Speak up, or there's going to be an unpleasant odour of roast meat wafting through the bath-house.'

'Th-there was a man who came in here after you left a few days ago.' The slave spoke hurriedly. 'He said he knew you and that you might have left something for him. I told him I didn't know anything about that, but that you left marks on the wall.'

Macro hissed with anger. 'You told him that?'

'They're only chalk marks, master,' the slave whined. 'What harm could it do to tell him?'

'Plenty of harm, you old fool. No doubt he paid you for the information?'

The slave lowered his gaze, and Macro dragged his head to one side and threw him to the ground, then stood over him, pointing the dagger at his face. 'If this man ever comes back, you are to tell him nothing. You are to deny you have seen me, or my friend. Then you are going to follow him and see where he goes. And report back to me the next time I am here. Do you understand?'

'But, master, I must maintain the fire. If I do what you say and the owner of the bath-house finds out, he'll have me whipped.'

'That's the least of your worries, my friend. If you try and mess with me again, you'll end up with this knife in your guts. But if you find out where this other man is living, there'll be a reward in it for you. Is that clear?'

'Y-yes, master!'

'Now what did this man look like?'

The slave thought quickly for a moment. 'Tall, dark features. He had a beard. Wore a brown tunic and cloak and military boots.'

'A soldier?'

The slave shrugged. 'I couldn't say for sure, master.'

Macro snorted and sheathed his blade. 'You've got your orders now. You'll do as I say, if you know what's good for you. Now get back to work.'

He turned away and strode over to the lean-to as the slave struggled back to his feet, rubbing his head where Macro had wrenched his hair. Ducking under the tiled roof, he searched the spot where he and Cato had previously left their marks for each other. There was his 'M' from two days ago, but nothing else besides. He slapped his thigh in frustration and returned to the middle of the yard, where he stood in thought as the slave went back to work, casting anxious glances in the centurion's direction as he fed more logs into the open door of the oven.

Macro was shocked by the revelation that someone must have been following him for some days without him being aware of it. Either the man who had bribed the slave, or companions of his. Or perhaps they had followed Cato here. He felt a new surge of alarm for the safety of his friend. Perhaps Pallas had already captured him, and was preparing to put him on trial. If that was the case, then Macro must track down and find Priscus, and force him to confess to the murder of Senator Granicus.

Fired by his sense of resolve, he strode out of the yard and into the street. Mindful of what he had learned, he took a winding course, stopping regularly and retracing his steps twice to see if he was being followed. But there was no sign that he had been tailed, so he resumed his usual route and returned to the Praetorian camp, making his way directly to the barracks of the Second cohort. Now that he was the acting commander, following Cato's disappearance, he had had further duties heaped on his shoulders, and there was little time to spare for the ongoing search for Priscus. And little time to spend with Petronella. That must be remedied as soon as possible, Macro thought, before her affection for him began to cool.

Optio Metellus stood up from his desk and saluted as Macro entered the office.

'At ease,' Macro responded as he took off his cloak and hung it on the back of the door. 'All in order, I take it?'

Metellus nodded. 'The duty roster is up to date. The last of the wills of the men we lost in Hispania have been filed at the Temple of Jupiter. I've been notified that the cohort will be getting the first batch of new recruits and transfers by the end of January. We won't be fully up to strength, but not far off. On the bad-news side, all leave has been cancelled. That's not popular with some of the lads, sir.'

'I can imagine.' Macro felt for those who had been hoping to leave the capital for a month or so to visit their families in the towns and countryside of Italia, but the simmering tensions in Rome between the supporters of Nero and those of Britannicus required the presence of every soldier. 'Any word from your friends at headquarters about a new commander for the cohort?'

Metellus shook his head. 'Seems that Burrus is struggling to find a replacement, sir.'

'Trust me, no one can replace Prefect Cato. Still less some chinless wonder appointed directly to tribune just because his father has friends at the imperial palace.'

Metellus nodded with feeling. Both of them were familiar with the rampant nepotism within the Praetorian Guard, at every level. The professional soldiers who had been transferred in from the legions did little to conceal their contempt for some of their comrades who were directly appointed to the Guard. The fact that the men still referred to Cato by his previous rank of prefect of an auxiliary cohort, rather than his official rank of tribune, was proof of their respect for him.

'Well, let's hope that his name is cleared soon and that he can return to duty. The way things are going, we're going to need him.'

'Yes, sir.'

Macro sat down at another desk. 'You got anything else for me?'

'Yes, sir. Punishment log.' Metellus picked up a slate. 'Two men drunk on duty, two charges of insubordination with officers from other cohorts, and eight men charged with fighting in barracks.'

'Let me guess, this is all to do with the bonus payments, or lack of them.' There was still a palpable tension between the men who had received their bonus from the new emperor and those who had not. Arguments were common and fights had broken out between men from different cohorts.

'I'm afraid so, sir.' Metellus hesitated before venturing a further opinion. 'If the palace doesn't sort it out soon, we're going to see a lot more of this kind of thing. Not good for discipline, nor morale, sir.'

'Quite. Then let's hope that Nero discovers a magic money chest any day now and sorts the lads out with the silver they are due. If he can afford the kind of lavish banquets he has been hosting, then he can damn well afford to find the money for his soldiers.' Macro paused and shot a sharp look at the optio. 'That last comment was between us two only.'

'Of course, sir.'

'There's one other matter,' Macro continued casually. 'That business of the guardsman I reported for insubordination. The one who gave his name as Priscus. Have you found out which cohort he is in?'

'I have, sir. I had a word at headquarters and it seems he's a ranker in the Fourth Cohort. Or at least he was.'

'Was?'

'He went absent without leave over a month ago, sir. Seems he was in a fight and killed one of his comrades. Hasn't reported back to barracks since. Nor has anyone seen anything of him. And the funny thing is, no charges have been raised against him yet.'

Macro could not hide his surprise. 'What? After a whole bloody month?'

'Yes, sir. I made quite sure of that. Never heard the like. Nothing like that would happen in the legions, or even the sloppiest auxiliary cohort in the army, for that matter.'

'Damn right. So, what's the story? Why has this Priscus been given a free pass?'

'Seems his tribune hasn't had the time to sign off on the charge.'

'Bollocks. There has to be more to it than that.'

Metellus clicked his tongue. 'If there is, then I'm not privy to it, nor any of my mates up at headquarters. Sorry, sir. Wish I could be more help.'

'Ah, you've done what you can, lad. Who is the tribune of the Fourth, by the way?'

'That's just it, sir. Small world, as you might say.'

Macro glared at the optio. 'Just tell me.'

'It's Cristus.'

'When did that happen?' Macro leaned forward. 'I thought he went on leave.'

'Apparently not. He was transferred to the Fourth as acting tribune after the prefect's appointment to our cohort was made permanent. The current commander of the Fourth is a drinking companion of Nero. He's hardly ever in barracks, and certainly takes no interest in his men. So Cristus has got the job, and for my money he's little better, given that he's done nothing about Priscus, sir.'

'All right, then. I'll have a word with him myself when I get the chance . . .'

* * *

It was dark by the time Macro had finished with the discipline reports and checked on the men taking the first watch. He let Metellus know he was leaving the barracks for Senator Sempronius's house and made his way back through the darkened streets, brooding over the failure of Cato to meet him in the bath-house, the identity of the man who had appeared at the yard where their signals had been left, and the failure of Tribune Cristus to take action against Priscus, who according to regulations was effectively a deserter. His heart felt heavy at the fact that Priscus had gone missing, thereby lengthening the odds against Cato's innocence being proven.

As he strode through the streets deep in thought, he nevertheless made sure that he kept an eye open for any sign that he was being followed. Not that it made any difference if he was being watched, as his nightly return to his unofficial billet at the senator's house had become a set part of his routine. All the same, he was keen to know who exactly was following him, and on whose orders.

When he reached the house, the doorkeeper was waiting on the steps and stood up quickly the moment he saw Macro approaching.

'Thank the gods, master . . . Please, come quickly!'

'What's happened?' Macro demanded as he followed the man inside.

'In the kitchen, master. Petronella's waiting for you.'

'Petronella? What's she doing back in Rome?'

'She didn't say, master.'

Macro left his cloak with the doorkeeper and hurried through the main house and across into the service quarters. The door to the kitchen was slightly ajar and he heard faint conversation and sobs as he approached. He swung the door in and stepped down into the large room, the far wall of which was lined with ovens and grills for those occasions when the senator was entertaining a large party of guests. This night, only one fire was lit, and in front of it, sitting on stools, were Petronella and two others, with their backs to him: a man and a woman.

Petronella stood up the moment she saw him, her face wrought with anxiety. The others turned to look round, and Macro took a moment to recognise them in the dim light. The man's head was bandaged and his face bore livid bruising. But there was no mistaking the woman. It was Petronella's sister, and the man was her husband.

'Macro.' Petronella rushed over and grasped his hands. 'It's Lucius. Someone's taken him . . .'

255

CHAPTER TWENTY-FIVE

'Taken him?' Macro growled. 'Explain yourself.'

Petronella was taken aback by his cold glare and recoiled, releasing his hands. He took her arm and steered her over to the others, sitting her back down before standing in front of them. They exchanged glances as Macro scrutinised their expressions closely.

'Tell me, Petronella.'

She clasped her hands together in her lap as she began. 'It was yesterday, at dusk. We were about to eat when there was a knock at the door. Marius went to answer it.'

'Marius? Then Marius had better speak for himself.' Macro turned his piercing gaze on the man. 'Well? What happened?'

Marius cleared his throat nervously and did his best to meet Macro's gaze. 'There was a man, and a cart outside the gate. He said they had been attacked by brigands and his friend was injured and he needed help to get him in from the back of the cart. I ran across with him and through the gate, and that's when the others jumped me. Knocked me down, kicked me and then held a knife to my throat and demanded to know who was still inside the house. I told them.' He flinched helplessly. 'What else could I do?'

Macro gave no response, so Marius was forced to continue. 'They dragged me to my feet, pinned my arms behind my back and kept the knife at my throat as we returned to the house. I saw Lucilla at the door. She screamed as soon as she saw what was happening. Before she could do anything, the first man had pushed her aside and entered. By the time I was taken to the kitchen, he had drawn a sword and the others were in the corner. He demanded to know if there was anyone else in the house. I told him not. He then asked if Lucius was the son of Prefect Cato. I said he was my nephew. So he hit me with the flat of his sword.' Marius indicated the dressing around his head, and now Macro could see a large dark stain in the linen. 'He then threatened Lucilla with the sword, but she was too terrified to speak.'

Macro turned to Petronella. 'Is that what happened?'

She nodded. 'I was trying to protect Lucius, and it was he who spoke first. He said he was Cato's son, bold as brass. Told the men to go before his daddy got cross with them.' A sad smile flitted across her face. 'Poor little mite didn't understand what was happening.'

'If he's his father's boy, he understood,' said Macro. 'Go on.'

'The leader took him. I tried to stop him but he punched me in the guts. I couldn't even breathe. They threw Marius down. He was bleeding badly from the head. Then the man told us to stay put and said they'd kill us if we made any attempt to follow. They left with Lucius. After they were gone, Lucilla and I saw to Marius, and then I got his cart hitched and we made directly for Rome. I had to let you know as soon as I could.'

Macro thought a moment and nodded. 'You did well . . . What about the men who took the boy? Did you recognise any of them?'

'No.'

'What about you two?'

Marius and his wife exchanged a glance and shook their heads. 'Never seen them before.'

'What did they look like? Anything that set them apart? Scars, or tattoos maybe?'

Petronella wrung her hands. 'They were just men, Macro. Like any on the streets of Rome. And it happened so quickly. They were gone before I could think clearly.'

Macro puffed impatiently, frustrated by their lack of wits. But they were civilians, he reminded himself. Surprise and swift reaction were more his stock-in-trade. But there was something not quite right about this. He had taken every precaution to see that they were not followed when he, Petronella and the boy had set off from Rome. He stared hard at Marius.

'I'm wondering just how they happened on your farm, and knew that the boy was there.'

It took only a moment for Marius to be aware of the direction the centurion's thoughts were taking, and he sat up abruptly. 'Now wait, you can't be thinking I told anyone?'

'I am thinking precisely that. I can see just how tempting it might be to take advantage of the reward being posted for information leading to Cato's arrest. With his son captured, he'd be forced to give himself up. That would be worth good money to Pallas. Well?'

'For Jupiter's sake, I gave you my word that we'd care for the boy.'

'Wouldn't be the first time someone gave me their word and then went back on it. And didn't live long enough to regret the mistake—'

'That's enough!' Petronella cut in sharply. 'I would trust my sister with my life, and Marius too. They are no more likely to betray Lucius than I am.' She pointed a finger directly at Macro. 'Or don't you trust me either?'

Macro pressed his lips together briefly. 'I trust you. However, it's been my experience that if you spend much time in Rome, you soon discover that there's hardly anyone who isn't prepared to do you in as long as the price is right . . . Have you told anyone else yet? Senator Sempronius?'

'Hardly. I had no idea how he reacted when he discovered Lucius and I had gone.'

Macro recalled the evening he had spoken with the senator about the need to move Lucius to a safe place while his father was being hunted. Sempronius had scarcely been able to conceal his anger, but had conceded that Cato had been right to be concerned for his son and for Macro to remove him from Rome. And now the boy had been abducted at the point of a sword . . . Macro coughed awkwardly before he replied. 'I'd better let him know. Meanwhile, I want the three of you to stay here. Don't tell anyone about Lucius, and keep out of sight.'

Marius stirred. 'What about the farm? We can't just leave it.'

'If I were you, I'd think twice about returning there for a while at least. If Lucius is in the hands of the man I think is responsible for grabbing him, you should know that he's not the kind who likes to leave loose ends. You've seen the faces of the men he used for the job. It's a wonder they didn't kill you on the spot. It's your choice, but in your boots, I'd make sure I kept a good blade at my side at all times from now on.' Macro rubbed his brow and let out a long, low sigh. 'Well, I'd better speak with the senator. Jupiter knows how he's going to react to this turn of events.'

* * *

'This is not an acceptable state of affairs, Centurion,' Sempronius said at length, with forced calmness. 'First my grandson is removed from my home without my consent. Secondly, you say nothing of the attempt by you and my son-in-law to track down the real culprits behind the murder of Senator Granicus, and now this. Did it not occur to you both that I might be able to help with your search for justice?'

'Cato took the view that it was best not to implicate you, sir. The less you know, the better. For your own good.'

'Really? Or is it that you and Cato did not feel you could take me into your confidence?'

'Sir, he felt it would put you at risk.'

'We are all at risk these days. Whether we are blameless bystanders or fully committed conspirators.' Sempronius took a deep breath. 'Be that as it may, we must concentrate on finding Lucius and rescuing him.'

'Yes, sir. Absolutely,' Macro agreed vehemently, happier to be on less questionable ground.

The senator leaned back in his chair and stared past Macro to the shelves laden with scrolls that lined the wall of the study behind the centurion. 'Very disturbing though the news of his abduction is, there are a few crumbs of comfort we can draw from it.'

'Sir?'

Sempronius glanced back at Macro. 'Think it through, Centurion. Why snatch the boy unless he can be used to put pressure on his father? That at least proves that Pallas has not got his hands on Cato. Not yet at least. You can take comfort from that, even if you have not heard from him for some days, as you say.'

'I suppose so,' Macro responded uncertainly.

'Then there's the fact that Lucius's nurse and the others were left alive. That was a deliberate act. Whoever is responsible, they wanted to ensure that they rushed back here to break the news to you as soon as possible. And the only reason they would want that is so that you could communicate it to Cato. I'd be wary of trying to meet with him for a while yet, just in case they are waiting to follow you straight to him. Even if you do manage to avoid being followed, Cato would be bound to want to protect Lucius, and would be willing to trade his life for that of my grandson. Either way, they have a way to get at him . . . Clever. You have to hand it to Pallas. Very clever.'

'Too clever in my book, sir. The bastard is lower than the belly of a fucking snake. And the best way to deal with a snake is to cut its head off.'

Sempronius raised his eyebrows at the brutal tone in Macro's voice before he replied. 'Or you step carefully round it and let it slither on its way, then tackle it when it's no longer paying you any attention. And then cut its head off.'

Macro considered this for a moment and shrugged. 'Either way, the bastard loses his head. That's all that matters to me.'

'Well, yes. I can see that's important to you.'

'Not half.'

Sempronius folded his hands and rested his chin on them for a while, then nodded as he appeared to come to a decision. 'We'll need to offer protection to the boy's nurse and the others, for the present. Now that they've served their purpose, I dare say Pallas will feel free to dispose of them. So it wouldn't be safe to return to their farm.'

'I suppose not, sir. And thank you.'

Sempronius thought hard for a moment before he continued.

'I need you to stay here for an hour or so. There's someone I have to speak to about this. Someone we can both trust, you have my word. I won't be long.'

He rose from his desk abruptly and left the study. Macro listened to his footsteps fade along the corridor and then sat down heavily on a couch below the shelves and let out an exasperated sigh. He prayed to the gods that the senator was right and Lucius's abduction was proof that Cato had not yet been captured. But with the boy in the hands of their enemy, it was only a matter of time before the imperial freedman used him as bait to lure Cato into a trap. After that Cato was as good as dead, and Lucius's fate would be uncertain. Such a prospect fired the blood in Macro's veins, and he sat and seethed as he waited for Sempronius to return.

It was well after dark when the senator came back; Macro calculated that it must be the third hour of the night. The door to the study opened and Sempronius stood on the threshold. Macro was surprised to see that he was wearing a sword, the scabbard hanging from a shoulder strap. Before he could comment, the senator gestured to him.

'Come with me.'

He did not wait for a reply, and turned away and strode off down the corridor towards the rear of the house. Macro hurried after him, and they crossed the garden to the walled yard beyond that housed the slaves' living quarters as well as stores and stabling. A litter was waiting by the gate, together with the bearers and a small escort of slaves carrying sturdy clubs and torches, which they lit as soon as they saw their master approaching. Petronella was standing ready with two plain brown cloaks folded over her arm. She bowed her head as she handed the first cloak to Sempronius and held out the other to Macro.

'Put that on and get in the litter,' the senator ordered.

Macro pulled the cloak around his shoulders and Petronella stepped up to fasten the clasp. She looked up at him anxiously, then took his face in her hands and drew it down to kiss him on the lips. 'Be careful, my love.'

'It's those who get in my way who should be careful.' Macro forced a grin. 'I'll be fine.'

He climbed into the litter and sat opposite Sempronius as the latter barked an order. 'Let's be off!'

The litter lurched as the bearers lifted it and paced towards the gates. Through the heavy folds of the curtains Macro heard the hinges grate as the gates were opened and the small procession entered the street outside.

'Don't get too comfortable,' said Sempronius as he cupped his hand over the pommel of his sword. 'Be ready to move as soon as I give the word.'

'What's going on, sir?'

'All in good time. For now, just do as I say without question. Clear?'

Macro hesitated, unsure of what was happening, and not liking it any more than most of what had happened since he and Cato had returned to Rome. Sempronius noted his expression and leaned closer. 'Do you trust me, Centurion?'

Macro chewed his lip. 'You're a good man, sir. But I've had my fill of politicians in Rome. However, Cato trusts you, and that'll do for me.'

Sempronius regarded him sternly by the dull glow of a torch flaring beside the litter. 'All right then, do what I ask for Cato's sake.'

The litter continued along the street and turned into a wide thoroughfare, shadows of passers-by flitting over the folds of the curtains. It slowed as it reached a junction, and a voice outside muttered, 'Get ready, master.'

Sempronius pulled the hood of his cloak over his head and drew his knees up. As the litter turned to the right, the curtain was whipped back and held aside, and he swung his boots round and heaved himself out. Directly in front of him a door was being held open, and he dashed inside, swiftly followed by Macro. Glancing back over his shoulder, the centurion saw one of the escort drop the curtains back as the litter continued on its way.

As soon as Macro was through the door, it closed behind him and a bolt slid home. By the light of some candles perched on a shelf, he saw that they were standing in a bakery. Racks lined the side walls, carrying a range of loaves, rolls and pastries. The man who had locked the door kept his face close to the grille and peered out on to the street as Sempronius attracted Macro's attention and raised a finger to his lips. Macro nodded and turned his attention to their host. He was squat, and wore a skullcap perched on his head. The ties of an apron looped from the small of his back.

All remained still for a while before the baker's neck craned slightly as he turned to watch something pass by the front of his shuttered premises. He took one last look and eased the flap of the grille back before he turned round.

'Seems you were right, sir. There were two of them, following the litter. No mistake about it.'

Sempronius glanced at Macro. 'Now you see why I am taking precautions.'

'With respect, sir, I still have no idea what's going on.'

'We're going to the home of a friend of mine, and it's important that we're not followed there. Hopefully it'll be a while before our tails realise they are being led on a wild goose chase around the back streets of Rome. Meanwhile, Matthias here is one of my clients. He used to be a slave before I freed him many years ago and started him up in this business.'

'And I thank you for it, master.'

Sempronius waved aside his gratitude. 'We'd better leave by a different door, just in case.'

'Certainly, follow me.'

Matthias led them through a door at the back into a storeroom full of large jars of flour, seeds and other ingredients, then out into a yard. Three large ovens stood in a row, the doors open and the glow of dying embers visible within. Then they passed through another door into the home of the baker, surprising his wife as she breast-fed an infant while three other children jostled noisily in a shared bed. They barely paused to look at the strangers passing through, and Macro tipped them a brief wink before Matthias led the way down a short corridor ending with another door.

'This gives out on to the street of the silversmiths. Go left to the junction, then right, and you'll know the rest of the way, master.'

Sempronius patted him on the shoulder. 'My thanks.'

The baker slid the bolt back and opened the door cautiously before peering both ways. 'It's clear.'

Macro followed the senator out into the street and they hurried off as the door closed behind them. He was anxious to find out what was going on, but reluctant to question his superior. Sempronius led the way down to the Tiber, flowing under the baleful loom of a crescent moon. On the far side, they took a street climbing up the Janiculum Hill. By now, Macro had guessed their destination from a conversation he had had with Cato several days earlier.

They were admitted to the back door of Vespasian's property and escorted through the slave quarters to the main house by an elderly retainer who, Sempronius explained, was unable to speak, having had his tongue excised by a former master when he was but a boy.

'Some pay a high price for discretion,' the senator explained.

Macro nodded in pity. 'So I can see.'

Sempronius shot him a look. 'I meant that he cost Domitia a pretty denarius.'

'Oh.'

They entered a colonnade facing the garden and approached a large door leading to an inner hall, lit by numerous oil lamps and candles. A small group of men were lying or seated on couches around a low table on which stood some fine glass decanters and glasses, as well as a handful of waxed tablets and styluses. There was a woman there as well, and as she turned towards the sound of the new arrivals, Macro saw that it was Vespasian's wife. She rose from her couch to welcome them.

'My dear Sempronius. And you, Centurion Macro.'

'A pleasure, my lady,' he responded with a slight bow of his head. 'Or it might be, if I had a clue as to why I have been brought here.'

'Why? Rome needs the help of every patriot, and one amongst us has vouched for you in that respect. He said that if Rome ever needed a good man to save her, that man is you, Macro.'

'Bollocks, if you'll pardon me.'

'Bollocks?' Domitia's brow furrowed, but there was a mischievous twinkle in her expression as she continued. 'I have to say, I fear you may have misled us about your friend's quality, Prefect.'

She stepped aside, and Macro could see two men breaking off an exchange to look round at him. His heart lifted as he caught sight of his friend, clean shaven and neatly dressed, and his lips began to frame a smile, then froze.

'Fuck me . . . Why in Hades aren't you dead like you're supposed to be?' He tapped the handle of his sword. 'I can soon put that right, if no one objects.'

There was a shocked silence from the others in the hall before Cato shook his head. Narcissus glanced at him and smiled nervously before responding to Macro.

'I am charmed to be reacquainted with you too, Centurion. That I am alive is due to my making preparations against the possibility that Pallas would attempt to have me disposed of. When the time came, I explained that I was ill and needed to rest at my country estate near Capua. I had a slave there who bore a remarkable resemblance to me. When the time came, he was intoxicated and his wrists were cut. The Praetorian death squad took the head back to Rome, and corruption of the flesh took care of any question over its identification. I remained in hiding for a few days before making my way to Rome, and the shelter offered by Lady Domitia. As you can see.'

'Might have guessed there'd be some poor sod who bit the blade so that you could continue to live.'

Narcissus shrugged. 'The good of Rome requires sacrifice from us all, one way or another.'

Domitia took Macro's arm before he could respond further, and steered him to sit on a couch with Cato positioned between him and Narcissus. 'We're all on the same side now,' she said smoothly. 'There's no need for you to be introduced to my

267

guests, Macro, since Cato has told them all there is to be said about you.'

'Really?' Macro arched an eyebrow. 'Not quite all, I hope.'

Cato laughed. 'They know enough to trust you, my friend. It's good to see you again.' He held out his hand and they clasped forearms before Macro nodded at the others. 'And might I know who the rest of you are? I already know the senator, and Lady Domitia.'

Some of the men bridled at his directness, until their host cleared her throat and spoke up. 'Every one of us is loyal to the ideals of the Republic, Centurion. Therefore, patriots all. We are dedicated to the ending of the line of emperors who have caused so much dishonour to the glory of Rome.'

'And how do you expect to do that, my lady?'

'By deposing Nero, his mother and their corrupt little entourage. We will replace him with Britannicus, who will reign for the interim while arrangements are made to bring back the Republic.'

'I see.' Macro nodded slowly. 'And what happens if Britannicus decides he prefers to be emperor rather than a citizen?'

One of the other guests rounded on him. 'I have known Britannicus all his life. His heart belongs to our cause. He has sworn a sacred oath to serve the same cause we have pledged to give our lives to, if need be. I think you might reflect on that before you disparage his motives.'

Macro turned to Cato. 'Have you sworn this oath?'

'Not yet.'

'Then you may want to think very carefully about it.'

'Why?'

'I've got news for you, lad. Bad news, I'm afraid.'

Cato saw the sorrowful expression on his friend's face and instantly divined the worst. 'Lucius?'

Macro nodded. 'He's been taken. Pallas has him.'

CHAPTER TWENTY-SIX

'That's all the more reason for us to advance our plans,' Narcissus decided, after Macro had told his friend the details of his son's abduction. 'Given what we heard earlier.'

'Earlier?' Sempronius leaned forward. 'What's happened?'

'There was an attempt on Britannicus's life,' Narcissus explained. 'Someone attempted to knife him on his way to the theatre this afternoon. If it wasn't for our man intervening before the assassin broke through his escort, Britannicus might have been killed. In that event our plans would have come to nothing. We need the prince alive if we are to have any chance of disposing of Nero.'

Sempronius nodded. 'It all depends on keeping Britannicus in play. And if Pallas already feels confident enough to make an attempt on his life in public, then we can expect him to try again as soon as the chance presents itself. We're running out of time. We have to act, and soon.'

'What about the would-be assassin?' asked Domitia. 'Is he in our hands?'

Narcissus shook his head. 'He died at the scene. Our man had to act quickly and get away before the escort could seize him. We can't afford to have one of our own being taken into custody and Pallas finding out. He'd waste no time in putting his torturers to work. They can break any man, or woman,' he added with a nod to Domitia. 'As it is, we were lucky that the attempt failed.'

'Where is Britannicus now?' asked Sempronius.

'He's returned to his mother's house. He'll have to remain there for a while, now that it's clear Nero and his followers want him dead. The prince has surrounded himself with German bodyguards. They were loyal to his father and have sworn to protect him with their lives.'

'Maybe, but that didn't save Claudius,' said one of the other plotters, a bald man with heavy jowls.

'Claudius was poisoned by his wife, Senator Sulpicius. Britannicus is wise to that danger. And now he knows he can't venture abroad safely.' Narcissus paused to refill his cup. 'That's good for us. He's safe enough where he is, but we have to assume that Pallas is already making plans to find another way to get at him. And that is why we need to bring forward our own arrangements. We can't afford to wait until the prince's birthday. We should send word to Legate Pastinus to get his legion to Rome at once. By now they should be on the way. If the Sixth force-marches then the legion can reach the city within the next ten days.'

'It's too soon,' Sulpicius protested. 'Far too soon. We need time to win over as many in the Senate as possible. We can't afford to have people questioning Britannicus's legitimacy once we put him on the throne.'

'I don't think anyone will be questioning the outcome,' Domitia intervened with a thin smile, 'once they realise that we have the Praetorians and the Sixth Legion behind us. The threat of cold steel has a way of winning over people's opinions, I think you'll find.'

'Assuming that we do have the backing of the Praetorians,' Sulpicius responded.

'That's where our friend Prefect Cato comes in.' Narcissus offered Cato a quick smile. 'Once he bring round the Praetorians, nothing can stand in our way.'

Sulpicius shrugged his fat shoulders. 'He's going to find that a little difficult to achieve while he is wanted for sticking a knife in the back of a respected senator, I'd say.'

Macro bristled. 'He's innocent. Cato sticks the knife into no man's back. That's more the speciality of your kind, and shit stains like Narcissus.'

Sulpicius sat back and shook his jowls. 'How dare you!'

Macro stared back coldly. 'Very, very easily . . .'

'That's enough, thank you, Centurion,' Narcissus intervened. 'No one is accusing Cato of murder. We know he was set up by Pallas, and the reason is obvious. The men in his cohort would follow him into the jaws of Hades, and where they would venture, many others would willingly follow. Particularly if his appeal to the men's patriotic instincts is backed up by the promise of a thousand denarii for each man.'

Sulpicius's eyes widened. 'A thousand denarii? That's preposterous! It's a king's ransom.'

'More like several king's ransoms.'

'Where would we get hold of such a vast fortune? We can't just wade in with promises like that. What happens when the Praetorians find out that there is no such bribe coming their way? There's already plenty of bad feeling up at the camp over those who have not yet been paid by Nero. If we make promises we can't possibly keep, they'll turn on us the moment they discover the truth.'

Narcissus smiled. 'But we can afford it, my dear Senator Sulpicius. You are a latecomer to our cause. We have been preparing for this occasion for years. From the moment Pallas convinced Claudius to marry his niece. That's when I first realised that it might not be in Rome's best interests to continue under the reign of the emperors. That is why I came to join your cause. We have been gradually amassing a war chest large enough to buy the loyalty of all the soldiers we needed to ensure that we succeeded in our aims. Great sacrifices have been made by many who support us. They have offered their lives, along with their fortunes. They have come to see, very literally, that there is a price worth paying to bring back the Republic. So when Prefect Cato appears before the Praetorians and asks for their support in overthrowing Nero, I want to make as certain as possible that we sweeten the deal with a bribe the soldiers can't refuse, and one that our rivals can't outbid.'

Sulpicius took this all in, and then pursed his lips and nodded. 'Very well. But a thousand denarii? No soldier is worth that.' He glanced quickly towards Macro and Cato. 'No offence intended.'

'None taken,' said Macro. 'After all, you're a politician, and you can easily be bought and sold. A soldier's loyalty is paid for in blood, but I don't suppose you'd understand that.'

'Ah, Macro, once again you evince the prickly sensitivity of your profession,' Narcissus mused. 'If only you were right. Sadly, it is all too evident that very many of your comrades *can* be bought. The Praetorians just happen to come at a premium. That is the only difference between them and the men in your precious legions. Ask your friend.'

Cato had been silent during the previous exchanges. Mostly because he was preoccupied by the danger Lucius was in, and was struggling to keep up with what was being said. He hurriedly composed his thoughts. 'We need to play this from every angle. Loyalty is both earned and bought. Money will only get your cause so far. You'll need men like Macro and me to see this through. And Narcissus is right. Our plans need to be brought forward. Nero and his followers are becoming bolder, and Britannicus's days are numbered. We need to act as soon as possible.'

Sulpicius regarded him steadily. 'And this has nothing to do with the news that Pallas has snatched your son?'

Cato rounded on him. 'For me, it has everything to do with that. But our needs overlap precisely, and for that you should be grateful. My only hope of seeing Lucius alive again is if this plot succeeds and Pallas is brought down along with Nero. Beyond that, I have only a passing interest in the merits of a return to the Republic. That is the concern of you and your friends once this is over. For my part, I have no desire to remain in Rome. I'll be looking to find myself a farm somewhere to raise my boy, or I'll return to the army. But I will not be a part of whatever regime replaces Nero.'

'A veritable Cincinnatus,' said Sulpicius. 'I do love a humble hero who saves Rome and then quietly hands power over when he resumes private life.'

Domitia clapped her hands together. 'That's enough, Sulpicius. We should just be thankful Cato is on our side, whatever his motive.'

The senator scratched the rolls of fat on his neck. 'If you say so.'

'Then it is settled. Narcissus will send instructions to Pastinus to get his forces to Rome as soon as possible. We'll strike the moment they are ready to enter the city. Prefect Cato will present himself to his men at morning parade, and declare for Britannicus and announce the bonus the prince promises them. When the Praetorians have been won over, they will join the legionaries and march on the palace and the senate house. Once Nero and his followers are arrested, the Praetorians will acclaim Britannicus, with the support of the Senate, and we will have won the day.'

'And what if Cato doesn't win over the Praetorians?' asked Macro. 'Even with the offer of a bribe?'

'Then we'll have to rely on the legionaries alone.'

Sulpicius winced. 'Even if that leads to conflict with the Guard?'

'Even so,' Narcissus intervened. 'Sometimes it is impossible to avoid bloodshed. The trick is to keep it to a minimum.'

He glanced round at the others to ensure that they had grasped the details of the situation. 'Then there's nothing more to be said tonight. We'll meet again as soon as Pastinus reaches the city. At which point we'll make our final preparations before acting. Clear?'

The others nodded or muttered their assent.

'Then farewell.'

While Narcissus reached for a bowl of olives, Domitia escorted her guests from the hall and arranged for some to depart by the rear entrance, and for all of them to leave intervals between venturing into the street. Senator Sempronius hesitated and hung back.

'Centurion, will you be staying here?'

'For the moment, sir. I need to talk with the prefect.'

'Very well. I'll let the nurse know.'

Macro nodded his thanks. He stared after the small group of plotters as they left the hall, and then shook his head. 'That lot don't inspire much confidence.'

'They're good people,' said Narcissus. 'They believe in the cause and they'll give their all to ensure its success.'

Cato looked at him and sniffed. 'Good people? And since when did you associate with good people and honourable causes?'

Narcissus affected a hurt expression. 'I have always done what is good for Rome. At times that entails shifting my allegiance from one faction to another. That is the reality of politics.'

'That is the reality of looking after number one, you mean. I suspect your alleged change of heart has rather more to do with you recognising that you were losing influence at the palace and needed to find a way to restore your position. When – if – Britannicus becomes emperor, you will resume your post as imperial secretary, right?'

'The young emperor will require the advice of experienced heads. If I am chosen, I will be honoured to serve.'

'I bet.'

'In any case, Cato, you aren't serving the cause out of fine principle. You are doing it to save your son's neck. So let's not question each other's motives. If I restore myself to favour and make more money, and you save your son and return to the army, and Rome becomes a republic again, then we all win. And what's so wrong with that?'

'What's wrong with it?' Macro interrupted. 'The bit where you get to live through it. That's what. You should have stayed dead.'

'And then who would have been around to oversee the efforts of those plotters you just said you had so little confidence in? The fact is that we are indispensable, all three of us. I am the brains and you two are the limbs. We need each other. Especially if Cato is to see his son again. If you don't want to fight for the cause, then fight for that.'

'The cause?' Macro snorted. 'You're just a bunch of mangy jackals scrapping it out in a soiled old sack.'

Narcissus's eyebrows rose a fraction. 'Clearly I misjudged you, Centurion. You have an almost poetic turn of phrase at times.'

'Better men than you have misjudged me.'

'That's quite enough, Macro,' Cato cut in. 'This bickering serves no purpose. And he is right. The cause is irrelevant. We're doing this for the sake of our own skins. It might stick in your throat as much as it does in mine, but there's nothing else we can do. Not without proving me innocent. And we can't do that unless we find Priscus.'

Macro sucked his teeth. 'And that ain't going to be easy. I did find out something about him.'

Cato leaned forward eagerly. 'Oh?'

'He's a soldier, like you thought. Only he's been absent without leave for over a month and there's been no report of his whereabouts. You're the only one to have seen him since then. That's where the trail ends for now.'

Cato's shoulders slumped in despair. 'Shit . . .'

The three of them sat in silence until Domitia returned and resumed her place on the hosts' couch. 'Do you need food, Macro? I can send for some.'

'No, thank you.'

There was another silence before Domitia shot an enquiring look at Narcissus and the freedman nodded slightly. She shuffled round to face Cato. 'There's something you need to know. I haven't been able to tell you before now. Not without putting our cause at risk. But since you are one of us now, I can speak.'

Cato's brow creased. 'What is it?'

'It concerns your late wife.'

Cato's frown deepened. The wounds inflicted by Julia's betrayal and loss were still far from healed.

'She was one of us,' Domitia continued. 'Like her father. In fact, it was through her that we recruited the senator.'

'When was this?' Cato demanded.

'While you were campaigning in Britannia. When she was expecting your child. I visited her at your home on a few occasions and we got to talking about who would succeed Claudius. One topic led to another over the days that followed, and she agreed to talk to her father because we needed all the support in the Senate that we could muster.'

'You recruited her deliberately then. You used her to get to Sempronius.'

Domitia nodded. 'I can assure you, Julia did not need much convincing in order to be won over. And she said that if you had been in Rome at the time, you would have willingly joined her.'

'I am not so sure about that.'

'No? But she was. She said you were a man of principle. That you would have done what was right for Rome. It was because of her conviction about you that she freely contributed to our war chest. Very freely.'

Cato sucked in a breath. 'Are you saying that the debts she left me with are due to her supporting your conspiracy?'

'Yes. And there's more. Julia needed a cover story. A reason to be seen in the company of one of the other members of our cause. A young tribune.'

Cato felt his stomach knot with bitterness as he grasped what she was saying. 'Cristus? So they became lovers because of your plot?' He felt his pulse quicken with anger. 'And you have the audacity to involve me even now? Have I not paid enough already? Have I not paid nearly all that I have?'

'Not quite all. There is still Lucius. If we succeed, he lives. If we fail, then yes, you lose all, including your life. But there's more you need to know. Julia and Cristus were never lovers.'

'But I saw their letters. I found them under Julia's bed.'

'They were written at my prompting. Julia needed to prove her cover story. We feared there might be an informer in Sempronius's household, and that there was a chance that Pallas might have his spies search your home. The letters were meant to be found. But not by you, Cato. And when you did discover them, what could we say without betraying ourselves?' She reached over and took his hand gently. 'I am so very sorry . . .'

He withdrew his hand sharply, his jaw clenched tightly as he glared at her.

'By the gods,' Macro said softly. 'Is there nothing you people will not do? Bastards, the lot of you.'

Cato closed his eyes and bowed his head, steeling himself to take control of the thoughts and raw emotions swirling through his head. He felt giddy with it all. At length he spoke.

'Are you saying she was not unfaithful to me? That I have endured a lie for the last year? That you broke my heart and let me suffer all that time, believing that the woman I loved as much as life itself had betrayed me?'

'We had to, Cato. Surely you can see that?' Domitia folded her hands. 'I'd have given anything to be free to tell you the truth, but I could not risk exposing our cause, and risking the lives of so many. What could I do? What would you have done, in my place?'

He was too appalled to reply. He was racked by guilt over the bitterness he had directed at Julia, and rage at the deceit that had been practised on him by Domitia and Narcissus. Why could she not have found a way to tell him? Why had she not left a message for him to explain it all? The giddiness began to give way to nausea, and he feared he might be sick. He swallowed hard, and opened his eyes.

'I should kill you both, right now. You deserve no less.'

Macro nodded, and began to draw his sword.

'And how would that help Lucius?' Narcissus asked. 'Julia is gone, but he still lives, and he needs you, Cato. Your only chance to save him is to work with us. You know it is true.'

Cato clenched his fists and let out a pained groan.

Macro's blade rasped free and he aimed the point directly at Narcissus. 'Let's kill this greasy little fucker and get out of here. We'll find the boy by ourselves. Whatever it takes. I swear it.'

'How will you find him, exactly?' asked Domitia. 'You have no idea where he is being kept. Cato is a wanted man, and Pallas will not rest until he is captured, forced to confess and executed. And do you imagine that once that has happened, Pallas will show the boy any mercy? Lucius would follow you into the afterlife as surely as night follows day. His only hope is that you work with us to overthrow Nero and Pallas.'

Macro's sword barely wavered as he growled, 'Just give the word, lad.'

Cato was silent, then he slammed his fist down on the couch. 'They are right, damn them to the darkest pits of Hades! Sheath your blade, Macro.'

'What?'

'Do it. Now. For the sake of our friendship.'

Macro hesitated a moment, and then angrily lowered his sword and returned it to its scabbard with a sharp metallic rasp.

Cato stabbed a finger at Narcissus. 'I will help you. I will do as you ask. And after I have found Lucius, there will be a reckoning.'

Narcissus licked his lips. 'If you say so. But you'd do well to remember who your new friends are, and what it will be in their power to do, for you as much as anyone else who furthers our cause. By the same token, they will show no mercy to anyone who poses a threat. It would be a good idea not to forget that.'

'There's no need for such talk,' Domitia intervened. 'Whatever happened before, we are on the same side now. The hour is late. I'll have quarters prepared for you, Macro.'

'We're not staying here,' said Cato. 'We'll go back to Sempronius's house.'

Domitia frowned. 'That's not safe.'

'Maybe, but I will not stay under the same roof as him.' Cato nodded in the direction of Narcissus. 'It would be in the interests of his safety that Macro and I leave now.'

Domitia and Narcissus exchanged a look before the latter gave a barely perceptible nod.

'Very well. But stay inside, Cato. Keep out of sight. And you, Macro, go about your duties as normal, until you receive further notice. We'll send for you both when the time to strike has come. Be careful when you return to Sempronius's house, in case the other side are still watching it. I suggest you take a haunch of meat from the kitchen and pass yourselves off as delivery men.' She stood up and gestured towards the rear of her husband's house. 'Go.'

Cato rose from the couch and together with his friend strode out of the loom of the lights and into the corridor. Neither looked back and neither spoke again until they were in the street, some distance from the house of the conspirators.

CHAPTER TWENTY-SEVEN

Cato looked up as Sempronius entered the small private dining room. There was no one else in the guest wing of the senator's house; it had been closed off for repairs to the roof, and the household slaves had been given strict orders not to enter to avoid the danger from falling tiles. The only exception was Petronella, who surreptitiously brought Cato food and drink when the other slaves were hard at work with their morning duties. It was dusk outside. Six days had passed since the meeting of the plotters, and aside from Macro's nightly visits, once he had returned from barracks, Cato had seen no one else. His patience had been sorely tested by the enforced isolation. His thoughts were consumed by anxiety for his son, and it took the greatest effort to force himself to think about other matters.

'Any news?' he demanded tersely.

Sempronius eased himself down on to a stool and nodded. 'The Sixth Legion is a day's march from Rome. It will camp outside the city by nightfall tomorrow. So we go into action the following morning. Everything is in place.' He looked at Cato and smiled wearily. 'All our plans come to fruition. Two days from now we'll have a new emperor, and begin the journey that will return Rome to being a republic.'

'We have to get through *that* day first,' Cato responded. 'And as you know well enough, given your military service, the plan is always the first casualty.'

'Which is why we have covered every contingency that we can think of.'

'It's the ones you don't think of that will kill you. There's no such thing as a foolproof plan. There is always a risk.'

'That may be so, but if it's the certainty of living under a despot against the risk of restoring the Republic, then the risk is worth it.'

Cato regarded him for a moment before he spoke again. 'Is that what Julia believed?'

'Julia?' Sempronius looked up and met Cato's gaze directly. 'Yes, that's what she believed, and what she convinced me to believe as well. If you had been here, maybe you too would have shared her convictions.'

'Maybe. But I wasn't. I was fighting for Rome in Britannia. All the time believing that I had a wife waiting to welcome me back to our home. Instead I came back and was led to believe that she was a faithless adulterer who had squandered what small fortune I ever had, and left me and our son to fend for ourselves. At no point did you tell me the truth.'

'I couldn't. I was sworn to secrecy. Just as my daughter was.'

'You could have given me something to cling on to. Some indication that she was not what she seemed. Something to save me the agony I endured.'

'I wanted to. I couldn't. For that I apologise with all my heart, Cato. You are as a son to me.'

Cato laughed bitterly. 'What kind of parent lies to their son?

What kind of parent denies the truth and causes the most unbearable pain and despair as a result?'

Sempronius thought a moment and then shook his head. 'I did what I thought was right.'

'The threadbare excuse trotted out by all those who have long abandoned integrity. You are no better than Narcissus, and you are certainly no father to me, Sempronius.'

'Cato, I beg you. Try to see this from my point of view. For Julia's sake.'

'Don't speak her name to me again!' Cato shouted. 'Not ever. Not if you value your life.'

'As you wish. All that matters now is preparing ourselves to act. We meet tomorrow, here in my house, to discuss the final arrangements. Be ready.'

Footsteps sounded in the corridor outside, and a moment later Macro entered the room, carrying a tray. He exchanged a cursory nod with the senator before the latter muttered a farewell and left.

'My girl's prepared you something to eat.' Macro set the tray down beside Cato's couch and took the stool Sempronius had vacated. He sat down heavily with a tired sigh.

'Busy day?' asked Cato as he lifted the plate and sniffed the warm odour of a cheese and onion tart.

'Burrus has had the Guard drilling hard the last two days. Every man that can be spared. Not just marching, but combat exercises, including street actions.'

Cato was about to take the first bite, but paused. 'Do you think Pallas has got wind of the plot?'

'Can't say. The word at headquarters is that this is an attempt to keep the boys busy so that they stop grousing about the delay in paying the bonus. The tensions over that are getting beyond a joke, I can tell you. It's almost like there are two Praetorian Guard corps right now, at each other's throats all the time.'

'Hmm. Well, that division may play into our hands. In any case, the moment they get a sniff of the bonus that Narcissus has been arranging for them, they'll come over to our side, meek as lambs.'

'I hope so, lad.'

Cato took a bite, chewed quickly and swallowed. 'I have my doubts over all this too, brother. But if there's any chance of saving Lucius . . .'

'Quite so. I'm with you all the way on that. We'll find him, Cato.'

The following evening, the conspirators reported their preparations. Sempronius read through the draft of his motion to be put before the Senate at the opening of business, to coincide with Cato's appearance at the Praetorian Camp. Narcissus and a party of Domitia's armed retainers would escort the bullion carts to the camp once Cato had won over the Praetorians, or at least enough of them to subdue the rest. While Sulpicius and the other senators supported Sempronius, Domitia would ride out to join Legate Pastinus as he led the men of the Sixth Legion into Rome and marched on the imperial palace.

Sempronius finished reading and rolled the scroll up.

'It's a bit wordy for my taste,' said Sulpicius.

'It's supposed to be. We need to buy time to let our opponents show their colours, and to ensure that the vote is taken after news of Nero's fall reaches the Senate. When the place is surrounded by armed men, they'll vote to save their necks, and the change of regime will have been endorsed by the Senate in the name of the people of Rome. That'll give us a veneer of legitimacy to use as the new regime takes control.'

'Fair enough.' Sulpicius nodded.

Narcissus rose to his feet. 'That concludes matters. We all know the parts we have to play when the morrow comes. Our spies are keeping watch on the emperor and his advisers; if there is any change of location at the last moment, I will be informed and we'll act accordingly. So it only remains to pray that the gods bless us with good fortune. I can see no reason why they wouldn't. After all, we have sworn to return Rome to the glorious days of the Republic and eradicate the scourge of the emperors who have so dishonoured us.' He looked round and punched his bony fist into the air. 'For liberty!'

'For liberty!' the others echoed.

Macro leaned towards Cato. 'For liberty, my arse,' he muttered. 'More like for saving his scrawny neck.'

Cato glanced at his friend. 'For Lucius, then.'

Macro nodded. 'For Lucius.'

The group began to break up, making solemn farewells to each other, and Cato was reminded of soldiers on the eve of a desperate battle. And so it was. If their cause failed, their enemies would be no more merciful than the most barbaric of tribes he had fought. Narcissus and Domitia were the last to leave, a short interval apart, and then Sempronius approached the two soldiers and clasped them by the arm in turn.

'I have given orders for us to be roused an hour before dawn. But I don't expect any of us will be sleeping tonight.' He smiled wearily. 'I'll be in my study. There are a few letters I need to write to friends and distant family members, just in case. I'll bid you goodnight.' He paused. 'Whatever may have happened, and whatever you may think, Cato, I have regarded you as the son I never had. I hope one day you can forgive me.'

Cato made no reply at first, and then sighed. 'In time, maybe.'

'Then I will live in hope.'

The senator left the room and Macro cracked his knuckles. 'Aren't you being a bit hard on the old boy, given the circumstances?'

'I don't think so. The truth matters to me, brother. When he deceived me over Julia, he crossed a bridge he will never be able to return across. A lie is a lie, and now there can never be trust again.'

'Cato, I hate to break it to you, but right now we're living in a world of lies. Being honest in Rome is as likely to get you killed as walking naked through Subura wearing only a heavy purse. All we can do is make the best of all this back-stabbing, find Lucius and get the fuck out of Rome for good.'

His friend looked at him and chuckled. 'Sage advice indeed.'

Macro tapped his head. 'It's not all porridge in there, lad. Right, best we get whatever rest we can. I'll see you before dawn.'

Cato raised his eyebrows at his friend's sudden alacrity to part company, before realisation dawned. 'Have you made plans for Petronella?'

'Aye, I've got a place for her and the others on the Aventine. Couple of rooms above a butcher's shop on a nice quiet alley. They'll stay there until I send for them. And if I don't, then they'll wait until things quieten down before returning to the farm. Marius sent a message to a neighbour to look after the place until they return.'

'Have they gone already?'

'No. They leave the house same time as us.'

'I'd better let you join them. Make the most of the time you have left, my friend.'

'Oh, I intend to!' Macro slapped him on the shoulder and

turned to leave. He paused at the door and gave a last nod in farewell, then he was gone. Cato waited a while longer, savouring the quiet, and then drained his cup, picked up an oil lamp to light his way and returned to his room in the empty guest wing.

As he lay on his bed and folded his arms behind his head, he could not help finding the silence oppressive. The next day might well bring the joyous dawn of a new age for Rome, and restore Lucius to him. But for now, his sombre surroundings felt more like a tomb, and he was filled with foreboding. It was typical of his nature, and he wished that for once he could believe that fortune was on his side. She had served him well enough in his life so far, but he could not help fearing that he had long exhausted her benevolent attention.

'Promise me you'll take care of yourself,' said Petronella as she stroked Macro's cheek. They were lying naked in his bed beneath a thick blanket to keep the chill of the night at bay. They had made love shortly before, and there was a clammy warmth between them that made Macro feel strangely comforted. They had an intimacy he had not experienced before, and he found that he rather liked it. Sure, he'd had sex with many women, mostly whores. But this was different. Better even than the rough and tumble he had once enjoyed during his brief relationship with that Iceni woman, Boudicca. At times that had been more akin to a wrestling bout, and he spared a moment's pity for anyone that ever got on the wrong side of the fiery tribeswoman.

'What are you smiling at?' Petronella drew his face round towards hers. 'My love? What is it?'

'Oh, nothing. Just thinking how you make me feel.'

'And how do I make you feel?'

Macro kissed her and ran his hand down her spine, gently squeezing one of her buttocks. 'That answer your question?'

She pushed him back. 'I'm serious. I may never see you again. I need to know how you feel before we part. I need to know what this means to you.'

Macro felt awkward. He was not used to the kind of unsoldierly sentiment that was brewing in his heart. It was hard to find words he was comfortable uttering. 'You mean . . . everything to me. You're my girl. I don't want to be without you.' He cocked an eyebrow. 'Is that the sort of thing?'

Petronella let out a deep sigh. 'What are you like? That's as much as I can expect, I suppose. But I'm serious about what I said just now. You take care of yourself, Macro. If it looks like it's all going badly, then you cut and run. You get out of Rome and go to the farm and wait for me there.'

'Not as easy as that. There's Cato, and the boy.'

'If things don't go to plan, there's nothing either of you can do about Lucius. I hate to say it, but it's true. I'm very fond of the boy, but if you two get all heroic about it, then you'll just be killed, and he'll be killed too. As long as you and Cato are alive, there's hope for Lucius.'

'Fair enough. I'll be careful as I can be. Happy?'

'No. Now kiss me.'

Macro reached round and drew her close, his lips pressing against hers. Once again he reached down her back and this time she moved her hips against him and he felt the light brush of her groin against his thigh.

A loud crash sounded from the heart of Sempronius's house. They froze.

The sound came again. This time Macro pulled himself free and swung his legs out of the bed. 'There's trouble.'

'What's happening?'

'Don't know. Get your clothes on. Then find your sister and Marius and leave by the back gate, at once.'

'Macro . . .'

'Do as I say,' he snapped as he slipped his tunic on, grabbed his sword belt and made for the door. There was another sound, the splintering of wood, and now the first cries of alarm from the other people in the house. Petronella rose hurriedly and shuffled into her stola, joining him at the door to the room. Macro steered her in the direction of the slave quarters, where her sister was sleeping. 'Go!'

There was just time for a quick squeeze of her hand, then Macro ran towards the front of the house. Other figures emerged from nearby rooms, and when he reached the atrium, he saw Sempronius talking urgently with a man in a cloak. Three of the household slaves were heaving an upturned couch against the front door as axe blows thudded against the outside. Cato came running out of the corridor opposite, lit by the glow of the lamps burning in the atrium. He was fully dressed, still in his boots, with his sword hanging from its strap across his shoulder.

As Sempronius saw the two soldiers, he indicated the man beside him. 'Attalus has come straight from the palace. Got to us just ahead of the Praetorians.'

'What's happening?' Cato demanded.

Domitia's agent turned to them, eyes wide with alarm, chest heaving with the exertion of his race to reach the senator's house in time.

'We are betrayed! They know about the plot. They're coming for us!'

CHAPTER TWENTY-EIGHT

'Betrayed?' Macro grabbed a fistful of the spy's cloak. 'Who's betrayed us?'

'It doesn't matter,' Cato cut in. 'Later. Right now we've got more immediate problems. They're going to be through that door any moment.'

'What do we do?' asked Sempronius, wincing as a fresh blow sent a length of wood flying over the heads of the slaves into the atrium. The heavy iron bolt that secured the door was already beginning to give under the furious battering from the men outside.

Cato turned to Attalus. 'Do they know about the others?'

'I don't know. I was watching the main gate of the palace when I saw them come out of their watch-house. Pallas was with an officer, and I overheard the order to come and arrest the senator.'

'No one else?'

'Just the senator.'

'All right, then we have to get a warning to Domitia and Narcissus. Sempronius, send one of your men. Someone you can trust and who is swift on their feet.'

'Shouldn't we get out of here?'

'We have to buy the others some time, or all is lost. Macro, Attalus, on me!'

He led the way to the entrance and pointed to a large chest. 'There, let's get that up against the door. You men, keep the couch in place.'

The nearest slave nodded and crouched low, pressing his shoulder against the bottom of the couch as he and his companions strained to keep pressure on the door. Cato and his companions sheathed their weapons and dragged the chest away from the wall and over towards the door. All the while the axe blows continued, and more splinters flew over the heads of the slaves bracing themselves against the couch. The chest was almost in position to press forward when a large section of the damaged door gave way and an axe burst through the shattered timber, striking one of the slaves on the crown of his head. The skull gave way with a crunch, and blood and brains splashed over the men on either side. Instinctively they recoiled and the couch lurched back a few inches.

'Get him out of there!' Macro ordered, and as soon as the slaves had dragged their comrade into the atrium, the chest was shoved forward tightly against the couch. There was a large gap in the door now and the flickering light of torches outside was clearly visible, as well as the faces of the Praetorians and the glint of their weapons as they waited for the door to give way. The next blow caused the locking bolt to burst from the woodwork and clatter between the chest and the couch.

'Stand firm!' Cato grunted as he crouched low and pressed his shoulder against the chest. A moment later the door thudded against the couch and the three of them just managed to hold their ground.

'What are you bastards waiting for?' a voice barked from outside. 'Put your backs into it!'

The pressure increased, and Cato could hear the grunts as the Praetorians heaved at the wrecked timbers.

'We can't hold them,' Attalus growled through clenched teeth.

Cato nodded. 'One more heave, then we fight it out. Ready? On my command . . .'

His companions braced themselves.

'Heave!'

They thrust back with all their strength and won a few inches of ground as the chest grated over the flagstones. Then Cato yelled, 'Get back!'

He leapt away from the chest and swiftly drew his sword, his comrades following his lead as they prepared to defend the makeshift breastwork blocking the entrance. Cato glanced at the slaves cowering beside their mortally wounded companion.

'You two, grab what you can and help us.'

There were a couple of thick staves near the door, and they snatched them up and took their place alongside the other defenders. Sempronius pushed himself forward at Cato's side, sword in hand.

'I've sent a man to warn the others.'

'Good. We'll hold these bastards off as long as we can.'

The senator swallowed and readied his weapon. 'It's been a while since I was a soldier.'

'You know the drill then, sir,' said Macro. 'One battle's the same as another.'

'Hate to admit it, but this is the first time I have ever drawn a sword in anger.'

'Seriously? Shit . . .' Macro shook his head. 'Then watch where you swing that blade, eh?'

There was no time for the senator to respond as the Praetorians surged again, pushing the shattered doors aside and flooding the atrium with the flare of the torch flames and the leaping shadows of crested helmets and raised weapons. An optio pressed forward, sword raised to strike; Cato lifted his own blade to parry the blow and the first clash of steel echoed off the walls of the atrium. More soldiers forced their way through the splintered doors to engage the defenders. To Cato's right, the senator swung at the man next to the optio, and the very tip of his sword glanced off a helmet and forced his opponent to recoil.

'That's the spirit!' said Cato.

To his left, Attalus was sparring with a bulky guardsman, wielding his sword skilfully as he blocked a blow then slashed the Praetorian's forearm open with a deep cut. The man snarled in pain as he tried to force himself back, away from the couch, but his comrades were packed behind him and he was helpless as Attalus leaned forward and punched his sword deep into the soldier's shoulder. He twisted the blade, then tore it back and held it up in the guard position as he waited for his next opponent to step forward. Beyond him Macro stood his ground, exchanging sharp ringing blows with a wiry foe. The slaves were not yet in the fight and stood back uncertainly until Macro yelled at them.

'Get stuck in!'

The nearest grasped his stave and thrust it at the face of the man opposite Macro. The Praetorian swatted the blow aside with a contemptuous snarl and then slashed at the slave's knuckles, cutting through skin and bone. With a shrill cry of agony the slave dropped his stave and backed away, nursing his wounded hand.

'Take his place!' Macro ordered the other slave. But the man shook his head and retreated a pace before throwing his stave down and turning to run towards the far side of the atrium, closely followed by his surviving companion.

Macro took advantage of the Praetorian's distraction and struck at him, stabbing into his chest. The point of the sword caught on his chain-mail vest, winding the man but not cutting through the metal rings. He staggered aside, clutching his breast, as one of his comrades pushed past him and engaged Macro.

The couch and chest continued to lurch inwards, forcing the defenders back, and Cato saw at once that the Praetorians would be able to edge round the barrier at any moment. He punched his sword forward; the point tore into the optio's cheek, cutting through to the bone below the eye, and he flinched back. The chest ground across the flagstones again and Cato saw one of the Praetorians working his way through the narrow gap between the upturned couch and the wall. Sempronius turned to deal with him, making a clumsy cut with his sword, and succeeding in striking hard with the edge into the angle between the man's shoulder and neck, cutting deeply. To the other side of Cato another Praetorian thrust at Attalus and caught him low in the chest, below the ribs, the swordpoint tearing through tunic and flesh and deep into his vitals.

'Fall back!' Cato called out. 'Sempronius! Look after Attalus. Make for the back gate. Go!'

Attalus staggered back as the senator disengaged and rushed to support him, and both men hurried across the atrium, blood staining the spy's tunic. Cato used the extra space he had been given to swing his sword in a wild arc, left and right, clattering off the weapons of the Praetorians in front of him.

'You now, Macro.'

'Fuck that, you go!' Macro sidestepped, shouldering his friend aside and letting out a roar as he hacked and slashed like an enraged barbarian, daring the Praetorians to close with him.

Cato staggered away, then recovered and, after the briefest of hesitations, followed the others, who had reached the entrance to the corridor leading off the atrium and were running through the house to the garden. Macro made a last wild slash and his eye caught the stand to one side where four oil lamps still burned. He leapt towards it and swung it down so that it fell across the chest. Oil spilled on to the couch, where several sword cuts had slashed the covering to expose the tightly packed horsehair stuffing within. A flame flowed across the oil and on to the couch and instantly set fire to the horsehair, and flames leapt as acrid smoke billowed across the doorway.

Macro backed away, spare arm raised against the glare of the flames. Seeing that he had bought himself a little time, he turned and followed the others. Cato had caught up with the senator and Attalus and supported the spy as Sempronius stopped and urged the other men down the corridor. 'Go!' A moment later Macro was at his side, turning to face the Praetorians who had been driven back by the flames.

'You too,' Sempronius ordered. 'Give Cato a hand. I'll keep them occupied.'

'Sir?'

'You heard me. Go, Centurion!' He thrust Macro after the others. There was too little time to think, and Macro just nodded a farewell and ran after the dim figures retreating ahead of him.

The senator stepped out of the corridor into the lurid glare of the flames and made his way round the atrium towards another corridor leading off into the guest wing. He paused by the alcove opening on to the small shrine of the household gods lined with the wax death masks of his ancestors and his wife, and there, directly above the modest altar, the pearly-white face of his daughter. Reaching out and stroking the firm wax curve of the cheek, he smiled sadly.

'Julia . . . I will see you soon, my child.' He looked round at the other death masks. 'And the rest of you.'

Then he moved on and stood at the entrance to the guest wing. The flames on the barrier flared as the Praetorians braved the heat to push it aside. They surged around the glare and began to spread out across the atrium. Sempronius took a step forward so that he would be seen more easily.

'Over there!'

One of the Praetorians had thrust an arm out towards him. Behind him stood the optio, a hand clasped to his cheek. He drew a deep breath and bellowed, 'You there! Drop your sword.'

Sempronius turned to call over his shoulder. 'Run for it, boys! I'll hold 'em back.'

Then he stiffened his back, raised his sword and tilted his head slightly as he faced the Praetorians with a contemptuous expression. 'You want my sword? Come and get it!'

'As you wish, you old fool,' the optio responded. 'Take him, lads.'

The Praetorians paced across the atrium and Sempronius lowered himself into a slight crouch as he retreated into the entrance of the corridor to protect his flanks. The first of the guardsmen cautiously advanced on him and raised his blade.

'Last chance, mate. Drop it.'

Sempronius clenched his jaw, and a slight smile formed on his lips as he shook his head.

The Praetorian feinted and the senator slashed wildly to block the blow, his sword cutting through the air as the soldier neatly disengaged and thrust at his body. He recoiled just in time to avoid the point and swept his sword back. The blades met with a loud clang, and sparks flew before each man recovered his weapon. The senator braced himself and then sprang forward.

'Death to tyrants!'

He swung his sword at the Praetorian's head. The soldier managed to sweep his sword arm up to deflect the blow, and as the senator lumbered on, he struck the older man on the side of the head with the pommel of his weapon. Sempronius staggered back, dazed and bleeding from a gash on his temple. The Praetorian contemptuously battered his blade aside and rested the point of his own sword in the notch just below the senator's throat.

'Drop it, you fool.'

Sempronius's breath came in rasps as he stared back for an instant and then made to swing his weapon. There was a soft explosion of air from his lips as the Praetorian drove the sword home, tearing through his windpipe and jarring against his spine. Sempronius's jaw sagged as he tried to speak a few last words of defiance, but he was already choking on his own blood and only managed a gurgle before he felt a warm gush from his lips.

The Praetorian recovered his sword and took a step back. Sempronius staggered away, dropping his blade and clasping his throat with both hands as the gore pulsed out in thick gouts, splattering down his tunic. He felt his legs tremble then collapse beneath him as he slumped down on to his knees. Already he was feeling light-headed, but he was aware of no pain, just a numbness in his throat, as if he had been punched hard rather than stabbed. Darkness folded in from the periphery of his vision, and the last thought that passed through his mind was a brief prayer that the gods might yet spare his comrades and let them see the downfall of Nero. Then he pitched forward on to his shoulder and his body convulsed, then finally relaxed in death as the blood pooled around his head.

CHAPTER TWENTY-NINE

They hurried out of the rear gate and down the street, supporting Attalus as they fled from the raid. Not a moment too soon, as the sound of boots pounding along a side alley alerted them to another squad of Praetorians moving round the house to cut off the defenders. They rushed into a narrow passage between two houses further down the street just before the soldiers came into view.

'Sloppy work,' Macro grunted as they continued along the dark way, damp with the sour smell of rotting vegetables. 'They should have covered the rear of the house first.'

'I guess they weren't expecting a fight,' Cato responded. 'Just a quick arrest.'

They turned into an alley leading away from the house and followed it for a safe distance up the hill before stopping to catch their breath.

'Which way do we go?' panted Cato as they leaned against the wall either side of Attalus. Domitia's agent was breathing in short, ragged pants as he clutched his hands to his stomach. They were several streets away from Sempronius's house and a faint orange bloom in the sky above the surrounding rooftops told of the fire that was burning there. They could hear the shouts in the distance as the Praetorians continued their search, and the muffled clang of a bell as one of the privately owned fire carts already rumbled towards the blaze, hoping to sell its services to the hapless owner of the property for a premium.

'We can't stay here for long,' Cato continued. 'We need shelter.'

'Vespasian's house?' Macro suggested.

'No. The Praetorians are between us and there. Besides, we don't know if it's safe. Pallas could have sent men to arrest them as well.'

'No . . .' Attalus said through gritted teeth. 'I overheard them. They were only after Sempronius.'

'We still can't risk it. Not with you wounded. We need to get you to a place where we can look at that. Need to stop the bleeding.'

Attalus nodded.

'Do you think Sempronius got out?' asked Cato.

Macro recalled the resolute expression on the senator's face as he had urged him to escape. 'I don't think so. He wanted to go down fighting.'

'Let's hope so. It would be better that they don't take him alive. It won't take Pallas long to beat the information out of him. Better that Sempronius is dead.'

'You're all heart, lad.'

Cato pushed himself away from the wall. 'We need to go.'

'All right, we're not too far from the place where I sent Petronella. We could try there. Except I'm not keen for us to attract any attention that might put her and the others at risk.'

They were interrupted by more shouting, closer now.

'Too bad,' Cato decided. 'We need to get off the streets as soon as possible. Let's move.'

With Macro navigating, they made their way up to the thoroughfare running from the ridge of the Esquiline Hill to the Aventine. They were obliged to duck out of sight a few times as they saw the approach of patrols from the urban cohorts, lighting their way by torches. And once they encountered a gang a footpads, several men who blocked their way until Cato and Macro drew their swords and dared them to bar their passage through the city. At length, just as the first glimmer of the coming dawn smeared the sky beyond the hills to the east, they reached the block of apartments where Macro had sent Petronella.

'This is the place,' he announced, breathing heavily from his efforts. 'We'll get you sorted out now, Attalus.'

The agent nodded his gratitude and the small party made their way up some steps to the entrance. It was a poor neighbourhood and most of the landlords weren't prepared to cover the cost of a doorkeeper. Which was just as Macro wanted it. No one to snoop on the comings and goings of Petronella and any visitors. They climbed the stairs to the apartment on the second storey and knocked lightly on the door. There was no immediate reply, and Macro tapped again and muttered, 'It's me. Macro.'

A moment later the bolt slid back and the door opened, and Petronella peered round the edge, lit by the glow of a lamp inside. The relief on her face quickly faded as she saw Cato and the wounded man. The door opened fully and they shuffled past her before she closed and bolted it behind them. The interior of the apartment was furnished with two bedrolls, a table and two benches. Lucilla and Marius were sitting on one of the bedrolls, huddled together, and watched anxiously as the two soldiers took off Attalus's cloak and lowered him on to the other.

'Who's this?' Petronella asked.

'He's one of ours,' Macro explained. 'And he's been wounded. Is there any water, spare cloth?'

She nodded and disappeared into the adjoining room, returning with a wicker basket and a pail.

'Good. Now get the lamp over here.'

She held the lamp over the bedroll while Macro and Cato crouched either side of Attalus. The agent's face was strained as he clenched his jaw. His tunic was saturated with blood, and Cato gently eased it up over his loincloth. By the pale glow of the lamp he took a rag and wiped away the blood to reveal a tear about four inches in length. Macro leaned forward and sniffed, then glanced up at Cato. 'Smell that?'

Cato lowered his head and inhaled through his nose. The odour of garlic and onion mingled with the sweet metallic smell of blood. 'Like a soup wound?'

Macro nodded.

Petronella nudged him with her knee. 'Soup wound?'

Macro turned his head away from Attalus to whisper his reply. 'Some of the German auxiliaries drink a stew laced with garlic before battle. Any wound in the guts that smells of the stew indicates that the stomach is pierced. That's usually fatal.'

'Charming.'

Cato saw that Attalus had closed his eyes and gave him a gentle shake until they flickered open again. 'We'll do what we can for now. First thing is to stop you bleeding out. This is going to hurt, so brace yourself.'

He took out his sword and cut the hood from Attalus's cloak, pressing it lightly into the wound and then folding it over as the agent's body tensed and he let out a keening groan.

'Hold that in place,' he told Macro, and cut a broad strip of cloth from the cloak to hold the makeshift dressing in place, tying it off tightly on the opposite side. When he was finished, Attalus slumped back and breathed deeply.

'Fuck . . . that hurt all right.'

'Told you it would. We've stemmed the flow of blood, but we'll need to get you to a physician to have the wound treated properly.'

Attalus nodded, and licked his lips. 'Could do with something to drink.'

Cato looked round and saw a shelf below the shuttered window. There were a couple of leather beakers and some wooden platters. He crossed the room for one of the cups and dipped it in the pail before offering it to the agent. Attalus shifted round so that his back was supported by the wall and reached for the cup. As he raised his arm, Cato glimpsed a mark near his shoulder. He took the lamp from Petronella, and as he moved it round slightly to illuminate the agent from the side, he froze, a sudden chill of recognition tightening the muscles of his neck. There in the glow of the lamp was a scorpion tattoo, just as he remembered it from the night of Granicus's murder. He felt his muscles tighten, as if he was about to go into battle, and slowly moved the lamp back and set it on the floor beside the bedroll.

Attalus drained the beaker and his arm dropped to his side as he smiled faintly. 'Needed that.'

'You also need to rest a moment,' Cato said evenly. 'Stay there and try to keep still. It'll help stop the bleeding.'

He eased himself up and stared at the agent, his mind reeling with the implications of what he had just seen. Attalus relaxed against the wall and closed his eyes. Cato took a deep breath and spoke to Macro without taking his gaze off the spy.

'Macro, a word. We need to decide what we're going to do. Over here, so we don't disturb him. Petronella, keep an eye on him for us, eh?'

She nodded as Cato gestured towards the other room and led Macro across to the doorway. They ducked under the low lintel and stood in the shadows, where Cato could still see the agent. He lowered his voice to a whisper as he addressed his friend.

'We're in trouble.'

'You think so?' Macro responded wryly. 'Sempronius's place raided, the senator dead, and who knows what else to upset our plans. Yes, I'd call that trouble.'

'It's worse than that. Far worse . . .' Cato was still grappling with the thoughts racing through his head. 'The name of our friend in there is not Attalus.'

'I don't suppose it is. Not with all this secret plotting and conspiracy.'

'It's Priscus.'

'Priscus?' Macro repeated, then his jaw dropped as his eyes widened. 'Him?'

Cato nodded. 'The scorpion tattoo, it's on his shoulder. I just saw it.'

'Shit . . .' Macro frowned. 'But if he's Priscus . . . what in Hades is he doing working for Domitia and Narcissus? He must be spying for Pallas.'

Cato shook his head. 'Why would he have warned us earlier? Why did he fight with us? He would never have put himself at such risk if he was working for Pallas. No, he's one of Narcissus's men, I'm sure of it. He has been all along . . .'

'But why kill Granicus? Why set you up to take the blame?'

Cato felt nausea welling up from the pit of his stomach. 'Jupiter, I can see it all now.'

'See what?'

'Their scheming. Macro, they've been playing us all along.'

'Who?'

'Narcissus and the others. They wanted us to join their plot, and when we refused, they feared that Pallas would put pressure on us to work for him. That's why they wanted me accused of killing Granicus. To make sure that I would not be able to serve Pallas. And when I was on the run, they knew I'd be grateful of the offer of shelter. Attalus didn't rescue me from the fire because Domitia had ordered him to watch out for me; the bastard most likely started it in the first place . . . They needed to drive me out into the open, and into their arms, and then manoeuvre me into serving their cause. And they have Lucius. That's the last piece of the puzzle. The bastards have Lucius, Macro. They've taken my son. To make sure I play my part when they seize power.'

Macro glanced over to Attalus, who had opened his eyes again and was gently rubbing his head. Petronella was patting his hand and murmuring to him soothingly. He felt his heart burn with rage at the thought of Priscus's friends turning up at the farm to abduct the young boy and threaten the woman he loved. Yes, he realised, he did love her. And that scheming bastard Narcissus was behind it all, as ever. His hand dropped to his sword and he took a half-step towards the other room as he growled, 'I'll cut the devious fucker's heart out.'

Cato took his arm firmly and held him back. 'No, wait. Let me think a moment.'

'What's there to think about?'

'Macro, we have a choice here. We can still see the plot through, and when it's over, Narcissus will find a way to return Lucius to me while keeping up the pretence that it was Pallas who took him. But I'm starting to wonder if we're on the wrong side.'

'After what we've just found out? I should bloody well think we're on the wrong side.'

'Granted, but there's a more pragmatic issue. Who is more likely to survive the next few days? Nero or Britannicus? It's clear that Pallas has already discovered that something is happening. If he moves swiftly, he can crush the plotters. If not, it could go either way. The question for us is which side do we serve if we want to survive? Which side is most likely to win out and let us save Lucius?'

Macro pondered this briefly. 'I don't suppose Narcissus is going to feel safe around us once he finds out we're in the know about Senator Granicus.'

'I don't suppose he is,' Cato agreed. 'Which doesn't leave us much choice, does it?'

'Not from where I'm standing . . .'

'Then we'd better act while we still can.'

Cato returned to the other room and prodded Priscus with his foot. 'Come on. Get up. We can't stay here, we have to go.'

Domitia's agent jerked into wakefulness and he winced as he sat up straight. 'Go? Go where?'

'You'll find out soon enough. On your feet!'

CHAPTER THIRTY

The sun had barely risen above the roofs of the city's loftiest temples and basilicas and only a few shops and stalls had opened for business. The usual throng of tradesmen were waiting by the gates of the service entrance to the imperial palace, their carts heaped with groceries for the kitchens, as well as haunches of meat and jars of wine, garum and oil, carefully packed in straw to prevent them cracking against each other as the cartwheels negotiated the cobbled streets. They would only be admitted when the chief steward of the household emerged to inspect their loads and admit those whose goods met his approval, or who were prepared to bribe him enough.

The gates were open and a squad of Praetorians stood across the entrance as they waited for the stewards to appear. Suddenly there was a small commotion, and a moment later three men emerged from the crowd and approached the gateway. The man in the middle was supported by the others, and it was clear from his ashen face and bloodstained tunic that he was badly injured.

'Halt!' the nearest sentry shouted, advancing his spear. 'What is your business here?'

The three men paused as the youngest of them replied, 'We

need to see Marcus Antonius Pallas, at once. Make way.'

The Praetorian stood his ground. 'And who the hell do you think you are, friend?'

'He's Prefect Cato, commander of the Second Cohort!' Macro barked. 'And I'm his senior centurion, and you'll stand to bloody attention when an officer addresses you!'

Force of habit and training got the better of the sentry and he snapped to attention and grounded his spear. Some of his comrades did the same; others, with more presence of mind, hesitated, and one called for their optio. A moment later a tall, well-built man strode out and placed his fists on his hips. 'What's this? Has the imperial palace suddenly become a hospital without anyone bloody well informing me? You three, on your way.'

The sentry gestured towards Macro. 'Says he's a Praetorian centurion, Optio. And the other one's Prefect Cato. They want to see the imperial secretary.'

'Bollocks to that.' The junior officer stepped forward with a haughty expression and then stopped dead and stared at Cato before exclaiming, 'Bugger me, it is the prefect. Sorry, sir . . . Hang on, you're a wanted man. For murder.'

'I'm innocent, and there'll be time to explain that later. But we need to see Pallas at once. Let us in.'

The optio frowned briefly and then nodded. 'Let 'em through, lads.'

His squad stood aside to admit Cato, Priscus and Macro, then the optio shouted an order to close the gate. Howls of protest rose from the assembled traders and he rounded on them and jabbed a finger. 'None of that, or the lot of you can just piss off. Now keep it down, and wait for the bloody steward.'

As soon as the gates were closed and bolted, he turned towards Cato and pointed to some benches beside the guardhouse. 'Wait there, sir. I'll send for the centurion in charge of today's watch.'

'No!' Cato snapped. 'I need to speak to Pallas right now. It's a matter of the greatest urgency.'

'Sir, with respect, you are wanted for murder. Now I'm sure the centurion will know what to do.'

Cato ground his teeth. There was no telling who was in on the plot and who wasn't. The centurion might be loyal to Narcissus. So might this optio. He dared not speak with anyone but Pallas.

'Look here, if you don't get Pallas at once, it may be too late. And if that's the case, heads will roll, and yours will be amongst the first. I won't tell you again, Optio. Send for Pallas.'

The optio thought briefly. 'Can't see any harm coming of it.' He turned to one of the sentries. 'Right, you, off to the imperial freedman's office and tell him I've got Prefect Cato here.'

The Praetorian saluted and hurried off. Not quickly enough for the optio's liking. 'Shake the fucking lead out!'

As the man broke into a run, the optio turned to Cato. 'Sit on the bench, please, sir. All three of you, and don't move. And I'll have your swords and any daggers, if you please.'

They handed over their weapons and eased Priscus down, then slumped either side of him. The agent's breathing was laboured and Cato felt for the pulse in his neck. It was weak and irregular and he gave Priscus's shoulder a gentle shake. 'You stay with us. Keep your eyes open.'

The agent nodded, blinked and looked round the yard. 'Where are we? This is the palace.'

'That's right.'

Priscus stirred anxiously. 'I thought you were taking me to get help for my wound.'

'Sure. There's none better than the physicians here. They'll see you right. Once we've had a little chat with Pallas first.'

The agent's expression became alarmed, and he went to sit up, then groaned in agony before leaning back, face strained with the effort of keeping the pain under control. 'Fucking traitor . . .'

Cato rounded on him. 'I'm no traitor. I didn't sign up for your cause; I was tricked into it. I know who you are, Priscus. I know you were ordered to murder Senator Granicus so I'd be blamed for it. I know you work for Narcissus. And you are going to confess all of that to Pallas when he gets here.'

Priscus smirked. 'I don't think so.'

'You'll do it, because you'll die in agony if you don't.'

'I'll die anyway. I ain't going to spill my guts to you or anyone else. Least of all that oily bastard Pallas.'

Macro nudged him. 'Spilling your guts may well come into it, if I'm any judge of Pallas and his methods. Just saying.'

'You don't scare me.'

'Not trying to scare you, big man. Just letting you know what you're in for.' Macro shrugged.

'You don't owe Narcissus anything,' Cato continued. 'I dare say he paid you well enough for your services. Now that you're here, he'll wash his hands of you.'

'Nice try, Prefect. However, I believe in the Republic. It's a cause I'm willing to die for, like all the others. And I'll not betray them, nor the cause.'

'Brave words. We'll see. Right now, I want you to answer one question. Where's my son?'

'I don't know.'

'Liar.' Cato reached down and pressed hard on the dressing over the wound, and Priscus gasped in torment until he eased up. 'Try again. Where is he?'

'I swear by Jupiter, Best and Greatest, I don't know where they're keeping him.'

'Then they do have him?'

'Yes. I was with the men who took him. We didn't harm him. Just took him to the lady, like we were told to.'

'Domitia?'

Priscus nodded. 'That's the last I saw of him.'

Cato stared into his eyes, looking for any sign of dishonesty, then glanced at Macro. 'What do you think? Is he telling the truth?'

'He'd better be. Or I'll pull his guts out with my bare hands and throttle him with them.'

Priscus swallowed and tried to recover his nerve as he spoke again. 'It's too late to stop them now. They'll come for Nero, Pallas and both of you. And your boy.'

Cato felt his anger flare up and he instinctively reached for his sword before recalling it had been taken from him.

'You'd kill my son, would you?'

'What does it matter? One more body in the foundations of the new republic. A small price to pay.'

Cato grabbed him by the neckline of his tunic and wrenched him closer so that their faces were no more than an inch apart. 'He's my son. There is no price I will not pay to make sure I find him. Understand? If the price of your republic is the life of my boy, then it means nothing to me. *You* mean nothing to me.' He thrust the man aside, then stood up and took a couple of steps away from the bench, not trusting himself not to harm him. The agent smiled grimly.

313

'If I mean nothing to you, then kill me now.'

'No chance.'

The optio approached them. 'Sir, back on the bench, please.'

Cato faced him with a dangerous expression and the optio raised a hand. 'Fair enough. Just don't cause any trouble.'

They were not kept waiting long before the Praetorian returned with Pallas. The imperial freedman could do little to conceal his surprise at discovering that the man who had eluded those scouring the city for him had now voluntarily handed himself in.

'So, Cato, here you are. And now we can bring you to justice and ensure that you pay the price for murdering Senator Granicus. Have you anything to say before I have you taken away and thrown in a cell? I imagine you must, since there is no other reasonable explanation for you being here that I can think of. Well?'

Cato quickly marshalled his thoughts. There was too little time for more detail than was absolutely necessary. He leaned close to Pallas and spoke softly so that they were not overheard. 'There is a plot to depose the emperor, and have him, his mother, you and the rest of his faction arrested, and no doubt murdered.'

'There's always a plot,' said Pallas. 'Which is why I have spies everywhere. I don't think you have anything to say that I don't already know.'

'Oh? Then you will know that there is a conspiracy to turn the Praetorian Guard against Nero, and that your enemies have raised a fortune to ensure that the Praetorians' loyalty is bought. You will also know that Legate Pastinus and the Sixth Legion will enter Rome to support the plotters . . . I assume that you are aware of all this, as well as whatever information you gleaned about Sempronius that caused you to raid his house in the night. Tell me, how far have you got in rounding up the rest of his co-conspirators?'

Pallas's expression darkened. 'I don't have their names yet. But I will, soon enough.'

'Not soon enough to save your neck. Unless you act immediately.'

Pallas narrowed his eyes and stared at Cato, then glanced at the two men sitting on the bench. 'I see you have Centurion Macro with you. He's never far from your side. I wonder if he was an accomplice to the murder of Granicus . . . I don't recognise the other fellow, but he doesn't look like he's long for this world.'

'He isn't. Which is why you need to speak to him. His name is Priscus. He is, or was until recently, a Praetorian. These days, he is spying for Narcissus.'

Pallas half laughed and half sneered. 'Seems like that reptile is determined to undermine me from beyond the grave. We won't see his like again.'

'Be careful what you wish for. Narcissus is alive.'

'Alive? Impossible. I saw his head for myself.'

'You saw *a* head, but not his. Narcissus duped you. He knew his days were numbered the moment Claudius named Nero his heir. So he planned to fake his death so that he could co-ordinate the plot to undermine the overthrow of the new emperor without worrying about you sticking the knife in his back. He is very much alive, I can assure you. I've seen him for myself.'

'Where?' Pallas demanded. 'I don't believe you.'

'You don't have to believe me.' Cato jerked his thumb at

Priscus. 'Believe him. He's Narcissus's man. He was ordered to murder Senator Granicus in such a way that I was blamed for it.'

Pallas considered this. 'You arrested Granicus and brought him to me. You expect me to believe that these plotters knew in advance which room he would be placed in when you reached the palace? That's a fetch.'

'Not really,' Cato countered. 'Not if they had one of their men working here in the palace, someone who knew Granicus was to be arrested. Someone who may even have informed you that he was a traitor so that you would issue the order for his arrest. It could all be arranged easily enough.'

'It could,' Pallas conceded. 'And I'll speak to the man involved soon enough. But there's a larger question here. Why? Why try to frame you?'

'Because I had already been approached by the conspirators and refused to help them. They weren't prepared to take the risk of me staying loyal to the emperor, so they set me up to ensure I could not oppose them when they make their move against Nero. They let me stay on the run just long enough that I would be desperate and accept their help when it was offered.'

Pallas folded his hands behind his back. 'If you knew about their plot before they set you up, then it was your duty to inform me. Why didn't you?'

'Because I am a soldier, not a schemer, and I wanted nothing to do with them, or you. It is my duty to defend Rome from its enemies, not its own people.'

'It is your duty to defend Rome and the emperor. That is the oath you swore. If any here in Rome plot against the emperor, then they are, by definition, your enemies. You do not get to choose, Prefect Cato, precisely because you are a

316

soldier. Your finely tuned sense of integrity may not save you when this plot is crushed.'

'*If* it is crushed,' Cato responded. 'Much as I'd like to spar with you all day, you need to act now. Have Priscus questioned before he bleeds out. Your enemies must already know of the raid on Sempronius's house. They may already be moving to pre-empt you.'

The imperial secretary nodded. 'I need to hear this from your spy, assuming that's what he is. For all I know, he may be someone set up to divert attention away from you. I'll find out soon enough. Optio!'

'Sir?'

'Have that wretch taken into the guardhouse. Wait . . . Have any of your men been trained as interrogators?'

'I was, sir. Back in the Tenth Legion. Pretty good at it, if I say so myself.'

'Then you're the man I need. Get him inside. The rest of you guard the prefect and the centurion.'

The optio leaned his staff against the side of the guardhouse and roughly pulled Priscus to his feet. The agent let out a pained groan as his arm was pinned behind his back and he was steered into the gloomy interior. Pallas followed him inside and closed the door. Cato sat down beside Macro with a deep sigh.

'Out of our hands now,' said Macro. 'Let's hope the optio is as good as he thinks he is.'

Cato leaned forward and rested his elbows on his knees. 'He'd better break Priscus quickly. There's no time to lose. Narcissus will already be making new plans, you can bet on it. And we need Pallas to crush the plotters as soon as possible if we're to have a chance of saving Lucius.'

'Why didn't you tell Pallas about that?'

'Because it's bad enough that Narcissus knows my weak spot. Best we find Lucius and get him out of Rome for good. I have no intention of letting Pallas take him hostage to force me to work for him when . . . if Narcissus and his friends are caught.'

Their exchange was interrupted by a cry of agony from inside the guardhouse. It rose in intensity for a moment before Priscus began to run out of breath and it died away, and then rose again, and again. Neither Cato nor Macro nor the Praetorians tasked with guarding them affected to notice the man's torment, and they all waited in silence, broken occasionally by Macro cracking his knuckles.

At length the door to the guardhouse opened and Pallas emerged, trying to rub a series of blood spots from the hem of his tunic. Cato stood up and confronted him. Over the imperial secretary's shoulder he could see Priscus writhing feebly in a pool of blood on the floor. The agent had been stripped of his tunic, his bandages removed and his wound reopened, along with fresh cuts to his flesh.

Cato forced his gaze back to Pallas. 'Well?'

'He bears out what you say. He doesn't know much more than you already told me. Small fry really. But he's given us enough names and locations to work with. I'll write the orders for the ringleaders to be rounded up, and then have the emperor sign the necessary death warrants. Best way to nip this in the bud is to cut the bud off completely.' Pallas paused and looked at Cato directly. 'You've done me, and your emperor, a great service, Prefect Cato. Rome needs such men.'

'Rome I'll serve willingly. You, never.'

'We shall see. Meanwhile, I'll call off the dogs. You are an innocent man, after all.'

'Of course he fucking is,' Macro intervened, standing at his friend's shoulder. 'Did you really think he'd be capable of cutting down an old man in cold blood?'

'Centurion, all of us are capable of such things. It merely requires the appropriate incentive to commit the prospect of any such deed to action. Now, time is of the essence, so—'

'Sir! Sir!'

All three looked round to see a clerk racing down the steps from the rear of the imperial palace.

'Thank the gods I've found you, sir!' the man panted as he drew up in front of the imperial secretary. 'Burrus is looking for you. He wants you in the audience chamber at once.'

'What's the matter?'

'There's a report from the sentries on the Flaminian Gate . . . They can see soldiers marching towards the city, sir. Thousands of 'em.'

Pallas looked to the north-east, towards the gate, as if he might see the approaching threat for himself. He frowned. 'Soldiers? What soldiers?'

'It's the Sixth Legion,' said Cato. 'They arrived early. And now they've been ordered to enter Rome. It seems that Narcissus has decided to make his move.'

CHAPTER THIRTY-ONE

The commander of the Praetorian Guard was already surrounded by officers and palace servants as he attempted to grasp precisely what was happening. He was listening to a fresh report from a breathless messenger from one of the urban cohorts as Pallas, Cato and Macro entered the audience chamber.

'. . . the entire legion, sir. I'm sure of it.'

'Any sign of Legate Pastinus? Or any word from him?'

'No, sir.'

'Then he may be being held by his men, or they could have killed him and the other senior officers. How close were they to the gate?' Burrus demanded.

'No more than three miles off when I was sent to report, sir.'

'They could reach the city within the hour. Very well, I want you to go straight to the Praetorian camp. Find the senior officer there and tell him to call a general assembly. The men are to be fully armed. They are to wait for me to join them, or to receive further orders. But mark me, they are not to answer to anyone else. They will do nothing unless I order it. Clear?'

'Yes, sir.'

'Then go. Stop for nothing.'

The soldier saluted and turned to run from the room. Burrus stared after him for a moment, his expression fraught, then he caught sight of Pallas and his two companions approaching.

'So, you've caught Cato. That's something at least. Best have him held somewhere until we can deal with him. Now is not the time . . . Is that blood on your tunic?'

Pallas glanced down and gave a nod before responding. 'It turns out that Cato did not murder Senator Granicus. But there is more you need to know. Far more. A quiet word with you—'

'Not now,' Burrus interrupted. 'We may have a mutiny to deal with.'

'Oh, it's far more serious than mere mutiny. This is treason, Burrus.' Pallas lowered his voice. 'We don't know who we can trust. So, a quiet word. At once.'

Burrus seemed to be about to dismiss the notion, then he glanced round the room and saw a number of officers and palace staff looking at them curiously. 'Very well.'

He turned and strode to the corner of the room, where a wide arched doorway led to a balustrade balcony that overlooked the heart of the city. As soon as he was certain they could not be overheard, he stabbed a finger into Pallas's chest. 'Out with it.'

The imperial secretary swiftly explained what Cato had told him and Priscus had confirmed. Burrus listened with an intense expression, and when Pallas had finished he nodded at Cato and Macro. 'And why should I believe them?'

Cato could no longer restrain himself. 'Because the Sixth Legion is marching on Rome to enter the city and seize the palace. They are acting under the orders of their legate, and

Pastinus is acting on the instructions of his fellow conspirators. They are probably already on their way to the Praetorian camp to bribe your men to abandon Nero and proclaim Britannicus emperor in his place. There is no time to question the evidence before your eyes. You must act, sir. At once. Before it is too late.'

'He's right,' Pallas added. 'They've stolen a march on us already. And if we lose the Praetorians, then it's all over. But first we must try and round up the ringleaders. Start with Senator Vespasian's house.'

There was a commotion from the audience chamber and Cato looked back through the arch to see a squad of German bodyguards forming up around the throne dais. When they were in position, a palace steward rapped his cane on the marble floor.

'His imperial majesty, the emperor!'

Four more of the fierce-looking bodyguards entered from a door at the side of the chamber, and then came Nero, wearing a purple tunic embroidered with elaborate designs in golden thread. At once those already in the chamber bowed low towards their ruler and Burrus and the others followed suit. Nero climbed the small flight of steps to the dais and sat down on the throne, resting his hands on the gilded lions that formed the armrests. As soon as he had settled, the soldiers and palace servants straightened up and looked to him in silence, waiting for his instructions.

'Where is Prefect Burrus?'

The commander of the Praetorians strode back into the chamber and stopped in front of the dais. Pallas beckoned to Cato and Macro and they followed him, hanging back a short distance from Burrus.

Nero leaned forward, a frown on his brow. 'I am told that there are legionaries approaching the city.'

'Yes, sire,' Burrus replied.

'Might I enquire why they are doing so?'

Burrus hesitated. 'I . . . I feared it may be a mutiny, sire. Now it seems the matter is more serious.'

'Serious? What could be more serious than a mutiny?'

Pallas advanced and stood half a step in front of Burrus. 'Treason, sire. It is my understanding that the legionaries and their commander are part of a plot to depose you and place Britannicus on the throne.'

Nero stared back, his jaw slackening slightly, and then he laughed and shook his head. 'Preposterous! No one would ever dream of such a thing. You must be drunk, Pallas. You and Burrus both.'

'No, sire,' Pallas responded firmly. 'The plot against you is very real, and it is already under way. The legionaries are merely one strand of the conspiracy against you. There are many senators and others here in Rome who are your enemies. Amongst them, I bitterly regret to say, your brother.'

Nero shook his head. 'Not Britannicus. He has all the ambition of a mouse. The very idea of the little bookworm taking up arms against me is laughable.'

'Then let's assume he is being manipulated by these plotters, sire. Either way, their sworn aim is to replace you with him. And they are in the process of doing that right now. I appreciate your surprise at this turn of events. And your shock at the betrayal of those who pretended to acclaim your accession to the throne, all the while plotting your downfall. But those are the facts.'

'Who says so?'

Pallas half turned to indicate Cato. 'Prefect Cato, sire.'

Nero shifted uneasily. 'The murderer of poor old Granicus? Why isn't he in a dungeon?'

'Because he came to me to reveal the plot.'

'And how did he come to know of it, might I ask?'

'Cato was caught up in the plot, sire. The conspirators murdered Granicus in order to force him to go into hiding, and then manoeuvred him into joining their cause. Once he discovered the truth, he came directly to the palace to warn me. Just in time to foil the plot, I hope. But we must move to crush the enemy immediately, sire. Even now, they are attempting to suborn the Praetorian Guard. Our enemies are also likely to appeal to the Senate to support them. By which time, they hope that Legate Pastinus and his men will have taken control of Rome, with the help of the Praetorians.'

Cato watched as the young emperor digested the information and then leaned back and rubbed his hands together anxiously. 'Then we . . . we must do something. What do you advise, Pallas?'

The imperial freedman responded at once, and Cato could not help being impressed by his instant assessment of the situation.

'Firstly, we must send orders to the men on duty at the city's gates. All of them must be sealed at once. We may be too late to prevent Pastinus forcing his way in through the Flaminian Gate, but at least we'll know where to concentrate the men who remain loyal to us. Second, we must arrest the known conspirators immediately. Third, we must take Britannicus into protective custody to keep him out of the clutches of the plotters until we can ascertain precisely how deeply he was involved in their treason . . . or not. Fourth, Prefect Burrus must return to the Praetorian Camp at once to take control of his men and prevent them deserting to the enemy. Fifth, you and Empress Agrippina need to remain here in the palace. Keep your German bodyguards close. They can be trusted. But be ready to flee the city at a moment's notice. If need be, go to Ostia and take a ship to Misenum. Lastly, you must give the order to clear the streets and tell people to remain in their homes until the plot is crushed.'

Nero listened attentively and then nodded. 'See to it. Issue the orders. But I will not flee. I refuse to leave Rome. I am the emperor, and I will not be cowed by a handful of traitors skulking in the shadows.'

'The boy's got more guts than I thought,' Macro whispered at Cato's side.

'Lot of good it'll do him if the plotters take Rome,' Cato replied, thin-lipped.

Pallas folded his hands. 'There's one other thing, sire. Narcissus.'

'What of him?'

'He's the brains behind the conspiracy.'

'Impossible! Narcissus is dead.'

'According to Prefect Cato, he is very much alive. He faked his death.'

'But I saw his head.'

'The head was that of a slave, purchased by Narcissus for precisely this purpose. The man closely resembled him, and several days of decay did the rest. We were fooled, sire.'

'Fooled . . .' Nero clenched his fist. 'I will make that wretched scoundrel die a thousand deaths next time.'

'Yes, sire. We can deal with that later. But now you must strike the first blows.'

'Yes. Of course. Proceed with all you said.'

Pallas was about to give the necessary orders when Nero spoke again. 'Burrus will stay here, with me.'

'Sire?'

'I need a good soldier at my side. Someone I can trust.'

'But, sire, Burrus must take control at the camp. He must leave at once.'

'If the enemy are already turning the Praetorians against me, then it is too late. We may be sending Burrus to his death. Better he stays here where he can do some good.'

'Burrus is a soldier. It is his duty to take risks.'

The commander of the Praetorian Guard puffed out his chest. 'If the emperor commands it, then my place is at his side, sword in hand, ready to defend him with my life.'

Pallas struggled to hide his anger. 'Your place is at the head of the Praetorians. We need to send someone there to take control, while we still have a chance.'

'Quite so,' Burrus agreed, then turned and pointed at Cato. 'Send him. We already know that Prefect Cato commands rather more respect in the ranks than I do. If anyone can rally them to support the emperor, it is him.'

'Are you mad?' Pallas retorted. 'They still think he is being hunted down for the murder of Senator Granicus.'

'Then send Centurion Macro with him. The men respect him almost as much, and if he vouches for Cato, they'll listen. If the emperor sends his personal standard as well, then who can doubt that Cato speaks in the name of Nero?'

'Very well.' Nero spoke up. 'Prefect Cato?'

Cato stepped forward, bewildered by the pace of events. 'Yes, sire.'

'You and the centurion will go to the camp at once. I will

send ten of my Germans with you to guard the standard. You
will win over the Praetorians and order them to crush the
traitors of the Sixth Legion, and anyone else who betrays me. Is
that understood?'

'Yes, sire. But . . .'

The emperor frowned and leaned forward. 'At once,
Prefect.'

'Yes, sire.'

Burrus glanced at the two officers. 'You'd better draw some
kit and get yourselves down to the main gate. I'll have the
standard and escort meet you there. May Fortuna march with
you, Cato. The fate of Rome rests on your shoulders.'

CHAPTER THIRTY-TWO

Macro lifted his right arm and Cato adjusted the buckle and shifted the back- and breastplates until he was satisfied the fitting was good. He himself was similarly equipped, with greaves, military boots and the plumed helmet of an officer besides, and their swords had been returned to them.

'For an individual charged with commanding the finest unit in the Roman army, our friend Burrus is remarkably lacking in spine,' said Macro. 'I've seen braver lawyers than that, and we all know what oily, lying weasels they are.'

'Quite.' Cato stepped back and patted Macro on the back. 'You're ready for the fight, brother.'

'True, but when I signed up, I rather expected to be fighting barbarians, not Romans.'

'We're soldiers. We don't get to choose our enemies.'

'It seems like they get to choose themselves.'

Cato laughed. 'An interesting perspective. As it happens, I'm grateful we won't have Burrus interfering. You saw what he's like. This will require a lot of front, and our friend the prefect lacks the bottom for it, if you'll pardon the mixed metaphors.'

'The what?'

'Never mind.' Cato glanced round the columned entrance to the palace. There was no sign yet of the imperial standard or its escort. 'Where in bloody Hades are they?'

'Running on palace time, I imagine. Bunch of slackers. That's what life in Rome does for a man: sucks the soldier out of him and leaves only the neat uniform and polished armour behind. This lot wouldn't last an hour in battle against a decent legion.'

'We may have to put that to the test very soon.'

The crunch of boots on flagstones announced the arrival of the men they were waiting for. There were twenty of the Germans, big men armed with long swords and axes in the fashion of their people. Even though they had been serving in Rome for many years and could speak Latin fluently enough, they looked like the barbarians they were – long-haired, bearded and wearing patterned tunics and leggings. Their appearance was intended to intimidate the city's inhabitants, and with no ties to political factions, and generous reward, their loyalty to their paymaster was absolute. Good men to have at your side in the circumstances, Cato mused. With them came a Praetorian bearing Nero's personal standard.

'Oh, the shame of it,' said Macro. 'Here's me, ten years on the Rhenus frontier fighting Germans, and now I have to march with these dogs. Still, needs must.'

The optio in charge of the Germans saluted Cato and addressed him in thickly accented Latin. 'Prefect Cato?'

He nodded.

'My orders are to act under your command, sir.'

'Very good, then hear me.' He raised his voice. 'Stay closed up, and do not draw your swords, or strike, unless I say. If Fortuna smiles on us, there will be no need to shed blood. But if we are opposed, then let no man stand in our way. Cut them down. Is that understood?'

The Germans let out a deep-throated roar and shook their shields. Those carrying axes rapped the heads against the shield trims and the din echoed off the walls either side of the palace gate. Cato gave his chin strap a final tug to ensure the helmet sat firmly on his head, and then called out to the section guarding the gate.

'Open!'

The men heaved the heavy timber locking bar into its receiver and then drew the gates inwards to reveal the Clivus Palatinus sloping down towards the Temple of Venus and Rome at the east end of the Forum. Macro fell in alongside Cato as the latter raised his arm and swept it forward, and the small column broke into a gentle trot as they passed out of the gate and down the ramp into the heart of the city. The civilians ahead of them turned towards the tramp of boots and jingle of equipment and quickly moved aside to let them by. Cato was aware of a few curious expressions, but there were no cries of support at the sight of the emperor's standard, nor any insults hurled from a safe distance. It seemed that the people of Rome sensed the precariousness of Nero's short reign and were waiting to see if he survived or went the way of the similarly youthful Caligula.

They reached the bottom of the ramp and tramped over the open ground between the columned facades of the Temple of Venus and Rome and the Temple of Peace. Cato spared himself a small, cynical smile as he reflected that he had rarely known any peace at all since he had joined the army. Nor had Rome, and now she faced the peril of civil strife yet again. Clearly the spirit of peace was a fragile creature who rarely deigned to put in an appearance.

By the time he and his men turned on to the street leading up the Viminal Hill towards the Praetorian camp, the chill of the morning had been worn off by the exertion of jogging in full armour. Cato's breathing began to labour and he felt the first slight burn in his thigh muscles, but he forced himself to keep the pace steady, concentrating on what he must do when they reached the camp. It would be up to him to speak to the Praetorians and appeal to them to remain loyal to their emperor. It was a daunting task. Cato was no politician raised by expensive tutors and teachers of rhetorical technique and tricks designed to win the hearts, and occasionally the minds, of his audience. He could only speak to them in the blunt language of a fellow soldier and pray that they would respect his record and his rank enough to give him a fair hearing. Otherwise, his reprieve from the inevitable death sentence for the murder of Granicus was likely to be of very short duration.

It was just over a mile from the palace to the camp, and soon Cato could see the towers of the south wall, further down the road. He was sweating freely and his heart pounded inside his chest as he forced himself on. Twenty paces ahead was a crossroads with a public fountain at the centre where a handful of civilians had gathered to sit and gossip. A litter emerged from the side street and turned towards the camp. A small escort of men followed the litter, and there was no mistaking the hidden weapons bulging under their cloaks. Then came a covered cart. Such a vehicle was not an unusual sight, even though it was illegal for wheeled traffic to be on the streets of the city in daylight. However, the rule was rarely observed when the guilty party had the muscle to beat down any who objected to its breach. More armed men came after the cart and Cato began to slow his pace as he stared at them, realisation flooding into his mind.

'What's up?' Macro panted at his side.

'That's them, the plotters, ahead of us.'

Macro squinted as he took in the details of the litter, the cart and the men escorting them. 'You sure?'

'As sure as I can be.'

'What'll you do?'

There was no doubt in Cato's mind. 'Take 'em down, now. The bullion's in the cart. We can't let them get to the Praetorians.'

Cato drew his sword and Macro followed suit as they swiftly began to catch up with the rear of the group moving on past the junction. The streets were filled with the usual cacophony of street hawkers, market criers, women shrieking at children and men shouting at the women to quit shrieking, as well as the clatter of metalworkers and the hammers of tradesmen. All of which covered up the sound of Cato and his men coming up behind the plotters. At the rear of the group, one man paused by the fountain to reach down and scoop up water to splash over his face. He shook his head from side to side, spraying droplets, and then froze as he caught sight of the imperial standard weaving from side to side above the soldiers bearing down on him. He turned to shout a quick warning to his comrades before sweeping aside his cape and drawing a sword. Ahead, the rest of the men escorting the litter and the cart turned back and formed up across the street. They moved quickly and had the poise of experienced soldiers, Cato saw. Army veterans, then. Behind them the litter stopped and was set down, and a man stepped out and climbed some steps beside the street for a better view.

'Narcissus,' Macro grunted. 'Cato, d'you see?'

'I see him.' Cato turned his head to shout an order. 'Close up on me!'

He slowed his pace to allow the leading Germans to catch up with him and Macro and form a front across the width of the street as they rapidly closed the distance to Narcissus's escort, all of whom had drawn their swords. Some brandished iron-studded clubs in their spare hands as they braced themselves for the fight. Macro was to his right, and two Germans on either flank, shields to the front and swords raised as they bared their teeth.

'In the name of the emperor,' Cato shouted, 'drop your weapons and stand aside.'

'Fucking make us!' one of the veterans jeered.

Those in the square realised the danger and were already running for cover, grabbing their children and abandoning baskets. The hawkers snatched up what they could and ran out of the path of the German bodyguards as they pounded across the open space. In the last ten paces the optio bellowed his war cry and his men roared in response, mouths gaping amid the flow of their beards as they charged.

The impetus was with the Germans as they punched their shields into their opponents, battering their limbs and driving them back. Cato and Macro had no shields and just had time to parry aside the blades waiting for them before they crashed into the men beyond, thrust forward by the Germans coming up behind them. Cato tripped and pitched forward and would have fallen had the press not been so compact. He managed to plant his boots securely and heave forward, squeezed on all sides. No more than inches from his face, one of Narcissus's escorts wrestled his left arm free and began to raise his club.

Cato saw the danger and tried to recoil, then realised that would only give his opponent a greater space to swing his club. He held his nerve, and the moment the club began to fall he threw himself forward, smashing the peak of his helmet into the man's forehead. At almost the same instant he felt the shaft of the club harmlessly strike the armour on his shoulder.

'Bastard . . .' the man grunted, as blood welled up from a gouge in the skin below his fringe. Cato jerked his head back and slammed it forward again, angled this time so that he crushed the man's nose. To his side, Macro had managed to get the point of his sword into his foe's guts and was pushing it home, twisting the blade savagely from side to side as he did so. His victim could do nothing but gasp and groan, his head hunching forward. The Germans were pressing into their shields and steadily gaining ground as the air filled with the strained breathing of the men of both sides.

Cato shoved hard, then craned his neck and saw that the rear of the cart was only a short distance beyond the maul. Narcissus was still watching from his step, his expression anxious. Now he turned to the men still standing beside the empty litter.

'Get that out of the way! Let the cart past. Do it!'

The slaves bent down, took hold of the litter, then straightened up, carrying it ahead and then into the opening of a courtyard. The cart driver cracked his short cane on the rumps of the mules and the cart lurched forward, picking up speed as it went.

Narcissus looked back along the street and his gaze met Cato's; immediately he thrust an arm out and shouted, 'Kill the officers! They mustn't get to the camp! Kill them!' Then he scrambled down into the road and hurried after the cart. There was a turning to the right a short distance beyond, and he desperately pointed it out to the cart driver, who hurried to snatch up the halter of the leading beast and steer it round the corner and out of sight.

Meanwhile, the leader of the veterans urged his men on before shouldering his way into the packed bodies of his comrades as he made for the crested helmets of the two officers at the head of the German mercenaries. Cato saw him coming, sword held high, ready to strike, but there was little he could do to avoid the approaching threat. Directly in front of him, the face of the man he had head-butted was now covered in blood, dripping from his brow on to his cheek as he tried once again to swing his club. This time it connected with the top of Cato's helmet with a ringing noise, and his teeth snapped shut under the impact. There was little time to act, but Cato managed to raise his left hand and squeeze it up between their bodies. Bracing himself, he spread his fingers and thrust the man back as hard as he could. At the same time he managed to free his sword arm enough to turn the blade towards his foe and stab upwards at an acute angle, feeling the cloth and flesh resist briefly before the point tore through and into the man's guts. It was not a deep wound, or even disabling, but the man's expression turned to panic and he tried desperately to work himself free. As Cato pressed his advantage, punching the blade home, he caught a flicker of polished steel and glanced up just as the veterans' leader swung at his head.

'Down, lad!' Macro bellowed, grabbing Cato's shoulder and pulling him to the side. The blade swished through his crest and cut deep into the head of the German fighting beside him. The man's skull gave way with a soft crack, and blood, gristle, bone and brains sprayed over Cato's shoulder and arm as the German slumped and slid down between the men surrounding him. One of his comrades roughly pulled him back, away from the fight, as another German surged into the gap and slammed his shield into the nearest of the veterans. Cato nodded his thanks to Macro, then rose warily to his feet.

He saw the enemy's leader clearly now, one rank back, raising his sword to strike again. Cato tore the point of his own sword out of the stomach of the man in front of him and thrust him back with his left hand as he raised the weapon to head height, blade parallel with the ground, and thrust over the man's shoulder into the face of the leader, smashing through his teeth, through his mouth and out the back of his neck. The veteran's eyes rolled down as he attempted to focus on the flat of the blade just below his nose. Then he spasmed before his legs collapsed beneath him and he slumped down, dragging Cato's sword with him.

'Porcinus is down!' a voice cried out from towards the rear. 'Run for it, lads!'

'Run!' Macro bellowed, taking up the cry.

A fresh series of war cries from the Germans added to the din, and the veterans fell back nervously, those at the rear turning to flee, following the cart. Without them there to defend their comrades still skirmishing with the Germans, there was no way to hold back the advance. The last of them fell under a savage axe blow and the rout was complete.

Cato stepped over a body to retrieve his sword from the mouth of the enemy leader, bracing the sole of his boot on the man's forehead before he worked the blade free. Macro stood by him, breathing heavily, as the Germans swept past on both sides to pursue Narcissus's henchmen. The standard bearer came up, and Cato gestured for him to remain at their shoulder as he and Macro hurried to the corner of the street and looked down a gently sloping thoroughfare.

The cart was already nearly a hundred paces away, trundling over the cobbles, the driver trying to control his mules as people ran from their path, crying out in panic. Narcissus was sitting on the driver's bench, holding on tightly. He stared back at the two officers for a moment before turning away. The veterans straggled behind the cart, running for their lives as the Germans pursued them with bloodthirsty whoops of triumph.

'The cart!' Macro thrust his arm out. 'We have to take that. And that bastard Narcissus.'

He made to start down the hill, but Cato held out his arm to stop him. 'No. We're almost at the camp. We need to deal with the Praetorians first. The silver can wait.' He was gasping and had to take a deep breath before he called out: 'Optio! Optio, recall your men!'

The Germans' officer was near the front of his men, whirling his sword overhead and bellowing encouragement to his comrades as they swept down the street, butchering any of the veterans too slow to escape them. Cato cupped a hand to his mouth and called out again, but the optio was too far gone to hear him.

'And that,' Macro panted, 'is why those hairy-arsed bastards don't get to serve in the legions. Fine in a skirmish. A liability in a battle.'

There was no point in chasing after them and trying to restore discipline, Cato realised. It was too late for that. By the time their bloodlust had been sated, the Germans would be halfway across the city. He would have to do without them. It was a pity that Narcissus had escaped with the treasure. But there was some comfort for Cato in the fact that the plotters had failed in their attempt to bribe the Praetorians.

With an impatient hiss, he sheathed his bloodied sword, then stood erect, shoulders back, and pointed along the street towards the camp. He glanced at Macro and the standard bearer.

'Just the three of us now.'

Macro returned his own sword to its scabbard. 'Then let's hope the Praetorians are still prepared to honour the imperial standard, otherwise you'll find yourself in chains for the murder of Granicus, if you're lucky. If you're not, your head'll be decorating the gatehouse of the camp within the hour.'

Cato glanced at his friend and frowned. 'Thanks for that encouraging thought. All right then, let's go.'

CHAPTER THIRTY-THREE

'Lower the standard, and cover it,' Cato quietly ordered as they approached the sprawling expanse of the parade ground in front of the camp.

The standard bearer hesitated and Cato snapped the order again. This time the man lowered the standard to the horizontal, shifted his grip and then covered the head with his cloak. With the wolf pelt over his helmet and the staff in his hand, no one would mistake him for anything other than his rank, but then there were scores of standard bearers in the Praetorian Guard, and one more would not attract attention.

Three cohorts had already formed up on the parade ground and more men were spilling from the arches of the main gate to take up their positions. Most were already fully kitted up, but others still struggled with buckles and ties as their mates carried their weapons for them. A familiar enough scene in every corner of the Empire, Cato reflected as he, Macro and the standard bearer made their way across the parade ground.

'Why hide the standard?' asked Macro. 'Thought we were here to get ourselves noticed?'

'Not until we have some idea of the lie of the land,' Cato

replied. 'For now, we're just officers going about the daily routine.'

They weaved a path through the throng of men spreading across the parade ground, exchanging salutes with the rankers and nods with other officers as they went. At the gate, Macro barked a warning.

'Make space! Officers coming through!'

The Praetorians obediently parted, and a moment later the three men were inside the camp. Cato gestured to his companions to step to one side so that he could give his instructions. He saw the nervous expression on the standard bearer's face and addressed him first.

'What's your name?'

'Herius Rutilius, sir.'

'Fine. Now listen to me, Rutilius. You are the emperor's standard bearer. You were chosen for this honour because you have distinguished yourself. Now your emperor needs you to do the same again. Do exactly as I say, without hesitation, and we'll get through this. Let anyone see a flicker of doubt in your expression and we're dead men, likely as not. Understand?'

'Yes, sir.'

'Then shoulders back, chest out and head held high. And when I give the order, you make damn sure that the imperial standard is held up where everyone can see it.'

'I will, sir.'

'Good. Macro, I want you to head to our barracks. Gather your century and join me at headquarters. Dismiss the sentries and replace them with your men. Don't let anyone stop you entering the main building. I want you and the rest of the century ready to back us up if this doesn't play out the way we hope.'

Macro clicked his tongue. 'Things haven't worked out the way we'd hoped ever since we were appointed to the Praetorian Guard. Why should anything be different now? Still, I'll be there, lad. Don't you worry.' He patted Cato on the shoulder and turned to trot towards the barrack block of the Second Cohort.

Cato gestured in the direction of headquarters. 'Here we go.'

He and Rutilius advanced along the main thoroughfare, to one side of the stream of men emerging from their barracks and heading towards the main gate. Cato kept his head tilted forward slightly to try and conceal his features from those passing by. Harassed by their junior officers, they barely had time to spare the two men more than a glance, and Cato and the standard bearer reached the arched entrance to the headquarters complex without incident.

There were two men standing sentry duty on either side, and they snapped to attention as Cato strode through. The other side of the arch opened on to a large colonnaded courtyard, on the far side of which rose a long three-storey building. Four more Praetorians stood outside the columned entrance, and Cato kept his pace steady as he crossed the courtyard and climbed the short flight of steps.

Inside the main hall, beams of light shone across the vaulted space from windows high above. A table stood just inside the entrance and an optio rose hurriedly as he caught sight of the approaching officer. Cato reached for the small waxed slate stuffed into his waistband and held it up for the optio to see.

'Orders from the palace. For the senior officers. Are they in the briefing room?'

'Yes, sir. In accordance with Prefect Burrus's orders.'

Cato nodded and turned towards the corridor leading to the officers' mess.

'Wait, sir! Aren't you Prefect Cato?'

Cato felt his stomach tighten, but forced himself to remain calm as he confronted the optio. 'That's right. I imagine you haven't heard the news that the murderer of Senator Granicus has been caught and my name has been cleared.'

'Er, no, sir.'

'Well, now you know. I'm here under the direct orders of Prefect Burrus and the emperor. Rutilius, it's time to show our colours.'

The standard bearer swept the cloak aside and raised the staff so that the golden disc bearing the face of Nero above a blazing sun design on a blue background was visible. As the staff was hoisted up, the disc was caught in a beam of light and gleamed brilliantly amid the floating motes of dust.

'You recognise the imperial standard?'

'Yes, sir.'

'Then you have all the proof you need of my authority. Remain at your desk and ensure that I am not interrupted.'

'Yes, sir.' The optio saluted and bowed his head to the standard as Cato gestured to Rutilius to follow him.

The two men passed the open doors of the mess and approached the door to the briefing room. Cato slowed and took a deep breath before he grasped the handle and pushed. A dais stood at the far end of the long room and benches were arranged in rows in front of it. The air was filled with the gentle hubbub of conversation from the assembled centurions and tribunes waiting for Burrus to arrive and brief them on the purpose of the morning's general assembly. As Cato entered, those at the rear of the room turned towards him.

He paused to undo the ties of his helmet and remove it.

'Bloody Jupiter . . .' A centurion half rose from his bench. 'It's him, Prefect Cato.'

More heads turned as the conversation died away. Cato marched between the benches to the dais and climbed the two steps before facing the gathered officers. He indicated to Rutilius to stand to his right, two paces away. As his gaze swept over the room, he noted the surprised and astonished expressions on the faces of those staring back. No alarm or hostility, yet. He singled out a junior tribune he recognised in the front row.

'Caecilius, come here.'

The tribune stood up uncertainly but did not approach, looking to his superior officers for a cue.

'Quickly, man!' Cato snapped.

The tribune hurried forward and took the waxed slate Cato held out to him. 'Read it out. Loudly and clearly.'

Caecilius coughed and drew a breath. 'His imperial majesty commands that all officers and men of the Praetorian Guard are to obey the orders of the bearer of this message, who acts in the emperor's name and carries out his will. Those who refuse to obey will be accounted traitors and condemned accordingly. I, Nero Claudius Caesar Augustus Germanicus, confirm this with my seal . . .' The tribune lowered the waxed slate. 'It is countersigned by Prefect Burrus.'

Cato retrieved the slate and set his feet firmly apart as he addressed the officers. 'Those are my credentials, gentlemen, and they are confirmed by the presence of the imperial standard. I have been appointed temporary commander of the Praetorian Guard. You are all under my orders.'

'Where is Burrus?' a voice called out from the middle of the room.

'Aye!' echoed another. 'Where's the prefect?'

'Quiet!' Cato shouted, glaring. 'Burrus is guarding the emperor during the emergency.'

'What emergency?' Tribune Tertillius, commander of the Third Cohort, stood up and pointed directly at Cato. 'What's going on here? Last I heard, you were wanted for murder.'

There was a chorus of shouted questions from other officers as Cato filled his lungs.

'SILENCE! Silence, damn you!'

The voices died away, and he continued. 'There is no time to question the emperor's orders. Nor is it your place to do so. Suffice to say I have his complete confidence, and therefore you will do exactly as I order, until otherwise notified. As I speak, traitors are attempting to take over the city, depose the emperor and replace him with Britannicus, to act as the puppet ruler of those leading the conspiracy. The Praetorians will protect the imperial palace and take control of the Senate, the city's gates and the riverfront. They will also round up the traitors and hold them until the emperor decides their fate.' He paused. 'You should also know that a number of Praetorian officers and men are numbered amongst the traitors. They will be dealt with alongside the others. But you must be on your guard against them. Meanwhile you will obey my orders, and only my orders, without hesitation. Is that clear?'

Tertillius raised a hand. 'Cato, I'm sure that I speak for more than a few of us here when I question why the order is not in your name explicitly. You might have intercepted the original bearer and taken it from him. For all I know, you might be working for those plotting against the emperor.'

Cato indicated the imperial standard. 'That is why Rutilius is here with the standard. Some of you will recognise him, and know that he has earned the trust of Burrus and Nero. To answer your question, I was not the only officer sent here to raise the alarm.' He indicated the dried blood splatters on his face and breastplate. 'If I had not made it, my companion would have taken command in my place.'

Tertillius shook his head. 'That's not good enough. I'm not prepared to trust your word on any of this. I want confirmation from the imperial palace before I lift a finger to do as you say.'

Some of the others nodded in support and Cato set his jaw as he responded. 'As has been pointed out, that will be regarded as treason. Besides . . .'

The tramp of boots in the main hall carried to the ears of those in the briefing room, and Cato smiled thinly as Macro and his men appeared at the door a moment later. The centurion directed them to line the walls and face the officers before they grounded their spears.

'I think that answers any questions about my authority,' said Cato. 'If Tertillius or anyone else here wishes to defy me, make yourselves known now . . .'

The tribune made to reply, then shook his head instead. No one else spoke, and Cato nodded. 'Fine, I'll assume that there are no more questions. I'll address the men now, and you'll have your orders immediately afterwards.' Then before anyone could offer any further interruption, he gave the order: 'Dismissed!'

There was no attempt at a ceremonial pace as Cato hurried up the steps of the review stand and approached the rail. The other senior officers formed up behind him, and the last of the centurions dressed their men and fell in at the right of their units. Macro and his men stood behind the review stand, in case any of the senior officers had a change of heart and tried to cause trouble. All was still on the vast parade ground, save for the gentle ripple of the standards and the glimmer of sunlight playing off polished helmets. Nearly six thousand men all told, and Cato felt the full weight of his task settle on his shoulders, like Atlas hunched by the burden of the world. One false step and it would crash and shatter. As a boy, he had often read of the great speeches given by Roman statesmen before the Senate and people of Rome, or generals addressing their men prior to battle, and he had never dreamed that one day it might fall to him to follow in that tradition. There was terror in such a moment that he had never considered, and it gripped his body like an icy fist as he gazed out over the ocean of faces.

He took a deep breath and eased himself away from the rail as he raised his right hand and called out in his best parade-ground voice: 'Comrades of the Praetorian Guard! I am Quintus Licinius Cato, tribune of the Second Cohort and prefect of auxiliaries.'

As he announced his name, there was a stirring in the ranks and a faint muttering, the tone of which Cato took to be dangerous. He continued quickly. 'Some of you have served with me when you were legionaries. Many more served with me in the recent campaign in Hispania when the Second Cohort defied the might of the rebel host at Argentium, and was honoured for their bravery by Emperor Nero. The rest of you will know that Emperor Claudius awarded me a silver spear for my deeds in Britannia. I need no man to vouch for my loyalty to Rome, to the people of Rome and to its emperor. I have proved it by standing shoulder to shoulder with my comrades and shedding my blood alongside them. Rome is my master, and to Rome I pledge my loyalty and my life . . . As should every soldier. Every Roman. To our dying breath. Yet there are traitors in our capital. Those who would betray sacred Rome and the emperor the gods have chosen to rule us.'

He gripped the rail in both hands and leaned forward as he continued. 'Brothers, I tell you that these traitors are amongst us now! At this very moment they are conspiring to take our emperor from us. They are conspiring to replace him with a usurper they will control like a puppet. They are conspiring to hand power to a corrupt clique of politicians!' He raised and shook his fist. 'Will we let them do that, my brothers?'

'No!' a voice cried. 'Long live Nero!'

Some others took up the cry, but Cato saw that it was not enough. Most stood still and held their tongues. A few jeered, before they were rounded on by their officers.

'Very well,' Cato muttered to himself. Appealing to patriotism was not quite enough, it seemed. He would have to strike closer to the hearts of these men. He raised his hands and waved them down to command silence, then continued his address in a controlled, calm tone. 'Brothers, let me tell you that these conspirators not only betray their emperor, they plan to betray us . . . They want to disband the Praetorian Guard and send us to the legions!'

This time there was a more general reaction, a mixture of gasps of surprise and cries of outrage. Cato let it run its course before he called them to silence again.

'Yes, brothers. And what is worse, they will not honour the reward that Nero has sworn to pay to every Praetorian here today! Our emperor has heard of this. He shares your rage and he has sent me to tell you that he has sworn a sacred oath to pay the promised reward in full, and more besides. This he vows with a certainty as firm as the rock upon which the Temple of Jupiter stands. Every man who counts himself the brother of Nero shall be richly rewarded, as any brother should be. This he swears! Are you with him, brothers?'

This time there was a rousing cheer, and hundreds of men raised their spears and shook them so that the parade ground looked like the surface of a lake in a rainstorm.

Cato thrust his arms up towards the heavens. 'Are you with him, brothers? Then call his name! Let our enemies hear his name, and know that we are loyal to our emperor Nero!'

Thousands of mouths opened to bellow the name, and it echoed off the walls of the camp and the surrounding buildings, amplifying the din of the cheering as it rose to a crescendo. Cato joined in, punching his fist into the air to emphasise the rhythm. He continued for a moment before he lowered his arm and backed slowly away, turning towards the assembled tribunes. His expression became cold and deadly.

'There is no conspiracy here. Those men will tear apart any officer who fails to show complete loyalty to the emperor – and at this moment, that means me. Is there any man here who questions my authority to command the Praetorian Guard?'

No one demurred.

'Good, then I will give you your orders. See to it that they are obeyed to the very letter.' He paused and looked over their faces again. 'Where is Junior Tribune Cristus?'

'Cristus is not in camp,' Tertillius responded.

'Then where is he?'

'He had orders to take half his cohort to the Flaminian Gate. First thing this morning.'

Cato stepped closer. 'What orders?'

'To provide an honour guard to welcome Legate Pastinus to the city. At least that's what he said.'

Cato clenched his jaw. It was already too late. By now Narcissus and his conspirators would have opened the way to Pastinus and his entire legion to enter Rome and seize power.

CHAPTER THIRTY-FOUR

There was only one unit that Cato could entirely trust to carry out the task of retaking the Flaminian Gate: his own men of the Second Cohort. He decided to take the Third Cohort, commanded by Tertillius, to support him, and most of the other units were sent to secure the other city gates in case there was more treachery. The remaining cohort, the Tenth, was dispatched to guard the imperial palace.

'Why bring Tertillius with us?' Macro asked as they quick-marched along the street running atop the crest of the Viminal Hill. Ahead of them civilians glanced up at the din made by the tramp of military boots and hurriedly retreated indoors.

'You know the saying. Keep your friends close, but your enemies closer still. I don't trust Tertillius.'

'And that's a good reason to have him covering our backs?'

'If there's any sign of treachery, I'll cut him down with my own sword and find someone else to command the Third. Now save your breath for the enemy.'

It was a crude way to prevent conversation, but Cato's mind was racing to consider all the forces in play. The defences of Rome existed in name only. The city had outgrown the Servian Wall over two hundred years ago, and though it still stood, much of it had been assimilated into other structures. The gatehouses remained, and were manned by soldiers from the urban cohorts – trained and equipped to prevent civil unrest, but wholly incapable of defending Rome against the hardened professionals of the legions.

Beyond the line of the old wall, the city sprawled across the Pincian Hill all the way to the Tiber, and the only barrier standing directly in the path of the Sixth Legion was the toll gate on the Flaminian Way, close to the river. That, and a ditch and watchtowers constructed to police those entering and leaving the city and ensuring that they paid their toll accordingly. Unless Cato intervened, Legate Pastinus and his men would brush the men of the urban cohorts aside with ease and march straight down the Flaminian Way into the heart of Rome. Nothing would stop them until they reached the line of the wall at the Flaminian Gate. That was where the success or failure of the conspiracy would be decided, Cato realised. That and the life or death of Lucius.

The thought spurred him on, and he was tempted to order his men to quicken the pace to a trot. But unlike the men he had faced with the German bodyguard, Pastinus's troops were heavily armed, and it was vital that the Praetorians were not tired out by the time they came upon the enemy.

At the same time as he was marching to deal with the Sixth Legion, Cato was aware that the emperor and his advisers were engaged with other elements of the coup, and he was frustrated by not knowing how the rest of the struggle was playing out. For all he knew, Nero was already dead, along with Pallas, Burrus and the others, and he and his men were about to engage in a futile battle with the legionaries. Despite his words about loyalty and honour delivered from the review stand, Cato would be prepared to switch sides once again the moment it was apparent that the conspirators had won the day. He had been contaminated by the cynicism of those playing politics for personal gain, he reflected. But there was also the realisation that a futile struggle would only result in the deaths of hundreds of his comrades, and no officer had the right to send his men to senseless destruction if it could be avoided.

Ahead rose the vast tiled roof of the Forum of Augustus, close by the Flaminian Gate. Two men in tunics were waiting at the junction at the end of the street; Cato recognised them as the Praetorians he had sent out ahead of the column. He held up his hand to halt the two cohorts behind him, and then beckoned Macro forward as he went to confer with the scouts. Once the men were still, he could hear the muffled tramp of more soldiers close by.

The waiting optio sent his man forward to keep watch as he made his report to Cato.

'We're too late, sir. Prefect Cristus and his men have taken over the gate, and the leading elements of the Sixth Legion are already through the wall.'

'How many men in the city so far?'

'They were already marching past by the time we got in position, sir. I can't say how many.'

Cato grimaced and stroked the bristles under his chin. 'There's nothing for it. We'll have to attack at once. The gate has to be closed.'

'Two cohorts against ten?' Macro tilted his head. 'Not great odds, sir.'

'But good enough given we're not fighting in the open. We'll make use of the streets to even things out. Defeat them in detail, if we can.' Cato turned to the optio. 'Go back down the column and find Tribune Tertillius. Tell him to take his cohort three streets up and then make ready to cut across the Flaminian Way. He's to wait until he hears us make our move against the men on the gate. And tell him he'll be fighting on two fronts. He's to hold off the men already in the city, and have half his men fight their way back to the gate to link up with me. Got that?'

'Yes, sir.'

'Go.'

As the optio ran back up the street, past the closed-up ranks of the Praetorians, Cato glanced cautiously round the corner of the junction. The other scout was a short distance further along, crouched behind a cart piled with bales of animal feed.

'Macro, bring the other centurions forward. I'll be back in a moment.'

Cato trotted towards the scout, untying his helmet and tucking it under his arm to prevent his crest from being spotted. When he reached the cart, he peered round the iron-rimmed wheel and saw that the street continued for another fifty paces before it was crossed by the broad thoroughfare of the Flaminian Way. Legionaries, four abreast, were marching past the end of the street. To Cato's right was another street, running into a small yard that backed on to the wall. Bracing himself, he sprinted across the gap. Just before the entrance to the yard was a narrow alley running towards the gate; at the end of it, he could see some of the men from Cristus's cohort guarding the gateway.

There was no time to get a better understanding of the lie of the land, and he hurried back to the column to give his orders. Macro and the other centurions were waiting, and Cato hurriedly formed his plans, describing the layout of the streets and assigning the roles each century was to play.

'Petillius, Porcino, you take your men across into the alley and then charge down on to the gate. Stop for nothing and go in hard. I know those men are our comrades, but we cannot hesitate in doing what we must. It is vital the gate is closed. We'll strike in the interval between cohorts as they enter the city. That'll give us the best chance of success. Clear?'

'Yes, sir.'

'The rest of the cohort will charge down the nearer street. Macro and Placinus, you will go left and drive into the rear of the legionaries already in the city. Keep pushing them back as long as you can. I'll lead the others in charging the gate. Ignatius and Nicolis, your men will follow Placinus and go right. We'll be hitting Cristus and his men from two sides. With luck, it'll unnerve them long enough for us to take back the gate, seal it and cut off the cohorts still outside the wall. Questions? No? Good luck, gentlemen. As soon as you hear the trumpet, go in fast.'

The other centurions turned and trotted away, leaving Macro at Cato's side.

'I'd be a liar if I said I'm happy at the prospect of fighting our own,' Macro commented.

'Can't be helped,' Cato replied tersely, then glanced at his friend. 'But you're right. It stinks. Let's hope Narcissus and his cronies are called to account for every drop of blood that is spilled today.'

'Fat chance of that. The man is as slippery as a greased pig and has more lives than a bloody cat. He needs to be nailed down. Preferably to a cross.'

'If it comes to that, I'll take a hammer to him personally. But that's for later. We've work to do. Get your men forward as far as that cart. Have the trumpeter at your side.'

Cato left Macro to organise his men and returned to the cart, crouching down next to the scout. 'Still the same cohort?'

'Yes, sir. Though there can't be more than two centuries to go by before the next one.'

Cato nodded as he rested his shoulder against the cart's yoke, angled up when the cart had been parked at the side of the street, outside a farrier's premises. Glancing down, he saw a pair of chocks bracing the larger wheels at the rear of the cart. The crunch of boots announced the arrival of Macro's men, and the centurion waved them to the side of the street and quietly passed the word for them to prepare to charge before he joined Cato.

'The lads are ready.'

'Good. Wait here.' Cato eased himself between the cart and the wall, hoping that none of the passing legionaries spared a glance in his direction. There was an arch into the farrier's yard and he hurried inside. One wall was lined with the tools of the trade, hanging from wooden pegs and iron hooks. A charcoal oven stood in the middle of the yard, a thin trail of smoke eddying from the hearth. In the corner was a broomstick, and he snatched this up and returned to the oven. Using one hand to work the bellows, he thrust the head of the broom into the oven and watched the blown air raise sparks and a glow along the edge of some of the smouldering lumps of charcoal. A flame flickered into life, and a moment later the head of the broom was alight.

'Oi! What the fuck are you doing?'

Cato looked up and saw a large bearded man emerging from a shed on the opposite side of the yard, pulling his tunic down from the waist.

'Shut your mouth,' Cato hissed, 'and get back inside.'

355

'Sod that.' The man crossed towards him, forearms like hams. 'You'll get out of my yard now if you know what's good for you.'

Cato pulled the broom out of the oven and drew his sword. 'And you'll fuck off back inside if you don't want trouble.'

The man drew up and raised his hands. 'Easy, friend.'

Cato backed away from him, keeping the burning broom at a safe distance. At the entrance of the yard he worked his way round to the front of the cart. Macro shot him a curious expression as Cato shoved the head of the broom into the piled feed bales. Smoke curled round the shaft of the broom, then flickers of orange flame spread to the feed. Cato released the broom and gestured to the scout.

'Get ready to remove those chocks. Macro, here. Help me with the yoke.'

Together they reached up and heaved the sturdy length of timber down, then Cato took his place closer to the cart. 'You steer, Macro.'

The flames were spreading quickly and smoke swirled across the width of the street. Cato braced his boots. 'Remove the chocks.'

The scout dashed forward, snatched up the first block of wood, then rushed round the back of the cart and used it to knock away the second chock and free the cart's wheels. At once it lurched into motion, rumbling down the slight incline towards the legionaries marching past the opening of the street. Macro held the iron hitching collar tightly, keeping the smaller front wheels aligned as he and Cato pushed the cart to help it build up speed. The flames crackled and smoke billowed back over the two officers as the cart accelerated.

'Stay with it!' Cato ordered, determined not to let the heavy

356

vehicle swerve out of control before it burst out of the side street. The rush of air over the cart fanned the flames into an intense blaze that stung his exposed flesh, and he tightened his grip and concentrated on not stumbling as the cart accelerated. Through the smoke he glimpsed the end of the street no more than ten paces away.

'Macro, let go!'

He released his grip and stepped aside to watch the impact. There were shouts of alarm from the street and then the cart ploughed into the side of the legionaries, crushing men under the wheels and knocking aside others before the front axle lurched round and the cart swerved and rolled over, spilling blazing bundles across the road. Cato grabbed Macro and shoved him back up the slope as he called to the scout.

'Give the signal!'

There was a pause of a heartbeat, and then the trumpet rang out and with a roar Macro's century charged round the corner in a dense mass. The two officers snatched out their swords and joined the Praetorians as they raced down the street and out on to the Flaminian Way. Ahead of them the weathered and rutted flagstones were covered with burning feed and injured legionaries. Others stood, shocked by the impact of the cart and now the sudden appearance of the Praetorians, and before they could react the charge struck home, spear tips darting out to tear into the flank of the disordered legionary column.

Macro crashed into the back of a man who had turned to run and now went flying face first on to the street even before he could draw his sword. The centurion left him there and turned on his next opponent: an optio cupping his hand to his mouth to rally the scattered men of his century. A quick cut to the side of the man's helmet laid him out before he could utter a word, then Macro paused to look round quickly, sword raised, ready to strike at any threat. He saw that his men had cut through the middle of the tail of the cohort marching through the gate. To the left, the ranks were becoming disordered as men stopped and turned to look back.

'On me!' Macro bellowed. 'First Century on me! Form up on me!'

He thrust his way through the loose melee until he was clear of the burning debris from the cart, then raised his sword and circled it overhead. The century's standard bearer hurried to his side along with more men until they filled the road from side to side. As soon as he had enough to fill out four ranks, Macro gave the order to advance in the direction of the palace.

'Advance spears!'

The front rank of Praetorians raised the shafts of their weapons overhead so that they could strike down and not risk injury to the men behind them. In front of them some legionaries turned to fight, but most fell back from the oval shields and darting spearheads. Macro could see the officers frantically attempting to turn their men about and form a line. No easy thing in the heat of battle when a formation had been broken. And the shock of attack was not yet over, he smiled grimly to himself. The trumpet was still sounding from the street nearby, and a few heartbeats later there was another full-throated roar as Tertillius and his cohort struck out two hundred paces further along the Flaminian Way.

'We have 'em, boys!' Macro yelled to his men. 'Keep pushing the bastards back. Don't give them a chance to recover.'

The First Century tramped forward another twenty paces, dealing mercilessly with those that dared to stand their ground. It was not long before they came up against the first organised resistance, as a line of heavy legionary shields barred their way. The blades of short swords pricked out between the shields, and above the trims, Macro saw the determined expressions of men preparing to strike back at their ambushers.

The easy part was over, he realised. Now came the close combat in which Rome's legions excelled. This would be the true test of the Praetorians' mettle.

'Steady, boys! Dress the line!' Macro halted and held his arms out, waiting for his men to settle into even ranks. He turned to the man behind him and took his shield, then hefted it round and up, in line with the Praetorians on either side. 'For the emperor! Advance!'

The First Century rolled forward with Macro calling the step, and the gap between the two sides narrowed and then vanished as the lines of shields thudded home against each other. As the shafts of spears darted to and fro overhead, the blades of the swords struck out at waist height. Macro, caught in the very middle of the dense press of bodies, braced his boots, gritted his teeth and leaned into his shield, trying to claw his way forward. But neither side gave ground, and the air was filled with the sound of men grunting with effort, the light rasp of snatched breaths and the rippling thud of shields, overlaid by the clash and clatter of spearheads and sword blades as the two sides struck out at their foe.

A bright gleam darted close by Macro's face as the legionary ahead and to his right made a stab at him. Only the chance jostle of a comrade shoved him aside and spared him a terrible wound. In return, he thrust diagonally up with his sword and caught the legionary in the flesh just above the elbow, cutting deep into the muscle. The man grimaced and tried to pull his arm free, but only succeeded in tearing the wound open further.

His fingers flexed involuntarily and the sword dropped from his hand, bouncing off Macro's hip before it hit the flagstones with a dull metal clang.

Further to his right, Macro caught sight of a spear tip plunging into the eye of a legionary, the man's helmet snapping back under the impact before the soldier slumped down out of sight. Almost at once, the Praetorian to Macro's left let out an explosive gasp and folded forward as he was stabbed in the groin. He was eased aside by the man behind him and thrust back through the ranks until he was clear of the fight and could slump down and tend to his wound. More of the Praetorians fell, and Macro knew that the heavier oblong shields of the legions were more than a match for the lighter oval shields of the guardsmen. Only the greater reach of the spears went some way towards evening the odds. Already the Praetorians' advance had stalled, and now, Macro knew, it was primarily a test of strength as each side tried to press the other back.

Cato drew aside from the skirmish and climbed on to the pediment of a small statue to some local worthy in order to get a clear view of the situation. Macro's two centuries were holding their own. In the distance he could see that Tertillius's cohort had cut through the legion and trapped several hundred men between the two Praetorian formations. Beyond that they were rolling up the head of Pastinus's column. In the other direction the men of Ignatius and Nicolis's centuries were mopping up the rear of the cohort they had ambushed, while the remainder of Cato's unit had pressed Tribune Cristus and his men back against the gate. Beyond that, the road was clear for fifty paces before the head of the next cohort. Even as Cato watched, the officer in charge halted his legionaries while he trotted forward to investigate the sounds of fighting beyond the gate. There was only the briefest opportunity to take advantage of the man's caution, he realised.

Jumping down into the road, he beckoned to the imperial standard bearer to stay close to him, and pushed his way through the ranks to where his men were fighting the disorganised mass of legionaries. Cato stepped forward and called out: 'Second Cohort, disengage! Disengage!'

Ignatius and Nicolis repeated the command, and their men broke contact and retreated out of range of the legionaries' swords.

'Soldiers of the Sixth Legion, you are committing treason! Whatever your commander has told you, the truth is that he is a traitor who aims to overthrow our emperor! The emperor you have sworn to serve. Save yourselves. Throw down your swords and surrender, or you will be cut down where you stand.' Cato paused to let his words sink in. 'Do it now!'

There was a brief stillness, and Cato focused his attention on a young soldier in front of him. The man's sword arm was trembling. Cato took a step towards him and spoke gently. 'Why should you die for a gang of traitors? Come on, my lad, this is no end for a brave legionary. You should be fighting for Rome, not against her. Put down your sword and I swear no harm will come to you.'

The legionary hesitated and then lowered his sword, crouching and laying it on the road, together with his shield.

'Good man. You did the right thing.' Cato turned to another legionary. 'Now you.'

He held the man's gaze unflinchingly, and this soldier too lowered his sword and shield. More followed suit, and Cato spoke calmly over his shoulder. 'None of our comrades of the

Sixth Legion are to come to any harm. Disarm them and get them off the road. There's a farrier's yard up the street there. Hold them in there until further orders. But remember, no harm is to come to them, or you'll answer to me.'

Centurion Ignatius led his men forward, rounding up the prisoners and helping the wounded to their feet. Nicolis gave orders to collect their weapons, remove the bodies from the street and douse the flames on the cart and the bundles of feed that still blazed around the overturned vehicle. But a small knot of officers, standard bearers and veterans barred the way to the ongoing skirmish in front of the gate. Cato approached them warily.

'There's no point in fighting on. Your troops have surrendered. Follow suit or I will have my men cut you down.'

The cohort's senior centurion sniffed with contempt. 'You know the score, sir. You don't get picked to be a centurion because you're the kind that gives in. I only obey orders from the legate, sir. That's how it is.'

Cato glanced at the other men around him, no more than a dozen in all. 'And what about the rest of you? Do you want to die?'

There was no reply, only grim defiance in their faces. Cato felt his heart sink at the waste of such good men. But there was no time to try and persuade them. The gate had to be shut before any more men from the Sixth Legion entered Rome. He sighed and nodded to Centurion Nicolis.

'Try to take them alive, but kill them if you have to.'

Nicolis waved his men forward, and the Praetorians closed round those who had chosen death over dishonour. As the first clash of blades rang out through the haze of smoke from the burning feed, Cato hurried on towards the gate. The remaining centuries of his cohort had already cut down most of Cristus's men in the first onslaught. Now the survivors had drawn into a tight arc in front of the arch looming above the Flaminian Way. Cato could see the crest of their commander as he stood by the standard and called out encouragement to his men. But he was outnumbered, and the defenders were being driven back steadily.

'Push 'em hard, boys!' Petillius cried out above the cacophony of battle.

The centurion nodded a greeting as Cato trotted up to his side.

'They won't hold out much longer, sir.'

'Long enough, maybe,' Cato responded as he saw the follow-up cohort from the Sixth Legion doubling towards the gate. He retrieved a shield from one of the fallen and called to two of the sections still formed up behind the battle line.

'You lot. On me!'

A short distance from the rear of the melee was a heavy wooden trough used to water horses and mules as they entered the gate. Cato ordered the first section to tip it over, and the water gushed over the road, churning up the dirt and refuse into a brown swirl that flowed briefly across the flagstones. Then, spears discarded, and slipping the straps of their shields over their shoulders, the eight men picked up the trough and Cato led them through the edge of the fight, along the road. Pulling his men back and shoving them aside, he cleared a path to the battle line, then paused to give his orders.

The men on the trough were given a twenty-pace run-up, and stood poised as Cato forced his way to the front, smashing his shield into an opponent's and then swinging it out wildly to knock the man off balance. It was a risky move, as it laid his torso open to a quick strike, but he slashed his sword out and to the right in an arc to keep Cristus's men back. As he recovered both shield and sword, he roared the order.

'Ram them, boys!'

The section carrying the trough broke into a run, picking up speed. At the last moment, Cato pushed himself out of their path and the trough splintered the shield of the Praetorian directly in its path, knocking the man down. Glancing blows drove those behind him to the right and left, and then the section carrying the trough burst through the enemy line, followed up by Cato and the second squad. At once Cato turned towards the flank of Cristus's men.

'Roll them up!'

With a lung-straining roar, he charged the rear of the enemy line, felling a man with a brutal swing of his shield. As his opponent fell on his back, Cato slammed the edge of the shield down on to his chest, driving the air from his lungs and leaving him gasping. The two sections with him hurled themselves on their foe, battering them and cutting them down with quick, savage sword thrusts. Praetorian on Praetorian. It wrenched Cato's guts to behold, even though he knew there was no alternative.

As they became aware of the brutal assault on their flank, Cristus's men began to fall back, breaking away from the fight. Some stood their ground and fought on. Others turned to retreat through the gate and flee along the Flaminian Way, towards the safety of the oncoming legionaries.

'Stand fast!' Cristus shouted after them. 'Stay and fight, you cowards!'

But the fight was already over. Those who could were fleeing. The rest started to surrender, throwing down their weapons as they backed away from Cato's men. Cato thrust his sword at the tribune. 'Take him. Don't let him escape!'

Cristus heard the order. He was still for an instant, then he turned and ran back through the gate, untying his helmet strap and flinging the helmet aside as he bolted into an alley and disappeared from view. He could be caught later, Cato decided. There was a far more immediate task that needed to be addressed. Running through those Praetorians who had surrendered, he sheathed his sword and cast his shield aside as he reached the gates and pressed his shoulder to the solid timbers.

'On me! Give me a hand here!'

More of his men rushed over, discarding their own shields and spears, and heaved at the ponderous gates, which had settled on their iron hinges. Then, with a deep, grating squeal, the doors began to grind across the flagstones. Cato looked up to see the nearest of Pastinus's soldiers no more than thirty paces away, running hard to retake the gate and keep the way open for the rest of the legion to enter the centre of Rome. The gap narrowed and the gate closed, and as the locking bar was hauled across into the brackets on each gate and then into the socket on the far side of the arch, a few futile blows sounded from outside. But it was too late. The men of the Sixth Legion beyond the Flaminian Gate would play no immediate role in the battle raging in the Forum beneath the towering bulk of the imperial palace.

CHAPTER THIRTY-FIVE

The road was strewn with the bodies of the dead and wounded as Cato doubled towards Macro and his men. He had left Ignatius and Nicolis to guard the prisoners and hold the gate while he led the centuries of Petillius and Porcino to join the struggle taking place around the Forum. As they approached the rearmost ranks of their comrades, Cato halted the column and pushed his way through towards the standard of the First Century, close to the battle line. Macro stood nearby, urging his men on. Cato joined him, breathing hard, and they exchanged a nod of greeting.

'What's the situation here?'

Macro was bleeding from a cut on his top lip, and he spat a gobbet of blood before he responded. 'We're holding them back, but only just. There's at least a cohort of them between us and Tertillius and his mob. But they're already using the alleys to try and work round us. I've had to send Placinus and his men to cover our flanks.'

Cato glanced to the side, as if he could see the skirmishes being fought out amid the surrounding tenement blocks. He smiled briefly at his foolishness and then concentrated his mind on the fight. With two more centuries to hand, Macro would be more than able to hold his own in the confined space of the Flaminian Way and the surrounding alleys. Tertillius, on the other hand, was caught between two forces and was badly outnumbered. But Cato had no way of knowing from the limited view afforded to him how the tribune was faring. He glanced up at the tenement blocks on either flank and slapped Macro on the shoulder.

'You take charge here. I'll be back.'

Before Macro could reply, he turned and pushed his way through to the side of the street, and found the entrance to the nearest building. The door was bolted, and Cato braced himself and kicked hard at the hinges. It took several blows before the aged wood gave and the door crashed inwards. He thrust the shattered timbers aside and entered the gloom. There was a small hall, with a few doors to one side of a narrow staircase. He ran up the steps to the first floor, just in time to see an anxious face at one door before it was slammed shut. He ran to the end of the landing and climbed the next flight of stairs, pounding on the door of an apartment overlooking the Flaminian Way.

'Open up! In the name of the emperor!'

There was no response, and Cato stepped back and lashed out with his boot. This time the door yielded on the first blow and he charged inside. There was a shriek of terror, and he turned to see a wild-haired woman with three small children huddled in a corner.

'Spare us,' she whimpered. 'For pity's sake.'

Cato looked away, towards the light entering a low doorway that led on to a flimsy balcony. Rushing across the room, he stepped out above the roadway and gazed down on the frenzied glimmer and glitter of armour and slashing weapons. Men were locked in conflict all the way down to the Forum. He leaned on the rail as he tried to get a clearer view, and the whole balcony shifted alarmingly beneath him. With one hand firmly grasping the door frame, he took in the view. As Macro had said, there were perhaps four or five hundred legionaries caught between the Second Cohort and Tertillius and his men. They were closed up, with their standards in the middle, and showed no sign of giving way. Further off, Tertillius and his Praetorians were also caught between two forces, but they were crushed together in a dense mass and Cato could see at once that they were in danger of being cut down unless the pressure on them was relieved. Before that could happen, the legionaries facing Macro and his men had to be dealt with.

There was one storey above Cato and then the tiled roof of the tenement block. His heart and mind were racing as he ducked back inside and dashed back to the door, ignoring the fresh pleas for mercy coming from the woman. He ran down the stairs and back outside, calling Petillius and Porcino to him.

'Centurion Petillius, take your men down the alley there, and then take the first junction parallel to the Flaminian Way. Push forward and try to make contact with the lads from the Third Cohort. If you come across any of the legionaries, cut 'em down. Porcino, I want your lads to follow up, and enter the buildings along the street. Get 'em up on the roofs and use the tiles to bombard the enemy. Make it count. Unleash an avalanche on the bastards and bury them! Go!'

The two centurions saluted and ran back to their commands, leading them at the double out of the main thoroughfare. Cato could see that Macro's century had been forced back a few paces by the time he returned to his friend's side, just as Macro pulled back from the fighting line and stood, chest heaving, spattered with blood.

'They're starting to . . . get the better of us,' he grunted.

'Just need to hold them a little longer,' said Cato, gesturing to the roofline above the street. 'They're in for a nasty surprise.'

'Eh?'

'You'll see. We just need to hold our ground.' Cato cupped his hands to his mouth, filled his lungs and bellowed. 'Hold firm, Second Cohort! Don't give the bastards another inch! Rome belongs to the Praetorians!'

'Heave!' Macro added. 'Push 'em back, lads!'

For a brief moment the Praetorians renewed their efforts, boots scrabbling for purchase on the flagstones as they threw their weight behind their shields. The legionaries recoiled no more than a pace before they pressed forward again. There was little room to wield weapons in this trial of strength, and only snatched chances to thrust into any small gap that opened between the shields grinding against each other. Step by hard-won step, the legionaries began to force the Praetorians back, and Cato knew that if his men broke, the gate would be retaken and the way would be reopened for the rest of the Sixth Legion. He looked round and snatched up a shield from one of the fallen, then glanced at Macro and the imperial standard bearer.

'On me!'

He led the way forward, pushing through as close to the front rank of the cohort as he could go. Holding his sword high, he stabbed out over the shoulder of the man ahead of him, and the point glanced off the helmet of a legionary beyond the squared trim of his broad shield. Cato rose up on his toes, adjusted the angle and stabbed at the opening over the man's ear. He felt the point pierce flesh and bone for a short distance, and the legionary tried to recoil, but there was no space behind him. Blood gushed from the wound as Cato snatched his arm back before it became a target and thrust his weight behind the Praetorian, winning back half a pace of ground. On all sides he could hear the gasps and grunts of the men straining against each other, and he snatched a breath before he called out: 'Hold fast! A moment longer!'

Macro bunched his shoulders and worked himself forward. 'Give me space! Let me at them, lads.'

As he slammed himself against the nearest legionary and then crouched low enough that he could stab the man in the foot, one of the Praetorians laughed loudly. 'Bloody centurions. Glory hunters all!'

Some of his comrades echoed his laugh, and Cato wondered if they had been drinking before they reached the parade ground. Or was it that they were intoxicated by the frantic immediacy of battle?

A flicker of movement caught his attention, and he looked up just in time to see a roof tile spin lazily through the air not ten paces ahead. It disappeared from sight with a crash as it shattered over the helmet of a legionary. An instant later there was a sharp rattle from the roofline above and to the left, and a slew of tiles tumbled out and crashed amongst the enemy's ranks, followed by a shower of loose mortar and lengths of weathered wooden batons. Cries of alarm rang out as more tiles slithered from the roofs further along the Flaminian Way and smashed into the tight mass of the legionaries, striking many of them down and causing fear and panic amongst the others as they struggled to raise their shields to protect themselves.

'Ha!' Macro shouted with glee. 'That's the stuff! Knocking the fight out of 'em now. Press on, lads! Forward the Second!'

The Praetorians took up the cry and renewed their efforts. They began to push the legionaries back, a step, then two, and then steadily advanced as their opponents gave ground. Craning his neck, Cato could see men peeling off from the rear of the pack of legionaries still holding the line and scurrying away from the barrage of tiles and debris raining down from the top of the buildings lining the street. One of the centurions stood out in the open, trying to rally his men to the cohort's standard being held aloft by its bearer. A handful of men, shamed by his example, began to gather. Then a fresh avalanche of tiles felled both the officer and the standard bearer, and as the dust swirled about the bodies, their men turned and ran into a side street. More followed their cue, and soon no more than forty legionaries barred the way.

'Break off!' Cato shouted suddenly. 'Second Cohort, halt!'

Most men obeyed the order, but a handful, carried away by battle rage, took advantage of the sudden open space to use their swords, stabbing and hacking at their opponents. Macro took a few steps towards the enemy, teeth gritted and eyes blazing, before stopping himself and backing away to rejoin Cato.

'Why are we halting, sir? We have 'em on the run.'

A handful of tiles smashed into the street just short of where Macro had been standing, and exploded in fragments. Fortunately none struck those Praetorians reckless enough not to pay heed to their commanding officer's order. Now some paused and glanced round sheepishly.

'What are you waiting for?' Macro shouted at them. 'The chance to have your thick heads caved in? Get back in formation, before I put you on a bloody charge!'

Macro's century dressed their ranks, and Cato continued to hold them back as the last of the tiles fell into the road. He waited until he was certain it was safe, and then ordered his men forward to the next building and halted again. The ground was littered with the bodies of legionaries, mostly wounded and stunned as they lay amid the shattered roof tiles. A haze of dust hung in the air, and the men of both sides coughed and spluttered. Through the haze Cato could make out the remaining legionaries backing away from Tertillius's cohort and throwing down their shields and swords as they surrendered.

Turning to one of his men, he ordered him to find Porcino and get the troops off the roofs and back into the main body of the cohort. The tiles had done their work, although Cato wryly anticipated that some landlords in Rome would be sure to protest to the emperor as soon as order was restored to the streets.

'Macro, detail some men to get the prisoners rounded up and marched off to the camp. The wounded will have to wait for now.'

'Yes, sir.' Macro saluted, and Cato crossed the street to the buildings occupied by the Praetorians. A handful of loosened tiles continued to fall as he picked his way forward, past the legionaries who had surrendered, until he reached Tertillius's men, some of whom were already covered in a patina of dust. The tribune was standing to the rear of the detachment of men who were still fighting the vanguard of the Sixth Legion. Ahead, the road sloped down into the centre of the capital, though the temples and basilicas obstructed any clear view.

'How are you faring?'

'Better now that we aren't caught in a vice.' Tertillius pointed down the street. 'We're holding them back. I've got men out in the side streets to block them off. With the Tenth Cohort holding the palace, Pastinus and his boys are nearly hemmed in.'

Cato nodded. 'Good. I'll call for reinforcements from the other cohorts along the city wall. We've got the bridges covered. Then we should have enough men to close the trap and drive the enemy into the warehouse sector. With their backs against the river, they'll have to surrender, or drown.'

'And if they choose to fight?'

'Let's hope good sense wins the day,' Cato responded. 'There's been more than enough blood shed in Rome today.'

Tertillius clicked his tongue. 'The day's barely started, sir.'

'All the more reason to finish them off as soon as possible,' Cato said coldly. 'As soon as the reinforcements arrive, we push forward into the Forum and drive Pastinus out. And we stop for nothing until the last of the traitors is in our hands, or dead.'

CHAPTER THIRTY-SIX

It was noon, as near as Cato could tell, and a quiet hung over the centre of Rome following a lull in the fighting. By mutual consent, the two sides had broken contact and were resting in open sight of each other. Bodies littered the streets, almost all of them soldiers from the legion and the Guard. The civilians had stayed off the streets, bolting their doors and waiting anxiously for the contest to be decided. A handful of small fires had broken out in the confusion, and the men of the urban cohorts had been assigned to put them out, while the better-trained and armed soldiers continued to fight. The senate house had been taken, and most of its members had been escorted to the imperial palace. They had been told it was for their own protection, but no one was in any doubt that those who were part of Britannicus's faction, or who even expressed support for him, were unlikely to leave alive.

Most of the senior officers of the Praetorian Guard were gathered along the waist-high wall surrounding the Temple of Jupiter on the Capitoline Hill. Below them lay the sprawl of warehouses and markets of the Boarium, where Pastinus and the remaining men of his legion were holding out. The bridge to the island in the middle of the Tiber had been barricaded and was held by the Praetorians. Downstream, more of Cato's men were holding the Temple of Minerva and preventing any access to the barges and other small vessels of the wharf district.

There was no escape for the legionaries, Cato concluded. All that remained was to call on them to surrender, or wipe them out if they refused. Their only glimmer of hope was that the units who had been cut off at the Flaminian Gate might find another way into the centre of Rome and come to the relief of their comrades. But Cato was confident that the Praetorians would keep the remainder of the legion at bay. In any case, the latest report was that the rear elements of the Sixth Legion had worked their way around the Servian Wall and had halted across the road to Ostia, making no attempt to attack the city. Cato could clearly see the glimmer of armour away to the south, no more than two miles in the distance. He had added the information to his own report, which he had only just sent to the imperial palace, where Burrus, Pallas and the rest of Nero's inner circle waited anxiously for the danger to pass.

Cato pointed out the limits of the perimeter held by Pastinus and his men. 'I would say there are no more than fifteen hundred of them left. Perhaps as few as a thousand. Not enough to fight their way out. They're trapped, and they know it.'

'So why don't they give in?' asked Tertillius.

'Because they're good men,' Macro responded. 'They're legionaries. They'll fight on as long as Pastinus tells them to. More's the pity.'

The tribune sneered. 'That didn't seem to be the case back on the Flaminian Way.'

'They were ambushed and caught by surprise. That won't happen again. And if the Sixth is like any legion I've ever served with, they'll be thoroughly pissed off about that and more determined than ever to redeem themselves.'

Tertillius shook his head. 'You men from the legions have a pretty high opinion of yourselves.'

Macro looked round at the other officers, some of whom had also been transferred into the Guard, and saw from their grim expressions that they shared his understanding of the unyielding spirit of those legions tasked with defending the frontiers from the wild barbarians who lived beyond the control of Rome.

He shrugged. 'Just telling it like it is, sir.'

'We'll see. I'd wager they'll throw down their swords the moment we're ready to make a fresh assault on their positions.'

Macro's lips lifted in a mocking grin. 'I'll take that wager, sir. What sum did you have in mind?'

'Hopefully there will be no need for an assault,' Cato intervened wearily. 'While you bring your men up, I'll try and reason with Pastinus. His troops deserve the chance to live. They're only obeying orders. Most of them don't even know the truth about the part they are playing in this conspiracy. From what the prisoners have said, they think that the Praetorians have overthrown the emperor, and that they've been sent to put down a revolt.'

'That's too bad for them,' said Tertillius. 'I doubt the emperor is going to be quite as understanding as you are, Prefect Cato.'

'That's as maybe. But for now I am in command and I'll do what I can to put an end to this pointless bloodbath. So get your men in position, and wait for me to come back. If anything happens to me, you take command, Tertillius, and finish the job.'

'Yes, sir.'

Macro glanced anxiously at his friend. 'What's to stop Pastinus taking you prisoner or killing you, sir?'

'That.' Cato pointed towards the imperial standard. 'From what little I know of the man, he is a good soldier, and he'll honour a parley under a symbol blessed by the priests of Jupiter. You willing to carry that for me, Macro?'

'It'd be an honour, sir.'

'Thank you. And if I'm wrong about the legate, then he'll bring down shame on himself and his family line for as long as the name of Pastinus is remembered.' Cato smiled. 'Roman aristocrats are a precious bunch. Seems legionaries aren't the only ones with a high opinion of themselves. The difference is that they've done more to earn it. Come on, let's go.'

He turned towards the ramp leading down the hill and ordered one of the trumpeters to follow him. Macro chuckled and shook his head before he picked up the imperial standard and set off after his commander. As they rounded the slopes of the Capitoline and approached the Boarium, the Praetorians in the street stood and watched the small party curiously. They passed through the lines and crossed a small square towards the first of the rebel lookouts, and Cato gestured to the trumpeter.

'Sound two notes, count to five and keep doing it. Clear?'

'Yes, sir.'

The soldier raised the mouthpiece of the bucina to his lips and blew deeply. The blasts cut through the air, announcing their approach. The nearest of the lookouts called a warning down the street and then moved out to block Cato's path.

'Halt! What do you want?'

Cato paused to examine the man. He looked to be in his mid thirties, his features lined and scarred, and there was a look of steady defiance in his expression that vindicated what Cato

377

had said about the iron-hearted men of the legions just a moment earlier.

'I am Quintus Licinius Cato, acting commander of the Praetorian Guard, and prefect of auxiliaries. Before that, a centurion of the Second Legion. This is Centurion Macro, from the legions before he was a Praetorian.' He saw the lookout purse his lips in grudging respect at their credentials, as he had hoped. 'I wish to parley with Pastinus.'

'The legate's down there, sir.' The legionary turned and pointed. 'In the lawyers' courtyard at the entrance to the Boarium.' He cupped a hand to his mouth and shouted towards a squad of legionaries resting halfway down the street. 'This lot want a parley with the legate!'

An optio waved them forward and the lookout returned to his duty as Cato and the others made their way past him. The trumpeter went to raise his instrument again, but Cato stopped him and told him to return to his unit. 'No point in risking any more lives than necessary. Go.'

He and Macro continued towards the waiting optio, who looked them over and seemed satisfied there was nothing to be suspicious of.

'Follow me, sir.'

He led them past his men and turned the corner at the end of the street. On either side the tenement blocks gave way to warehouses and merchants' offices and the first of the specialist markets where the luxuries and necessities of the Empire were bought and sold. Here, the men of the Sixth Legion were hard at work barricading the streets and blocking alleys. A large party of men were using ropes to pull down a row of decrepit tenements that dated back to the days of the Republic. The ruins of those already demolished would greatly impede any attack made by the Praetorians, as well as supplying the defenders with chunks of masonry to hurl from their makeshift barricades and the walls surrounding the warehouses.

'I hope our friend the legate accepts that the game is up,' Macro muttered. 'Otherwise we're going to lose a lot more men.'

Cato nodded. 'Quite.'

The optio led them on, through the stalls of a cloth market, some of which were still piled with wares, so hurriedly had their owners fled from the fight raging through the streets. In the colonnaded courtyard of the capital's lawyers, scores of wounded men were sitting or lying on the open ground as the legion's medical orderlies attended to their injuries, or made the mortally wounded as comfortable as they could before they passed into the shadows. The most sumptuous-looking premises in the courtyard had a sign hanging above the entrance: 'Marcus Antonius Cephodius – the most silver-tongued advocate that silver can buy! All cases considered, regardless of guilt!'

The optio halted on the threshold. 'Praetorian officers want a parley, sir!'

'Really? Send 'em in.'

The optio stood aside and waved Cato and Macro through. The lawyer's office was large and well appointed, with scrolls neatly shelved and cushioned stools for clients arranged around an ornately carved desk of some dark wood. The legate was sitting on the corner of the desk as a medic wound a dressing about his head. Pastinus was a thin man in his forties with a narrow face and deep-set eyes. His breastplate, once polished, was now grimy and streaked with dried blood. He sat still so that the medic could continue his task. There was one other occupant of the room: a short, overweight man in a neat striped tunic. He had a large head, with thinning grey hair combed back and oiled. He sat in the corner, hands clasped together anxiously as he regarded the confrontation between the legate and the Praetorian officers.

'And who might you two be?' asked Pastinus.

'Prefect Cato, sir. And this is my second in command, Centurion Macro.' Cato eased himself up to his full height. 'I have come to ask for your surrender.'

'Indeed? Don't you think that is somewhat presumptuous as things stand?'

'Hardly, sir. We have you surrounded. The river is at your back. Your position is untenable, and continued hostilities will only lead to thousands of deaths amongst your men and mine. That would be pointless, sir. I am sure you can see that.'

'Of course. So why don't you and your men do the right thing: stop fighting against us and start fighting with us against that tyrant Nero and the scoundrels he surrounds himself with? Do that, and I am sure I can persuade my people to overlook your untimely change of sides in this matter.' The legate's eyes twinkled. 'Oh yes, Prefect Cato. I am fully aware of the role you should have played in these unfortunate proceedings. If you had done as you were supposed to, this would all be over now. Nero would be dead and the Senate would be proclaiming Britannicus emperor as we speak. Any man with a claim to a sense of honour would join our cause without a moment's hesitation. It is not too late for you to throw in your lot with us.'

Cato shook his head. 'It is far too late for that, sir. As well you know. Besides, I was never a willing party to your conspiracy. I was forced into it by your accomplices. The same people who kidnapped my son and tried to frame me for the murder of Senator Granicus, while pretending that it was the work of Pallas. I hardly think that is the work of those with any sense of honour at all.'

The legate winced slightly. 'Fair enough. Let us not talk of honour then. You claim to have the advantage, but half of my legion is still outside the city wall. It is only a matter of time before they find a way through and link up with my men here.'

'The rest of your legion is positioned on the road to Ostia, sir. Unless I miss my guess, they intended to wait there until they learn of the outcome of the contest here in the city. They won't save you.'

Pastinus took this in and reflected a moment before he responded. 'I may not live to see Nero fall, but fall he will. There are other forces in play.'

'Other forces?'

'Surely you did not think that the full scale of the plot was limited to those details made known to you? I had heard you were smarter than that, Prefect Cato. In any case, it is of no account to me. If the rest of my legion cannot cut their way through to me, then I am as good as dead already. That hardly inclines me to embrace the notion of surrender. I am no fool, Cato. I know how this ends for those who play for the highest stakes in the Empire and lose. Knowing Pallas as I do, it is certain that if I surrender, my death will be extremely painful and prolonged.'

'Yours is not the only death to be considered,' Macro interrupted. 'What about your men?'

'What about them? The vast majority come and go and leave no trace. They might as well not have existed. Men like you, Centurion. Even men like your prefect. Who will remember Cato in the generations to come? Only the names of the greatest families endure.'

'You aristocrats . . . you make me fucking puke, so you do.'

'Macro, that's not helpful.' Cato stepped between them. 'Sir, if you surrender, I give you my word that you will be accorded a trial. Your treason is unquestionable, but you will have the chance to state your case. With honour. If you choose to force your men to die with you, needlessly, then your name will merely live on in infamy.'

'A trial?' Pastinus laughed coldly and turned to the man sitting in the corner. 'Let's ask my host over there about a trial. I caught him skulking in this office, about to make off with his ill-gotten gains. What do you say, Cephodius? Surely a professional parasite like yourself with no more than a passing acquaintance with the truth, let alone any sense of justice, would leap at the chance to take my coin and lie on my behalf. Would you defend me?'

The lawyer cringed at the suggestion. Then he licked his lips nervously and replied in the modulated tone of the well-bred but morally destitute manner of his trade. 'I am not sure I am the best man for the job, sir. May I recommend my colleague Longinus?'

'Let me guess, less proficient but more expendable than yourself?' Pastinus shook his head in disgust. 'It's a pity that I may not be around to see the fall of Rome. First thing I'd like to have done is kill all the lawyers.'

'You wouldn't be the first to wish it, sir,' Macro said with feeling. 'Nor the last by a long way, I should think.'

The legate and the centurion shared a brief smile of common feeling before the medic tied off the dressing and Pastinus waved him out of the room. 'I shall not be surrendering to you, Prefect Cato. Though I thank you for making the offer. I suspect you are a more merciful man than those who command you.'

'Sir, I beg you to think again.'

'My decision is made. I would ask you to leave now.'

Cato made to reply, but saw that there was no point. He nodded sadly. 'As you wish, sir. Come, Macro.'

'Wait!' Cephodius rose to his feet. 'Take me with you.'

'Sit down!' Pastinus barked, thrusting out his finger. 'You move from that corner once more and I'll cut your throat myself.'

The lawyer shrank back like a whipped dog and resumed his position and Pastinus smiled at Macro and Cato.

'If there's one good deed I do before I meet my end, it'll be to take this oily weasel with me . . .'

Cato saluted the legate, and Macro followed suit, and then the two men turned and marched out of the office, across the courtyard and into the street that led back towards the Capitoline Hill. The legionaries regarded them silently as the two officers passed by, and Cato's heart was weighed down by the prospect that more good men were about to die as a result of the legate and his fellow conspirators.

When they returned to the temple they discovered that the emperor and his closest advisers had joined the officers looking out over the Boarium. Nero had chosen to dress in armour over his purple and gold tunic, but the military garb only served to emphasise his skinny physique and weak chin. A loose line of German bodyguards screened the imperial party and blocked Cato's way.

'Let them pass!' Burrus ordered, and the mercenaries stepped aside. The prefect of the Praetorian Guard was wearing a silvered breastplate that gleamed like a mirror, over a spotless white tunic. Cato could not help being conscious of the contrast between Burrus's appearance and that of himself and Macro, grime caked on their faces and kit, along with the spattered blood from the desperate fight for the Flaminian Gate.

'I understand you asked that traitor Pastinus to surrender.'

'Yes, sir.'

'Well?'

'He has refused to accept the terms I offered.'

'Then he will die. And most of his men with him,' Burrus concluded. 'A pity. But if that's the path he has chosen, then I can do nothing about it. Come, the emperor wants to speak with you.'

He led them over to Nero, who stood apart from the others, hands clasped behind his back as he looked down on the ground held by the survivors of the Sixth Legion.

The prefect of the Guard coughed softly. 'Sire, Cato has returned, along with the imperial standard.'

Nero turned and leaned his hip casually against the parapet. 'You've done well, Cato. Saved the day, in fact. But for your actions, those traitors might have seduced my Praetorians over to their side.'

'I was just doing my duty, sire.'

'Spoken like a loyal soldier. Now your emperor thanks you and you can return command of the Praetorians to Prefect Burrus.'

'With respect, sire, the danger has not yet passed. We must still defeat Pastinus and his men.'

Pallas, who had been standing within earshot, joined them. 'That is being taken care of. The orders were given while you were talking to Pastinus.'

Cato glanced towards Burrus. 'Orders?'

'We're going to burn them out,' Pallas continued. He licked his finger and held it up. 'The Venti are on our side; there's a nice breeze blowing towards the river, so we can contain the damage.'

Cato exchanged a glance with Macro before he responded. 'But there are over a thousand men in the Boarium, and no doubt many civilians still sheltering in the area.'

Nero clicked his tongue. 'That's too bad. One can't make an omelette without breaking a few eggs in the process.'

'Many of those eggs are innocent, sire.' Cato swallowed and forced himself to remain calm. 'And it's possible that my son is down there, amongst the conspirators.'

The emperor stared at him without a flicker of emotion. 'That's not my problem, Prefect Cato. Nor is it my fault. If your son is there, I will grieve with you when the time is right.'

Before Cato could think how to respond to this callous dismissal of Lucius's life, the imperial secretary interrupted.

'I doubt the boy is down there. It's more than likely that he is with Britannicus and the rest of the traitors who have already fled the city.'

Cato rounded on Pallas. 'What do you mean?'

'While you were dealing with the Praetorians, other elements loyal to the emperor were dealing with the conspirators. Many senators have been arrested, and their houses raided. One of the first was Vespasian's home. We found the body of his wife, Domitia, in a bath. She had opened her veins. There was a letter addressed to the emperor stating that her husband had no knowledge of the plot. That remains to be seen, of course. Vespasian will need to be closely questioned to determine the truth.'

'What about Lucius?'

'He was not found at the house, nor at any others we have searched so far. However, I have to tell you that Narcissus escaped the city. He was seen leaving by the Ostian Gate, with an escort and a cart. There was a small boy seated with him on the cart. I fear that may well be your son.'

Cato felt torn between the agony of helplessness and the desire to obliterate Narcissus. An image of Lucius, wide-eyed and terrified, filled his mind and paralysed him with anxiety for a moment. 'Are you sure?'

Pallas shrugged. 'I am only telling you what was reported to me. What is certain is that Narcissus, and some others, escaped capture and are making for Ostia with the cohorts of the Sixth Legion that failed to enter Rome.'

Cato hurried to the parapet and leaned out to see past Nero. Sure enough, the glimmer of armour from the men on the Ostian Way had vanished. And with them Narcissus, Lucius and the cart carrying the silver bullion. It was too late to bribe the Praetorians, but there was more than enough there to ensure the loyalty of the survivors of the Sixth Legion. And enough besides to bribe others, Cato realised.

His thoughts were interrupted by the emperor, who was grinning as he pointed down towards the Boarium. 'It's started!'

The others looked on as smoke billowed from a yard on the fringe of the area held by Pastinus and his men. Then they saw the glitter of flames leaping up amid the smoke.

'And there!' Nero leaned forward.

More fires started along the perimeter of the buildings held by the Sixth Legion, and the light breeze fanned the flames and directed them towards the river. One building after another caught fire as the blaze spread. Now Cato could see figures fleeing from the flames, retreating through the streets as they were pushed back by the heat. Some legionaries, and civilians, managed to find a way through to the bridge and fell into the hands of the waiting Praetorians. Those wise enough to throw down their arms were spared. Those who hesitated or resisted were cut down without mercy.

'How beautiful,' Nero mused. 'It is like a basket of rubies come to life.'

Cato looked on and shook his head. There was no beauty, no poetry in the inferno that was engulfing Pastinus and his men, and a broad swathe of one of the most ancient districts of Rome.

Pallas stood beside the emperor, a satisfied expression on his face. 'We may destroy Pastinus, sire, but there will be much damage to repair.'

'Repair? No. We can erase the whole area and build something better, something beautiful, in its place. We should embrace the opportunity that this fire has given us,' Nero mused as he turned to look speculatively at the rest of the city sprawling over the surrounding hills.

'Rest easy, Cato,' said Burrus quietly. 'I have the men of the city watch and the urban cohorts standing by to extinguish the flames the moment the fire has seen to Pastinus and his men. There won't be any more damage than I can help. You look exhausted. Perhaps you should return to barracks and rest. You and Macro. He can hand the standard over to one of the Germans now.' He turned and called one of the emperor's personal bodyguards over to relieve Macro of his burden. The centurion hesitated and glared at the German.

'I ain't used to handing Roman standards over to

barbarians . . .'

The German shrugged and grasped the polished wooden staff in both hands. Macro held it a moment longer, out of defiance, before he released his grip with a disgusted grunt.

'There, you hairy-arsed bastard. Look after it.'

Pallas leaned back from the parapet and folded his arms. 'And now it only remains to chase down Narcissus and the remnants of the conspiracy, and the matter is concluded.'

Cato shook his head. 'No . . . it's not over yet.'

'No?' Pallas cocked an eyebrow. 'What do you mean?'

'Something Pastinus said. "There are other forces in play." Those were his words.' Cato frowned as he recalled the insouciance of the legate in the face of his death and the almost certain failure of the conspiracy. It had not seemed quite right at the time, and Cato had put it down to the arrogance that came with the social class Pastinus had been born into. But now, on reflection, there was more to it. 'Besides the Sixth, are there any other units in transit across the Empire? Any other legions or auxiliary cohorts?'

Pallas considered the question and gently rubbed his throat. 'Yes, as it happens. The Twelfth Cyrenaica are on their way to Pannonia to put on a show of strength to the locals. They have a few auxiliary units with them, as I recall.'

'Pannonia? And are they stopping anywhere on the way?'

Pallas nodded. 'Brundisium. To pick up supplies. Why do you ask?'

Cato sighed. 'That's what Pastinus meant by other forces. I'm sure of it. If Narcissus and the surviving members of the plot can get to the Twelfth Legion, together with the silver and Britannicus, they'll have more than enough men to march on Rome and finish the job they started.'

The imperial secretary's expression became taut with concern. He called Burrus closer and made Cato repeat what he had just said.

'What in Hades should we do?' Burrus asked. 'We were lucky enough to survive today. If they bring in more men, we're fucked.'

'What about sending for our own reinforcements?' asked Pallas. 'We can summon a couple of loyal legions to stop the traitors.'

'The nearest legions we can count on are the other side of the Alps. They'd never reach us in time.'

Cato breathed deeply. 'Then we have to catch and destroy Narcissus and the others before they can link up with the Twelfth Legion. But we'll have to act at once if we are to stand any chance of stopping them.' He glanced at Burrus. 'What are your orders, sir?'

The commander of the Praetorian Guard looked away towards the dense smoke rolling across the Boarium and the river beyond. 'We need to take stock. I have to prepare the city's defences for a siege . . .'

Pallas caught Cato's eye and arched an eyebrow before resting a hand on Burrus's shoulder. 'One thing's certain. The emperor needs you at his side. No one else can protect him as well as you, my friend. You must stay here in Rome to ensure that the city is safe.'

Burrus nodded. 'You're right.'

'The task of pursuing the traitors can be handled by one of your subordinates. Cato seems to be the obvious choice. He knows Narcissus. Knows how he thinks. And you can spare him.'

'Yes. I suppose I can. For a while at least. Long enough to

chase 'em down.'

'Exactly,' Pallas said encouragingly. 'So, Prefect Cato, how many men do you need? Will half the Guard suffice?'

Burrus looked alarmed. 'That's too many. We can't afford to leave Rome thinly defended.'

'Four cohorts then?' Pallas suggested.

'Together with the mounted contingent,' Cato added. 'I'll need them to harass the enemy and slow them down.'

Burrus looked from man to man uncertainly and then nodded in resignation. 'Very well. But deal with them swiftly and return to Rome as soon as you can. Is that understood?'

Cato nodded. 'Yes, sir. You can rely on me.'

Burrus smiled. 'As you have already proved. Take your cohort, together with those of Tertillius, Macer and Pantella.'

His cohort was already under strength, even before the fight for the Flaminian Gate, Cato reflected. Tertillius had lost men too. Only the last two units were fresh. But it was likely to be a waste of precious time asking Burrus for more men. Cato saluted.

'I'll gather the men and set off at once, sir.'

'The gods go with you.' Burrus returned the salute and hurried to the emperor's side as Nero watched the fire with a look of fascinated glee.

Pallas sighed. 'All right, you have what you need. Do the job and return to Rome as soon as possible. I'll handle the emperor and Burrus for now.' He held out his hand and clasped Cato's forearm. 'I hope you find your son, Cato.'

There was something in his tone that caught Cato's attention, and at once he understood why Pallas had manoeuvred Burrus into choosing him to hunt down the traitors. With the fate of Lucius at stake, there was no officer in the army more motivated to carry out the mission. And if Lucius was killed, then no officer would exact revenge on the traitors as completely as Cato would.

'One final thing.' Pallas stared into his eyes fixedly. 'Bring Britannicus back alive. But make sure that Narcissus is eliminated. I want there to be no doubt that he is dead this time. Swear it.'

Cato nodded. 'Before all the gods, I swear that Narcissus will die, and that I will not rest until he is dead.' He pulled out his dagger and drew it across the palm of his spare hand, deeply enough to open a shallow cut. Then he clenched his fist as the first drops of blood ran down his wrist. 'I offer this blood to the gods in token of the certainty of my oath. Narcissus will die.'

CHAPTER THIRTY-SEVEN

Dawn was breaking over the hills to the east as Cato and Macro reined in their mounts on a rise overlooking the final stretch of road leading to Ostia. Ahead lay the great port through which passed all the luxuries bound for Rome, as well as the vital supply of grain that kept the masses fed. Inside the wall lay tightly packed apartment blocks, and beyond loomed temples, basilicas and warehouses lining the Tiber and the harbour. The masts of ships rose dark and needle-like. Behind the two officers rode one of the mounted squadrons. The other three squadrons of the Praetorian cavalry had been launching hit-and-run attacks on the enemy column through the night in an attempt to slow the legionaries down. Four miles behind Cato marched the main column, striving to catch up with their prey, but now he could see that it was futile. Narcissus and those of his companions who had escaped Rome would reach Ostia well ahead of their pursuers.

The head of the enemy column had already entered the port, and the rest of the cohorts had closed up and were easily fending off the feints and sudden charges of the Praetorian cavalry.

'That's made things tricky,' Macro commented, as he pulled

the stopper from his canteen and took a slug of the acrid wine he preferred to drink when he needed to sharpen his wits and fend off weariness. He winced as the liquid burned its way down his throat, then coughed and spat to one side. 'Once they're holed up in Ostia, we're going to have trouble winkling them out. Especially with the number of men Burrus provided. We'll not have nearly enough to launch an assault on Ostia. Unless you've got a plan up your sleeve.' He looked at Cato hopefully.

'No plan at present, alas.'

'Then we'll just have to starve them out.'

Cato shook his head. 'That won't be an option. It's clear enough that Narcissus and his friends won't be sitting on their hands waiting for the Twelfth to relieve them. Not if I am any judge of the man. He'll want to go to them before Nero gets the chance to try and buy them off. It's no accident that Narcissus made for Ostia. He's after the ships to take his followers down the coast. They'll make for Brundisium, or perhaps land at Cumae or Misenum and cut across to the Appian Way to join their reinforcements. With the fortune in that war chest of theirs, the traitors will have enough silver to buy the loyalty of more than enough soldiers to win the day.'

Macro considered his friend's calculations and yawned with exhaustion. 'If they take to the ships then we'll have to follow them. Nothing else for it.'

'Not quite nothing. If the fleet at Misenum is still loyal to Nero, we might be able to head them off.' Cato turned in his saddle and ordered the nearest of the cavalrymen to come forward. 'I want you to ride to Misenum. Find the admiral and tell him that the emperor commands him to use his ships to block any vessels making passage to the south. All ships are to be held in port until further orders, or sunk if they resist. If he questions your instructions tell him what has taken place in Rome, and remind him that those who fail to respond to the emperor's orders will be treated as traitors and share their fate. Don't stop for anything on the way.' Cato rubbed his eyes for a moment. 'You'll need remounts. Take two horses from your men. Is all that clear?'

'Yes, sir.'

'Then go now.'

The Praetorian saluted, wheeled his horse around and headed back to his men, barking an instruction for the last two riders to dismount.

Macro rolled his shoulders to ease the tension in his back before he spoke again. 'What happens if the admiral is in on the conspiracy?'

'Then we'll have to hope that we can find ships fast enough to overhaul Narcissus before he reaches Misenum. Otherwise he'll escape and we'll have failed. In which case we'd better hope that Britannicus shows us mercy, because I doubt Narcissus will. Not after I thwarted him back in Rome.'

'Do you know anything about the admiral?'

'Nothing. The navy's a different world, Macro. I don't tend to keep up to speed on naval matters. It's been enough of a challenge trying to keep abreast of who I can trust amongst the men around me ever since we were transferred to the Guard. Present company excepted.'

'So I should bloody think. It'd take more treasure than the Empire can afford to get me to stick a knife in your back.'

Cato looked at him. 'How reassuring it is to know that everything has its price.'

'Ah, come on. Just trying to lighten the mood.' Macro's

smile faded as he saw the drawn features of his friend. He reached across and patted Cato on the shoulder. 'We'll find Lucius. I swear it. We'll find him.'

'Yes . . .' Cato closed his eyes and bowed his head. He felt impossibly tired. His limbs were leaden and even the simplest, most routine thought was an effort. He craved sleep as never before, and yet he was driven on by the thought of his son, still alive and in need of him. He dared not dwell too much on Lucius's fate, because he knew it was possible that he was already dead. The only reason for Narcissus to keep the boy alive was that he might still have some value as a hostage. Cato forced himself to sit erect in the saddle and open his aching eyes. 'Macro, ride back to the column and hurry the men on. I need them in Ostia as soon as possible. As many as you can. The stragglers can catch up later.'

Macro cocked his head slightly. The men had not rested since the night before, and since then many had fought their way through Rome and marched on Ostia without any break. Amongst them were the walking wounded who had refused to abandon their standards when the cohorts set off. That was true of every man in Cato's cohort who could still put one foot in front of another. And their example inspired the rest, all keen to follow the new emperor's chosen hero of the moment. But for all that, Macro knew that his friend was driven solely by a father's desire to save his child from harm.

'I'll keep the lads on the go. About time they had to do some proper marching instead of traipsing round Rome looking to get laid.' The centurion saluted and turned his horse, spurring it back past the squadron in the direction of the capital. Cato took a last look ahead and then raised his arm and waved the mounted men forward.

They cantered down from the rise towards the rear of the enemy column just as the legionaries drove off another attack by the three squadrons who had been sent forward to harass the fugitives. Several Praetorians had already been lost, and as Cato approached, he saw one of his men turn away too slowly and the legionaries quickly fall on horse and rider, slashing at the beast's legs as it staggered and then collapsed, spilling the rider from his saddle. The man landed heavily and rolled to one side, and then was lost from sight as the legionaries closed over him and stabbed him to death.

Reining in a safe distance from the enemy rearguard, Cato called the other squadrons to him with a hoarse shout. The horsemen re-formed their units as the sun crested the hills and cast a ruddy light across the open country in front of Ostia. The dull colours of a moment ago were now lurid in the beams of sunlight, and long shadows stretched out from the lines of horsemen, where steamy breath plumed from the flared nostrils of the mounts. There were barely a hundred of them, Cato estimated with frustration. Not nearly enough to risk any further attacks on the enemy, let alone to force their way into the port. All they could do was keep the legionaries under observation until Macro came up with the infantry.

Cato gave the command to advance in column and the other squadrons fell in line behind his as they moved parallel to the road leading to the gates of Ostia. His gaze swept the enemy ranks, but there was no sign of the cart, or any civilians amongst whom Lucius might be present. They must have been at the front of the column with Narcissus, he guessed, and had already entered the port before dawn had broken.

As they got closer to the city, they saw several bodies dumped on the side of the road; the men assigned to the town's night watch, Cato surmised, hastily dispatched by the vanguard of Narcissus's column as they entered Ostia. The centurion in charge of the rearguard shouted an order, and his century halted and closed up, presenting a rectangle of shields. Another order set them on the move again, covering the rest of the column as it passed through the gate and out of sight. The Praetorians could only look on helplessly as the legionaries tramped along the road and entered the city. A moment later the gates closed in the faces of the pursuers and the gleaming helmets of soldiers appeared in the tower over the arched entrance.

Cato halted his men and leaned against his saddle horns as he scrutinised the port's defences. To his right lay the steady flow of the Tiber; the wall ran down to its banks and ended in a fortified tower. In the other direction it ran around the edge of the port for well over a mile before ending at the mouth of the river, where another tower rose. A ditch separated the wall from the scattered buildings that grew up along the other routes that led to Ostia. If Narcissus had ordered the other gates to be seized and defended as well, then there was no way in to Ostia for the present.

Not by land, at least.

Cato turned and looked out towards the river. A handful of barges and skiffs were already abroad. Two large craft were being drawn upstream by yoked oxen, while another empty barge was approaching from the direction of Rome. It slowly passed behind a screen of trees and disappeared from view. Cato had seen that there was no way to conceal a party of men aboard the barge; they would be seen from the tower on the bank of the Tiber at once. But one more man would not be noticed . . .

He wheeled round to face the senior decurion. 'Take all four squadrons forward. Ride up and down in front of the main gate, kicking up as much dust and making as much noise as you can. Challenge them to a fight. Just keep their attention on you for as long as you can until Macro arrives. When he does, tell him I've gone ahead and I'll be in Ostia waiting for him.'

'Sir?'

'Just say that I'll see him on the wharf.'

They exchanged a salute, and Cato walked his horse to the rear and waited until the decurion gave the order to approach the gate. A moment later, the decurion called on the squadron's trumpets to sound to add to the distraction. A nice touch, Cato thought, as he steered his mount towards the belt of trees growing along the bank of the Tiber and urged it into a canter. As soon as he reached the cover of the trees, he dismounted, tethered the horse and ran through the morning shadows until he came to the water. The barge was fifty paces downstream, and he turned and ran towards it, calling out to the crewman at the stern, who was heaving his pole into the riverbed to keep the vessel on course.

The man turned as Cato caught up with the barge. He looked alarmed at the sight of the haggard and bloodied soldier hurrying towards him. Given the previous day's events in Rome, his reaction was understandable.

'What d'you want?' he demanded.

'Pull into the bank.' Cato slowed down to catch his breath. 'Do it now.'

'Who are you?'

'I'm acting on the emperor's orders . . . Now let me come aboard.'

'Nero, eh?' The man nodded, and then called out to his companion in the bows. 'Paulinus, get us to the bank!'

His friend glanced over his shoulder, hesitated a moment as

he caught sight of Cato, then shrugged and braced himself against his pole, heaving until the bows eased round towards the reeds at the edge of the river. Cato was too tired to attempt to jump from the bank to the barge in full armour, and instead eased himself down into the muddy shallows and waded towards the middle of the barge where the beam was lowest. He managed to heave himself up and swing a leg aboard, then rolled over the side and into the bottom of the barge and lay there gasping for breath. The man at the bows pushed off, and the barge edged back into the current as his comrade made his way forward and squatted down beside Cato.

'So what's this about, then?'

Easing himself up, Cato undid the buckles at the side of his breastplate and eased the armour off with a sigh of relief.

'I need to get into Ostia. I take it you're aware of the conspiracy against the emperor?'

The man nodded. 'I could hardly have missed it. Soon as that fire kicked off, I got my boat out of the city as fast as I could. Paulinus and I will wait it out in Ostia until things have settled down. That was the plan, at least.' He scratched his cheek. 'But seeing as how there's soldiers all over the place, I ain't so sure. What's your business in Ostia, mate?'

'The traitors are there and I need to get inside the port without them seeing me. Will you help?'

'I don't know much about traitors. But I like the new emperor well enough. He saw to it that there was free bread and wine at the last races in the Great Circus. So he'll do me. Yes, we'll help you. Best you lose that armour if you don't want to attract attention.'

Cato nodded gratefully, and the bargee picked up the breastplate and stuffed it under a pile of empty sacks near the stern. Then he picked up a weathered cloak and tossed it to Cato. 'Put that on. It'll hide the sword and make you look like one of us.'

Cato did as he was told, trying to ignore the musty, sweaty odour coming from the soiled folds of the cloak. He pulled it round his torso and went aft to sit on the empty sacks as the barge cleared the line of trees. The level of the Tiber was high enough for him to see over the bank at this point, and he watched as the Praetorian cavalry surged around the gate and walls on either side, brandishing their spears and shouting challenges and insults to the legionaries above them.

'That's your lot, I assume?' the bargee commented.

Cato hesitated before he replied. Although the man was doing him a favour, it was possible he might be tempted to betray Cato for a reward if he realised his rank. So he gave a nonchalant nod. 'My mob, yes.'

'Well, they ain't going to get in by acting like that, are they? Bloody ponces, them Praetorians. Present company excepted.'

Cato raised a smile and then settled back, trying to appear unconcerned by the events outside the gate as the barge glided down towards the tower that loomed over the river at the end of the town wall. As they got closer, he could make out the bolt thrower mounted there. A relic from the days when pirates still dared to raid the mouth of the river, to be sure, but if it was still in working order, it could sink the barge easily enough. Already a few faces had appeared along the parapet, staring in the direction of the vessel as it drew near. But with only three men aboard, and no possibility of a landing party being concealed in the empty hull, they took no action as it passed by and made for the wharf, where scores of similar craft were tied up. Paulinus thrust his pole down and heaved the bows round, and the current carried the barge gently towards them. At the last moment he shipped his pole and reached out to grasp the side of the nearest vessel, holding fast. The man at the stern followed suit and nodded towards a coil of rope close to Cato.

'Take that and put a loop round the other boat's cleat, then fasten it off on ours. Got that?'

Cato nodded and made his way forward to do the bargee's bidding. A moment later, they were securely rafted alongside, and Cato glanced across the other barges towards the wharf. There was no sign of any soldiers; just a handful of other crewmen aboard some of the barges, and civilians hurrying in and out of the warehouses opposite. The tense atmosphere of the capital and a desire to get off the streets and away from the soldiers had spread to Ostia, Cato noted. He would have little chance of blending in as he made his way through the port, and would need to proceed with caution.

He thanked the bargees, then clambered over the intervening vessels until he reached the wharf. Two hundred paces to his right was the short mole that marked the deeper waters where the seagoing vessels were moored or lay at anchor, their masts and yards a profusion of angled lines against the clear morning sky. Sunlight gleamed on the helmets and armour of the soldiers standing on the mole, and more were searching the nearest of the barges for equipment and loot. Cato made his way towards them along the near-deserted street that ran between the wharf and the warehouses. A short distance from the nearest soldiers, he turned into an alley and made his way into the centre of the port, along the side of the vast granary that received the grain from Aegyptus and Sicilia that fed the teeming population of Rome.

Soldiers were passing at the end of the alley, and Cato turned back to work his way round the granary, continuing to head towards the part of Ostia where the ships berthed. If his suspicions were correct, that was where Narcissus and his companions would be organising the loading of their forces to make their escape by sea. And Lucius would be with them. Increasing his pace, he worked his way round to the Temple of Hercules, close to the wide thoroughfare that cut straight across the centre of the port. The streets around it were packed with soldiers heading for the docks. Some units were held together by their centurions and optios, and marched by in narrow columns. Others, who had become separated from their units, made their way singly or in small groups. Some paused to break into the small shops lining the street and steal whatever portable valuables they could find, as well as wine and food. The priests of the temple had closed and barred the door, and watched the passing soldiers through small grilled windows either side of the entrance.

Cato stood amongst a cluster of civilians on the highest of the steps rising from the street. His companions looked on anxiously as the legionaries streamed past.

'Always thought that lot were supposed to defend us,' one man complained quietly to his neighbour as he pointed out a legionary with a bale of silk across his shoulder. 'Not act like conquerors.'

'Bloody soldiers,' the other replied bitterly. 'Good-for-nothing thugs. No better than the other scum who tried to kick Nero out. They're the real villains. Setting Roman against Roman. And unleashing those dogs on us.'

Cato carefully pulled his cloak closer to his body to make sure his sword was not seen, and edged round the small crowd and down the steps at the side, moving on through the alleys until he emerged between two warehouses on Ostia's main dock. The wharf was crowded with legionaries, and Cato eased himself back behind the corner and peered out cautiously. He could see parties of legionaries embarking on ships, while more parties went aboard other vessels and cut away the rigging and slashed sails that were stowed on deck. Still others were loading combustible materials: tubs of pitch and bundles of kindling and flax from the nearest warehouses. He took all this in while he scanned the wharf for any sign of Narcissus and the other plotters, and hopefully Lucius too.

As he watched, a cluster of litters appeared a hundred paces away and several figures emerged, the unmistakable bald pate of Narcissus amongst them. Narcissus gestured towards one of the handful of warships moored close by, and the party hurriedly boarded the ship and made their way to the covered shelter at the stern. Cato craned his neck and stood on his toes to search for his son, but he could not see over the heads of the intervening soldiers and the sailors they had pressed into service. Still, if Lucius was anywhere, he would be close to Narcissus and the other ringleaders. There might be a chance to rescue him if Cato could only get nearer.

He ran down the alley, then turned into another behind the warehouses and followed that in the direction of the warships. When he judged he was close enough, he slowed and looked for a way into the nearest warehouse. There was a small door at the rear of the yard beside it, and he tried the handle. Though the timbers of the door were old and weathered, they held firm, and the bolt on the far side rattled but did not budge. Cato glanced round to make sure there were no witnesses, then took out his sword and feverishly worked the point into the gap at the edge of the door frame, splintering the wood until the bolt on the far side was exposed. Then he worked the edge of the sword on the bolt, shifting it fractionally each time, until at last the end came out of the receiver and the door swung open with a dull squeak from the hinges.

Beyond was a narrow yard at the rear of the warehouse with a loading platform and a wide opening to a cavernous interior where large unglazed jars were piled on wooden racks. From the pungent smell of the place, it was clear that the main product stored at the warehouse was garum. Cato heaved himself up on to the platform and entered the warehouse, passing between the racks as he made for the front of the building. There were a number of arched entrances opening on to the wharf, but all the doors were securely bolted. A flight of stairs led to an office, and he saw that there were windows either side of a balcony. He approached the nearest window and gently slipped the latch, then eased the shutters apart to afford him a view over the wharf.

Directly in front of him, lines of soldiers snaked towards boarding ramps leading on to two large cargo ships. Shifting his position, Cato could see that more ships were being loaded on either side; beyond them, several had already moved away from the wharf and were being propelled towards the entrance of the harbour by long oars. Smoke trailed across the gentle swell in the sheltered waters, and Cato saw that some of the vessels further along the wharf had been set on fire to deny their use to the loyalist forces advancing on Ostia. Moving to the other side of the window, he looked for the warships he had observed earlier and then felt a surge of panic when he saw that their berths were empty. He reached out and opened the shutters a bit further, willing to risk being spotted by the soldiers below. That was when he saw them: three biremes, slowly manoeuvring to point their rams at the entrance to the harbour.

On the nearest, he spotted Narcissus standing at the rail as he looked out over the ramshackle fleet heading to sea. Beside him was the tiny figure of Lucius, hands reaching up as he tried to peer over the side. Cato felt his throat constrict in pain as he saw his son. There was relief too, that he was alive, but now there was no hope of effecting his rescue. It was too late, and Cato felt as if his heart was being torn apart.

As he looked on in despair, he saw Narcissus glance down at the boy and ruffle his hair. Then he bent to pick Lucius up and lifted him so the boy could see better. Lucius pointed out at the ships and looked up to Narcissus, and a moment later they shared a smile. Cato felt his grief turn to nausea and bitter, bitter hatred of Narcissus. The kidnapper of his son. The vile, cunning traitor who had used the boy to force Cato into betraying the emperor. And there he was, handling Lucius like some doting uncle.

There was no manner of death, no matter how humiliating, agonising and lingering, that Narcissus did not deserve, thought Cato. The man was steeped in the blood of his victims. He had destroyed the fortunes of all who stood in his way. He had manipulated Cato and Macro to carry out his dirty work. All along he had claimed that what he did was for the good of Rome, and all the time the only purpose of his malignant actions was the aggrandisement and enrichment of himself. He was as vile a specimen of all that was ignoble, mendacious, selfish and cruel as ever walked the earth, and he must be exterminated, Cato resolved.

Cato ground his teeth as he glared at the sight of his son in the arms of the monster who had blighted his life ever since they had first met. The monster who had poisoned Cato's marriage and who had now stolen his son away from him. It took all his self-control not to roar with rage and scream out a challenge to Narcissus to turn about and fight him man to man. But that would only bring down death on Cato, and he would die not knowing if Lucius was safe. Instead, he forced himself to back away from the window. To close the shutters and retreat back down the stairs and out of the warehouse.

As he made his way back to the main route through the port, he set his mind to organising the pursuit of his enemy. Most of the legionaries had already reached the harbour, and only a few stragglers remained. More of the civilians dared to emerge from their homes now, their anxiety aroused by the columns of smoke rising from the direction of the sea. Cato pushed past them, heedless of their protests and the insults hurled after him. He knew that he must reach the gate and ensure that the way was opened for Macro and the column of Praetorians marching on Ostia.

The towers of the gatehouse were in sight when he saw people rushing aside a short distance ahead of him. A moment later, he caught sight of the crest of a centurion's helmet, and then the forty or so men trotting behind him. The final element of the rearguard assigned to hold the gate while the main force made for the ships in the harbour. Cato stood and watched as the legionaries passed by, their boots tramping loudly on the flagstones as their accoutrements jingled and slapped against them. Then they were gone, and he turned and ran towards the gate. He was breathing hard by the time he reached it, exhaustion of heart and body making his limbs tremble. Still, he managed to work the locking beam free, and bracing his feet, he hauled the gates open and stumbled out of the city.

The cause of the rearguard's hurry to reach the remaining

ships was immediately clear. Fifty paces away, the Praetorian cavalry were formed up on either side of the road leading to Rome. And marching down that road at a lively pace came Macro and the four Praetorian cohorts. As soon as he saw his friend, the centurion broke into a run, and a moment later he was supporting Cato as the latter leaned against the inside of the arched gateway.

'Are you all right, lad? Are you wounded?'

'I'm fine. Just need a breather. Then I'll be all right.' Cato closed his eyes and took a few deep breaths before he continued. 'Lucius is alive.'

'Alive? Thank the gods.'

'I saw him. With Narcissus. At the harbour.'

'Then let's go.' Macro turned to call out to the men marching along the road towards them. 'Second Cohort! At the double! On me!'

Without waiting for the men to catch up, Macro and Cato entered the port and hurried along the main street, all the way down to the wharf. As they emerged into the open, they saw the last of the legionaries scrambling aboard a cargo ship, then the crew slipped the moorings and used their sweep oars to push the vessel away from the wharf. All around lay the ships with cut rigging swinging uselessly from masts and spars. Many ships were on fire, and the first sailors were already emerging from the alleys to try and save their livelihoods as the smoke rolled over the warehouses and the sea. Thick coils swirled up into the sky like writhing serpents. Through the gaps in the smoke, Cato could see the ships commandeered by Narcissus and his followers rounding the harbour mole and turning to the south. At the head of the motley squadron were the three biremes, oars rising, sweeping across the swell and splashing down in a steady rhythm as they drove the warships forward.

Cato strained his eyes to make out every detail of the lead ship, and then turned as the first of the Praetorians reached the scene.

'We need ships. I want those fires put out and the rigging repaired at once. Then we'll chase those bastards down and crucify every last one of them. As surely as night follows day.'

CHAPTER THIRTY-EIGHT

The evidence of the sea battle that had taken place the day before was clear to all. Several ships lay beached or washed up on rocks. Timbers, spars, shreds of sailcloth, debris and bodies wallowed in the gentle swell as the ships carrying Cato and his soldiers sailed towards the humpbacked promontory beyond which lay the naval base of Misenum. Cato and Macro were aboard the largest of the cargo ships that had been hurriedly repaired at Ostia and now led the fleet of other vessels acting as troop transports. They were not the only ships at sea this morning. Five small warships, liburnians, lay hove to, forming a loose screen across the approaches to the bay that stretched from the promontory to the cape at Surrentum some thirty miles beyond.

'Looks like your message got through to the admiral,' said Macro as he surveyed the scene. 'The navy put up quite a fight.'

Cato nodded. 'The question is, which side won? Are those ships waiting for us ours or theirs?'

Macro shaded his eyes and squinted at the liburnians before he responded. 'Ours. Surely?'

'I wonder.' Thanks to a good night's sleep curled up under a cloak on the deck, Cato's mind was fresh and alert to potential dangers. 'We've no idea where the admiral's loyalties lay. Nor if there were any traitors in his fleet. For all we know, the traitors won the day and those warships have been ordered to watch out for us. Maybe even attack us. We'll know soon enough. Look, there.' Cato pointed out the vessel that had just raised its oars and turned towards them. A moment later the banks of oars on either side rose and fell in unison, and a small spray of white showed where the ram was cutting through the sea.

'Shouldn't we signal the other ships to heave to?' asked Macro. 'Until we know for sure?'

'No, we keep going.'

Until they knew what had become of Narcissus, Cato was determined to drive his men on, pursuing the enemy like wolves snapping at the heels of sheep.

Macro glanced at his friend, concerned that Cato seemed to have abandoned his usual calculated caution. But then again, the life of his son was at stake, and that was more than enough reason for Cato to behave in this way. But if that put the operation and the lives of the men at risk, Macro knew that he would have to intervene, and he was not comfortable at the prospect of confronting his close friend and, more importantly, superior officer.

The wind was from the north and the Praetorian flotilla closed rapidly with the liburnian. When the latter was no more than a quarter of a mile off, it began to turn. Macro looked on suspiciously as the bows of the warship aimed directly at them for an instant. Then, in a neatly executed manoeuvre, the liburnian swept round and drew up alongside Cato's ship, reducing its speed to match that of the ponderous cargo vessel.

'Thank the gods for that,' said Macro. 'I thought for a moment there the bastard was going to come at us.'

'The thought had occurred to me too,' Cato commented wryly. 'But it seems we're safe, for now at least.'

An officer on the stern platform raised a speaking trumpet. 'Is there a Prefect Quintus Licinius Cato aboard?'

Cato cupped his hands to his mouth to make his reply. 'That's me.'

'May I come aboard, sir? Admiral Lemillus ordered me to report to you the moment you reached Misenum.'

'By all means.' Cato turned to the captain of the cargo vessel and ordered him to heave to. The sailors hurried to release the sheets as the steersman turned the vessel up into the wind. The rest of the flotilla began to follow suit as the warship lowered a skiff over the side and the officer climbed down with two crewmen, who shoved off and quickly stroked the small craft over the gentle swell to the side of the cargo ship. A moment later the naval officer climbed through the side port, where Cato and Macro were awaiting him.

'Navarch Spiromandes, sir.'

'Make your report,' Cato responded curtly. 'We saw wreckage. I take it the admiral managed to intercept the traitors?'

'Aye, sir. Your messenger reached the base just before they were sighted from the watchtower on the point. The admiral gave the order to put to sea as swiftly as possible. Most of the ships are drawn up for winter maintenance, but we managed to get the rest out just as the enemy rounded the promontory. The admiral ordered them to surrender, but their leader produced Britannicus and said that he was the true emperor and that he ordered the fleet to stand down to let them pass. The admiral refused and ordered our ships to attack. We were outnumbered three or four to one, but they only had a handful of warships so we were able to sink several of theirs for no loss

411

before they slipped through and cut across the bay. We pursued them and captured a few more, but at least half escaped.'

'Escaped? Where?'

The navarch pointed south. 'Caprae, sir. They managed to make the harbour and landed their soldiers on the island. The admiral has them blockaded there and orders that you join him with your men at once.'

Macro glanced at Cato. 'Sounds like someone wants to assume command of the operation.'

Cato stared at the naval officer for a moment before he issued his instructions. He had visited the island briefly some years before and from what he could recall it would be an easy place to defend since the island was mostly surrounded by steep cliffs. 'We will make for Caprae. Meanwhile, take your ships and sail ahead of us and tell your admiral that I require him to report to me the moment I arrive. He is not to attack before then, save only to prevent the enemy from attempting to leave the island. You will also inform him that I am acting under the direct orders of the emperor and that Nero has authorised me to command whatever forces I deem necessary to crush the traitors. That includes the fleet at Misenum, and its commander.'

Spiromandes raised his eyebrows. 'The admiral may not like that, sir. The chain of command places only the emperor above him.'

'I understand. As far as the admiral is concerned, I am acting in the name of the emperor, and you will tell him that he will obey me as if I was Nero himself. If the admiral . . . What is his name again?'

'Gaius Lemillus Secundus, sir.'

'Fine, if Admiral Lemillus wishes to query my authority, he is to hand over command of the fleet and make his way to

Rome to confer with the emperor directly. If he is considering obstructing me, then he should know that the emperor has decreed that anyone who aids the traitors, even by omission, will be regarded as one of their sympathisers.' Cato paused. 'I don't think I need to spell out what that might entail for your admiral, or any of his officers that get in my way. Do you understand?'

The navarch chewed his lip and nodded. 'Yes, sir.'

'Then be on your way.'

Spiromandes saluted and quickly climbed down into the skiff, ordering his men to row back to the warship. Shortly afterwards the liburnian's oars were powering the vessel forward and it swiftly pulled ahead of the cargo ship. A signal pennant ran up the mast and the other warships turned about and began to follow.

'If you're in such a tearing hurry to get at Narcissus, you could have gone ahead with them,' said Macro.

'No. Better to let Admiral Lemillus understand his position before I reach the scene. He may not like it, but it's better than me springing in on him the moment I board his flagship.'

As the Praetorian flotilla rounded the promontory, the vast bay opened up ahead of them. To the left rose the towering peak of Vesuvius, the tip of which was just visible through the haze. Along the shore nestled a series of small towns and fishing villages. Despite the season, there were a number of craft on the waters of the bay – fishing boats and cargo ships – and Cato could not help marvelling at how peacefully the world went about its business while great affairs of state and personal tragedies were played out at the margins. It mattered not a jot to most of the people living along the shore of this bay whether Nero or Britannicus was emperor. Any more than it mattered whether Cato rescued his son or not. The life of any person not destined to be inscribed in the annals of history was a brief, intimate thing, he reflected. And most of it was spent struggling to survive, coping with tragedy and disappointment. Happiness of any sort was no more than a brief interlude, therefore it should be treated like the windfall of fortune it was. He had loved and lost Julia. And now it was possible – nay, likely – that he would lose Lucius as well.

He tried to push such thoughts aside and lifted his nose to breathe in the clean, salty air, so different from the sweaty stench of Rome. He turned to Macro and made himself smile as he decided to turn his mind from his darkest concerns.

'So, what are your plans for you and Petronella?'

'Plans?' Macro frowned, then laughed. 'By the gods, what brought that on? We're fresh from the fight and on the trail of one of the most dangerous traitors Rome has ever seen, and you're wondering about my domestic arrangements.'

'Why not? We're not going to reach Caprae for a few hours. Nothing useful we can do until then.'

Macro shrugged. 'I suppose not. You've been thinking about Julia, haven't you?'

'You know me too well.'

'I know you enough to know when you're troubled. And usually what it is that troubles you too. So . . .'

'You're right.' Cato's expression softened. 'I was wrong about Julia. I cursed her name and made myself hate her. I shouldn't have done that. It has poisoned my memories of her.'

'That's not your fault, lad. That was the work of Narcissus and his friends.'

'I know. But it's taught me a lesson. The fact is that our situation is precarious. And it always seems to be, for that matter. So we owe it to ourselves to take what rewards come our way. If you care for Petronella, then cherish the time you have with her. Every moment of it. If we get out of this alive, make sure you make her your wife.'

'Wife? A wife for me?' Macro clicked his tongue. 'Now there's a laugh. I've got something of a reputation. I go and get married and the boys in the officers' mess will piss themselves laughing. Mind you, might be worth it just for that.'

Cato glanced at him and smiled lightly. 'I know you well too, my friend. And I know that your lady is worth rather more to you than that. I'm just saying that you should do something about it.'

Macro shrugged. 'Well then, maybe I will. Now if you don't mind, if there's nothing important to discuss, I'll take a nap while I can.'

'As you wish.'

Macro went aft to the steps leading up to the steersman's small deck and wedged himself in the angle between the steps and the siderail. He folded his legs and arms and closed his eyes, and in moments his chin had slumped down on to his breast in sleep. Once again Cato envied his friend his ability to sleep so easily. He had never developed a knack for it himself. Troubled thoughts and a restless mind always plagued him at such times. He made his way forward and stood at the bows, holding on to the stem post, carved and simply painted with the likeness of Neptune. The heights of Caprae were just visible through the haze now, rising above the horizon, and Cato felt his stomach tighten at the prospect of a final reckoning with Narcissus.

Admiral Lemillus made no attempt to conceal his disdain for the young Praetorian officer acting as his temporary commander.

He was a tall, weathered man with wrinkled features, and his deep-set brown eyes missed little as he briefed Cato and Macro on the deck of his flagship, an old trireme that looked as if it might have seen action at the Battle of Actium. The *Pegasus* rode the swell comfortably as it lay less than a quarter of a mile from the island's harbour. The remainder of his small fleet was spread out on either side; behind them were the cargo ships carrying Cato's troops.

Caprae measured nearly four miles from end to end. A line of sheer cliffs ran across the middle of the island, cutting it in half. The eastern side, closest to the mainland, provided a gentle-looking saddle between the cliffs and the steadily rising ground that led up to the narrow tip upon which Emperor Augustus had constructed a villa where the traitors were no doubt holed up. The villa had been massively expanded by his heir, Tiberius, to take full advantage of the spectacular views of the bay. It was a home worthy of a god, and for that reason it had become known as the Villa of Jupiter. It was reached by a steep track leading up from the harbour. Cato had visited the island once before and knew that the route would be easy to defend since there was no other approach to the villa. But the more pressing difficulty was making a landing on the island itself. Apart from the harbour in front of them and another tiny harbour on the far side of the island, which only had a dock large enough to take one ship at a time, Caprae was protected by sheer cliffs.

'A frontal assault on the main harbour would be suicidal,' Lemillus explained as Cato gazed at the masts of the ships behind the mole. Barely a dozen of the vessels that Narcissus had seized from Ostia had made it to the safety of the harbour. But once inside, and having taken control of the defences, they were safe enough. The admiral pointed towards the solid guard towers either side of the entrance to the harbour. 'As you can see, there are catapults mounted on each tower, and a battery of bolt throwers on top of the cliff to the left there. There's smoke rising there too. So we can assume they have incendiaries ready to shoot at any vessels attempting to enter the harbour. In addition there are bolt throwers mounted at intervals along the mole. The simple truth is that we would face very heavy casualties if we attempted to take the harbour by force. Any ship that does get through will land its troops in the face of overwhelming odds, and those men will be massacred.'

Cato sucked his teeth. 'Nevertheless, we must take the island and capture the conspirators. We cannot risk them slipping away under cover of darkness and making their way to join up with the reinforcements coming up from Brundisium.'

'Well, what do you suggest then, Prefect Cato? That I sacrifice the fleet in a futile attack? And not just my fleet, but your men as well?'

'Of course not. There has to be another way of landing forces on the island. How well defended is the harbour on the other side?'

'It's easy enough to get a ship to the pier there, but there's a fortified gatehouse across the end of the pier. And catapults too. A handful of men could hold off an army.'

'And there's nowhere else we can attempt to land?' Cato asked.

'No,' Lemillus replied bluntly.

There was a brief silence as the officers contemplated the formidable defences of the main harbour. Then Spiromandes braced himself before he addressed his admiral.

'There is another possibility, sir.'

'Be quiet,' Lemillus snapped. 'I did not ask you for your opinion.'

'Wait,' Cato intervened. 'I want to hear this. What do you mean, another possibility?'

The admiral glared at his subordinate as the navarch elaborated. 'There is a very small cove a short distance to the east of the smaller harbour, sir. The local fishermen use it from time to time when they are caught out by squalls. Apart from that, it's a place where youngsters go to drink and eat on public holidays.'

'How do you know this?' Cato demanded.

'I was born on Caprae, sir. Lived there until I joined the navy.'

'And how does this cove of yours help us?'

'There's a track that goes down to the cove. It comes out a short distance from the track between the villa and the port. It's steep and only wide enough for one person. And if the rebels know about it—'

'Not rebels,' Cato interrupted. 'Call them what they are. Traitors.'

Spiromandes nodded. 'Yes, sir. Traitors then. If they know about this path, they'll be able to defend it with a handful of men.'

'Then it's of no use to us,' Lemillus decided.

'On the contrary,' said Cato. 'If Narcissus is not aware of it, this path may be the only way we can take the island. Even if he is made aware of it, we might still be able to win through. If not, we'll have to pull back and think of something else. The emperor will not be pleased with any of us if we fail to take the island and capture the traitors as soon as possible. I for one am not keen to put the will of Nero to the test. Are you, Admiral?'

Lemillus pressed his lips together and refused to meet Cato's eyes, or even answer the question.

'Very well, then,' Cato announced. 'Unless there's any other suggestion, we'll give this cove of yours a go, Spiromandes.'

'And when do you propose to do that?' asked Lemillus.

Cato fixed him with a steady stare. 'When? Why, tonight, of course. You'll assault the main harbour to draw the enemy's attention. And if all goes well, we'll take the villa, complete with the traitors, in a dawn attack.'

'And what if it doesn't go well?'

'In that case, Macro and I will probably be dead. And it will fall to you to explain it all to the emperor.'

CHAPTER THIRTY-NINE

The sounds of the first attack were muffled by the mass of the island, but Cato could still make out the crack of catapults, the blare of trumpets and the faint battle cries of the sailors and marines as the warships swept forward out of the night and began to unleash a barrage of missiles against the harbour's defences. There was the barest sliver of a moon to add to the loom of the stars, and so the defenders would not have had much warning of the assault. By contrast, the harbour and port buildings, as well as the route up to the villa and the villa itself, were all illuminated by torches and braziers. Which had made it easier for the naval forces to manoeuvre into position under cover of night.

While Lemillus commanded the majority of the fleet, as well as the ships carrying the two cohorts Cato had left in reserve, Spiromandes had taken his squadron of liburnians and the ships transporting the other two cohorts in a wide arc around the eastern tip of the island during the late afternoon, as if to make for the mainland. Once the sun had set, they doubled back to approach the small harbour and the fishermen's cove. Inevitably, several of the ships had lost their way in the darkness, but enough had worked their way round to the south of the island to make Cato's plan feasible.

Spiromandes had been the first to go ashore in a skiff, feeling his way in towards the small strip of beach. Once he had landed, he set up and aligned the two shielded lamps to guide in the cargo ships' tenders as they ferried the Praetorians across. Cato and Macro were in one of the first boats to be rowed towards the dark mass of the island. Around them the sea, mercifully calm, broke against the rocky cliffs with a light thud and rush, although it sounded deafening and perilous to Cato's ears and he had to force himself to sit calmly at the stern in order to set an example to the soldiers in front of him. Now, of all times, it was essential that his men had absolute confidence in him. He had never embarked on such a risky enterprise. So much could go wrong in a night attack, and doubly so for a seaborne operation like this. The dark cliffs reared up ahead and to the sides, and Cato felt sure they must hit some rocks at any moment. Only the wavering glow of the lamps offered him any reassurance.

'How much further?' Macro whispered hoarsely, his throat dry with anxiety. 'Where's that bloody beach?'

'Quiet now,' Cato replied calmly. 'It can't be far.'

Sure enough, the soft hiss of water on shingle came to his ears, and then he saw the faint outline of figures moving in the barest loom of the oil lamps.

'Easy oars,' the mate of the cargo ship ordered, and the men rested their oars just above the water as the boat glided forward, then grounded on the shingle.

'Thank fuck for that,' Macro muttered before he raised his voice just enough to be heard by the other men. 'Over the side, lads. Form up on the beach and wait for orders.'

They picked up their shields from the bottom of the boat

and slipped over the side with a series of splashes, and then surged through the surf up on to the shingle. Thirty or so men had already landed and were being marshalled into formation by their officers as Cato and Macro made their way up the beach to where the furthest lamp burned. As arranged, Spiromandes was waiting for them there.

'Where's this path then?' Macro demanded.

The navarch turned and gestured unhelpfully at the foot of the cliff. 'Just there. Easy enough to follow when the time comes.'

'We'll have to move up as soon as we can,' said Cato. 'Lemillus won't be able to keep his feint up for long. We need to be well on the way by the time he withdraws, and at the top of the path before first light.'

'I can get your men up there, sir,' Spiromandes insisted. 'Trust me.'

'Any sign of lookouts?'

'No, sir. I've scouted ahead almost to the top of the path. There's no one.'

'Good.' Cato turned to face out to sea. He could hear more boats approaching, then the thud of a collision and a muttered oath. His guts twisted anxiously as he waited for the alarm to be raised, but all remained peaceful, on this side of the island at least. More men joined the landing force and Cato was conducting a count when he heard the blare of a trumpet away to the west, in the direction of the small harbour. That was the second feint, intended to satisfy the enemy's suspicion that the navy might conduct a two-pronged attack. While their attention, and hopefully their reserves, was diverted to meet the new threat, Cato would lead the real strike force up the steep slope to take the villa. With Britannicus, Narcissus and the other leaders of the conspiracy in the bag, the remaining cohorts of the Sixth Legion would be leaderless, and therefore almost certain to surrender. If Cato and his men were spotted, however, it would be a simple matter to block their path and inflict heavy casualties before they were forced to withdraw. Then there would be no second attempt possible once the enemy had been alerted to the danger posed by the path winding down to the cove.

In accordance with their orders, the five liburnians were making as much noise as possible as they rowed in towards the small quay and the gatehouse beyond. The light bolt throwers mounted in their bows cracked sharply as they launched their missiles at the defenders, and their drums sounded loudly, beating the rhythm for the men at the oars.

'That should keep the bastards busy,' Macro said cheerfully.

'I hope so,' Cato responded, then strained his eyes to try and pick out the transports lying offshore, as well as the boats bringing his men ashore. But it was still too dark to see, and he could only hope fervently that he could gather a sufficient number of men for the attack on the villa before dawn came. Already he was aware that the sounds from the other side of the island were growing fainter, and he mentally cursed Lemillus for not staying the course. The admiral had no doubt decided to play no greater part in the operation than he could get away with.

'Damn the man,' Cato said under his breath. He thought quickly and nodded to himself. He was committed to the attack now, and not just because he feared for his son. A great many more lives hung in the balance, and it was his duty to prevent the outbreak of the inevitable civil war should Britannicus avail himself of the forces advancing from Brundisium.

'All right,' he concluded. 'It's time to move up. Spiromandes, you lead the way. Macro, pass the word to the officers. I want each boatload of men to follow us up the path as soon as possible. They're to keep the men moving off the beach, unless they get fresh orders.'

'Yes, sir.'

'Once you've passed on the instructions, find me and we'll march together.'

Macro crunched down the shingle to the shoreline and Cato turned back to the navarch. 'Take me to the start of the path.'

Even by the faint light of the stars and the crescent moon, Cato could easily see the gully that Spiromandes led him to, a route well worn by the islanders. No more than fifteen feet in, it turned sharply and narrowed as it climbed parallel to the cliff.

'And this zigzags all the way to the top?'

'For most of the way. The slope gradually becomes more gentle as it reaches the crest. There is another track that branches off it and runs parallel to the main path leading to the villa, winding along the top of the cliffs. It's not the most direct route. Better make sure that no one takes it by mistake.'

Cato thought a moment. 'No. We'll use that too. If more of us turn up from yet another direction, it'll keep the enemy off balance.'

'Very well, sir. I'll make sure to point out the track when we get to it.'

Macro returned to them and Cato looked over the dark mass of men waiting at the foot of the cliff.

'Lads, there may be no chance to form up when we reach the top of the path. This is going to be desperate stuff. Centurion Petillius?'

'Sir?'

'You take the first thirty men and turn left to block the track leading down to the port. Don't let anyone get past you. Hold on until the last man if need be.'

'Yes, sir.'

'I'll be taking a small party along a side track. The rest of you will follow Macro towards the villa. Stop for nothing. Anyone you come across who is holding a weapon and isn't a Praetorian is to be cut down. There will be no quarter given. The enemy will show us no mercy in any case. We either win tonight or we die . . . May Fortuna watch over us all. Let's go. Spiromandes, lead off.'

As the navarch entered the gully, Macro muttered, 'Nice rousing speech. Liked the do-or-die touch. Just what a bunch of nervous lads need to hear when they'll be jumping at every shadow.'

'They need to know the stakes, Macro, for when the fighting begins. Come.' Cato hefted his shield and followed Spiromandes. After him came Macro and then the Praetorians, one man at a time, winding their way up the steep path. They proceeded in silence, the only sounds the crunch of boots, the soft chink of loose equipment and the laboured breathing of men weighed down by their arms and armour. The noises of battle from the main harbour had died away completely, and now the only action came a quarter of a mile to the west.

After they had climbed the first two hundred paces or so, Cato could see along the coast to where one of the liburnians had landed some men by the light of a brazier burning at the end of the pier. But they were crouched behind mooring posts and sheltering behind their shields from a steady barrage of arrows and slingshot from the gate at the far end of the pier, and could make no progress. Even as he watched, a bolt slammed through a shield, skewering the marine behind it and carrying him away over the side and into the harbour. He could just make out the other warships lying close by, shooting back with their own artillery pieces. The attack was doomed to fail, and was not intended to be more than a feint, but Cato hoped it would draw the enemy's attention long enough for the Praetorians to get sufficient men on to the island to swing the struggle in their favour.

A short time later, Spiromandes stopped and turned round. Cato turned and gave the order to halt before he approached the naval officer. 'What's up?'

'We've reached the other path. That way.' Spiromandes pointed to a barely visible line of soil and gravel cutting through the darker vegetation.

Cato glanced at it. 'How far does it run?'

'No more than half a mile; it comes out a hundred paces from the entrance to the villa.'

'Macro, you'll take over the main column now. Good luck, brother.'

They clasped arms briefly and then Cato headed down the smaller path, followed by the first twenty men, while Macro gestured for the rest to follow him and the navarch as they continued up the steep slope. Further along the coast, and far below now, the marines began to withdraw from the pier, and the small warship thrust away and then backwatered into the night with a final exchange of missiles. Only the distant pitiful cries of the wounded and the muted crash of waves carried on the cool, light breeze.

As the track turned back on itself, Macro stared in the direction Cato and his party had gone, but he could not pick them out in the darkness. Cato was on his own now, and Macro hoped that when the fighting was over, his friend would find his son alive. But now he needed to concentrate on the part he himself was to play in Cato's daring and desperate bid to put an end to the conspiracy that threatened to topple the Empire into a bloody civil war.

The gradient began to ease, and now Macro could see the faint line of the saddle that formed the middle of the island. A short distance ahead, just beyond a wide, even stretch of ground, Spiromandes crouched down and indicated to Macro to halt the column.

'Stop here,' he whispered. 'We're no more than fifty paces from the road that leads to the villa.'

Macro nodded and turned to order his men to spread out over the even ground and await further orders. The Praetorians continued to file forward and gather in a formless mass. He caught sight of the crest of Petillius's helmet as the centurion approached him.

'Gather the men you need,' Macro said. 'And make ready to take position across the road the moment I give the order. After that, you're on your own.'

'I understand. I know what we have to do.'

'Right. You keep the rest of the lads here. I'm going forward with Spiromandes to see the lie of the land. If the alarm's raised for any reason, bring all of 'em forward at once.' He turned to the navarch. 'Let's go.'

Rising from the edge of the small depression, they kept low as they crept towards the road. The flames of braziers flickered every hundred paces or so, marking the line of the road as it stretched between the port and the villa. By their light Macro could pick out a handful of sentries along the way, and then a larger group of legionaries standing higher up the road, staring out towards the main harbour where Lemillus had made his feint. Spiromandes led the way along the path towards a small cluster of terraced olive trees, through which the main route ran. As they passed into the trees, they heard a brief laugh a short distance ahead, and then a muted exchange and another laugh. The navarch froze, and Macro eased himself into position beside him. 'I'll go first,' he whispered.

Creeping through the shadows, testing each step he took to ensure that he made as little noise as possible, Macro edged forward until he saw the track open out on to the road. A short distance to his right, two legionaries were facing downhill, shields grounded and javelins to hand as they chatted quietly about the feeble attack the navy had just mounted on their island fortress. Macro hunched down and glanced both ways, but there were no other legionaries visible.

'We have to get rid of them,' he whispered. 'Then use these trees as cover to form up our men before we go on the attack.'

'Get rid of them?'

'Just follow my lead.' Macro eased his sword from its scabbard and slowly rose to full height. 'Put your hands on your head and walk ahead of me. Ready?'

The navarch did as he was told, and both of them stepped out on to the road and approached the legionaries. As soon as they heard the crunch of boots, the sentries turned towards the sound.

'Who goes there?'

There was no trace of alarm in the man's voice, and Macro took a breath and called back, 'Easy there, lads. Just taking a prisoner up to the villa.'

'Prisoner?'

'Bagged him when his lot tried to land on the mole. Rest of

the bastards are dead, but we got ourselves an officer here.'

Macro held his sword arm slightly back as he approached so the weapon was out of sight. The legionaries' attention was on Spiromandes as the two men approached. They stepped to one side to let them pass, and before they even realised the danger, Macro had swept his sword round and thrust it up under the first man's chin, driving the point into his skull.

'What the f—' the second man gasped, and then his voice was cut off as the navarch hurled himself forward, snatching out his dagger. Both men tumbled to the ground beside the road before the naval officer stabbed the man in the face with a frenzied series of blows.

Macro hesitated a moment before he spoke. 'I think you've got him . . .'

Spiromandes stuck his blade in one last time, then twisted it and pulled it free before easing himself up on to his feet, breathing hard.

'First kill?'

'Yes . . . first time,' the younger man replied. 'The navy doesn't get to see much action these days.'

'Hmm,' Macro grumbled. This was not the time to make a point about which service had the tougher job. Instead he sheathed his blade and patted Spiromandes on the shoulder. 'You did well. Some hesitate the first time, and that's usually their last time, if you see what I mean. Now go back and bring the men forward. Nice and quiet like.'

While the naval officer was gone, Macro dragged the bodies a short distance into the trees in case any more legionaries came by. As he waited in the shadows, he noticed that there was a faint smudge of lighter sky towards the east, clearly outlining the towering heights of Vesuvius on the far side of the bay.

Time was running out. Cato's plan depended on striking in the darkness and causing confusion to hide the smaller numbers of the Praetorians.

He started at the sound of rustling close by, and then Spiromandes appeared with Petillius and his men.

'This will do for your position,' Macro decided. 'Stay out of sight for as long as you can. If one or two of them slip by, let them pass. Only engage if they are sending reinforcements up to the villa. You should be getting more men coming up from the cove all the time. Once most of the rest of our detachment is landed, then you can press forward to the main harbour.'

Petillius nodded and then gestured to the east. 'Dawn's almost on us.'

'I saw. Better get moving.'

Besides the twenty men assigned to Petillius, Macro saw that he had perhaps another hundred for the attack up the road. It all depended on the defenders having positioned the bulk of their forces to cover the two harbours. If they had kept any sizeable reserve back to protect the ringleaders up at the villa, then the operation was doomed.

Well, there was only one way to find out, he told himself. Drawing his sword, he ordered the men to form a column two abreast and took his place at the head. He looked back to make sure they were ready, and even now he could make out more detail as the frail light began to grow.

'Second Cohort,' he announced automatically, and then smiled at his mistake. These men came from both cohorts that had been assigned to the attack. 'Praetorians, on me! Forwards!'

He broke into the gentle trot that soldiers were trained to use to cover ground swiftly and not be too blown to fight effectively when they made contact with the enemy. The small column followed him, emerging from the olive grove and tramping up the paved road towards the villa perched on top of the eastern cape of the island. Ahead of them Macro saw the next pair of sentries nearly two hundred paces away, clearly visible as they warmed themselves by a brazier. The road inclined more steeply just before them, and a smaller brazier lit the way.

At the sound of tramping boots, the sentries turned to look, and as Macro and the leading ranks of his column passed the smaller brazier, the nearest man yelled: 'Praetorians!' Then both men turned and ran up the road, shouting ahead to raise the alarm and alert their comrades.

'Here we go, boys!' Macro called over his shoulder. 'The fight's on!'

CHAPTER FORTY

The legionaries were still forming up across the road as Macro and his men rounded an outcrop of rock no more than twenty paces away. The centurion commanding the force reacted instantly.

'Loose javelins!'

Before the first missile could be readied and thrown, Macro shouted an order of his own. 'Shields up!'

The men behind him swung their oval shields to the front and then angled them up above head height. In front of them the legionaries hurriedly braced their feet and hurled their javelins at the oncoming Praetorians. There was no time for an organised volley, and the shafts arced briefly before their iron points struck home. The range was so close that it was impossible to miss the target. Most of the javelins were deflected by the curved shields, but some punched through, splintering wood and passing on until brought to an abrupt halt by the joint between the shank and the wooden shaft. The main weight of the barrage struck the column several ranks behind Macro with a rolling series of crashes and thuds. Some men were injured as the javelins pierced their shields, others by deflections off the shields of the men beside them. The wounded went down on the road or staggered to the side and covered their bodies from further strikes as best they could as their comrades rushed past them.

There was no time to give the order to charge. In any case, Macro and his men instinctively broke into a dead run and struck the enemy line even as the last of the javelins arced over their heads. At the last moment Macro burst into a sprint, and then his shield smashed into the enemy with a force that jarred his arm and nearly knocked him off balance. But his vast experience of battle had sharpened his instincts enough for him to adjust his balance instantaneously, and he battered his opponent back into the rank behind, at the same time thrusting his sword to the right, punching the point right through the sword arm of the legionary next in line.

The impetus carried the attackers forward a short distance into the centre of the line of legionaries, driving a wedge into the enemy formation, before the melee pitted sword against spear. Short blades thrust between the larger legionary shields and the leaf blades of the spears stabbed overhead, while those pitted directly against each other thrust their weight behind their shields and struggled to hold their ground. Macro felt the familiar fire of battle burn in his veins as he gritted his teeth and his lips twisted in a ferocious snarl.

Alone amongst his men he fought with a short sword. He gave the man he had charged into no time to recover, but pulled his shield back and punched it forward again, advancing another pace as he pulled his sword free from the man he had wounded and then smashed the weighted pommel against the side of his helmet, jarring his neck and knocking him senseless. The legionary crumpled on to the road and a Praetorian stabbed down at his face with his spear, and then stepped over the man and thrust the point at another man.

Even though there was no mistaking the gradual increase in the light as dawn approached, it was still too gloomy to see clearly and Macro was aware of the frenzied movement of shadows all around him, and the grunts and gasps of men striking and receiving blows. He sensed that the impetus of the charge had passed, and now his men needed encouragement to push forward and press on. Snatching a breath, he bellowed, 'Forward, Praetorians! Grind those bastard traitors down!'

'Traitors he calls us!' a voice cried out from behind the legionaries. 'Liar! Hold 'em, lads! In the name of Emperor Britannicus and Rome!'

There was an instant when Macro was struck by the tragic absurdity of Roman soldiers fighting against each other. Some of these men might even have served together, but now they were bitter enemies, thinking of nothing but cutting each other down. Then he thrust such thoughts aside as he brutally hacked at another legionary's arm and cut through flesh and bone so that the limb was almost severed, flopping like butchered meat as the sword dropped from nerveless fingers. Aware that he was forward of his men and vulnerable, he held his ground and let the Praetorians close up on either side.

The legionaries had fully recovered from the charge now and were resolved not to give another inch of ground as the two sides pressed forward, compacting the front ranks into each other in a tight mass of flesh and armour, shield to shield. And then Macro heard the enemy centurion's voice again.

'Here they come, lads! More of our boys! We'll have 'em on the run now!'

* * *

434

It was not easy going on the path that ran along the southern cliffs. The trail was narrow and followed the contours for the most part, dipping and rising. At times Cato had to feel his way forward, always conscious that time was running out. If dawn found them strung out and exposed, they would be easy enough to pick off with arrows and slingshot from above. In any case, he reminded himself, if dawn found them in such a predicament at all, they would already have failed. So he led his men on as swiftly as he could. At length the path began to climb steeply, then passed through a cluster of cypress trees and abruptly joined the road.

Cato just had time to stop and halt the men behind him before they blundered out into the open. A short distance to his right was the gateway leading to the villa. It was nothing more than ornamental and posed no obstacle. Beyond, by the glow of the torches illuminating the outside of the villa, he could see steps and a ramp leading up to the building. Closer to, the true magnificence of the place was more apparent, impressing Cato now as it had years before when he had last briefly visited the island. The structure dominated the heights at the eastern end of the island, atop cliffs that dropped straight down to the sea a thousand feet below. The sky was growing lighter behind the villa, and the walls and roofs were outlined clearly against the velvet backdrop.

There was a shouted command from beyond the gate and a small body of legionaries, thirty or so, came running out. Cato waved his men down and crouched beside the trunk of one of the cypress trees as the soldiers hurried past. He waited a moment to make sure there were no more to come before he rose and cautiously stepped into the road, looking in both directions. There was no further sign of movement from the villa, and down the road he saw the soldiers who had passed by a moment before. Just beyond them he made out a knot of figures in front of a rocky outcrop and his heart quickened anxiously as he realised that must be Macro and his party trying to cut their way through to the villa.

As Cato quietly ordered his men to come out from the trees and form up, he was uncertain how to proceed. Ahead lay the villa, where Lucius was still held prisoner. His intention had been to directly attack any men he came across to add to the enemy's confusion, but the only legionaries he could see were engaging Macro. He was also close enough to his son to be sorely tempted by the prospect of rushing the villa at once. But there was no knowing how many legionaries remained to defend Narcissus and the others.

'Your orders, sir?' one of the Praetorians prompted.

Cato cast a last glance towards the villa, weighing up certainties against possibilities, then turned down the hill and gave the order. 'This way, at the double.'

He led the men along the road, hardening his heart to the delay in rescuing his son and fixing his attention on the imminent fight. With luck the enemy would think the Praetorians were on their side until the last moment. Cato was counting on the element of surprise to break the will of the legionaries and clear the way for Macro to join him in a final assault on the villa. They covered the distance quickly and the clash of weapons grew louder as Cato quickened the pace. To one side of the road he saw the transverse crest of a centurion and angled towards the officer, determined to cut him down in the first rush and deprive the enemy of their leader. A few faces at the rear of the melee turned as they heard the sound of boots, and the centurion cried out, 'Here they come, lads!

More of our boys! We'll have 'em on the run now!'

At the last moment, Cato filled his lungs and shouted, 'For Nero! For Rome!'

His men echoed the cry and readied their spears, fanning out behind Cato as he drew his sword and held it level with the ground, ready to strike. In the faint light he saw the centurion's jaw drop slightly as he began to turn towards the Praetorians charging at his men. Then Cato's shield slammed into him, knocking the breath from his lungs with a hoarse gasp. In the next instant Cato struck him in the side of his chest, the point of his sword breaking through some of the rings of the mail vest and penetrating a short distance into his torso. It was only a flesh wound, but the impact knocked the centurion off balance and he stumbled against the back of one of his men and crumpled to the ground. There was no hesitation in Cato's savage follow-up as he hacked down into the back of the officer's neck, shattering the spine and cutting deep. The centurion threw out his arms and fell flat on his face without a sound.

On either side of Cato his Praetorians thrust with their spears at the unguarded rear of the enemy line, striking men down before slamming their shields into the press of bodies driven forward against Macro and his men. Several went down in the first moment of the charge, while others tried to turn and fight, swinging their heavy shields round, inevitably clipping or tangling with their comrades and falling victim to the darting iron spearheads.

'Kill 'em all!' Cato shouted. 'Kill the traitors!'

Macro repeated the cry, and his men joined in and renewed their own onslaught. The first of the legionaries on each end of the line began to draw away from the fight, stumbling into the undergrowth at the side of the road. Their fear instantly spread to their comrades, and the battle line broke up as each man looked to his own safety and tried to escape the thrusts of spears from front and rear. Some, braver than their companions, or just more fired up by the fury of battle, tried to stand their ground, but were quickly dispatched as the triumphant Praetorians closed round them. Others tried to surrender and threw down their swords and shields but were shown no mercy and were slaughtered where they stood.

'Cato!'

He looked round as Macro hurried up to him, grinning with delight.

'Fine work, sir! The bastards are bolting like rabbits.'

Cato could see several of his men rushing after their opponents and knew that he must regain control of them at once.

'Praetorians, on me! Form on me! On me, damn you!'

Macro quickly grasped the need for swift action, and the two officers hurriedly assembled their remaining men on the road a short distance from the bodies and discarded equipment scattered on the ground. No more than fifty men left, Cato estimated, hoping that it was enough for one last effort. One last attempt to save Rome from tearing itself apart as two boys and their armies fought for the imperial crown.

'Advance!'

With Macro at his side, he jogged up the road, past the cypress trees and on to the gateway. A short distance beyond was a series of short flights of stairs that led up to the massive foundations of the villa. Cato could feel his limbs burning from the exertion of climbing the cliff and now this final approach. As the Praetorians scaled the last steps and reached the ramp stretching up to the entrance to the courtyard, he heard a cry of alarm and glanced up to see a signal tower at the corner of the complex. Several figures were looking down towards the harbour, but now one was pointing directly at them, and Cato could make out enough detail to recognise the man at once.

Tribune Cristus.

More shouts followed, and as they neared the arch, a squad of legionaries hurried forward to bar their way. Cato hefted his shield to the front and hunched his head down a fraction as he closed the distance. There was no question of another charge. Not up the slope, as weary as the men were. So they slowed to a walk and approached the legionaries as if this was a sparring exercise on the parade ground. Cato picked the man on the end and feinted with his shield before thrusting his sword in a shallow arc. His opponent was no raw recruit and recognised the feint for what it was. He parried the blow and swung his shield hard, knocking Cato back against the wall running up the side of the ramp. The impact drove the breath from Cato's lungs, and he just managed to throw himself to the side as the legionary's sword scraped past on the stonework, sparks leaping in its wake. Then one of the Praetorians thrust himself between his commander and the legionary and their shields slammed together.

By the time Cato had clambered back to his feet, the Praetorians had pressed their enemy back through the arch and into the courtyard. More soldiers came rushing out from the hall and the other rooms giving on to the courtyard, and the surrounding walls echoed to the scrape of blades and the jarring crash of shields as the struggle became a confusion of running duels. Cato's lungs were straining to draw enough air in as he held his shield up and made his way around the edge towards the hall. That was where he guessed the ringleaders would be, close to the watchtower where he had seen them a moment before.

The Praetorians, though tired, had superior numbers and had reached the courtyard together, whereas the legionaries had charged pell-mell from their quarters, some in armour, some not, with no chance to form the battle line that made them such effective combatants in a more formal setting. But there was nothing formal about the fight in the courtyard. It was a savage skirmish in the thin light of pre-dawn. Neither side asked for quarter as the Praetorians fought their way across the open space, and bodies fell and spilled their blood and guts across the white marble in front of the great hall where the emperors held court.

As Cato approached the wide flight of steps leading up to the entrance, a figure emerged between the studded doors, sword in hand and bareheaded, and he saw that it was Cristus. At the same instant the tribune's eyes locked on Cato and his lips stretched in a thin smile of satisfaction as he came down the steps and hefted his blade. At the edge of his vision Cato saw a Praetorian charging towards Cristus from the side.

'Leave him!' he bellowed. 'This one is mine.'

The Praetorian stopped in his tracks, and then turned to look for another opponent, leaving the two officers in a patch of open ground in front of the steps. Cato readied his shield and sword and advanced warily as Cristus waved his sword in a loose ellipse.

'You should have stayed in Britannia, Cato.'

'I don't think so. It seems that barbarian tribes aren't the only enemies of Rome.'

'I am no enemy of Rome. I am a patriot.'

'You are a traitor, Cristus. And there is only one fate for

traitors.' Cato kept his gaze fixed on the weaving blade in his enemy's hand as he spoke. Suddenly the tribune sprang forward and unleashed a series of violent blows that cracked off the surface of Cato's shield as he gave ground before the wild onslaught. Each strike jarred his arm, but Cato held on, absorbing the attack as Cristus hacked clumsily. Then, reading the next blow, he whipped his shield out of the way. The tribune's sword cut through the air, then continued down and struck the flagstones. At once Cato rushed forward, catching Cristus with the full weight of his shield and sending him staggering back, off balance. He followed up with a flurry of attacks, ending with an undercut to avoid the tribune's parry. His point dropped and thrust forward, catching his opponent in the groin and stabbing deep into his flesh. A swing of the shield knocked Cristus back, and his heel caught the bottom step so that he stumbled and fell.

Cato loomed over him, poised to strike, and Cristus held up his sword to ward off another blow.

'Drop the sword,' Cato ordered.

'What for? Like you said, there is only one fate for me now.'

He was right, Cato knew. The only choice in the matter was whether he died at Cato's hand, or that of an executioner.

Cristus slowly lowered his sword. 'I may be a dead man,' he sneered, 'but I will die with honour, while the likes of you and that pleb Macro serve Nero like the common curs you are.'

'As you wish . . .' Cato raised his own sword to strike.

'Wait. You may think you've won the day. But I can win one small victory of my own before I die. Your wife. Julia . . . You think she was unfaithful.'

'Not now. I heard the truth from your friends in there. That your relationship was a cover.'

'Is that what they said?' Cristus chuckled. 'Do you believe them? Why should you, given the other lies you were told?'

Cato froze, then spoke through gritted teeth. 'Did you?'

'Did I fuck her?' Cristus laughed. 'Maybe I did. I'll leave you with that doubt, Cato. You'll never know one way or the other. That'll be the sweetest revenge for my death, eh?'

He suddenly reversed his grip on his sword and placed the tip under his ribcage, grasping the handle with both hands.

'No!' Cato shouted.

With a savage motion Cristus rammed the blade up into his heart. His jaw snapped open as he let out a shrill cry, and he fell back hard, his skull cracking against a step. Cato dropped to his side and let go of his own sword as he clenched his fist in the tribune's hair.

'Tell me! Tell me the truth!'

Cristus stared up at him, eyelids fluttering. There was blood on his lips from where the blade had sliced through a lung. He smiled as he muttered, 'Fuck you . . .' Then the light in his eyes faded and he slumped back, his chest sinking as blood bubbled from his sagging jaw.

Cato shook his head. 'Tell me . . .' But it was too late. He released his grip and picked up his sword as Macro came towards him.

'We're done here, sir. The courtyard is ours.' He looked down. 'Cristus? He killed himself? I wouldn't have thought he had it in him to do that.'

'Nor me.' Cato tore his gaze away and pointed towards the entrance to the audience chamber. 'Come on, bring the men.'

Leaving Macro to gather the remaining Praetorians, Cato climbed the stairs and eased one of the doors open with his shield. Inside, the hall was lit with braziers along each wall. The floor and walls were covered in marble slabs, and thick columns supported a vaulted ceiling. The only other people in the chamber were at the far end. A throne stood on a dais, and Britannicus sat there, an imperious tilt to his chin. At his side stood a handful of senators Cato recognised from the secret meeting at Domitia's home. Lowering his shield, he undid the ties under his chin and removed his helmet so that they would recognise him.

'Where is my son?' he demanded, and then he realised that someone else was missing. 'And Narcissus. Where are they?'

No one replied, and he strode towards them, his footsteps echoing off the walls. As he drew near, Britannicus pointed at him and spoke calmly. 'How dare you approach your emperor without showing due respect?'

Cato climbed on to the dais and stood over the boy. Behind him he heard more men entering the chamber.

'You are not the emperor, Prince Britannicus. Nor will you ever be.'

The boy glared at him, but before he could express more outrage, Cato raised a hand to still his tongue and demanded again, 'Where are they?'

'Outside,' Senator Sulpicius volunteered anxiously. He pointed to a door at the rear of the chamber. 'He took the boy and went outside. That way.'

Cato looked over the faces of the conspirators and then walked past them towards the door Sulpicius had indicated. He heard Macro's voice behind him.

'Arrest this lot.'

'You dare to—' Britannicus began.

'Shut your mouth, boy. Unless you want a thick lip. I've had enough trouble for one night.'

The door was ajar. Cato pushed it open and saw that there was a narrow covered way leading from the back of the villa through a neatly tended garden. At the end he emerged on to a wide path that stretched from one side of the island to the other. It was quite bare, except for two figures away to his right, standing watching him. Narcissus rested his hands on Lucius's shoulders and waited as Cato turned and strode towards them. Now he could see that he was approaching a circular open area with a number of couches arranged so as to make the most of the spectacular view over to the east. On the mainland, Vesuvius and the hills stretching out on either side were rimmed with the golden hue of the rising sun, still hidden from sight. Behind Narcissus it was only a short distance to the edge of the viewing platform, and then a void.

Cato stopped ten paces away and sheathed his sword before he spoke. 'Let Lucius go.'

The boy made to take a step towards him, but Narcissus tightened his grip and the child winced in pain.

'I said let him go.'

'I don't think that would be a good idea,' said Narcissus. 'He is all I have left, now that Britannicus's cause has come to nothing.'

'You're wrong. You have nothing left. Nothing at all. The boy cannot help you.'

'No?' Narcissus took two steps back, dragging Lucius with him. He glanced over his shoulder and stopped when he was no more than four feet from the edge. 'Think again, Cato. If you want to see your son grow up into a man, you'll do what I ask.'

'And what do you ask?' Cato replied, taking a step towards them.

'That's close enough,' Narcissus snapped. 'Hear me out. I don't care about the conspiracy. I don't care about my fellow plotters, and I could not care less about the spoilt brat sitting on his throne inside the villa. I only care about staying alive. So if you want your son, you'll let me go. You'll find a way to get me off this island and let me escape into quiet obscurity.'

'You don't get to escape and leave all this behind,' Cato replied. 'Not with the blood that is on your hands.'

'Well, given how much blood is already on my hands, what's a little more to me now?' Narcissus took another step back and to the side, and held Lucius closer to the edge. Cato felt his heart lurch and had to force himself to stand still.

'What do you want from me?'

'Your word. I know you well enough to believe that you are a man of honour and integrity, Cato. Rare qualities in our world, but real enough to count. Give me your word that you will help me escape, and I will give you the life of your son.'

'Don't listen to him, lad.' Macro spoke from behind Cato's shoulder as he strode towards them. 'He's never honoured a single promise he ever made us. Besides, you vowed that you would kill him.'

'I know . . . But what can I do? He has Lucius.'

Macro halted beside his friend and kept his eyes fixed on Narcissus. 'Give the boy up, you piece of shit. You know you can't escape. Are you seriously saying you'll die and take Lucius with you?'

'That's precisely what I am saying. Unless your friend gives me his word. Well, Cato?'

Cato winced and looked down at his son, seeing the terror in the little boy's expression. Mortal terror, and he felt his heart aching with the longing to love and protect Lucius. He swallowed before he responded. 'I give you my word. If you will only let him go.'

'Swear it. On the boy's life. Before Jupiter, Best and Greatest, swear it.'

'I swear, by almighty Jupiter, and on the life of my only son, that I will help you escape.'

Narcissus's eyes narrowed momentarily, and then he released his grip and Lucius pulled away and ran to his father. Cato whisked him up off his feet and held him close, wrapping his sword arm around him as he cradled the soft curls of his head with his other hand.

'Daddy . . .' Lucius whispered softly into his shoulder. 'My daddy.'

Narcissus stepped away from the edge of the cliff and smiled. 'Such a touching reunion.'

Then before either Cato or Narcissus could react, Macro sprang forward and grabbed Narcissus by the arm, swinging him round. The freedman tried desperately to pull himself free, his slippered feet sliding as he tried to get purchase on the ground. Macro took a step towards the abyss and swung again, and this time his momentum carried Narcissus towards the edge and Macro released his grip. With a shrill scream of terror, Narcissus was launched backwards, waving his arms wildly, and snatched from sight. Macro stepped to the edge and watched as the freedman plummeted down the cliff, still shrieking. His body struck an outcrop, bounced a short distance from the cliff and continued falling, until at last his broken, ruined corpse splashed into the sea far below and he was gone.

'Definitely dead this time,' Macro said with satisfaction. 'Thank the gods.'

'Macro, I gave my word,' Cato said in a pained tone. 'On the life of my son.'

Macro retreated a safe distance before turning to his friend. 'So you did. But you also vowed to kill him. And I didn't make any promises to anyone. So no harm done, eh? At least not to the three of us.'

At that moment, a wash of bright light spilled over the tiles of the villa, making them glow bright red with an intensity that instantly drew the attention of both men.

'Going to be a fine day,' said Macro. He reached up and ruffled Lucius's hair. 'Ain't that right, lad?'

But the boy flinched and hugged his father tightly and muttered into Cato's ear: 'Please, Daddy, take me home . . .'

Cato looked over his son's shoulder and saw the bittersweet expression on his friend's face. Macro was perceptive enough to recognise that his days as the boy's putative uncle had at last been eclipsed by Lucius's discovery of his unquestioning need for his father. And he felt glad for his best friend.

He cleared his throat, but his voice was still hoarse as he growled, 'Come on, Cato, let's get away from the edge of this cliff, before I fucking cry.'

CHAPTER FORTY-ONE

'Not exactly the happiest of birthday parties, is it?' Macro commented as he gazed around the banqueting hall of the imperial palace.

Several days had passed since the action on Caprae. All the conspirators were dead. Those who had refused to take their own lives had been executed, and only Britannicus had been spared, as ordered. Cato had brought him back from the island, along with the remnants of the Sixth Legion and the men of the Praetorian cohorts. The return of the prince to Rome had been handled discreetly, and Nero had announced that he had chosen to show his adoptive brother mercy and forgiven him his treachery. Such magnanimity had astonished the population of Rome, commoners and aristocrats alike, and most held this to be proof of the golden age that the new emperor had promised to usher in from the outset of his reign. Moreover, Nero had proclaimed that he would hold a feast to celebrate his sibling's coming of age, and that henceforth Britannicus was to be his closest adviser, confidant and heir.

Anyone with a shred of common sense believed none of it. Britannicus least of all. Cato looked towards the raised table that dominated the feast. Nero sat in the centre, surrounded by his family and his cronies, a mix of actors, musicians and poets. To his immediate right sat his mother, Agrippina, looking bored by the conversation around her as she picked one grape after another from the bowl in front of her. To the emperor's left sat Britannicus, looking down at his hands with a haunted expression. Every so often Nero turned to him and made some jocular remark or slapped him amiably on the back, which only caused the younger boy to jolt violently with shock, as if he had been stabbed.

'How long do you give him?' asked Macro. 'A sestertius gets you ten denarii that he's still alive when the year is out.'

'I wouldn't even take those odds,' Cato replied quietly. 'The poor little bastard . . .'

'I suppose . . . By the way, how is Lucius?'

Macro had deliberately kept his distance since they had returned to Rome. Cato and his son were living in the part of Sempronius's house that was undamaged by fire. Not that it would be referred to in those terms much longer. The senator had died with no living relatives other than his grandson. In the normal course of events the house, and the senator's entire estate, would have passed to Lucius. But these were not normal times, Cato reflected. Nero, on the prompting of Pallas, had confiscated all of Sempronius's property – a common fate for those who committed treachery against Rome. He had then peremptorily – and against the advice of his imperial secretary, who had hoped to gain from the confiscation – awarded the entire estate to Cato in recognition of the role he had played in crushing the conspiracy.

'He's doing well,' Cato replied. 'Better than you would imagine given what happened to him.'

'That's kids for you. There's no tragedy that can't be fixed by buying 'em a new toy. All the same, you should spend as much time with him as you can. He needs his father now. In any case, you're all he's got.'

Cato nodded, and decided to change the subject. 'And how are things with your lady love?'

Macro grinned. 'Good. Better than good. Every meal she cooks me is a banquet. And every night she humps me to within an inch of my life. Most mornings, too. I think I could get used to it. Not a bad life, eh?'

'Doesn't sound bad to me. And what next? You going to marry her? Settle down, maybe?'

'I could be tempted.'

'Really?' Cato arched an eyebrow. 'I thought you had yourself down as a soldier for life.'

Macro scratched his chin thoughtfully. 'I don't know. If there's one thing I've learned, it's that no one is anything for life. I'm not getting any younger. My best soldiering days are behind me. The longer I stay in the game, the more likely some barbarian toerag is to cut me down. That, or some injury or sickness. And what with Petronella's charms being what they are, I figure I might just think about leaving the army, unless I can tempt her to be an army wife. I've got savings, plus more than a little put aside for my pension fund from the odd bit of looting I've done over the years. Petronella and I could afford to open a nice little business in a quiet corner of the Empire. Maybe even go in with my mother and her place in Londinium.'

'The army would miss your talents. So would I.'

'Bollocks. There's nothing more I could teach you, lad. You're as good a soldier as I've ever met. You can manage without me.'

'I'm not so sure. It'd be like going into battle with one arm tied behind my back. If you ever get tired of married life, there'll always be a place for you in any unit I get to command. Although I don't suppose I'll be going into battle much more, now that I've asked for our transfer to the Praetorian Guard to be made permanent.'

'Smart move. Now that you've won the emperor's gratitude, the command of the Guard will be yours for the asking if anything happens to Burrus.'

'I know. And he's none too pleased about it. But I can't help that. I'll just bide my time and enjoy my life in Rome. Besides, I'll have quite a time of it raising Lucius.'

'It will be good,' Macro agreed. 'He's a fine lad, smart too. Just don't go and spoil him with too much reading, eh?'

'We'll see.' Cato gestured to one of the slaves lining the edge of the hall and indicated his goblet and Macro's. When the slave had refilled them, Cato raised his to make a toast. 'To wives and children.'

'Yes . . .' Macro took a sip. 'Julia's forgiven, then?'

'I'm not sure about that. I still don't know if there really was anything to forgive or not, thanks to Narcissus and those bastards. And I don't suppose I ever will.'

Just then one of the imperial clerks approached and leaned forward to address Cato discreetly. 'Prefect Cato, sir. My master wishes to speak with you.'

'Pallas wants to see me now?'

'Yes, sir.'

'Can't it wait?'

'I suspect not, sir. He does not make such requests lightly.'

Cato sighed and set his cup down. Swinging his legs over the side of the couch, he stood up and nodded to Macro. 'I'll make this quick.'

451

'Don't worry. There's plenty of wine to keep me company.'

Cato followed the clerk along the side of the banquet hall and out into one of the service corridors, stopping to let a small column of slaves laden with fruit baskets pass by. A short distance along the corridor was the office of the palace quartermaster, and the clerk showed Cato inside. Pallas was sitting on the corner of the table, and he stood and smiled as Cato entered, then held out his hand. Cato ignored the gesture.

'What do you want? Make it quick. I've a decent wine waiting for me.'

'Your pleasure at seeing me is so touching.'

Cato shrugged.

'I imagine you are delighted with the way things have turned out for you,' Pallas continued. 'You have your son, a fine house, a goodly fortune and the gratitude of the emperor. What man could wish for more?'

'You have all those yourself, yet I don't see you satisfying your appetite for more of the same.'

'My rewards are commensurate with the services I provide to this emperor, as well as the last.'

'Of course they are. Now let's not waste any more time on unpleasantries. Why have you called me away from the feast?'

'It's something of a delicate matter. You and I both know that the men of the Praetorian Guard hold you in high regard. Too high, some might say.'

'Is that a problem?'

'It might become a problem. At present you enjoy the emperor's regard. But I can't say the same for Burrus and some others. And they might be inclined to make trouble for you. Besides, if it was felt that the men owed their loyalty to you first and foremost, then someone might be concerned that if ever there was another conspiracy, you might be tempted to play politics.'

'Someone? You mean Nero?'

'Nero, or one of his inner circle. Now, I'd hate to see that happen. So I have a proposal for you. Something to help ease away any potential friction between yourself and Burrus.'

'And what might this proposal be?'

'You've heard of Legate Corbulo?'

Cato recalled the name, and some details. 'I know of him. He's a respected officer. Does things by the manual and is hard on his men, but no less hard on himself. He shares the same tents, the same rations, and so they regard him as one of themselves. Last I heard, Corbulo had been sent to the east to raise an army.'

'That's right. There's been some trouble on the frontier. Parthians stirring things up once again. Not to mention rumours of a rebellion in some regions close to the frontier. Corbulo has asked for more men. More officers. It seems you have enough of a reputation that he would be grateful to have you serve with him. So I have made arrangements for you and Centurion Macro to be transferred to his command to help train the troops and lead them into battle. It's a good opportunity to win yourself more acclaim.'

'While making sure that I'm not around in Rome for my popularity with the men to embarrass Prefect Burrus. Or alarm the emperor.'

'Something like that.'

'I'll give it some thought, but I tell you now, I'd rather remain here in Rome.'

'It's not a request, Cato . . .'

'I see.' He thought for a moment. 'Give me a little while to sort things out. I think I have earned that. I have family duties to attend to, and I dare say Macro might not be so eager to take you up on this. I'll let you know as soon as I can.'

He turned to leave, but just as he was about to close the door to the office, Pallas called after him.

'I wouldn't leave it too long before you set off, Cato. I really wouldn't. Rome can be a dangerous place for those who lack the political nous to understand how it works.'

By the time he returned to Macro, a fresh course had been served to the guests. Bowls of snails in a rich wine sauce. Macro had helped himself to most of them already, and steered the bowl towards Cato with a guilty expression.

'So what did he want?'

'He offered us a new posting, far away from Rome, where we won't attract too much unwanted attention to ourselves. He wants us to leave for Asia Minor to help train Corbulo's army to prepare it for a campaign against the Parthians.'

'You tempted?'

'I said I need some time first.'

'And what did he say to that?'

Cato helped himself to a snail. 'He said not to leave it too long.'

Before he could continue, there was a cry from the end of the hall, and faces turned towards the raised couches of the imperial entourage. Nero seemed to be absorbed in a conversation with his coterie of artists. On the other side of him, Britannicus had curled into a ball and was crying out in pain as he clutched his stomach. The conversation in the hall died away quickly, save for the emperor and his associates, who could not help being distracted by the agony of the emperor's adopted brother even as they tried to follow the thread of Nero's comments.

'What's eating him?' Macro whispered.

Britannicus suddenly sat up, raised his head and screamed, before dropping back on his couch and writhing in agony, lashing out with his feet. Most of those closest to him looked on in horror as Nero ignored the plight of his brother. Then Britannicus let out a long, drawn-out groan and slumped, still and silent. No one said anything, Cato noted. No one dared to. They all looked to Nero for their cue, but he continued his conversation and paid no regard to his adopted brother's body.

Some of the guests began to get up and leave, slipping away without saying a word. Cato looked closely at the snail in his fingers and then hurriedly returned it to the bowl. Even though Macro had eaten from it and exhibited no signs of being affected, Cato could not bring himself to take the risk. Already there was no doubt in his mind that Britannicus had been poisoned.

'I think we might just want to consider taking up Pallas's offer after all . . .'

THE END

AUTHOR'S NOTE

The troubled reign of Claudius

The reign of Emperor Claudius endured rather longer than that of his predecessor. Indeed, it lasted longer than the next six emperors that followed him. That is no small achievement, given that he was constantly undermined by the Senate (many of whom paid the ultimate price for underestimating the ruthlessness of Claudius and those who surrounded him). Rome at this time was a hotbed of intrigue; elements of the aristocracy were still reluctant to accept being ruled by emperors and hankered for the days of the Republic, when the senators were the undisputed masters of Rome. Relations between the Senate and the emperor were not improved by Claudius forcing the retirement of many senators who no longer met the property requirement, and replacing them with fresh senators recruited from the Gallic provinces. The latter were regarded with considerable disdain by the more senior members of the Senate, adding yet more tension to relations between them and their ruler.

The choice of Claudius's successor

In recent centuries we have become used to the generally painless process of one monarch succeeding another. But back in the days of the Roman Empire, the succession was more like the process of replacing a Mafia boss. Devious manoeuvring and deadly interventions were the stock-in-trade for those involved in deciding who became the next emperor.

Despite having a natural son, Britannicus (named in honour, of the province that Claudius had added to the Empire in order to cement his martial credentials), the emperor may have felt that the boy was tainted by the scandalous behaviour of his mother, Messalina, who had been executed in AD 48 after plotting against Claudius. So Britannicus's prospects of inheritance languished. All the more so when the emperor was persuaded to marry his niece, Agrippina, and adopt her son as his own. Now Britannicus's fortunes reached a low ebb. His newly adopted brother was clearly the preferred choice to succeed Claudius, especially as Agrippina used her considerable sexual allure to keep control of her husband. In time, though, Claudius grew wise to her scheming and was heard to lament his poor choice of wives, indicating that his affections were swinging in favour of his natural son. Fearing that her ambitions might not come to fruition, Agrippina took pre-emptive action and murdered the emperor, presenting Nero to the Empire as their new ruler. Not everyone was pleased with this turn of events, not least the faction that surrounded Britannicus . . .

The Praetorian Guard

The other political reality that had become a crucial consideration for those playing for the purple was the influence of the Praetorian Guard. Originally created to serve as the bodyguards of senior Roman officers in the field, the Praetorians took on a more permanent role as the Roman army professionalised. By the time of the emperors, they had become an elite unit billeted in Rome.

It did not take long for the Guard to start making its political power felt, firstly through the machinations of Sejanus, the commander during the reign of Tiberius. It was Sejanus who had the camp built and increased the strength of the Guard. It was also under Sejanus that the Guard's death squads were regularly used to eradicate political opposition. Ultimately, it was the limitless ambition of Sejanus that proved his undoing, and he was executed.

One might imagine that subsequent emperors might have learned to stay on good terms with the Praetorians. However, Tiberius's sucessor, Caligula, went out of his way to humiliate senior officers, who duly murdered him and his family and plucked Claudius from obscurity, forcing him on the Senate as the Guard's choice for emperor. Claudius repaid their support handsomely by awarding 15,000 sestertii to each man – a fortune at that time. Henceforth such 'bonuses' – or more accurately bribes – were expected by the men of the Praetorian Guard and woe betide any emperor who failed to cough up the necessary reward to keep the Praetorians happy. It was an open secret from the age of Claudius onward; while the emperors might rule the empire, fear of the Praetorians ruled the emperors. The real power in Rome lay in the hands of the Praetorian Guard, and those who were able to control them.

Caprae

For readers of *Day of the Caesars* who have not yet had the pleasure of visiting Capri, may I recommend that you put it on your bucket list right now. Aside from its breathtaking beauty (I once sailed past it at dusk and have never forgotten the sight of the sun, softened by haze, slowly disappearing behind the sheer cliffs at the eastern tip of the island), it features the remains of one of the most dramatically situated palaces of the Roman Empire. The long walk up the narrow path to the site is well rewarded by the scale of the remains, and their situation atop cliffs overlooking the stretch of sea that separates the island from the southern arm of the Bay of Naples.

When I last went there, I was fortunate enough to have the place to myself for an hour or so, and sat close to the edge of the cliff to take in the view. There was a sense of complete serenity about the place, and I could well understand why the emperors spent so much time in such a setting.

Definitely a view to be killed for.

Looking down, I could see the dots of seagulls and other birds wheeling far below, and the white V of a boat passing soundlessly across the azure waters at the foot of the cliffs. The setting and the ruins spoke to me of Roman times far more clearly than most archaeological sites I have visited, and it is one of those places where history truly comes alive to those who are receptive to such things.

If you enjoyed DAY OF THE CAESARS,
make sure you've read all of Cato and
Macro's adventures in the bestselling
Eagles of the Empire series . . .

Don't miss the gripping first novel in the Eagles of the Empire series

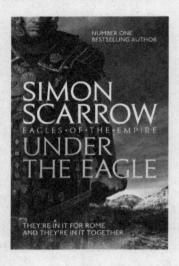

AD 42, Germany. Tough, brutal and unforgiving. That's how new recruit Cato is finding life in the Roman Second Legion.

Cato has been promoted above his comrades at the order of the Emperor and is deeply resented by the other men. But he quickly earns the respect of his Centurion, Macro, a battle-hardened veteran. They are poles apart, but soon realise they have a lot to learn from one another.

On a campaign to Britannia – a land of utter barbarity – an enduring friendship begins. But as they undertake a special mission to thwart a conspiracy against the Emperor they rapidly find themselves in a desperate fight to survive . . .

Available to buy in paperback or download in eBook.

THE EAGLES OF THE EMPIRE SERIES

The Britannia Campaign

UNDER THE EAGLE
AD 42–43, Britannia

New recruit Cato arrives in Germany to serve under the command of Centurion Macro in the notoriously tough Second Legion. Soon the long march west for a brutal campaign in Britannia begins . . .

THE EAGLE'S CONQUEST
AD 43, Britannia

The invasion of Britannia is underway, but the Roman army is desperately outnumbered by the savage Britons. Centurion Macro and young optio Cato begin a treacherous battle against the enemy . . .

WHEN THE EAGLE HUNTS
AD 44, Britannia

Camulodunum has fallen to the Roman army, but the joy of victory is short-lived as the family of General Plautius has been captured by the vicious Druids. Cato and Macro must race against time to find them . . .

THE EAGLE AND THE WOLVES
AD 44, Britannia

As the Roman army continues its quest to conquer the ferocious Britons, it is weakened by its own split forces. The Romans must recruit native tribesmen to fight, and Macro and Cato must train them fast before they are destroyed by the enemy . . .

THE EAGLE'S PREY
AD 44, Britannia

The campaign in Britannia has been far bloodier than predicted, and Emperor Claudius needs a victory. A battle against the barbarian leader Caratacus could finally be the triumphant end that the Empire desperately need . . .

Rome and Eastern Provinces

THE EAGLE'S PROPHECY
AD 45, Rome

A band of brutal pirates have captured scrolls holding secrets that could destroy the Roman Empire. Centurions Macro and Cato must join the navy and hunt down the scrolls before the Empire falls . . .

THE EAGLE IN THE SAND
AD 46, Judaea

The eastern provinces of the Roman Empire are under threat. Centurions Macro and Cato have arrived in Judaea to regain control of the region. But the revolt is strengthening and the army must return to its full force before these provinces are lost . . .

CENTURION
AD 46, Syria

Rome's old enemy Parthia prepares to unleash its might across the border into Palmyra. Macro and Cato are posted to Syria in a desperate quest to protect the Empire . . .

The Mediterranean

THE GLADIATOR
AD 48–49, Crete

Centurions Macro and Cato are sailing home after a harrowing campaign in the east. But an earthquake forces them on to the shores of Crete, a province in chaos. The men are faced with a rebellion that could ignite a disastrous uprising across the Empire . . .

THE LEGION
AD 49, Egypt

Rebel gladiator Ajax and his crew are threatening the stability of the Roman Empire. After a series of attacks along the Egyptian coast Macro and Cato are hot on Ajax's trail, but can they defeat him?

PRAETORIAN
AD 51, Rome

A shadowy republican movement threatens Rome and the Emperor Claudius. Treachery lurks within the Praetorian Guard and Cato and Macro begin to unravel more than one conspiracy against the Emperor . . .

> ## The Return to Britannia

THE BLOOD CROWS
AD 51, Britannia

The Roman army's fight to hold Britannia continues almost a decade after invasion. A campaign to resist the relentless natives begins, and Macro and Cato return to the perilous British shores to aid it.

BROTHERS IN BLOOD
AD 51, Britannia

Prefect Cato and Centurion Macro are pursuing barbarian leader Caratacus through the mountains of Britannia. Defeating Caratacus seems within their grasp, but the plot against the two heroes threatens their lives . . .

BRITANNIA
AD 52, Britannia

The western tribes prepare to make a stand and Centurion Macro remains behind in charge of the fort as Prefect Cato leads an invasion deep into the hills. Cato's mission: to crush the Druid stronghold. But has the enemy been underestimated?

> ## Hispania

INVICTUS
AD 54, Hispania

Cato and Macro have been recalled to Rome, but their time in the city is short. Soon they are travelling with the Praetorian Guard to Spain, where they battle for control in a land considered unconquerable . . .

SIMON SCARROW

THE EAGLES OF THE EMPIRE SERIES

Under the Eagle	£8.99
The Eagle's Conquest	£8.99
When the Eagle Hunts	£8.99
The Eagle and the Wolves	£8.99
The Eagle's Prey	£8.99
The Eagle's Prophecy	£8.99
The Eagle in the Sand	£8.99
Centurion	£8.99
The Gladiator	£8.99
The Legion	£8.99
Praetorian	£8.99
The Blood Crows	£8.99
Brothers in Blood	£8.99
Britannia	£8.99
Invictus	£7.99
Day of the Caesars	£7.99

THE WELLINGTON AND NAPOLEON QUARTET

Young Bloods	£8.99
The Generals	£8.99
Fire and Sword	£8.99
The Fields of Death	£8.99
Sword & Scimitar	£8.99
Hearts of Stone	£8.99

WRITING WITH T. J. ANDREWS

Arena	£8.99
Invader	£7.99

Simply call 01235 827 702 or visit our
website www.headline.co.uk to order

d availability subject to change without notice.